THE
UNPREDICTABLE
ADVENTURE

Utopianism and Communitarianism

THE UNPREDICTABLE ADVENTURE

A COMEDY OF WOMAN'S INDEPENDENCE

Claire Myers Spotswood Owens
With an Afterword by Miriam Kalman Harris

SYRACUSE UNIVERSITY PRESS

Syracuse University Press Edition 1993
93 94 95 96 97 98 99   6 5 4 3 2 1

The paper used in this publication meets the minimum requirements of American National Standard for Information Sciences—Permanence of Paper for Printed Library Materials, ANSI z39.48-1948. ∞™

Library of Congress Cataloging-in-Publication Data

Owens, Claire Myers.
    The unpredictable adventure : a comedy of woman's independence /
Claire Myers Spotswood Owens ; with an afterword by Miriam Kalman
Harris.
        p. cm.—(Utopianism and communitarianism)
    Includes bibliographical references (p.).
    ISBN 0-8156-2583-9 (pbk.)
    I. Title. II. Series.
PS3529.W436U55   1992
813'.52s—dc20   92-30746

Manufactured in the United States of America

To
that rare person,
a critic who takes an impartial,
impersonal, and passionate interest
in good literature;
the lucidity of whose critical mind
is equaled only by his kindness:

BURTON RASCOE

"GOETHE'S *mental health was attained by a long process of elimination from his consciousness of those fears and prejudices and trepidations, heritages from a medieval past, which beset him in his youth. . . . Goethe was sixty years writing* Faust. *It is a poetic record of a man's whole inner inexperience. It is . . . like life itself, an unpredictable adventure."*

TITANS OF LITERATURE, by Burton Rascoe

CONTENTS

PREFACE   xiii

ACKNOWLEDGMENTS   xvii

CHAPTER I. HOW AN UNWELCOME VISITOR DISTURBED THE
PEACE OF SMUG HARBOR, AND THE STRANGE PREDICTION SHE
MADE CONCERNING TELLECTINA   I

CHAPTER II. HOW TELLECTINA CONSULTED THE GUIDE TO THE
ROCKY MOUNTAINS OF CASUISTRY, AND THE GREAT EARTH-
QUAKE AND STORM ENCOUNTERED THERE   26

CHAPTER III. WHAT HAPPENED WHEN TELLECTINA WAS SENT
TO ROTE HILL TO TAKE THE CURE; HOW SHE DISCOVERED A
GREAT CARNIVAL, ENJOYED SECRET PLEASURES, AND MET THERE
HER NATURAL SISTER FEMINA   45

CHAPTER IV. HOW TELLECTINA LEAPT OVER THE WALL INTO
NITHKING; WAS ATTACKED BY OUTLAWS, LOST IN THE DOTBU DE-
SERT, AND RESCUED BY DREISER, BRIFFAULT, AND ROB-
INSON   67

CHAPTER V. HOW THE YOUNG EXPLORER WAS CAPTURED BY
CANNIBALS IN THE JUNGLE, SWAM AGAINST THE CURRENT OF
THE SACRED RIVER, PUBLI COPINION; AND FOUNDED THE COLONY
OF NEW CHIMERA   94

CHAPTER VI. HOW TELLECTINA WAS PURSUED BY THE THREE
WHITE HOUNDS; HOW RENAN ENTRAPPED GODSSON, CAB-
ELL RESCUED HER FROM ONEGOD, AND SHE OBSTRUCTED THE
WAY OF THE GREAT HOUND GODIDEA   129

CHAPTER VII. ADVENTURES IN CAPE COVERTURE; HOW TELLEC-
TINA FELL VICTIM TO TROPICAL FEVER AND ENCOUNTERED OLEV
THE THIRD   156

CHAPTER VIII. WHAT HAPPENED WHEN TELLECTINA BE-
CAME LOST IN THE GREAT JUNGLE OF OTHERPEOPLESIDEAS; AND
THE INCREDIBLE OCCURRENCE AT MANU MISSION ON THE MOUN-
TAIN TOP   223

CHAPTER IX. THE DISCOVERY OF THE SEVEN SIREN IS-
LANDS AND HOW THE EXPLORER INDULGED IN THE NATIVE OR-
GIES   241

CHAPTER X. HOW TELLECTINA WAS LURED TO THE SEV-
ENTH SIREN ISLE AND BELIEVED HERSELF TO BE THE FIRST
WHITE PURITAN EVER INITIATED INTO THE MYSTERY OF MYSTE-
RIES   271

CHAPTER XI. WHAT HAPPENED WHEN TELLECTINA MET SOME
STROLLING PLAYERS ON THE HIGHROAD; WHAT SHE SAW BEHIND
THE SCENES OF THE OLD MORALITY PLAY, "THE WORLD'S
WORLD"; AND THE PART SHE PLAYED THEREIN   301

CHAPTER XII. THE SEARCH FOR MT. CERTITUDE CONTIN-
UED; HOW MENCKEN SHOWED TELLECTINA HIS VIEW OF THE
LAND OF ERR, AND RASCOE ACTED AS OFFICIAL GUIDE TO THE
GREAT MOUNTAIN   332

CHAPTER XIII. A FIGHT FOR HER LIFE, AND THE PART PLAYED
THEREIN BY THE MAGIC POWER OF A STRANGE LITTLE PACKAGE
CONTAINING STRAWS AND PRAYER BOOKS   355

CHAPTER XIV. THE DISCOVERY OF THE HIGHEST MOUTAIN IN
THE WORLD, AND THE MANY STRANGE THINGS THAT BEFELL
TELLECTINA THERE; THE END OF HER QUEST FOR MT. CERTI-
TUDE, AND HOW SHE OBTAINED THE BEST VIEW OF BOTH
WORLDS FROM CABELL'S WINDOWS   375

CHAPTER XV. HOW TELLECTINA RETURNED UNEXPEC-
TEDLY TO THE LAND OF ERR; HER STRANGE ADVENTURES
THEREIN AND SUBSCRIPTION TO THE LAWS THEREOF; AND HOW
SHE RESORTED TO AN ESOTERIC DRUG FOR ALL HER MANY
ILLS   414

CONTENTS

AFTERWORD   459

GLOSSARY   497

WORKS CITED   509

PREFACE

As a graduate student, I read Elaine R. Hedges's afterword to *The Yellow Wallpaper*, by Charlotte Perkins Gilman, and knew I wanted to rediscover a "lost" woman writer whose work would be a valued addition to the growing canon of women's literature. Such an enterprise seemed not only vital to the overall feminist project but also an exciting adventure. At that time I could not have imagined that my adventure would prove to be so provocative, expansive, and unpredictable.

The first phase of my journey was short, a mere forty miles north from my home in Dallas to the Blagg-Huey Library at Texas Woman's University in Denton, which houses an impressive woman's collection and archive. There in Elizabeth Snapp's office, I discovered Claire through her portrait, which captivated my imagination. (I describe this initial encounter in detail in my chapter in *All Sides of the Subject*. See Works Cited.)

I began working through the Claire Myers Owens Collection, read Claire's published writings, and accumulated stacks of notes and photocopies of memorabilia. I discovered in Claire Myers Spotswood Owens a literary figure, a humanist, and a patriotic American with a feminist sensibility. Although she was not actively involved in either wave of feminism that surfaced during her long and productive life, women's issues and women's rights were the first and lasting passion informing her personal choices and her public commitments.

My first priority was to republish her 1935 fantasy, *The Unpredictable Adventure: A Comedy of Woman's Independence.* Carol Farley Kessler, editor of *Daring To Dream*, has called this book one of "the most significant of the nine utopias published by

xiii

United States women during the 1930s" (private correspondence, 1991). Drawing on her life experiences, Claire uses anagrams to establish an allegorical pattern satirizing cultural norms, and she demonstrates the hazards awaiting a woman who dares to think and act in defiance of the gendered roles assigned her. In a spirit of serious fun, the book examines female sexuality, the problems of marriage, work, religion, divorce, and the universal struggle of woman to achieve a balanced life, themes that anticipate contemporary feminist concerns. The protagonist's quest for self-realization is as vital and relevant to today's questing women as it was to women of the 1930s. Republishing this novel in the final decade of the twentieth century is a tribute to the accomplishments of the ongoing women's studies movement and a charge to future literary scholars, biographers, and historians to keep these "lost" women "found."

Like Claire, I am a firm believer in the Jungian concept of synchronicity. Just when I needed to broaden my understanding of my role as biographer and literary critic and to learn the approach for bringing this novel to public attention, I discovered an ad in the *Women's Review of Books* for a Women's Studies Summer Institute to be held in July 1988 at the University of London. With financial assistance from Sallie Bingham and the Kentucky Foundation for Women, I extended my journey across the ocean to England where I attended two seminars conducted by Dale Spender on writing feminist biography and the study of women's diaries and journals. Dale Spender's commitment to feminism and writing is an inspiration. Her wit, wisdom, and expert advise on publishing forgotten women's writings guided me through the subsequent phases of my quest.

The glossary provides translations of the anagrams and references to some of the many literary and historical figures the protagonist encounters throughout her journey. Our decision to include a glossary presents an interesting choice to the reader. On the one hand, it makes reading more accessible to those not having the patience to unscramble words or to research literary allusions, and it also functions as an educational assistant for use

in the classroom. On the other hand, it makes the reader's journey through the novel less an adventure. My impulse is to advise readers, at least for the first reading, to join the author in
her invitation to participate in the game, the search for meaning
en route to Mount Certitude. Ultimately, however, the choice
of approach is up to the individual.

I am indebted to the following mentors, colleagues, and friends
for their support and guidance: Nancy Tuana, Dale Spender,
Florence Ridlon, Margaret Moore, Saundra Snyder, Phyllis Prager,
and Larry Campbell. I thank Ulli Munroe for the use of her laser
printer, Carol Stephenson for her astute legal counsel, and Linda
Comess for her faithful encouragement in all of my work and for
her exquisite portrayal of Claire Myers Owens in *Mirrors: A One
Woman Performance*, which I wrote and she produced and performed. I also thank Wendy Kolmar and Lynette Carpenter for
their last-minute guidance regarding research materials.

As an expression of her commitment to the rediscovery of lost
women writers, Janet Mullaney, editor of *Belle Lettres*, published
my article on *The Unpredictable Adventure* and Claire Myers Spotswood Owens. By way of synchronicity, Carol Farley Kessler saw
the article and brought the novel to the attention of Cynthia
Maude-Gembler, executive editor at Syracuse University Press.
When Ms. Maude-Gembler contacted me, I knew Claire's book
had found a new home in the Utopianism and Communitarianism series. I feel privileged to have worked with the editors at
Syracuse who made writing the afterword and glossary an enjoyable experience.

Permission to quote from the unpublished manuscripts, letters, and papers of Claire Myers Owens in the Texas Woman's
University Library Special Collections is kindly acknowledged. I
am most grateful to Elizabeth Snapp, Director of Libraries, and
her fine staff at the Blagg-Huey Library: Dawn Letson, Head of
Special Collections, and Library Assistants, Kim Grover-Haskin
and Georgia Bonatis, who has become another Claire devotee

through her excellent work processing the archive. Georgia's help in solving the puzzle of biographical information goes beyond the call of duty. In the beginning phases of my work, Peg Rezac and Metta Nicewarner provided valuable and enthusiastic assistance. Ms. Snapp's personal contact with Claire during her life and her subsequent devotion to the Owens Collection made this project special to her. This book could not have materialized without Elizabeth.

From an early age, my mother, Frances Levy Kalman Rose, instilled in me a love of literature that is reflected in all of my work. My sisters-in-law, Rhonda Harris Polishuk and Janet Harris Rice, have celebrated with me each phase of this book's rebirthing. These three women are thus both family and friends.

The love and support of my closest family members function as a stabilizing force in my life. My children, Pepi and Earl, and my husband Stanley, an exemplary "without whom . . . ", have believed in this project since its inception. To them I express my deepest gratitude and love.

This edition is dedicated to Claire's colleagues and friends who have kept her memory alive. Kenneth Ring, professor of psychology at the University of Connecticut, welcomed me into his home for an interview in June 1989 and gave me his own copy of *The Unpredictable Adventure*, inscribed to him by Claire in 1979, to use in my work. (My resources at the time were limited to a photocopy of the book held in the archive.) John White, Literary Executor of Claire's estate, granted permission to republish this novel. His cooperation in working through the technical details made the process a positive learning experience. I feel certain Claire would be pleased to know that she left her work in the charge of a man of such integrity and honor. Claire's friends and colleagues affiliated with the Zen Center in Rochester, New York become characters themselves in the afterword: Audrey Fernandez, Margaret Lee Braun, Marion Rigney, Barbara Percy, Geoffrey Lister, and Dwain Wilder. My heartfelt thanks to all of you.

ACKNOWLEDGMENTS

THE author wishes to make grateful acknowledgment for permission to reprint material in this book, kindly granted by the following authors and publishers:

Robert Briffault
    for selections from his article "Nemesis."
James Branch Cabell and Robert M. McBride & Company
    for selections from *Jurgen, Townsend of Lichfield, The Lineage of Lichfield, Beyond Life, Something about Eve, Figures of Earth, Straws and Prayer-Books, The High Place,* and *The Cream of the Jest* (in the Storisende Edition).
Havelock Ellis and Doubleday, Doran & Company, Inc.
    for selections from *Little Essays of Love and Virtue.*
Aldous Huxley and Doubleday, Doran & Company, Inc.
    for selections from *Brief Candles.*
Walter Lippmann
    for selections.
H. L. Mencken and Alfred A. Knopf, Inc.
    for selections from *Prejudices* and *A Book of Prefaces.*
Burton Rascoe and G. P. Putnam's Sons
    for selections from *Titans of Literature* and *Prometheans.*
James Harvey Robinson and Harper Brothers
    for selections from *The Mind in the Making.*
Bertrand Russell, E. P. Dutton & Company, and D. Appleton-Century Company
    for selections from *What I Believe* (In The To-day and To-morrow Series) and *Why Men Fight.*
Carl Van Doren and Robert M. McBride & Company
    for selections from *James Branch Cabell* (in the Modern American Writers Series).

Dodd, Mead & Company
  for selections from *Appreciations of Poetry*, by Lafcadio
  Hearn.

Houghton Mifflin Company
  for selections from Ralph Waldo Emerson's *Essays*.

Mitchell Kennerley
  for selections from *Love's Coming of Age*, by Edward
  Carpenter.

Modern Library, Inc.
  for selections from Arthur Symons's translations of
  Baudelaire's *Poems in Prose*.

THE
UNPREDICTABLE
ADVENTURE

CHAPTER I

WELL, SHE MAY be old, but she certainly is not an old maid!"

"But, my dear wife, she's never been married, so——"

"And you needn't pretend for the smallest fraction of the smallest second that she *is* an old maid—even if she *is* your own sister!"

The violent motion of the woman's rocking chair was also intended to convey her annoyance to her husband; but neither the acerbity of her words nor the nervous tempo of her movements disturbed the slow leisurely rhythm of the chair beside her.

"You can't possibly have any way of knowing," the man persisted quietly.

"Know!" His wife brought her agitated rocking chair to an abrupt standstill. "I don't need to know anything about such women: my intuition is more than sufficient! Besides, weren't two of her books suppressed? What more do you want, in the name of goodness?"

While waiting on the veranda for the most momentous announcement of the day, Mr. and Mrs. John Christian were fervidly performing their noon ritual, which consisted of rocking unceasingly for the traditionally proscribed time both before and after dinner: a rite which was invariably followed by a similar one at supper time.

Their small daughter was seated on the low white steps that led into a luxurious and lazy old boxwood garden. The unwonted heat in her mother's voice had finally penetrated the delicious oblivion which enveloped the child whenever she was reading fairy stories. After slowly uncurling the long young leg folded carelessly under her, Tellectina reluctantly transferred her gaze from the book on her knee to the plump form of her mother.

"Who, Mother? Who is it you are talking about?"

There being no reply to her question, the child laid aside her book and with quiet determination approached her mother's chair. Immediately and jealously Mary Christian's arm encircled her daughter as though to protect her from some impending evil.

"Think what a terrible influence that sort of woman will be on this poor innocent child!"

"Who, Mother, who?" Tellectina insisted. "Oh, who *is* it, Father?"

"My dear," the man said to his wife in a tone of dangerous patience, "we will not discuss this matter further. I told you I did not invite her here: she simply announced that she was coming for a visit because she wished to see her namesake, Tellectina. You are perfectly well aware that she hasn't displayed the slightest interest in the child all these ten years, and it was only when *you* took it into your own inconsistent woman's head to send her a picture of Tina (who is the living image of her aunt, you must admit) that she came racing from the other side of the world."

The child was now standing beside Mr. Christian's chair plucking at his sleeve impatiently. "But, Father, you always tell *me* it's impolite not to answer when I'm spoken to."

"You imp!" John Christian laughed and pinched her cheek. "And I've also told you that a preposition is the wrong thing to end a sentence with. Ah, well, manners and grammar seem to be the two most difficult things for a child to learn—even such a willing pupil as my little Tina. But, if you must know, it's your aunt Sophie who's causing this sudden rise in the domestic temperature."

"Oh, what's she like, and will she bring her little——"

"Why, let's see now, honey: she's tall and slender—and pretty and gay. She laughs at absolutely everything, and yet her face seems sad, somehow."

"And will she bring her little girl for me to play with, Father?"

Mrs. Christian flashed her husband a warning glance, but he merely colored slightly and looked away from his daughter. "No, dear, she's—well, she has never married. She's an—an old maid."

"But I just heard Mother say she wasn't! Yet if a grown-up woman's not an old maid and not married either, then what do you call her?"

"A disgraceful hussy," Mrs. Christian muttered under her breath. "That's what *I* call her!"

At this moment, however, a gray-haired Negro servant appeared in the open doorway with the announcement for which they had all been eagerly waiting; whereupon the Christian family arose with unusual alacrity and passed indoors to dinner. And Tellectina's question, having been left unanswered, stuck like a burr in her young mind.

Early the following morning the child skipped gayly along the garden paths. On arriving at the great eastern gate she climbed the intricate ironwork to its height and peered eagerly down the main street of Smug Harbor, intent on catching a glimpse of the mysterious new aunt. From the south, where the garden gave onto the beach, the fog rolled in from the Dead Sea in such thick white clouds that it was impossible to see anything clearly. The child, however, was so accustomed to the continual fog that she scarcely noticed it.

Although ten years old, Tellectina had seldom been allowed to venture outside the grounds of this ancient family estate, unchanged by generations of Christians except for minor alterations. It lay sleeping confidently on the far western edge of

Smug Harbor, a large and prosperous seaport on the south coast of Err.

Eventually the aunt, Sophistica Tellectina Christian, arrived, two hours late. Her namesake stood shyly on the veranda while Mrs. Christian met her guest on the graveled drive with words of admonition: "Now, Sophie, for heaven's sake, be careful what you say in the presence of my child!"

As Sophistica stepped from the carriage she exclaimed, "Oh, dear Gawd, the fog, Mary, the Errorian fog! I'd forgotten that its ubiquity was surpassed only by that of its creator! I've been asleep ever since we crossed the Nithking border."

Mary Christian froze instantly. "Sophie, will you at least have the—the decency not to swear in front of this innocent child!"

Her guest hastened to apologize. "Oh, my God, but I'm sorry! Honestly, I'm damn—I mean, I'm terribly sorry, Mary! One forgets so much in ten years, you know."

"Evidently," her sister-in-law agreed icily as she dismissed the old coachman and led the way into the house.

When Mrs. Christian with cold courtesy showed her unwelcome visitor to the guest room the young Tellectina followed them up the steps, listening in rapt admiration to this tall beautiful woman with the low luscious voice which possessed a vibrant quality like the harp that she had sometimes heard played in church.

Standing in the doorway the hostess ran a practiced eye over the room. "Well, Sophie, I trust you'll find everything you need for your comfort, at least; but I'm afraid you will find the Christian mode of life very dull after the gay life you're accustomed to."

Turning around, Sophistica said, "My dear Mary Christian, you haven't changed one iota in all these years, have you? Except to grow more so."

"More—more what?"

"More of a Christian."

The older woman drew herself up stiffly. "I'm sure I don't understand you—but then I never did, anyway. But I'm proud of my name, if that's what you mean, and try very hard to live up to it." She held out her hand. "Come, Tina, your aunt is tired and wants to rest."

Sophistica smiled and likewise held out her hand. "Stay, Tina, your aunt is gay and wants to play!" She offered the little girl a large pink box. "See, my dear, here's an *enor*mous box of candy, enough to make you gorgeously ill for days and days!"

As soon as Mrs. Christian had gone down the stairs, the barrier of shyness melted to such an extent that it emboldened the child to step inside the room.

"Come here, Miss Tellectina Femina Christian, I wish to see if there's anything behind that pretty little face of yours. If there isn't, I shall weep—for myself; but for you—" Sophistica shrugged—"I shall rejoice."

Advancing, the small girl laid her hand timidly on the woman's knee as she sank to the edge of the bed. After they had conversed a short while, however, Tellectina summoned the courage to deliver herself of the question which was still pricking her young mind.

"Auntie, if a grown-up woman's not married and not an old maid, what do you call her?"

Sophistica threw back her shining black head and laughed until the tears sparkled in her eyes. "Out of the mouths of babes! Why, you funny little darling, I'd call her a damned intelligent woman! That's what I'd call her! To say nothing of natural and courageous and honest and glorious and a dozen other fine things besides! But do you realize, wise infant, that you touch upon the most ludicrous theme in all human history?"

"Hasn't she any kind of name?" the young inquisitor insisted; but before her question could be answered the child's puzzled expression suddenly changed to one of pride. "Oh, Aunt Sophie, I learned something yesterday! I know the difference now between Miss and Mrs.—and I didn't used to!"

"There isn't much difference—*now!* There used to be! You have it reversed, darling!"

"But 'Mrs.' means you're married and 'Miss' means you're

not, doesn't it?" Tellectina's perseverance had begun to evince itself at the early age of ten.

"Yes, duckie, those are labels which used to be one of man's little methods of distinguishing the sheep from the goats, but now——" Again there rose that effervescent laugh which came from a great store of well-seasoned merriment.

Leaning forward she touseled her little niece's long black curls affectionately, then, desisting abruptly, gazed out the window with a smile of secret amusement about her lips. "A thousand years from now, when civilization begins to dawn on this benighted planet, the world will wake up and rock with laughter at the outmoded purity myth. It is a primitive superstition which should have become extinct with the dodo or the dinosaur. It is absurdity on the grand scale, imbecility defying all human logic, injustice beyond human credence. For has not six inches of—of vacuity altered the entire course of human lives, wrecked homes, and swayed the destiny of empires? Ah, yes, women still hold the power of the world in the hollow of their little——" Laughter prevented her, however, from completing the sentence.

Rising she went to the dressing table. "Here, Tina, you sit in that chair and gorge yourself with candy while I dress this unruly hair of mine." Great cascades of shining black hair tumbled down her back.

With a chocolate poised in midair Tellectina exclaimed, "Oh, Auntie, your hair is so wonderfully long!"

"I know. Damned nuisance too. But men simply adore long hair, so—— Always remember, my dear, that a woman's hair makes an excellent net in which to ensnare unwary hearts—although each male has his own individual weakness. But to return to your original question: If a woman's not married and not an old maid, what is she called? Of course, she surely has some epithet, for the masculine sex is particularly adept at problems of female nomenclature. Now let's think."

Slowly and absent-mindedly she brushed out the long, luxuriant hair. "Apparently all down the ages men have classified men according to their profession, ability, or class, leaving to privacy that which was private. Their classification of women, however, has been based on what? Character, mentality, beauty, or breeding? No, in the very beginning they chose the most incredible, insignificant, and irrelevant basis imaginable: the use and disuse of a strictly private entry to a private estate."

Although the words bewildered the little girl, the melody of the voice held her entranced. With her comb still in hand, Sophistica, having completely forgotten the presence of the child, commenced to count on her fingers. "First in this ludicrous male system of nominalism comes the term which signifies the unused state of the entry; next, the one denoting desuetude due to prolonged drought; then comes the name meaning primarily that passage in and out is legal; and last, the term signifying payment of the specified toll."

Intent on solving her problem, the woman continued. "Certainly the lady in question could not be disposed of in any of those four major female divisions. The modern splendid pariah has necessitated a fifth. The truth is that it all resolves itself into a matter of property rights. Due attention has never been paid by the chroniclers of the human race to the parts played by these small passages. Why, the whole history of womankind could be written in terms of entry—and will be written some day!"

Pausing for an instant, Sophistica hastily scribbled a note on a slip of paper.

"Yes, it appears that where the right of way is not legally contracted for, nor the channel opened to the public, nor entered by force; where, in short, the generous owner merely grants the right of entry to some favored one because it gives her pleasure—there is for this kind of woman apparently no name. For her who is caught breaking the ancient law governing these small channels there is still a penalty but no appellation. How odd that no libelous term has yet been coined! A woman without a label—for the first time in the world—what an appalling oversight!"

Rising from the dressing table, Sophistica laughed and kissed her niece on top of her head. "There, there, my dear Tina, eat your candy and forgive me. I forget where I am and unconsciously drop back into Reasonese and get drunk on my own words."

Mischievous glee sparkled in her eyes as she stood smiling down at the puzzled face of the child, then suddenly she said, "But come, dear, tell me: what are we going to do this disgracefully hot, foggy, muggy morning? Let's play—what do you say?"

The little girl twisted her hands together uncertainly. "I'd like to, but—but it's Sunday, and I have to go to Sunday school."

"Sunday school!" The woman passed her fingers over her forehead as though attempting to revive a long dead memory. "Ah, yes, I remember, the school where you learn more sophistry in a day than you can rid yourself of in a lifetime! You poor infant!" She gazed earnestly into the child's eyes. "Tell me, do you honestly like to go to Sunday school?"

"I ought to, but I—oh, Auntie, why must it always make you feel so wicked, even after you've tried so hard to be good?"

Sophistica smiled. "It doesn't! What I mean, dear little Puritan, is that I see how I may be able to save you. But first, 'fess up, what do you like to do best in all the wide, wide world?"

Tellectina's face lighted up instantly. "Oh, why, go over to the island!"

"The island? What island?"

The light was suddenly extinguished. "Why, the Romanz Isle, of course."

"Come then, let's cut Sunday school right out of the calendar today like *that!*" She made a decisive stroke through the air. "I'll answer to your mother, and you conduct me to your marvelous island." Hastily coiling her hair on the nape of her neck she waited with outstretched hand.

Tellectina paused, frowned, took an uncertain step, and then, catching her aunt by the hand, ran quickly from the room with her. Down the steps, out of the house, and through the winding paths they sped until they arrived at the foot of the garden where it gave onto the beach. Rocking idly in the slow swell of the sea were two small rowboats of very curious rectangular design, with worn gold lettering barely discernible on their sides.

The child introduced her aunt to the three old boatmen. "This old blue boat belongs to Andersen, and this large red one is rowed by the Brothers Grimm. Will you choose the one you like best?"

Sophistica smiled as she looked from one to the other.

"I admire their skill very much, but I fear they wouldn't be able to carry a big grown-up woman like me to Romanz Isle. Here's another boat, however, which looks as if it were just made for skeptical folk like me. With the aid of M. Voltaire and his offspring, Candide, I should reach the island almost as soon as you do."

Sophistica gave herself into the hands of the old Frenchman while Tellectina, although looking somewhat crestfallen, settled herself quickly in the stern of Andersen's boat. Almost immediately, however, the child began pressing her flat little abdomen with both hands. Abandoning Voltaire completely, Sophistica ran toward her niece in distress. "Why, Tina, whatever is the matter?"

There was no reply from the small girl, whose slender body was bent double with pain.

"Ah, yes, a tummyache, poor dear! Too much candy, I suspect."

"No, Auntie. It's one of those old conscience pains that Mother says is always such a good sign—though I don't know a bit what she means."

"So, you're afflicted with that chronic Christian ailment, are you?"

"I don't know, but she says it runs in our family. I'm always having attacks at the wrong time: I hate it because it's forever spoiling the nicest things I want to do."

"Well, my pretty Puritan, it's this damnable climate you live in: it gives me a pain, too—of quite a different sort! Conscience pains are unnatural in a healthy child. Smug Harbor is no place to bring up children."

"It's no use now, though, Auntie. I couldn't enjoy the trip a bit as long as I feel this way. Maybe if I go on to Sunday school it will get better, and then I can come back later." Still bent over, she stepped out of the boat and started up the beach, but paused to say, "I hate to leave you, but you'll excuse me, please?"

"Excuse you? You poor darling, I only wish to heaven I could do something to save you!"

"Oh, but I will be saved if I'm a good little girl, won't I, and always do right? And I always try to."

"Well, you know 'good' and 'right' are relative terms, my dear. What is right in Err is wrong in Nithking, where I've been traveling. But you should pray to your God to make you a stupid little girl: then you're sure to be saved."

"Pray to be stupid? Oh, no, Auntie, you don't understand! I study so hard in school because I want to know—oh, just *everything!*"

"Oh, you do—do you? Well, that will be your undoing some day, I do hereby predict. For she who increaseth knowledge, increaseth sorrow. But no matter, run along now and cure your conscience pain. If I don't save you in time, however, you'll be bitten by the pernicious desire to make a trip through that dangerous region whose true name is the Rocky Mountains of Casuistry, though it's invariably called otherwise by the ignorant."

The child cast a puzzled glance on her enigmatic relative and ran quickly back to the house. And sure enough, as she dressed hurriedly for Sunday school, the conscience pain disappeared entirely. There was no further opportunity, however, to return to the beach that day; for after church Mrs. Christian brought the minister home to dinner with her. As his hostess had been obliged to excuse herself for a few minutes, the Rev. Rationalizer found to his annoyance that there was no one in the drawing room to entertain him except the small daughter of the house.

"Well, well, so this is the *young* Christian, is it? I understand that you are one of our star Sunday-school pupils. Now I wonder if you can repeat the Ten Commandments for me—word for word—correctly."

"Oh, yes, sir." Instantly the child stood up and, clasping her hands behind her back, began: " 'I am the Lord thy God, which have brought thee into the Land of Err.' "

But while she was repeating the Seventh Commandment: " 'Thou shalt not commit adultery nor any other pleasure,' " Sophistica made her appearance in the doorway; whereupon Tellectina ceased, and the minister arose.

Advancing, he said, "Ah, Miss Sophistica, I'm so delighted to see you again after all these——"

After a hurried "How do you do?" she held up an admonishing hand. "I don't wish to interrupt. Tina was reciting something: I could hear her sweet little singsong voice out in the hall, so continue, my dear."

"Yes," the clergyman replied, "Miss Tellectina here was repeating the Ten Commandments as revised by the Puritans, and very well, too."

Sophistica moaned. "Dear Lord, will no one have mercy on this defenseless child?"

The Rev. Rationalizer stiffened perceptibly. "But, my good woman, all children should be taught the Ten——"

"I'm *not* your good woman, but I can quote scripture, nevertheless. 'And ye have heard that it was said by them of old time, the love of money is the root of all evil?' But I say unto you, stupidity is the root of all evil!"

At the bland blank face which the clergyman turned upon her, however, she shrugged and murmured, "Continue, my child, continue. (And, Sophistica, 'Forgive them, for they know not what they do.')"

The minister coughed nervously and said, "Just give us the last two and that will be all."

Hurriedly the child resumed her recitation:

" 'Thou shalt not bare thy body to thy neighbor, nor to thy neighbor's wife, nor his manservant, nor his maidservant, nor his ox, nor his ass; for all nakedness and all sex is obscene, lewd, lascivious, filthy, and indecent.

" 'Thou shalt not covet the joys of the senses, neither those of drinking nor smoking, nor yet those of seeing nor hearing nor feeling, nor anything that gives thee pleasure; thou shalt not lust after that wanton whom men call Beauty; for whosoever looketh on Beauty to lust after her hath committed adultery with her already in his heart.' "

"Very good, my child." Whereupon the minister advanced toward Sophistica. "Well, well, you're more beautiful than ever."

"Don't look my thirty winters, eh? You know it's *sin* that keeps me young and happy."

"Oh, Miss Sophie, you always were such a tease!"

Then the Rev. Rationalizer added reprovingly, "I'm sorry I didn't see *you* out to church today, Miss Sophie."

An impish gleam flashed in the woman's eyes, but her tone was very solemn. "Oh, well, you see, I suffer from deafness a great deal—especially in churches."

Announcement of dinner terminated their conversation. As they passed out of the drawing room Mr. Christian joined them and spoke to his sister in an undertone. "It is our custom, Sophie, after grace has been said, for everyone to quote a verse from the scriptures while heads are still bowed, so——"

Pursing her lips, Sophistica responded with mock severity, "Dangerous custom, my boy!"

After they were seated and grace had been said by the minister, Mr. Christian took the lead by mumbling in an inaudible voice, " 'The Lord is my shepherd, I shall not want.' "

The quoting made the rounds of the table, and when Sophistica's turn came she said in reverential and clearly audible tones,

" 'By night on my bed I sought him whom my soul loveth: I sought him, but I found him not.' "

Everyone squirmed in his chair except Sophistica and Tellectina, whose turn had now come and who was quoting in a small voice, " 'Judge not, lest you be judged.' "

Sophistica raised her head and with eyes of complete innocence gazed at the guilty faces about her. The Rev. Rationalizer coughed nervously.

There was no conversation for some time, for there was an excellent and abundant dinner: it being a religious custom devoutly observed in Err to feed the physical man generously on the holy Sabbath. Finally John Christian leaned back in his chair with a long sigh of satisfaction and said, "Well, Sister, you don't talk much, do you?"

"No, people of my age find peace a very pleasant thing."

Mrs. Christian looked up suddenly. "Speaking of peace, Sophie, did you know that my only brother is in the Great War and he may never—never——" She began to whimper.

"Now, don't cry, my dear," John Christian implored her. "How many times have I told you that you must be brave, and proud of having him give his life for his Fatherland? Remember, everything's always for the best."

The visitor from Nithking laughed softly to herself. "So that's the gospel according to John: 'Everything is for the best'; therefore we have wars and diseases and earthquakes and floods and —clergymen!" she whispered to her brother.

Mr. Christian reproved her with patient severity. "Now, Sophie, if you want us to understand you, you will have to speak our language. You know very well we only speak Halfish: it's quite good enough for us. What is this foreign tongue you've learned away from home, anyway? I don't like the sound of it myself."

"Oh, I forgot, I didn't realize I was speaking Reasonese again. I suppose all I intended to say was that all wars are stupid, and stupidity is inevitable because——"

"But this is not a stupid war," Mrs. Christian interposed.

"This is a war to end war—a war to make the world safe for peace. And God is on our side too!"

The Rev. Rationalizer agreed warmly. "Certainly He is on our side. He's always on our side."

With an air of finality he laid his napkin on the table— whereupon his hostess rose and led the way to the veranda.

But the Rev. Rationalizer carried the conversation to the porch, where it was resumed as soon as they were all comfortably seated in their rocking chairs and set in motion. The small girl sat on the steps, seen but not heard—yet hearing all.

"As I've said before, it's these foreigners who make this country what it is today. Err for Errorians! Down with all foreigners—that's what I preach!"

Such thick clouds of fog began to roll onto the porch from the Dead Sea that for a moment Sophistica choked, then, slowly shaking her head, murmured, " 'Peace on earth, good will to men.' 'Love thy neighbor as thyself.' 'Down with all foreigners.' Dear God, has their casuistry killed all Christianity completely!" Turning, she peered searchingly through the fog at one face after the other. Apparently, however, everyone was happily oblivious of the suffocating mist except the ex-patriot, who was gasping painfully for breath. Rising suddenly, she exclaimed defiantly to her brother, "Oh, the devil take this fog! I can't breathe in it! I'm leaving Smug Harbor tomorrow. And I don't think such an atmosphere agrees very well with a child like Tellectina, either. John, won't you allow me to take her to a higher altitude, where the air is purer and more stimulating? Where there's more sunshine too? After all, that's what growing children need. Why, you can't see an inch beyond your nose in this place! And it may stunt her growth irremediably."

Mr. Christian appeared uncertain. "Well, Sister, that's certainly very nice of you. I want my daughter to have all the advantages possible, but——"

"What!" his wife exclaimed. "Give up my only child to go and live among those pagans—those heathens! Never!"

"That was the chief reason I—I mean, my dear sister, Tina

looks so delicate and overstudious. Besides, she might benefit by learning some language other than Halfish. In fact, I have excellent reason to believe that she may exhibit a decided talent for Reasonese as she grows older. (She's not the image of her aunt for nothing, I hope.) She could be tutored privately, and I'd pay all expenses."

"Oh, let me go with her, Father—*please!*"

Sophistica urged with renewed zeal. "Do, John. I'd like to take her with me now to Mt. Ghaulot to spend the summer. The air might be too rarefied at first, but it would be the most wonderful atmosphere in which any child could grow up. It's the highest altitude habitable by man, you know. And you may not realize it, but the teachers there are conceded to be the best in the world—they have all been educated in Nithking. Eventually Tellectina will run away from home, anyway, if she lives up to her name; so why not now?"

The expression on John Christian's face changed, and he bristled slightly. "Run away! From a good home like this? Don't be ridiculous. And besides, I think our schools in Smug Harbor and our climate quite good enough for anyone."

The Rev. Rationalizer stopped his rocking chair with emphasis. "Why, Miss Sophie, you don't seem to realize that the Land of Err is God's own Country!"

"I realize it only too well, that's exactly why——" the aunt began when her brother ended the entire discussion:

"Let's talk about it no more. I know you meant well, Sophie." Turning to his sister he continued in an undertone, "After all, I don't want any child of mine to be too different from other people. Even superiority makes for loneliness."

"Ah, there speaks the brother I used to know! But, John, you may not be able to prevent it. To be a Tellectina is at once a blessing and curse. I predict wonderful and terrible adventures for this quiet little dreamer." She sighed heavily. "Ah, well, if I can't save her now, I must at least be on hand a few years from now, when she starts out alone to explore Nithking, the Forbidden Country."

"Nithking?" Tellectina inquired eagerly. "Where is that, Auntie?"

"Oh, some distance above Smug Harbor, outside the Land of Err, of course."

"But why is it forbidden?"

"That's a long story, darling." Sophistica yawned in spite of herself. "I'll tell you some other day."

The combination of the heavy Sunday dinner and the warm enervating humidity was overwhelming. Suddenly the minister, opening his eyes with a guilty start, rose, apologizing for having interfered with the ladies' siestas, and took his departure; whereupon the family retired indoors to the coolness of their darkened bedchambers.

Soon the entire household and even the house and gardens themselves seemed to be breathing the measured breath of sleep. Quietly, with the art of long practise, Tellectina climbed out her bedroom window, down the heavy wistaria vine, and sped noiselessly over the grass to the beach and Andersen's waiting boat. As she sailed happily away to the Romanz Isle the child was filled with an ever increasing perplexity at her aunt's belief that she should wish to explore Nithking or any other country, forbidden or otherwise, as long as it was possible to visit this glamorous island, dreaming its days away under a perpetual rosy haze. Some time prior to the next visitation of this exotic lady, however, Tellectina was destined to make a discovery concerning Romanz Isle which produced in her a feeling both of pride and of regret.

Three years elapsed before Sophistica's second visit. It was as brief and unexpected as the first one and remained in the child's memory like the passage of some gayly colored bird. The departing guest had insisted on having the carriage wait for her outside the great iron gate. While being accompanied through the garden by her niece, who was astonishingly tall and thin now, Sophistica stopped abruptly between the tall rows of box.

"Here, child—now that we're alone a moment. Here is your

birthday gift, but don't open it until tomorrow. And take care, for there is a letter in the back of it. And if you value your wicked old aunt's life, then don't let anyone see it!"

"Oh, Auntie, thank you!" She kissed her delightedly. "I just love secrets, but I *wish* you'd stay for my birthday cake and everything."

"Ah, but I couldn't—and hold my unruly tongue, for I know what the Christian delegation is planning to give you. And I must not get myself forbidden the house entirely."

"Oh, no, no! That would be terrible. But, Auntie, before you leave, you're—you're so different from all the people here in Smug Harbor! Couldn't we, just this one little once, sit on top of the garden wall over there? I know it's forbidden and unladylike but—I've longed to so much!"

"Of course it's forbidden and unladylike—all interesting things are—so let's do it!"

Together they scrambled up on top of the high ivy-covered wall which enclosed the Christian estate on three sides and looked over. The young girl raised her arms in an exultant gesture of overflowing happiness.

"Oh, Aunt Sophie, isn't everything outside this old Christian estate just too beautiful! I can hardly wait till I'm old enough to go out and see the world for myself!"

The woman stared at the ugly city on the left and the fog-covered gray sea on the right, then at the child. "Now this is becoming serious. I'm afraid Andersen and Grimm have a deal to answer for—if the psychologists only knew it. Tell me what you saw on that fatal Romanz Isle."

"Oh, so many wonderful things! I was very sorry, and yet I was proud too, when I got to be thirteen (at least, I'll be thirteen tomorrow!) and discovered that I'd grown too big to ride in Andersen's and Grimms' little boats. It was a wonderful place they took me to, but I think the great world out there looks far more beautiful!" Tellectina then described the fine princes, princesses, and good fairies she had known on Romanz Isle, where virtue was always rewarded and wickedness always punished, where Prince Charming invariably came, and everyone invariably married and lived happily ever afterward.

With her hand under Tellectina's chin Sophistica tilted the child's head back and gazed long and earnestly into her eyes. "You poor blessed child, you've been looking at things through that rosy haze much too much: the Romanz atmosphere has seriously affected your eyes. I can see that there is a film over them now, and its removal will be very painful."

"Removal? You mean operate, like when I had my tonsils removed? And will it bleed and hurt?"

"No, no, darlikins, nothing as crude as that. But there is a universal and inviolable law that these films must be removed by a series of treatments known as the Sillidinous process, because the substance used is derived from a poisonous vine of that name which grows abundantly in every part of the world —but especially in Nithking."

"But, Auntie, my eyes never hurt me except when I read too much, so why——"

"Because it's said to be a handicap, this film—prevents you from seeing things as they really are. I had mine removed years ago. I can see everything too clearly now. I sometimes wish— but no, the comedy is worth the pain. But you, my dear—to think that I must fly away tonight and leave you to your fate; for this damnable atmosphere still suffocates me. (Besides, I now have a husband somewhere in the offing.) Yet somehow I do not fear for you."

"Fear what, Auntie? I don't understand."

"You will, all too soon. But remember, don't revile life too much for having created a Land of Err. Otherwise there would be no Forbidden Country for young Tellectinas to explore, and your adventure would end before it began. For without fools there is no comedy, my child."

Although the small girl merely looked at this strange vivid creature beside her in bewilderment and admiration, her words were unconsciously being stored up to be recalled years later at the most unexpected times and places.

"Where are you going now, Auntie?"

"Back where I came from. Nithking."

"Is Nithking nice?"

"No, not nice—exciting. I've made the trip through it once, but it's a country which always affords new delights and new dangers." She sighed happily. "Ah, yes, there's no doubt about it—Nithking offers the greatest possible adventure in all life!"

"Oh, then you *are* an adventuress, just as my mother said!"

Sophistica smiled. "Yes, I am an adventuress—but not just as your mother said."

"But you don't have real adventures and real dangers, do you?—like climbing mountains and getting lost in jungles, the way men do who go to Africa?" the child asked skeptically.

"No dangers, no adventures? Why, my dear young thing, in Nithking the jungles are so vast that thousands of lost explorers wander in them for a lifetime; its sacred rivers are the most treacherous and turbulent in the world, and their banks are white with human skeletons; cannibals lie in wait to devour you, wild beasts spring upon you, and the deadliest cobras known to man coil themselves in your very path ready to strike you dead. But the attacks of wild beasts are nothing compared to the attacks of hunger, loneliness, fatigue, fever, and fear. And worst of all is the poison vine which infests the whole continent: even the wariest explorers never escape it and usually it poisons them for life. And the mountains, ah, the mountains in Nithking run up and nuzzle their cold noses in the very hand of God Himself, and the gorges are but the blackened antechambers of hell! No adventures? No dangers? Even those of wildest Africa can't surpass those of Nithking!"

"Then, if it's so dangerous, why do people go to Nithking?"

"Because the lust for adventure is in their blood, because they can't tolerate confinement, and curiosity consumes them like a fever; because excitement is the breath of life to them and they like to use their wits to save their lives; because in Nithking the adventures are unsurpassed by any other country on the face of the earth, the scope and grandeur of the views staggering, and the beauty almost unbearable. The very scent of its flowers makes one delirious, and the seas are fragrant with amorous perfume. In Nithking explorers reach heights that are absolutely intoxicating, but the chief reason they go is that every genuine explorer longs to find the highest mountain in the world and scale its peak."

"But my geography teacher says Mt. Everest is the highest mountain in the world."

"Your teacher is wrong—as usual. Obviously he has never known the joys of Nithking. Most great explorers maintain that it lies somewhere in Nithking, but as to its exact location and name, there is a regrettable difference of opinion: points over which people have been known to slay each other."

"But, Auntie, didn't you say you had found it?"

"Well, according to the instruments with which I measure heights, it is Ghaulot. But every young explorer worthy of the name refuses to accept the reports of other travelers: she feels the urge to investigate such an important matter for herself."

"I thought real adventurers were always men. Are there many women who go to Nithking?"

"Too damned few!"

"Oh, Auntie, it sounds terribly exciting—even better than Romanz Isle! But why is it that you never hear anything about Nithking in Smug Harbor?"

"Because to all one hundred per cent Errorians it is not only a forbidden country but even a forbidden subject. Most Errorians are Puritans, and although Puritans are the hardest and toughest and most long-lived of any race in the world, few have ever possessed the strength or courage to endure the hardships of Nithking."

"Well, when I grow up I intend to be an adventuress too."

"Then remember, my child, the greatest adventure of all is not tracking down lions and tigers in Africa, or flying over the South Pole, or invading the Forbidden City of Tibet, or scaling Mt. Everest—as men will tell you; or even collecting hearts —as women will tell you. No, it lies in Nithking. But my most sensible advice to you is to stay safely in Smug Harbor and be happy."

"No, no, Auntie, I long to travel everywhere and see everything."

"Ah, yes, you are under the curse too. But you'll be obliged to climb through the Rocky Mountains of Casuistry first, then over Rote Hill, before you can arrive at Nithking proper."

Just then Mr. Christian, followed by a servant who was carrying Sophistica's bags, was seen between the boxwood hedges; whereupon the two culprits slipped guiltily off the garden wall. The woman joined her brother, while the child sped on far ahead of the others and waited at the carriage.

After the departing guest had settled herself in the cumbersome old vehicle she held up a warning finger, "If I'm any judge of character, John Christian, there is someone here who leads a double life. Another life goes on behind that sweet little smile which is all she shows to an unsuspecting world. There is trouble ahead for you, my placid one."

While Tellectina raised a startled face to her aunt, John Christian replied confidently, "Oh, no!"

The child, however, was not listening to them, she was staring miserably at the occupant of the carriage, but that lady was busily absorbed in wrapping carefully about her feet the robe which the fogs of Smug Harbor always necessitated for one so sensitive to them as Sophistica. Tellectina wondered desperately how anyone had been able to discover her most jealously guarded secret of a double life. And she even kissed her aunt a little resentfully as she bade her good-bye.

Father and daughter strolled back through the garden arm in arm, laughing happily together. Suddenly, without warning, the first wind of autumn swept past them. It ran its cool fingers through the child's long curls, tugged at her dress, sang across her ears, teased, called, beckoned her to come and join her old playfellow.

"Looks like a storm, Tina," Mr. Christian said. "Better run into the house out of this terrific wind."

The child stared at the man incredulously. Did he know nothing of the strange thrill to be derived from running in the wind, with the wind? Quickly she darted away from him and into the great south garden, hearing behind her his admonishing voice, the violent banging of the shutters, and the loud confusion of the servants struggling to close the windows.

Another terrific gust from the north descended upon the indolent old garden. For a long moment Tellectina stood in the path amid the frenzied swaying of the trees and shrubs—motionless, expectant, breathless. The wind seized upon the trembling trees, violating them till they flung their arms wildly above their heads half in protest, half in ecstasy; it rushed on, flinging the dead leaves into the air with lordly abandon; stripping the petals from the flowers, leaving them naked and shivering. The wind quickened the child's pulse, caught up her spirit like a helpless leaf, bore it aloft in dizzy spirals, drawing her irresistibly into the wild autumn bacchanalia.

Intoxicated by her own joy, she knew not why, the small Bacchante flung her arms to the heavens and began to dance riotously in the wind, with the wind, against the wind, over the dead leaves, through the dead leaves, darting between the swaying bushes, over the green grass, laughing up into the face of the frightened clouds hurrying and scurrying before the long lash of the merciless wind.

Breathless, she paused and stood swaying drunkenly in the path. Again and again the wind swept through the taut strings of her heart, wringing from it an unearthly music that was wildly sweet. And rushing through all her being, a tumultuous lyric to the autumn wind sang itself in her young blood—wordless and soundless—but she lived it, she was song incarnate, a living lyric for one ecstatic moment.

Once more the north wind rushed down upon the waiting garden. Faster and faster, colder and colder whirled that invisible mystery all about her. The ravished trees groaned aloud in agonized pleasure. The girl's long hair flew out wildly on the wind, writhing above her head in great Medusa swirls, whipping across her face in stinging lashes. Delirious with this strange fearful ecstasy, she abandoned herself to the orgy with all the fervor of a whirling young dervish. The beauty of departing summer, the excitation of approaching autumn, whipped the child's senses into an erotic state of mystic exaltation.

Oh, to be a leaf whirled through space! Oh, to be a tree, a cloud blown across the face of heaven! Oh, to be the wind—to come from beyond the world, to rush across the earth and return to the illimitable! I *am* a leaf, a tree, a cloud! I am the wind! I AM THE WIND! . . .

And then, possessed by some fearfully sweet power, she felt the walls enclosing her personal identity crumbling away, her very self dissolving into the elements, her individuality being drawn up into the vast unknown—a foretaste of absorption back into the universe, a foretaste of sleep everlasting.

But ecstasy transcended itself—it was insupportable. Terror struck into the child's heart. Abruptly she stopped, again swaying drunkenly in the path.

Frantically she looked about her to find—herself. There was nothing anywhere save the flying clouds above, the frenzied trees around her, and the wind—everywhere, that invisible force, moaning, sighing, laughing—the merciless, sinister wind. Terrified, she turned away and, instinctively seeking human contact, rushed blindly through the garden. As she rounded the corner of the house, the sight of her father and mother standing calmly on the porch permitted her to breathe again. She was safe; but what had happened to her?

"Something's wrong with me!" she assured herself. "I'm sure of it. No one else gets so excited over just plain wind and green trees. They're grown people and so ought to know what's what. There's something queer about all this—this joy, that I don't understand. I've always loved to run in the first autumn wind —but this was the very best time. But I must never, never, as long as I live, tell a soul what the wind does to me; they would think I was mad—and maybe I am, a little."

With an elaborate pretense of calm she walked slowly up the

steps and started for the door, but her mother rushed toward her.

"Good heavens, child, look at your face!"

Guiltily Tellectina pressed her cold trembling hands against her burning cheeks.

"Why, it's positively purple! Oh, Tina, how many times have I told you——! Remember, I said the very next time that you ran in the wind like that you'd go to bed without your supper!"

Mr. Christian turned toward her. "Moderation, Daughter, you must learn moderation in all things."

The exasperated woman appealed to her husband. "Honestly, John, I don't know what we are going to do with that child! She does everything to excess. She studies too hard, reads too much, and even plays too violently. I simply can't understand her."

"Daughter, can't you run more—well, more quietly? It would be just as much fun."

The child stood with downcast eyes, saying nothing, panting violently, but locking the secret joy fast in her young heart.

Her mother, however, pounced upon the word fun with alacrity. "Fun! Well, young lady, you'll see how much fun it'll be to be deprived of your supper! Now, march yourself right upstairs and lie down and dash some cold water on your face before you burst every blood vessel in it!"

Tellectina obeyed automatically, too full of receding joy to protest. When darkness stole into her room, however, self-pity moved her to tears. It was the first time in her entire life of thirteen years that she had been deprived of supper.

Suddenly she heard someone coming stealthily into her room. The dim figure set a large bowl of milk toast on the bedside table and, laying her finger on her lips, whispered, "Don't tell your father, whatever you do!" Then Mrs. Christian departed as noiselessly and inexplicably as she had come.

All the adventures and misadventures of the day were soon forgotten, for, unaware that she would on the morrow be taking the first step toward that great adventure Sophistica had predicted for her, Tellectina began to make exciting plans for a secret excursion she intended to make the following day: a search for a famous mountain path on which, for some mysterious reason, all the people of Smug Harbor constantly bestowed their praise but seldom their presence.

CHAPTER II

"WELL, TINA," Mrs. Christian said at the breakfast table the following morning, "you've opened all your nice birthday gifts from everyone except Aunt Sophie. Why didn't you bring that down too?"

"It's just—just a book."

"Good heavens, you have too many books now! But I hope it is a proper book for a thirteen-year-old girl. You'd better let me have a look at it first."

"Oh, it's just sort of fables—called *Greek Myths for Young People.*"

Mr. Christian intervened. "That won't hurt her, Mother. They're charming stories."

"Well, I know what *I'd* like for her to read," Mary Christian murmured significantly as Tellectina left the dining room hurriedly.

Extracting the letter concealed in the back of the book, the child rolled under her bed to the farthest corner, that being the only place where reading or daydreaming could be indulged in without the violation of the eternally inquisitive maternal eye. Three times she read the disturbing letter.

My Dear Namesake:

If you ever wish to see your wicked aunt again in this world, then destroy this letter.

I've been searching for a book called *How to Be a Good Heathen* or *The Delights of Being a Pagan.* The best antidote I can find, however, to counteract the poisonous effects of the Holy Guide which they will inevitably force on you as a guide to Casuistry, is this *Greek Myths for Young People.*

The Greek imagination gave birth to the most delightful gods ever conceived by man—or woman either—compared to which the Hebraic gods are malevolent, mutable, peccable, and satanic—in short, merely great panjandrums.

I myself, however, am tempted to write an epistle to the Puritans, or at least to compile a set of rules to guide the young: to tell you that if you turn the other cheek, life will smite it twice as hard as she did the right cheek; that the meek do not inherit the earth, but a hell on earth; that life is your adversary, and a grand cantankerous old woman she is, too; that if you ask little of the old girl you receive even less, therefore demand much; and that the two cardinal sins are: to hurt others deliberately (though hurting is inevitable) and to fail to enjoy life as much as possible.

But I can only do my educational bit, and that surreptitiously. The instinct of love, of course, is to save you from the very struggles which may be the making of you, but I shall do you a kindness and let you suffer.

But why do I worry about you, anyway? If you are a Tellectina with the right stamina, you will work your way through their Rocky Mountains of Casuistry; and if you are not, my little dear, then it doesn't matter the smallest tinker's smallest dam. For in that case you will settle down in Smug Harbor and grow into a nice fat Christian and live stupidly ever after. So I waste my breath—but not my love, I hope.

Your loving aunt,
SOPHISTICA TELLECTINA CHRISTIAN (still!)

P. S. Read every word of your Holy Guide religiously. For, paradoxical as it may seem, that black book will lead you out of Casuistry more quickly than anything else—as certain shrewd

Catholic gentlemen discovered long ago, and as the protesting ones never have. (Being one of those unnatural females who writes books, I am still to be addressed by my maiden name, a fact which the male resents—naturally!)

Bewildered and yet fascinated by this strange letter in Reasonese, the young girl tore it into shreds, but its words were to haunt her for years to come.

After the elaborate noonday dinner and the cake with thirteen candles had been properly appreciated by relatives and friends, they all adjourned to the long drawing room for coffee.

The Rev. Rationalizer, clasping a black book in his left hand, rose from his chair and, shaking a fat admonishing forefinger at Tellectina, said: "My child, mark my words well. The time has now come when you are old enough to start on the Great Journey. Heed my warning, for you will find many paths to lead you astray. But scorn the broad well-trodden ways and the wide gates, 'enter ye in at the strait gate,' and beware of the many tempters who will endeavor to lure you off the straight and narrow path and lead you into their wicked pleasure dives; for therein are ceaseless dancing, gambling, drinking, smoking, and card-playing. And these dens of iniquity are but the way stations on the road which leads to the Pit of Lost Souls whence there is no return trip."

The child's eyes were wide and frightened, and she trembled slightly.

"But verily I say unto you, the worst temptation which besets every traveler in this world is the seductive primrose path which cuts directly across the straight and narrow. But I'm certain your good mother here has given you wise and private instructions on this point many times."

"Yes, sir," the child responded. "She said that every boy who crosses your path will try to kiss you, but that a kiss is sure to lead a girl into the primrose path that goes steadily down to the place of brimstone and eternal damnation and that every girl should guard her virtue with her life and that it is a woman's chief jewel."

"Ahem! Ahem!" The minister coughed violently several times, but wishing to make her proud mother even more proud of her, the little girl continued to repeat Mrs. Christian's lesson verbatim.

"And she said that the path of every young girl is beset by men and that all men are lustful beasts and nothing but wolves in sheeps's clothing anyway, ready to prey upon the first——"

"Tina! That will do!" Mary Christian commanded in tense, muffled tones, her face a vivid crimson.

"And—er," the clergyman resumed hastily, "better than any warning which we, the poor humble servants of the Lord Jesus, can offer, however, are the directions to be found in this divinely inspired guide book to Casuistry. So, Tellectina Christian, we, the assembled, the humble representatives, so to speak, of the Church, the home, and the school, do hereby present you with the Holy Guide." Here he laid the large imposing book in Tellectina's trembling young hand.

Emotion caused her childish voice to quaver as she said, "Thank—thank you, sir."

Shyly the bewildered and excited little girl thanked the donors successively, but while they were congratulating the Rev. Rationalizer on his presentation speech she slipped out of the door, unnoticed save by the other children, whose presence she had completely forgotten. On reaching a secluded part of the garden she leaned against a great flowering magnolia tree and drew a deep sigh of relief.

"He talked with that sobby voice just the way he does at revival meetings, and it always makes my insides sort of melt. But I guess it's only the spirit of the Lord stirring in me, as he always says. I'm glad it's got my name on it in big gold letters at the bottom. Everyone says that this guide book will show you how to walk on the straight and narrow path. And I feel that that's the only place where you can live a perfect life, and doesn't Jesus say, 'Be ye perfect even as your Father which is in heaven'? And I want so terribly to be perfect. I see no reason why I can't be, if I only try hard enough." Closing her eyes a moment she prayed silently. "Oh, dear Lord, help me to make myself perfect! And please help me to find the straight and narrow path."

Hearing footsteps on the porch, she sped lightly down to the gate, which she opened cautiously on its rusty hinges. The only sound in the sleepy afternoon streets of the town was that of her own skipping feet, which brought her quickly to the edge of the woods. She ascended the foothills at a run, for this was all familiar ground where she had frequently picnicked with her family. On arriving at the first mountain, however, she stopped abruptly: a strange dizziness came over her. She closed her eyes for a moment but the sensation of faintness was succeeded by a curious elation which she had never experienced before except in church during the most exciting part of some stirring hymn. Looking about her, she seemed to see broad well-worn paths leading in every direction—paths which surely had not been there a moment before. None of them, however, was straight or narrow or possessed of a strait gate.

Undecided as to which way to go, the child seated herself with her back to a tree and hastily consulted the first page of the Guide Book, which said:

"In the beginning God created the heaven and the earth.
"And the earth was without form, and void; and darkness was upon the face of the deep."

Unconsciously the young girl closed her eyes the better to feel the sonorous words roll about her ears—their sound was so lovely it made their sense difficult to grasp. Until now they had always constituted beautiful but fearful music to her, but for the first time in her life she wondered what on earth they meant. Where were the directions? What sort of guide book was this? She read on:

"And Adam . . . begat a son . . . Seth: . . . and Seth . . . begat Enos: . . . and Enos . . . begat Cainan: . . . and Cainan begat Mahalaleel: . . ."

The words sounded like the droning of bees in her ears. The sleepy murmur went on and on. . . .

After an hour had elapsed, the child awakened from her delicious nap with a guilty start. Overwhelmed with mortification, she rubbed her heavy-lidded eyes vigorously and hurriedly read on.

"And Lot . . . dwelt in a cave, he and his two daughters. . . . And they made their father drink wine that night: and the firstborn went in, and lay with her father. . . . For the Lord had fast closed up all the wombs of the house of Abimelech, because of Sarah, Abraham's wife."

Shocked and confused, the little Puritan hastily concealed the book behind a bush and ran away as though pursued. Shame sent the most painful blushes rushing to the child's face. Were these not the very subjects which she had been emphatically informed were too indecent to mention except in whispers behind closed doors! Then what were they doing in this sacred guide book?

She had not wandered far, however, when a violent conscience pain smote her, causing her to retrace her footsteps and consult the book once more. Having been bewildered by the first half, she turned guiltily but hopefully to the second part, where her eyes skimmed the pages in haste until they lighted on the last "begat," and there she began again. Although the story on the ensuing pages was interesting, it contained no directions for bewildered travelers. Finally there appeared words which caused her heart to leap with joy.

"Blessed are the meek: for they shall inherit the earth. . . .

"Blessed are the merciful: for they shall obtain mercy. . . .

". . . Whosoever shall smite thee on thy right cheek, turn to him the other also."

Rising, Tellectina walked on in smiling confidence. How simple it all was after all. Now she would assuredly find the straight and narrow path, the very obvious implication being that she should be meek and merciful and when injured turn the other cheek to her enemy, and such commendable actions would automatically lead her into the famous path on which everyone in Smug Harbor constantly bestowed his praise rather than his presence. Dusk having descended, however, she was obliged to return home, but went singing happily at every step.

In the days that followed, the natural exuberance of a happy healthy child with a keen zest for living made it difficult for her to be at all times meek. Daily she was torn between the desire to enjoy the pleasant activities of a normal child and the strange powerful urge which impelled her toward the straight and narrow path; but never at any time was she wholly oblivious of the oppressive shadow of Casuistry in which she dwelt.

One afternoon after school she stumbled up the steps of her house sobbing bitterly. "Oh, Mother, Mother, I'm disgraced! And I wasn't guilty, and I was punished just the same! It's not fair! And I hate that old Blithings woman!"

Mrs. Christian, who had been sitting on the veranda rocking gently as she embroidered, now rushed toward her daughter. Sinking to the steps Tellectina sobbed out the whole story in her mother's arms.

"Katie Dawson copied my theme yesterday—I saw her do it, and after school today that new teacher—that Miss Blithings, made us both stay in and write new ones."

Mrs. Christian stroked the long black curls soothingly. "There, there, pet, don't cry! Didn't you tell the teacher that Katie did it?"

"No, because I thought her conscience would make her tell the truth, and besides, I was trying to be—to be—I mean, I felt so sorry for Katie, she was crying and everything. But it's not fair and I'm—oh, I'm disgraced forever!" She began to sob afresh.

"Now, now, sweet, everyone knows that my little girl

wouldn't copy or cheat. It's because this is a new teacher, that's all. Your father will go to see her tomorrow, and then everything will be all right."

"It never *can* be all right! I was punished when I didn't deserve it!"

"Come on in and lie down. I'll have Liza fix my baby a big, big bowl of milk toast, and then you'll forget all about it."

Tellectina obeyed, but the instant her mother left the room, sat up to peruse again a certain passage in the Holy Guide lying on the table beside her bed. Yes, there it was in black and white:

"Blessed are the merciful: for they shall obtain mercy."

And until she finally fell into a troubled sleep that night after supper, the child continued to murmur over and over again, "But if I showed mercy to Katie, then why didn't *I* obtain mercy from the teacher? There's something queer about all this mercy business which I don't understand."

Not long afterward, while Tellectina was standing in line ready to march into the schoolroom, a mischievous boy reached forward and snatched the ribbon off the long braid of a red-haired girl and then gazed innocently off into space. Tellectina, who was standing directly behind the victim, promptly laughed, whereupon the angry girl slapped her on the right cheek.

Tellectina was momentarily too stunned to move, although through her anger ran the familiar words, "Whosoever shall smite thee on thy right cheek, turn to him the other also." The little religionist was struggling with her impulse to strike back and the longing to practise her Casuistry and offer the other cheek when the young redhead, egged on by the laughter of those around her, slapped Tellectina twice as vigorously on the left cheek. At this juncture the teacher came down the line to see what was causing the delay in its advance; whereupon the children sobered immediately and marched into the building before the young martyr could utter a protest.

After school she thought matters over in private. "No use staying at home: poor dear Mother would only try to solve my troubles with milk toast!"

Arriving at the first woods, she paused to verify an all important matter. Perhaps she had misread it. But no, she had memorized her guide book correctly.

"Whosoever shall smite thee on thy right cheek, turn to him the other also."

"That's almost exactly what I did, even though I wasn't guilty of anything. Surely this good deed will lead me to the path at once." She walked on confidently for some time, but finally exhaustion and disappointment compelled her to return home.

Could the Holy Guide Book be incorrect? That was impossible, surely. Yet where lay the difficulty? Why was her life such a failure? This remained an open question for years—unanswerable and increasingly painful.

A year flew by, however, in which the interest of new dresses, school, and flirting with the boys distracted her mind almost entirely from her desire to walk on the straight and narrow way. In fact, the mere joy of being alive and young submerged all problems for months on end. Finally, however, the cumulative discomfort of a dull conscience pain occasioned a resumption of the old search.

One fine spring day the little Casuist was toiling up a rocky incline when her thoughts were suddenly lured astray by the fragrance of flowers. "Oh, I didn't know there were any flowers in these mountains! And I've never in my life smelled anything so—so sweet that it is almost wicked!"

A voice startled her by replying, "Come closer!"

The voice had issued from the smiling face of a young boy about sixteen. Enticed by the strange irresistible fragrance of the flowers, Tellectina allowed him to lead her toward them by the hand. Opening a wide gate, he entered; but the girl hesitated, until drawing her to him suddenly with a rough awkward gesture he kissed her lightly on the forehead. A strange sweet

sensation ran like an electric current from the inside of her
forehead to her stomach and, circling around there deliciously,
slowly died away.

The girl blushed warmly and, drawing away hastily, protested, "Oh, you mustn't do that!" secretly hoping he would repeat the offense.

"Why not?" the boy asked, also blushing, but with his bold
bright eyes still on her face.

"Because it—it's not nice."

"Isn't nice? Why, I think it's about the nicest thing in the
world! And you're the prettiest thing in the world. Come, let's
walk farther down this way."

Lifting shy eyes, the girl beheld a broad well-trodden path-
way bordered with fragrant pink primroses which danced and
beckoned to her in the warm spring breeze. With slow, hesitant steps, she began to stroll down this path with the admiring
youth at her side never taking his eyes off her face. How pleasant it was after all the thorns and rocks of all the other paths!
The blood in her veins was behaving in the most extraordinary
way—it actually tingled and felt strangely delicious. Tremu-
lously happy and frightened, she flashed several sidelong glances
at him from the corners of her eyes.

The youth laughed sheepishly. "Don't look at me that way!"

"What way?"

"That way. It gives me the—the stomach-ache."

The girl laughed and looked at him again—that way, glowing with pleasure at her new-found power. She laughed mockingly into his eyes and tossed her head. The boy endeavored to
kiss her once more, but she fled back up the path and was
amazed to find herself confronted with a heretofore unseen
gate: a small strait gate leading into a narrow path overgrown
with brambles and thorns. It was steep and rocky and gave every
evidence of being neglected, even forgotten. The gate bore a
sign in large letters:

THE STRAIGHT AND NARROW PATH

The young girl stood with reluctant feet where the primrose path and the straight and narrow meet. The youth tugged at her hand, but the little Puritan of fifteen turned heroically away and entered in at the strait gate, at last aware that the path on which she stood was the very one she had been so diligently seeking for two years.

As she walked slowly along this dim trail, picking her way painfully over the rocks and through the thorny bushes, she felt excessively virtuous but not at all happy, as she had anticipated. Suddenly the perfume of the primroses was again wafted to her. Turning impulsively, she ran back down the narrow path and leaning on the strait gate gazed wistfully over the great field of pink flowers. Soon a girl whom Tellectina knew could be seen wandering there with the arm of a boy circling her waist. In response to Tellectina's call, she came to the small white gate on which the little Puritan was leaning heavily. In shy, frightened tones Tellectina whispered to the older girl, "What's that —that nice funny feeling in your stomach when a boy kiss— kisses you?"

"Passion," her friend whispered in reply.

"What is it called?"

"Passion."

"But you oughtn't to feel it, ought you?"

"No, but you wouldn't be natural if you didn't."

"Then how can you keep from it?"

"Will power."

"Will power," Tellectina repeated in an awed voice as the other youth arrived to reclaim the older girl.

With her hand on the latch of the strait gate, the little Casuist murmured, "I know it's wrong to walk on the Primrose Path —everyone says so; only, only, dear Lord, I can't quite see why you've made wicked things so pleasant, or how anything so pleasant as being kissed can be wicked. But give me will power. O Lord, give me will power! I know I'm going to need it. Oh, dear, there's something queer about this wickedness that I don't understand. Help me to understand, God, I want to understand *everything*. And I intend to some day—you'll see!"

This memorable day was followed by turbulent weeks indeed. Every night the bewildered little adolescent girl first indulged in the sweet memory of the birth of passion and then prayed earnestly for forgiveness and the strength to resist it at all future times. All her other senses were likewise awakening in strange troubling fashion. After having tortured herself almost to the breaking point, one afternoon she went to the mountain and sought help in prayer.

She sank to a kneeling position and clasping her hands convulsively began to speak with her eyes closed painfully tight. "O Lord, help me, help me! For a whole year now I've tried to do what I thought Jesus would do. I've tried not to let the boys kiss me—not even on the hand or hair. And I've tried—but oh, the trouble is I don't *know* what Jesus would do! Would he go to parties or take love notes from the boys in school or accept boxes of candy? I refused one from Jack, and so he gave it to Janet, and, Lord, you know how I love chocolate candy! Or would Jesus think it wrong to wear pretty red hair ribbons that go so well with my black hair? or to read books that weren't school books? or enjoy quotations from poetry which have no moral lesson in them? Oh, why—why, must I give them up? When I read them over they give me such a happy sad feeling all inside me—it's even better than that nice smooth feeling that chocolate candy gives you all the way down. It's almost as nice as that wicked sweet sensation you have when a boy holds your hand. O dear Lord in heaven, I try so hard to be good—to be perfect; but why do you allow me to have all these wicked feelings, and why did you make wrong things so nice? And why, why, did you make me such a weak and willing sinner? Help me, tell me what to do, Lord!"

The child waited. No answer to her supplication came. No answer seemed to be forthcoming at any time. Exhausted with doubt and despair, she sank back to a sitting position and remained motionless for a long time. Finally sighing heavily, she formulated her conclusions.

"I suppose the real trouble is that Jesus was a man and I am a girl, therefore my problems are different from his, and besides, times have changed since his day." In her inmost heart, however, she knew she had failed ignominiously; how or why, she could not fathom.

"And there is another thing which puzzles me," she announced to the indifferent mountains all about her: "Why is it that the wicked are not punished on this earth nor the good rewarded? I have seen with my own eyes that they are not. Three of the deacons in our church make shady business deals every week—my father says so. And why is it that the righteous people all look glum and sour and the wicked are the jolliest people in all Smug Harbor? And why is it that the more I try to be good the more miserable I become? There's something queer about this goodness which I don't understand." Slowly she rose and walked home.

For months Casuistry only vaguely troubled Tellectina until one Sunday morning the Rev. Rationalizer delivered such a moving sermon that the tears streamed down his own face as well as the faces of the entire congregation. The violence of her conscience pain propelled Tellectina toward the straight and narrow path that afternoon with the Holy Guide clasped firmly in her hand. Seating herself on a great boulder, she determined once more to place her confidence in the Holy Guide, and opening it, read:

"Therefore I say unto you, Take no thought for your life, what ye shall eat, or what ye shall drink; nor yet for your body, what ye shall put on. . . .

"For your heavenly Father knoweth that ye have need of all these things. . . .

"Take therefore no thought for the morrow. . . ."

After reading these instructions the young girl remained motionless for some time, as though arriving at some momentous decision. The sun began to sink behind the mountain top, but Tellectina arose with a beatific expression on her face; she did not turn back, she walked steadily on and up. The way grew steeper and rockier; the air grew uncomfortably chill; and the child became ravenously hungry.

"But I must not worry about any of these things because does not my heavenly Father know that I have need of a warm coat and some hot supper? Or perhaps He'll drop some manna down, the way the Sunday-school teacher told us He did long ago. Anyway, I'm certain everything will be all right: for it says in the Holy Guide that I need take no thought for the morrow." Thus reassuring herself at every step, she stumbled on, until hunger, exhaustion, and fear overcame her, and she sank to the ground. . . .

Early the following morning, when she awakened, it was not yet daylight. Her limbs were painfully stiff, but after great effort she struggled to a sitting position. At the sudden recollection of all the horrors of the night—the cold, the hunger, the fear, and the darkness—she covered her eyes and uttered a low wail.

"O Lord, why did you fail me? Oh, how could you, how could you? 'Hast thou forgotten me?' No manna was dropped, no warm coat provided; oh, what—what has happened?"

In a dazed way she looked about her. Then her eyes closed, and, supporting herself against a tree, she remained thus for what seemed an interminable time while her head insisted on swimming in a most peculiar fashion and her body went alternately hot and cold.

Suddenly there was a long deafening peal of thunder. The earth quaked beneath her, the lightning ran in blinding flashes across the sky. The young explorer trembled violently but was unable to flee. Overcome with fright, she sat there gazing with wide, fascinated eyes up into the heavens. The zigzag streaks of lightning formed themselves into gigantic fiery letters against the black storm clouds:

HOW DO *I* KNOW THERE IS A GOD?

Terror paralyzed the overwrought child. No human being she had ever heard or read of had dared ask such a question! She would be struck dead instantly for such blasphemy! With a mighty piercing noise the earth was suddenly rent open before her. A black chasm yawned at her feet. Out of the abyss sprang a man clothed in flaming red with a forked tail and horns. He was flourishing a trident as he danced about fiendishly on the opposite bank. Tellectina's senses reeled—her eyes closed—the earth slipped from under her—she plunged into the awful black void.

She felt herself falling—falling, through endless black space—down—down, and ever down to death—to destruction—to everlasting hell itself. Her mind reeled and went blank. . . .

Finally regaining partial consciousness, she forced her eyes open with a desperate effort and, realizing that she was suspended dizzily over the void about halfway down, caught frantically at the only thing in sight. For a moment the bit of old bee leaf saved the frightened child, but proved to be a rotten twig too weak to support her. Clinging blindly to the face of the cliff with all the passion of fear and despair she cried aloud:

"Give me a sign, O God! Do not destroy me! I do believe, I do believe! I have failed, but help me, lift me out of this abyss. Oh, *prove* to me that there is a God! A sign—a miracle—a vision, anything, only give me some sign that you are there! I can't take other people's word for it. I must know—know for myself! Oh, dear God, do not fail me now as you failed me last night with the manna and the coat! Oh, save me, save me from death in this awful black chasm!"

For a long eternity she clung there, waiting, breathless, motionless. At last the answer came, an answer more terrifying than all the thunder and noise of the rending earth: a great deafening silence that rang in her ears like a thousand bells. . . .

At length she managed somehow to climb out of the abyss, back to firm ground. She lay for an interminable time with her face to the earth, sobbing as she had never sobbed in her life. Something in her had died forever.

"There she is! There she is!" came the voice of Tellectina's mother shouting hysterically.

Mr. Christian ran forward and lifted the child in his arms. Both parents were speechless, though Mrs. Christian continued to weep audibly, so that the man was obliged to support her as well as the child. Several neighbors with lanterns still lighted gathered around.

One woman cried, "She's having a chill! It's chills and fever. See her shake—take her to bed quick. She'll get pneumonia. Here, put my coat over her!"

The searching party started down the hill at a brisk pace, but not too brisk for one old woman to rebuke Tellectina. "Why, child, aren't you ashamed to stay away all night and frighten your poor mother out of her wits? We've been searching for you all night. Thank goodness, none of my children ever did as queer things as this!"

"And to think she was so near home all the time, too," her father murmured brokenly.

"Whatever," a third neighbor asked, "do you suppose possessed a little girl to stay out all night in the mountains? Now, if it had been a boy playing at Indian or something——"

The woman beside her replied, "Guess she must have tripped or fallen or gone to sleep or something like that."

Mary Christian turned imploring eyes on her daughter. "That *was* it, wasn't it, dear?"

Opening her eyes, the child beheld two large, troubled, pleading eyes hovering above her. "Yes, I reckon that was it, Mother."

As Tellectina lay ill with pneumonia in the weeks which followed, there was one other phenomenon which puzzled her almost as much as the earthquake: the fact that her parents did not wish to hear the truth concerning that momentous night in the mountains. With recovery there came also the realization that never again would she feel quite the same. Apparently no one else noticed any difference in her; consequently she did not mention it, though she continued to feel a great deal of intermittent pain which she assumed was the result of some severe internal injury received from her fall into the abyss.

Besides that, Tellectina's sixteenth year was memorable for another reason: the discovery of a forbidden source of pleasure almost as satisfying as that of the Primrose Path. She had been indulging in it periodically ever since she was fourteen, but at sixteen it took fatal hold on her. Although her schoolmates and particularly her observant English instructor had frequently commented on its results the morning afterward, she had been able to keep it a secret until one night when her mother—to her horror—stumbled upon her in the very act.

The discovery that the use of a certain drug had the power to fill her with delight for hours on end was made, so Tellectina considered, quite by accident. She found it lying freely about the house, neglected by all members of the Christian family, who were apparently equally unaware of its potentialities either for harm or pleasure. It was many years before Tellectina learned that its proper name was Cianite Vitrgrew. It appeared to be merely a hard compact grayish powder usually contained in small yellow or brown cylindrical cases. One night she had been under its influence for about six hours when her mother appeared in the bedroom door.

"Why, Tina, what on earth do you mean—being up at this hour! It's two o'clock in the morning! Get into bed at once!"

The young girl lifted dazed unseeing eyes and stammered, "I—I can't yet because I haven't finished——"

Mary Christian snatched the yellow cylinder from her daughter's hand. "Give me that thing! Don't you know you'll ruin your health? I never heard of a young girl doing anything so foolish—you ought to be ashamed of yourself! How often have you been guilty of this before?"

"Well—er—I——"

"Don't tell me an untruth! I'm certain you have done it many times before, judging from the expression on your face. To think that a mother can't even go to bed and trust her own child! I'm thoroughly ashamed of you and understand once for all that I don't intend to allow you to form any such pernicious habit as this. It's unnatual, unhealthy, and unnecessary. Now, go to bed. I won't leave the room till you do."

Tellectina crawled meekly into bed, for the effect of the Cianite Vitrgrew had not yet worn off. As soon as her mother had angrily snapped off the light, however, the young girl rose and again attempted to apply the drug in the dark, with indifferent success. After this episode she carefully shaded her light so that the vigilant maternal eye could not see her weekly indulgence. And with continued use the visions came to her in such increasing abundance and intricacy that when transmitted to paper they elicited great amazement and praise from the entire school, to which they were read aloud, as a mark of especial merit, by the head of the English department.

One spring evening after supper Tellectina turned away from the piano which she had just been playing and said to her father, "Tell me what 'ravishing' means and also this word in the beginning of this other song, 'braes,' I guess it's pronounced."

With a gesture of finality Mr. Christian laid aside his book. "Come here at once, Daughter."

After examining her for some time, her father pronounced his diagnosis. "Tina, this constant shaking of the head which you've exhibited throughout this entire examination is a symptom of a disease we must endeavor to cure as soon as possible."

"Disease? Oh, no, Father!"

"There, there, child, it's nothing to be ashamed of. Cerebral Lethargica, as it's technically called, is simply a childhood malady with which we all have to be afflicted. Wouldn't you like to be cured of it before you grow any older? It's less painful if treated properly while young."

"If it doesn't mean operate——"

John Christian laughed and patted her on the shoulder affectionately. "No, no, honey, nothing so drastic. They don't take things out of you, they try to put things into you! And there are certain health resorts which make a specialty of curing young people. Your mother went to Veneer Bluffs as a young girl, but I have excellent reason to believe," and here he chuckled softly, "that Rote Hill is better."

"Rote Hill! Oh, I'd love to go there because I've heard some of the patients who've been there talk about all the fun they have dancing at the Casino."

There was great excitement in the Christian household throughout the entire summer, inasmuch as Mrs. Christian was outfitting Tellectina for her stay at Rote Hill. Sophistica wrote her niece that she trusted her struggle through Casuistry had at least proved to her that "an honest God's the noblest work of man"; and that after she was treated for Cerebral Lethargica she would be far stronger and more fitted to make the trip into Nithking. But Tellectina was so excited over the idea of going to a spa that she forgot, for the time being, both Casuistry and the fact that her aunt had predicted that climbing over Rote Hill would be merely her second adventure, preliminary to her supreme adventure in the Forbidden Country.

CHAPTER III

WHAT HAPPENED WHEN TELLECTINA WAS SENT TO ROTE HILL
TO TAKE THE CURE; HOW SHE DISCOVERED A GREAT CARNIVAL,
ENJOYED SECRET PLEASURES, AND MET THERE HER NATURAL
SISTER FEMINA

ON THE VERY FIRST NIGHT of her arrival at Rote Hill
a mysterious incident occurred which Tellectina realized
with some trepidation might be destined to change the course
of her life very radically.

Her first day at the spa had been a pleasant confusion of
kaleidoscopic pictures flashing across her field of vision in rapid
succession: vast rolling green lawns, incredibly tall trees, many
"Fine old buildings rearing their gray heads proudly above their
dark green coats of ivy," as her father expressed it in his impromptu poetry; and "Innumerable pretty girls flitting through
the October gardens like brightly colored butterflies."

Superimposed on these impressions were those of the imposing offices of the chief medical director, his highly disconcerting resemblance to her own pouter pigeons back in Smug
Harbor; the book of interminable rules he gave her; the doctor's
laughter at his own jokes about her ailment, Cerebral Lethargica, not being fatal as often as Encephalitis Lethargica, the
tropical kind of sleeping sickness; and the stream of technical
phrases which he poured over her father's polite head as they
left his office: "The catalytic action of the baths, the unexcelled
therapeutic agencies, the unparalleled mineral waters and justly
famous medical staff of Rote Hill."

After having inspected his daughter's room in the hotel, Mr.
Christian had stood on the spacious veranda bidding Tellectina

good-bye. She had been surprised when her own hard intact little heart had suddenly contracted with sweet pain, but even more surprised and puzzled at the melting tenderness glowing in her father's eyes—a look she was to see in so many men's eyes in the future—but one seldom intended for her.

That night after her first supper in a strange hotel among so many strange people, such a black loneliness suddenly descended on the sixteen-year-old girl that she rushed out of the building to seek the friendliness of the garden. And it was there that the mysterious incident occurred. She was sitting quietly on the marble rim of a fountain when she heard someone calling softly through the dusk. Lying on top of the high stone wall and half concealed by the leaves of the overhanging branches was a handsome young boy. Although aware that conversing with boys in the absence of a chaperon was a violation of the rules of the institution, Tellectina was unable to resist the magnetic power which drew her toward him. To her own amazement she found herself flashing her eyes at him in the most unaccountable fashion. The youth responded appreciatively by slipping down from the wall.

As he was advancing toward her, the most extraordinary thing happened. Slowly, subtly, surely, half of the girl's inner self stirred, tugged at her other self—loosened—uncoiled its tendrils from about her mental self like a vine being torn away from its support, and suddenly wrenched itself free.

It was some time before Tellectina realized that the young boy was holding her hand—and yet it was not her hand. For although she could feel the blood pulsing rapidly through it, she saw to her amazement that standing immediately in front of her and completely concealing her from the boy's view was another girl who had emerged mysteriously out of her own being—out of her own body; a girl who looked and sounded like herself yet was not herself; a stranger touching her so closely that she could feel the blood dancing in the other's veins; while Tellectina herself was left behind, sufficiently detached and intact coolly to observe the interloper.

The youth was addressing himself solely to Tellectina's feminine counterpart. "My name's Andrew Mereboy. I'm from that
boys' spa over there on the other side of the hill. I think you're
awfully pretty—what's your name?"

Before the astounded Tellectina could reply she heard a voice
that sounded like her own but was not her own, for it contained
a gay provocative lilt. "What's that to you?" it said.

"Aw, please tell me. I'd like to write to you."

With a toss of her head and a flash of her black eyes, the
strange girl answered him. "Well, try Femina Christian and see
what will happen!"

The soft tender look in the boy's pleading eyes enveloped
both girls in a warm golden intoxication such as Tellectina had
never before experienced in her life. It was a sensation more
delicious than she had ever dreamed existed in the whole world.
Frightened by both the boy and the mysterious girl and yet
curiously delighted, Tellectina turned away and sped swiftly
through the garden until she reached the hotel.

With her hand on the door of her bedroom, however, she
paused, for there close beside her stood the other girl. Leaning
weakly against the doorpost, Tellectina murmured in bewilderment, "Dear Lord, what have you done to me? Must I be
divided into two people just because I think one thing and feel
another? Which am I?—this Femina who rolls her eyes about
like a lunatic and laughs at nothing, who considers a boy her
rightful plaything, or——"

"Or," the impertinent stranger supplemented, "are you merely
Tellectina who longs to be cured of her sleeping sickness, who
studies and reads till she gets a headache and affects a supercilious indifference to all feminine matters?"

"But," Tellectina objected stoutly, "I love to read and study
better than anything else in the whole world!"

The other girl laughed gayly. "But *I* love to flirt and make
boys fall in love with me better than anything else in the whole
world, so there! And I had my first real taste of power tonight,
and I refuse to be kept imprisoned any longer!" Then she

laughed joyously. "Oh, I never dreamed what a girl could do to a boy simply with her eyes! Ah, it's delicious to be Femina!" And without so much as a by-your-leave she boldly opened the door of Tellectina's room and walked in. Tellectina slowly followed and locking the door behind her stood leaning against it, staring at the intruder in a sort of fascinated horror, as she might regard a beautiful serpent.

Running to the mirror over the dressing table, Femina gazed at herself intently. "So," she whispered, "I *am* pretty after all. I was never sure until tonight."

She tossed her head and watched the effect in the glass, looked through half-closed lids, opened them wide in an innocent stare, flashed a provocative glance from the corner of her eye as though practising on some invisible victim, then threw back her head and laughed mischievously. Suddenly screwing up her nose she made a face at her image and, turning away, walked slowly up and down the room, arching her back, moving seductively with one hand on her hip.

"Stop it!" Tellectina cried in disgust.

The intruder merely laughed and seating herself on the edge of the bed commenced to undress. Selecting one of her companion's most feminine and absurd nightdresses, she slipped it over her head and then, lifting her arms exultantly, murmured, "Oh, it's good to be free! And it's good to be Femina!"

"But," Tellectina protested, "how on earth can I explain your presence to other people?"

"Oh, we won't often appear simultaneously. In fact, I'll sleep most of the time—except when an attractive boy comes into view. But you might tell the simple truth and say that I am your natural sister."

Tellectina looked at her scornfully. "Either of my parents would be ashamed to own you! And besides——"

"Well, my better half," Femina said as she stretched her slim body diagonally across Tellectina's bed, "perhaps then you had better say to the world that we are cousins—newly discovered cousins."

"Oh, I don't see why you couldn't have remained in hiding where I could control you properly."

"There are a great many things you can't see—and there are going to be even more." The stranger laughed significantly, and turning over, dragged all the covers with her.

Tellectina looked down on her severely. "I warn you, Femina, I came to Rote Hill for a serious purpose, and I don't intend to put up with any of your nonsense."

"All I ask of you, my dear sweet sister, is a policy of non-interference. And I also wish that you wouldn't blur my bright eyes with that damned reading lamp of yours every night!"

This only served as a signal. At once Tellectina obstinately settled herself down in bed to read, as was her nightly custom. On this night, however, she spent most of her time gazing at her new-found sister and roommate with disapproval, bewilderment, and admiration.

The following morning at breakfast in the long glassed-in dining room which overlooked the sunny gardens and the rolling blue hills beyond, Tellectina and her unwanted roommate were introduced to some of the other patients who lived in the same hotel: a tall angular girl named Puritine afflicted with an extreme case of Lethargica; Eva, a voluptuous blonde, discharged from two other spas as incurable; and Tommy, a sad pale-faced girl who dressed and acted like a boy. There was one girl at the table named Clare, to whom Tellectina felt instantly drawn. And her admiration only increased with the discovery that the other's case was even milder than her own.

For the next few days confusion reigned over Rote Hill while the doctors and patients attempted to dovetail schedules for the hourly cures. Finally, with their schedule cards in hand, the girls trooped forth to find the various thermal establishments which were located about the grounds. Clare and Tellectina walked eagerly in front of the others, curious, excited, and a little frightened. On arriving at the first group of buildings, however, Tellectina received a surprise even greater than the sudden emergence of Femina.

But this discovery was too wonderful even to mention to her new-found friend, Clare. Nevertheless, the sparkling eyes and excited voice of each indicated to the other that she also had caught a glimpse of the same phenomenon; yet their young shyness caused them, by a tacit agreement, to keep it a sort of open secret. It was like first falling in love: they were too diffident even to broach the very subject uppermost in their minds, the very thing which drew them together and served to forge the bond between them.

Nor in the ensuing weeks did Tellectina confide in her parents, merely replying to the eager questionings in their letters that she was enjoying Rote Hill exceedingly, having found it even more exciting than she had ever dreamed. It was not until the sudden and unexpected visitation in the late spring of her aunt Sophistica, who had failed to communicate with her niece during the four years which had intervened since her last visit, that Tellectina divulged the secret she had kept religiously and fearfully locked in her breast for nine months. It was the last Sunday of the season, and when they strolled out into the garden a soft June moonlight enveloped them caressingly. To obtain privacy, however, Tellectina chose to sit on an old stone bench in the shadow of a flowering locust tree whose heavy fragrance made the young girl's heart almost burst with a sweet inexplicable joy.

"You know, Auntie," she said, twisting her hands nervously in her lap, "I'm afraid something's the matter with me. I don't believe I'm normal."

"I certainly hope not. Normality means mediocrity."

"But I've watched all the other girls here for nine months, and none of them seem to feel the way I do. Except my friend Clare, perhaps."

"She's quite the loveliest girl here—except my own little Tina, of course."

"But we're both queer, I'm afraid. I know I am, because I don't see things here the way the other patients do. The trouble

is, Aunt Sophie, I—well, I haven't found Rote Hill to be a
health resort at all—it's a—a sort of carnival—a new sort!"

The older woman squeezed the girl's arm violently. "You
lucky young devil!"

"You mean—you mean it's all right? I'm not queer or crazy
or anything?"

"Oh, you're queer all right, but you're not crazy or stupid
either! Of course it's a carnival—to some people. You darling
half-wit! But tell me more, more!"

That was all the happy, frightened girl needed. Suddenly all
the bewildering surprises and thrilling discoveries of the last
nine months she began to pour out in a torrent of words.

"You see, when we entered the first building last fall, we
thought of course that it was a thermal establishment and that
we'd have to be plunged into hot water and all that. Instead,
we—at least Clare and I—suddenly found ourselves in a little
car and being shot away up into the air. It was the highest,
fastest, largest shoot-the-chutes in the world, imagine! But it
wasn't like any of those Father took me to ride in as a child.
Things happened on this roller coaster which you can't even believe. Oh, it still makes my hair stand on end to remember the
excitement of it!"

"I know, you went above the clouds and under the earth."

"Oh, yes, yes, that was the kind, Auntie! So you've been on
one too! Well, our little car with that nice fat guide in it shot
out into the sunlight, and up and up a steep incline till I got
positively dizzy. We were swept higher and higher and faster
and faster. Then suddenly the most incredible things began to
happen. Without the slightest warning, right there in front of
our eyes, the common everyday air which we had breathed
every moment of our lives without a question began to separate,
its component parts rolling to each side. The guide informed us
that on the right was the oxygen and on the left, the nitrogen;
while behind us fell a little water vapor, and that floating off
into space was carbon dioxide, argon, and other gases. Oh, dear

Lord in heaven, Auntie, I never dreamed before that air was composed of anything but just air!"

"Most females still don't—go on."

"We shot up through damp white fog to find ourselves actually above the clouds. The wind blew the words 'cirrus,' 'nimbus,' and 'cumulus,' from the guide's lips; and many other odd names which I promptly forgot. Then we rushed down and up, down and up as if over the monstrous waves of a monstrous sea. When I had the courage to open my eyes again, a cool darkness enveloped us. Illuminating the walls of the earth with his flashlight, the guide pointed out the various strata that shot past us, the humus and loam, the clay and rocks and a confusion of other names. On and on through the dark underground passage we sped. It was only occasionally, however, that I was able to understand a few words such as 'Tertiary Era,' and 'Carboniferous,' and the more familiar terms such as 'chalk' and 'shale.' Suddenly we rushed up again into the blinding sunlight and soon found ourselves at a standstill at the very place from which we started. We climbed out of that car with weak knees and paid our exit fee with ken. That's pure gold, you know. Just before our departure we noticed some of the other girls, who were leaving what had been to them severe treatment in the hot baths, trying to pay with rote, but that's counterfeit, and they don't allow its use here."

"Oh, don't they! Rote is so common it's become the accepted currency in every spa; though of course it has never been recognized officially—even in the very place which bears its name, the philosophy of the ostrich being the motto of all health resorts."

"Oh, Auntie, I guess it sounds silly, but I was so excited that I lay on my bed for an hour afterward and forgot to eat lunch."

"Doesn't sound silly—it sounds too good to be true."

"But why didn't some grown person tell me I was coming to a carnival—why didn't you?"

"For several reasons. I had been putting on a little private circus of my own called marriage. And besides, if I had told you, you wouldn't have believed me. Only seeing is believing in this case."

"But everybody said this Cerebral Lethargica was a youthful disease which had to be cured painfully."

Sophistica laughed. "You don't know how painful the cure is to most girls, and even boys, and they don't get cured, either!"

"Well, I can't understand why all the girls don't discover the carnival, for it certainly is here. And it's a more efficacious and certainly pleasanter method of cure than being plunged into hot water every day and having bitter stuff forced down your throat. That's what the other patients tell me they have done to them. But the discovery that staggers me most is that there is a reason for everything and a name for it too! Honestly, I wasn't aware that I had a brain until it got waked up in that thrilling ride in the loop-the-loop!"

"And did you see the 'Greatest Magician on Earth,' too? I remember when I was your age I saw him perform the most——"

"Oh, yes, yes! Although I got awfully bored with his tricks this spring and paid half my exit fee in rote, I blush to confess, his performances at first were simply too marvelous!" Suddenly Tellectina closed her eyes and gripped her aunt's arm. "Oh, just to think of them again excites me terribly! I used to sit there trying to follow his sleight of hand, and I would get so excited that my hands turned to ice and the cold perspiration came under my arms!"

"Oh, you too!"

"Why, Auntie, cold chills used to chase each other up and down my seventeen-year-old spine. I simply never dreamed that common everyday things could be transformed into strange marvels!"

"And I never dreamed that cold chills could chase each other up and down my thirty-seven-year-old spine again, either! You renew my youth, Tina darling!"

"But you look so very young! Much younger, Mother says, than you have any right to look!"

"Tell me more—about the magician, I mean."

"Well, as a very little girl I used to be fascinated by the magicians at the street fairs when they tore plain white silk handkerchiefs into beautiful colored strips and produced rabbits out of empty silk hats. But this old wizard, Shicspy, as they call him, surpasses all other magicians on earth! His legerdemain deals with the most elusive thing in the world—ideas. He takes a simple idea like the boiling of water and tears it into five strange new ideas and shows us poor nitwits that it is actually composed of increase in temperature, acceleration of motion, molecules, intermolecular spaces, and size. Like the ignoramus I was, I thought water boiled just because it boiled!"

"And I presume you went smugly along through life taking for granted that you understood 'freezing,' 'melting,' 'light,' and 'color,' too. But when old man Shicspy began his wonderful prestidigitations with 'convection' and 'refraction' and 'absorption' and——"

"And solids and liquids and gases and heat and cold," Tellectina hastily supplemented, "it was just too thrilling, and I could see through those tricks. But when he began to perform so rapidly and use unfamiliar things like levers and siphons and solar spectrums, magnetization, and so on, I simply couldn't follow him. And they never allow us time after the performance to go up and ask the magician for an explanation. We are invariably rushed on to the next show because all these barkers are so jealous of each other."

"Exactly, and it's ludicrous even to a seventeen-year-old girl."

"The last part of old Shicspy's performance had no relation or resemblance to anything in everyday life that I had ever seen. Still, it was magic all right. But Auntie, why in the name of Jehoshaphat did no grown-up person ever tell me that there was magic in ideas: enough magic to keep you thrilled for the rest of your natural life!"

"How can people inform you of things which they don't know themselves? Ideas don't wake most persons up, they put them to sleep."

"Well, I can certainly inform you of one thing: he made my poor brains dance about so excitedly that I thought I should have to be cured of brain fever next! Oh, Aunt Sophistica, it's so wonderful to be able to talk to someone who understands me. No one else seems to, except my friend Clare—and sometimes my father, a little."

"Don't expect understanding, my dear, prepare to be always utterly alone in this world even when lying in your lo— I mean husband's arms. But what about the rules and regulations of Rote Hill—do you find those just?"

"Just? They are made for half-wits who wouldn't recognize a sense of honor if they met it in the road! The patients are not allowed to wear their dresses open in front more than an inch below the collarbone; not allowed to speak to a boy except on Sundays in the presence of a chaperon; and are supposed to go to bed at ten o'clock. Well, Clare and I have been studying Reasonese privately, and in that language it says that it is wrong to obey any rule which is stupid."

"Adhere to that rule of action, my dear Tina, and you will go a long way in life—and get into a lot of exciting trouble as you go. What about smoking and drinking and dancing?"

"Dancing is permitted at the Casino in the late afternoons and early evenings; in fact, that is the most popular spot in the entire spa. But drinking and smoking for ladies are still considered the handmaidens of Jezebel!"

"So of course you do both."

"Certainly. Because we figured it out that dancing is no more sinful than walking to music, drinking and smoking merely physical pleasures like eating chocolate candy, and card-playing an innocuous game like checkers."

"You've made an excellent beginning, Tina. But what about that large building over there in the center of the grounds—the one with the tall spire pointing to heaven like an accusing finger, or, rather, like a lingam?—though it looks so cold and white that I should think even the angels would object. Do they put on a good show in there, too?"

"I—well, I—you see, to be quite truthful, I particularly dislike musical comedies, but I'm the only person in the whole of Rote Hill who doesn't attend it religiously. I suppose I should, but——"

"You should do exactly as you think best about everything. Don't permit anyone to influence you—not even me. But I must tear myself away. A man waits for me. Since I saw you on your thirteenth birthday I have made the great mistake of marrying a strong masculine personality. I should have married a weak one. You should too—but you won't. I shall not go to Smug Harbor this trip, but I shall write your parents that you are improving so rapidly that at the end of three more seasons they won't recognize their own daughter."

After a hasty farewell Sophistica's brief visit came to an end, a visit during which Tellectina had carefully kept Femina concealed. A few days later, however, when the summer vacation arrived, Femina accompanied Tellectina home and was treated by Mr. and Mrs. Christian exactly as if she were their own daughter. In fact, they made no distinction at all between the two girls.

It was now Tellectina who slept through the long summer months while Femina enjoyed the innumerable parties and beaux. The latter, though reluctant to leave when fall necessitated a return to Rote Hill, was nevertheless hustled off by the eager Tellectina.

A few weeks after their return there was an inexplicable occurrence which both girls believed to be without precedence anywhere in the world. Tommy had come as usual to spend Saturday night with the two sisters. About seven o'clock Sunday morning she crept noiselessly out of bed and returned to her own room, as had been her custom for some time. The two sisters lay rigid and motionless after her departure—with their hearts pounding violently.

"Femina," Tellectina whispered in a shaken voice, "what has happened?"

"Noth—nothing."

"You can't lie to me."

Femina began to tremble while she whispered brokenly, "It —it all happened before I realized what was happening. I'm, oh, Tina, I'm so frightened, tell me what to do."

"Tell me everything first, and then——"

"Well, you know what a crush Tommy has had on me for a long time—even last season—and how she brings me candy and flowers just the way Andrew and the other boys do? But I never thought anything at all about it much and——"

"And she draws the bath and turns on the heat for us every morning, but we, especially you, are so spoiled and accustomed to being waited on that I never thought——"

"Neither did I. And you remember how last season she used to tuck me in every night and kiss me good-night and then go back to her own room. But so many girls sleep together on Saturday nights that when she asked me if she might stay with me I knew it would be uncomfortable, but I didn't want to hurt her feelings. Everything seemed all right until last night. She said it was easier for her to go to sleep if she could just lay her hand on my—my breast. I thought it was silly, but it made no difference to me one way or the other, but now that I think of it, Andrew has tried to touch me there, too."

The girl ran her hand curiously over her small childish breasts. "I wonder why anybody would wish to touch a girl's breasts? Well, anyway, I fell asleep almost immediately, but this morning I was awakened by her kissing me and snorting and breathing hard in that funny way a boy does when he tries to kiss you."

"Oh, Femina, how awful! I never heard of such a thing before in my life! And you know you shouldn't allow boys even to try to kiss you. But it simply isn't possible for a girl to kiss another girl with—with passion!"

"I drew away from her—it made me sort of sick and frightened. So then she rose and left the room without a word."

"Well, Femina, there is certainly something about this girl that I don't understand. But one thing I do understand: and that is, we must never allow such a thing to happen again."

"No, never! But what she needs is a beau: then she wouldn't get so excited about other girls. Poor thing, she's not at all attractive to men, she's too masculine herself, I guess."

"Well, we don't want to hurt her feelings, but I'll—I'll certainly stop it!" Tellectina shuddered.

Femina shuddered too. "It's so repulsive, somehow; not sweet as it is when Andrew kisses me."

"Femina, aren't you ashamed!"

"No, I'm ashamed only when I permit some boy to kiss me who doesn't love me. Of course, I've never allowed any boy to kiss me on the lips! And you can say kissing is wrong till you're blue in the face, but that doesn't prevent it from *feeling* pleasant, somehow."

"Kissing *is* wrong—but I wonder why. No one ever gives any reasons, though of course there must be plenty of them."

"What I wonder," Femina whispered, "is whether men and women are made the same—you know, down there. I reckon they are, but it's strange that you can never tell when a boy has his periods."

"Eva would know because she says she's been to that mysterious Show-for-Men-Only. But she won't tell us anything, just laughs and says we are too disgustingly innocent. But I'm just dying to know if——" Here the two sisters conversed in excited and guilty whispers.

On the following Saturday night Tommy found the door of Femina's bedroom locked, whereupon she sobbed softly and tiptoed away. The matter was never mentioned by anyone. Tommy continued her devotion but never again attempted to sleep with Femina.

Their second and then their third season flew by so rapidly that before they realized it Tellectina and Femina were back in Smug Harbor again for a third summer visit.

Although both her parents appeared very proud of the apparent improvement in their daughter's health, Tellectina herself realized that instead of her cerebral trouble being cured it had become aggravated. Having grown more conscious than ever of the acuteness of her case, she carefully concealed the fact. Her malady now assumed a somewhat different form, the remedy for which she was convinced could never be found at Rote Hill. There was a sweet, unfamiliar ache that plagued her body during all the long luscious hours of her nineteenth summer. On moonlight nights it became almost unbearable.

One midsummer night she lay by the open window looking out over the garden, grown suddenly so mysterious and unfamiliar in that unearthly light of pale heavy gold. It was unreal: an enchanted earth laid under a sweet but fearful spell— motionless yet vibrantly alive—waiting—waiting. The very air hung heavy over the garden weighed down with the perfume of the amorous Cape jasmine and tuberose. Then quietly the fickle summer breeze came: it touched the trees tenderly like a lover, played with their tremulous shadows, seductively caressed the girl at the window, ran across the grass, and was gone. Silence —the uncanny stillness, not of death, but of living things— hypnotized.

Frightened, the watching girl instinctively covered her eyes but, drawn irresistibly by the potency of the moonlight, looked forth again. Neither sight nor sound of human life anywhere; she was alone with the moonlight. And as it drew the fragrance from the night flowers, so it drew forth the essence of her own hidden desires. Simultaneously its beauty awakened hopes of a fabulous and unattainable happiness and stirred memories of sorrows she had never known, aroused old racial griefs long buried, until gradually a sort of sad rhapsody sang itself through all her being.

Was there any beauty on earth so compelling, so hypnotic as midsummer moonlight? Her very body drank in sight and sound and scent until her intoxicated young soul swam in a rich voluptuous sorrow. The poignancy, the yearning, was unbearable—softly the young girl wept. Ah, that terrible longing which persisted in rising and sweeping through her in mighty waves! What was it? Longing for love, for a lover? Yes, for love. Some day she would find perfect love, sweet beyond all dreams; and a lover, wonderful beyond all men; and they would marry and live happily ever after in the house of love. It was her due as a woman.

But love was not enough. She longed for more: for romance, for adventure, for the fullness of life. That consuming insatiable hunger to taste all the beauty, the pleasure, and joys, even the tragedies and sorrows; yes, even the ugliness and cruelty of life! Only to miss nothing! that would be the great tragedy without recompense—to miss life. If she could only know, know all things, experience all things—only that would bring her complete happiness. Ah, somewhere in the world there must be great Certitude where one found answers to all questions, and not until she had attained its summit would she know peace. Long and long she gazed into the beauty and mystery of the midsummer moonlight: it alone possessed the power and privilege of drawing forth her deepest desires.

Then, finally closing her eyes to sleep, the young romantic would assured herself that in one more year she would sally gayly forth into the great world to find all the lovely things, all the happiness, for which she longed so passionately and was so confident of finding.

When the season opened again at Rote Hill, those patients who had returned for their fourth year were allowed to give a large dance and invite the young men from a neighboring watering place. Although Tellectina knew no one to invite, Femina asked Andrew, the young man whose devotion she had smilingly tolerated ever since the strange episode in the garden three years before.

The evening had not progressed far when it became noticeable that Femina was dancing every other dance with the nephew of the chief medical director, a very handsome blond youth of twenty and the undisputed beau of the ball. Tellectina, speechless with wonder, observed her sister as she circled about the room. Femina would toss her head airily and laugh directly

up into the man's eyes, in which there soon appeared a hypnotized look such as Tellectina had never witnessed before except once in the eyes of a bird before a snake. Aware that
Femina had marked him for her prey and that he was helpless,
she pitied him, yet was amazed at his weakness and simplicity.

There was something provocative, inexplicable, and elusive in
Femina's laugh. She herself appeared to be intoxicated by the
sound of it as well as her victim. Under the warmth of his admiration the girl's charm uncurled like the petals of a rose, ex-
haling a seductive essence which Tellectina had not known her
sister possessed. Curiously proud of Femina for her unexpected
power over men, Tellectina was at the same time mortified that
any girl should descend to such wiles, though she soon realized
that it was so purely instinctive as to be almost unconscious.

After this dance Don Knight, the young blond admirer, called
on Femina regularly every Sunday, showering her with candy,
flowers, and love letters in even greater abundance than the
devoted Andrew. All masculine tributes, however, Femina
laughingly accepted merely as her just due as a girl. Although
she cautiously endeavored to conceal from Tellectina the fact
that Don had frequently attempted to kiss her, she assured her
dubious sister that his real name was Olev, that he swore eternal
love, and that Tellectina was not capable of appreciating the joy
of being ardently adored.

Their fourth and last season was drawing to a close when one
indolent spring day the two girls sank wearily to the steps of
the building from which they had just emerged. "It's all over,
Clare," Tellectina said. "One more week and we'll be going
home."

"Yes, but it's been wonderful. Which show have you enjoyed
most of all, Tina?"

"Our ride in that amphibian biplane, I think. Honestly, Clare,
my heart stood still in my breast when we rose so high that we
obtained a bird's-eye view of the whole world of Err at once!"

"Mine too! And didn't it make you dizzy—deliciously dizzy—

when we actually saw an oligarchy, a timocracy, and a democracy in operation one after the other!"

"Dizzy? The whole experience positively intoxicated me! The trouble is that in everyday life we are all so close to such important things as labor and capital, supply and demand, and marriage and divorce, that we only see their details. It's absolutely necessary to look at these things from a great distance before one can see them whole."

"And what a thrilling sight! You know, Tellectina, all the great human movements and forces of society had always been vague and confused to me until this biplane carried us so high that we could trace the origin and direction of social forces like great rivers running through the body politic. It all came as such a tremendous surprise and revelation—this first comprehensive view of the economic and political world! It made the physical world fade away into nothingness! Seen from such a height, didn't the whole world appear like a picture puzzle, properly fitted together or improperly, as the socialists and anarchists see it? One thing is only too plain, and that is the world is full of injustice, and I'd like to—to do something about it, Clare!"

Just then the tall brown woman who had piloted the biplane came along and stopped to bid the two girls farewell and to inquire about their future plans. When the conversation turned on Rote Hill, bitterness crept into the older woman's voice. "But how can the sick cure the sick? And all the so-called physicians here need treatment themselves—of another sort. And out of the three hundred patients we're discharging this season I predict that the remarkable number of two will have either the strength or courage to explore the Forbidden Country. Most of the girls will have a relapse of their original malady. Yet many of them are endowed with such constitutions that they might be made into perfect specimens of humanity; and all they do for most of them is to pour bitter medicines down their unwilling throats. Wastage—of time, money, and opportunity—that's what it is—and it's criminal! But after all, this is Err. This shouldn't be a health resort at all—it should be a pleasure resort. Rote Hill could be converted into a carnival for all, instead of a few fortunate ones like you two. I've been trying to do that for twenty years but—" she shrugged—"Errorians always win. Remember my words, though, girls: there is only one other experience in all life which can be more thrilling than this carnival on Rote Hill—and that is the exploration of Nithking. But it is a lonely trip." The tall brown woman with the sad enigmatic eyes turned and walked away abruptly without another word, while the two girls followed her with admiring glances.

Then they looked at each other and smiled fondly. "Oh, Clare," Tellectina murmured, "I'm going to miss you terribly!"

Her companion responded with a quick pressure of the hand. In confusion and embarrassment the two young girls looked hastily away from each other, for they now shared a happy secret. The silence in which they walked through the sunken garden to their hotel was vibrant with a sweet new emotion. When they parted at the door, Tellectina observed the same look in Clare's eyes which had so puzzled her in her father's, and in Olev's whenever he looked at Femina. It caused such a wave of tenderness to surge through her heart that it overflowed, seeming to envelop completely this person whom she suddenly realized she loved.

That same evening at dinner, when Femina exhibited a solitaire diamond and announced her engagement to Olev, even Tellectina was somewhat surprised. Noticing the hurt expression on Clare's face, she hastened to whisper, "It's really news to me, too. But I don't intend to allow her to marry for years yet. We must both see the world before we settle down to pots and pans and babies!"

During Olev's call after dinner, Tellectina held the conversational reins until the polite boredom of the young man became so apparent that she withdrew. Too excited to sleep, she paced the floor while waiting impatiently for Olev to take his departure.

When Femina finally burst into their bedroom she exclaimed, "Listen to me, Tina, I want you to stay out of sight when Olev is here. There is no necessity for you even to speak to him. He's not interested in your precious mentality, I assure you. In fact, he frowns every time you show yourself. He declares it annoys him to hear any woman attempting to speak Reasonese, that it's a man's language anyway, and I agree with him."

Tellectina nervously lit a cigarette. "None of the boys like me. It's such a great disappointment, because they speak Reasonese so much better than girls, and I enjoy conversing in something besides Halfish. But, no—they don't like girls with any brains—only silly, pretty flirts like you. Oh, why must men be that way?"

Femina threw back her head and laughed by way of answer as she seated herself at the dressing table, but her sister was serious. "Femina, you can't marry this man you call Olev. I don't believe it's his real name anyway. If you really loved him —but you only love his love for you. Besides, we're both too young to be tied down, so in all fairness——"

Femina smiled at her own reflection in the mirror. "Fairness? What's that got to do with love? I can't help it if he loves me, can I?"

"You certainly can—you forced him to fall in love with you. I saw you do it. Oh, Femina, how selfish and conceited and cruel you are! Is it possible that you are my own flesh-and-blood sister?"

As Femina sat before the mirror brushing her long black hair with slow caressing strokes, she said, "Last night when Olev put the ring on my finger, I allowed him to kiss me on the mouth. He wouldn't believe any girl of twenty had never been kissed on the lips—until he tried it. Then he laughed and said I kissed exactly like a little child and that he had a great many things to teach his innocent little angel. But kissing wasn't nearly as exciting as I had anticipated. By the way, Tina, Eva told me that when men and women married they did exactly the same thing they do at that Show-for-Men-Only down in the South Woods.

I know they get in bed together, but I can't find out what they do after they get there, besides kiss."

"I can't either; all the girls just call it, 'IT.'"

Femina sighed and turned out the light. "Maybe it's too indecent to have any other name, whatever it is."

"I suppose so. But remember, when either of us marries, the other one will be obliged to live under the same roof. And although this Olev is a sweet boy, I, Tellectina, could never be content to live with any man who disliked to have a woman speak Reasonese. So I've almost decided where I shall go after we leave Rote Hill. I can't prevent your accompanying me, but you must promise not to——"

"Oh, I'm not going to marry Olev for a long, long time. So you go your way and I shall go mine—and thereby hangs a tale. I shall, however, step onto your scene whenever *you* become seriously interested in some man. In the meantime——" She laughed significantly.

Through the darkness Tellectina's voice came in low, determined tones: "Remember, young lady, when Olev comes to call tomorrow evening, you must ask him if—you know what I mean."

Late the following night the two sisters sat on the edge of their bed dissolved in tears, making futile efforts to console each other.

"It's just too terrible," Tellectina said in pained bewilderment. "I thought Olev was so—so pure."

"But it's more terrible for me, Tina, to have to give him up: I love to be loved. He was so hurt when I returned his ring: he said he knew it was wrong for him to go to that side show, that Sex was really supposed to be for married men only. He nearly wept with remorse."

"Well, why shouldn't men keep themselves as—as chaste as they *demand* girls to be?"

Femina was sobbing. "Then he—he got angry and said I was a little fool to react this way and make a mountain out of a molehill, and that a pure angel like me couldn't understand how Sex tempted men, and that women just had to overlook men's weaknesses and forgive them."

"Well, let me tell you one thing, young lady! If you, the woman, had fallen so low as to go to a show like that before marriage, would he overlook your 'weakness'? Indeed he would not! He'd have broken the engagement so quick it would have made your head swim! How can a thing be right for a man and the same thing be wrong for a girl? You see, it simply doesn't make sense!"

But Femina was not listening, she had already sobbed herself to sleep. Tellectina turned out the light and sitting by the open window stared wide-eyed out into the sweet spring night, inaudibly murmuring, "What *is* this mysterious Sex? Why should everybody be so interested in it and yet so ashamed to talk about it? Who was omnipotent enough to decree that it should be a show for men only? A double standard in anything is unjust as a mere matter of principle. I believe in a single standard of conduct for all grown people. Why not make men live up to women's standard? Or do women have the same urge to enjoy this forbidden show as men say they do? If women are just restraining themselves because they think they should—is that honest? And is dishonesty ever moral? Or if women are born indecent, wouldn't it be more honest, more decent, to be indecent? Or does that make sense?

"What a muddle it all is! Oh, if I could only find someone who would explain this famous Show-for-Men-Only to me in Reasonese! It's all so mysterious. How strange that no one has ever written books about it—too indecent, I suppose. There's certainly something queer about this Sex which I don't understand—but I intend to find out, and that pretty damned quick!"

CHAPTER IV

HOW TELLECTINA LEAPT OVER THE WALL INTO NITHKING; WAS
ATTACKED BY OUTLAWS, LOST IN THE DOTBU DESERT, AND RES-
CUED BY DREISER, BRIFFAULT, AND ROBINSON

B UT, MOTHER," Tellectina protested, placing her hand in
exasperation on Mrs. Christian's rocking chair to arrest its
ceaseless rhythm, "boys don't go to the dogs the minute they
leave home, do they? Then why should girls? If you would
only listen to reason for one very little minute instead of merely
getting shocked, you would understand readily enough that a
girl's desire for economic and mental independence has no relation to morals at all. And as for smoking and drinking—good
Lord, they aren't immoral: they're simply physical and sensory
pleasures like eating chocolate candy—which *you* enjoy so
much!"

The Christian family was ensconced in its chairs on the
veranda this August evening in order to rock away the hours
between supper and bedtime. Every twilight of the last four
summers which Tellectina had spent in Smug Harbor had been
thus disposed of by her parents.

"Well, Daughter," Mary Christian said, "I simply can't understand you. The language you speak is decidedly foreign to me.
In fact, it sounds suspiciously like that ungodly tongue your
aunt used to speak."

"Exactly," her husband agreed emphatically as he moved his
rocking chair from the edge of the porch where the motion of
it had gradually carried him.

"But," Tellectina reiterated with weary patience, "it's all so

67

self-evident, so obvious and logical, Mother: I should think even a child could understand such elementary Reasonese."

Mary Christian bristled at once. "So you think your parents aren't as intelligent as children!"

"Please, please, Mother."

"If we had known," John Christian said, addressing his wife, "that they were going to allow her to pick up any such new-fangled radical ideas, or such an immoral, irreligious language at Rote Hill, we'd never have permitted her to stir one foot from her parental roof, would we?"

"I told you, John, that you should have sent her to Veneer Bluffs. Perhaps some day you will learn to take your wife's advice."

"Reasonese may be irreligious," the girl conceded, "but it's not immoral. And no one speaks it at Rote Hill, you can rest easy on that point! My friend Clare and I learned it all by ourselves," she concluded disdainfully.

"Oh dear, oh dear," Mrs. Christian lamented, "I never thought I'd live to see the day when a child of mine would bring disgrace on the name of Christian."

Suddenly acute pains in the head, chest, and abdomen attacked Tellectina, whereupon she arose and, advancing to the edge of the veranda, loosened her dress and bared her throat in an effort to obtain more air.

"Oh, there," her mother cried, "she's ill again! You'd better call a doctor at once, John!"

"No, no, no," the girl pleaded, "I've told you a dozen times he couldn't do anything for me."

Mr. Christian's concern prompted him to forego his rocking voluntarily. "Now, tell me, Daughter, what is the matter? What really ails you?"

"It's just that I can't breathe in the atmosphere of Smug Harbor, that's all. I must go away to some other climate, to a higher altitude. I've been here all summer now and I've steadily felt worse. If I don't go I shall suffocate."

"That's perfectly ridiculous! It's simply your imagination. This is the same air you've breathed all your life, and it has never discomforted you before."

"I know, Father, but I feel different since I went to Rote Hill —the altitude was higher there. This fog stifles me: it's so dense, so oppressive all the time. Anyway, I'm going away."

"I don't hesitate to inform you, Daughter, that I regret the day I ever sent you to Rote Hill. Personally, I can't imagine any finer place in the world to live than Smug Harbor. Remember, it's the capital of Err. It's the oldest and largest and most prosperous seaport in the whole world."

The girl threw out an angry hand. "Oh, it's a horrible place! How can people live in this continual fog from the Dead Sea! They mold, mildew, and decay, and don't even know it! And Halfish is the language of half-wits! I hate it, hate it! I'm going away, somewhere, anywhere! I can earn my own living—I'm eager to work. At least it will give me independence—I'm sick of asking for every cent I want and having to account for it too!"

John Christian rose abruptly and, drawing himself up to the full extent of his small plump stature, said with severe dignity, "Tellectina, what you've said is not only an insult to the city of your birth but also to your parents' home. Boys are expected to leave home—but not girls. Why, I've never heard of such an irregular thing. Why should a gentlewoman want to work? I've never refused you a cent you asked for. You're not ill, you're foolish and disrespectful and ungrateful as well—after all I've done for you. Therefore, if you feel that way, go—but never expect one red cent from your father. Remember, I have spoken —and the Christians are a stern race." And, turning, he walked into the house with a firm, righteous step.

Tellectina stood straight and rigid at the edge of the porch with her back to her mother, not daring to glance around even when she heard muffled sobbing.

"Oh, you foolish, foolish child, see what you've done to your poor mother now! You're not ill, you're just abnormal not to appreciate your nice home and what your parents have done for you."

The girl obstinately maintained the same position but clenched her hands and swallowed rapidly in an effort to restrain her own tears.

"Oh, Tina, you're my only child: what will your poor mother do without you? I gave you up for four long lonely years so you could go to Rote Hill. Your father and I sacrificed many things in order to send you to that expensive place; and I had hoped to have you with me now at last. I've waited all my life for this time, and now to lose you, my only child! And goodness knows what will happen to an innocent girl out in the world alone: it's full of wolves in sheep's clothing. Oh, dear, I simply can't understand you. None of the other girls are afflicted as you are: all they want is to get married. And if you'd stay at home your father would give you everything money could buy. Oh, don't go, dear, and break both our hearts."

Tellectina was muttering fiercely to herself, "I won't, I won't, I simply won't allow her tears to melt my resolve! Oh, help me to be strong, dear Lord!"

She blinked violently, but lacked the courage to face her sobbing mother. "Oh, surely you know, Mother, that—that I don't want to hurt you or Father either, that I—I love you both, only—that I do appreciate—but you—oh, you just don't understand. I don't want the things money can buy. I am ill, I can't breathe in Smug Harbor, I must have a different altitude."

For a long time Mrs. Christian pleaded with her headstrong rebellious offspring. Then finally she dried her tears with a resolute hand. "Well, if you must go, then here's—here's my watch to carry with you. It may be useful and remind you occasionally of your—your poor lonely——" But she was unable to say more; so, slipping the watch into the girl's hand, she ran quickly into the house with her handkerchief pressed firmly over her quivering lips.

Not until she was alone in her bedroom did the girl give way to her own sobbing and self-deprecation. Having regained her courage by bedtime, however, she shyly entered the room adjoining hers—that of her aunt Sophistica, who in her usual mysterious way had suddenly appeared on the scene the day before. Laying aside the book she was reading, the older woman sat up in bed attentively while her agitated niece rehearsed the scene with her parents.

"Ah, well, my dear, it is sad—but that sort of thing is inevitable. So," Sophistica murmured, gazing at the girl intently, "you've turned twenty, and the time has come at last, thank God! And look at her! Dressed in rough trousers like a boy with a pack on her back in true explorer style! And she's even cut her beautiful feminine locks! Well, you do mean business, don't you?" Altering her tone, however, she suddenly began to parry with the young girl perched precariously on the edge of her chair. "But, my dear, this little respiratory ailment you complain of may pass away; so why go dashing off to the ends of the earth—why not grow rich and fat and contented like other sensible girls?"

"Oh, but, Auntie, I don't want to be any of those things! I want to go to a place where I can breathe freely and see everything clearly. This eternal damnable fog—I'm sick of it! I long so—so desperately for the bright sunshine, and I want adventure—excitement—I want to be on my own—to see the world!" She flung her arms out in a confident young gesture. Then she whispered, "And—and I intend to find a place where—where only Reasonese is spoken!"

"Ah, but remember, my pretty rebel, there is a strict law forbidding the use of Reasonese in Err. It is spoken only sub rosa. Yet if anyone leaves the Land of Err, a heavy penalty is imposed on him, or her—though few women ever leave Err (since they yearn for safety as men yearn for adventure)."

"Oh, I'm willing to pay anything for my freedom, my independence. (I can't bear to be treated like a child any longer!) And pay handsomely too, for anything I want."

"Pay? What do you know of payment, you starry-eyed darling? Oh, God, she sits there like a delicately tinted flower, so tender and fragile and erect! Like a gayly colored fledgling, eager to prove her untried wings, and she will return looking like a——" The older woman covered her eyes with her hands for a moment. "No, no, I can't let you go, Tina, my child!"

Tellectina rose with quiet determination. "But I'm going. I have no destination as yet, but I shall travel 'everywhither' until I discover a place I like. And I'm eager to work even though my parents seem to consider it a disgrace. I'm leaving Smug Harbor early tomorrow morning. I've merely come to say good-bye to you, Aunt Sophie."

Sophistica waved her back to her chair. "There, there, my pet, sit down again. Don't heed my tears. I'm only a sentimental old fool: forty is a dangerous age, even to a Sophistica. But consider this step well, for in Err you'll have soft beds, abundant food, and a warm house, many friends, security, and safety—and fog. And if you travel beyond the fog, where will you go? There are only two worlds, and the other is Nithking, the Forbidden Country—a continent which to the young and inexperienced is wild, unknown, and dangerous. And if, and when, you arrive in Nithking, you will have none of the comforts you enjoy here. You may be attacked by cannibals, lost in the desert, drowned, frozen on the mountain tops, devoured by wild animals or, even worse, by loneliness and——"

The young explorer leapt to her feet. With shining eyes she ran to her aunt's bedside. "Oh, is there really a place as thrilling as that?"

The older woman sank back into her pillow. "Sweet Lord in heaven, how could I have forgotten that danger is merely fuel for youth's fire?" She took both of Tellectina's hands in hers. "Well, my dear young thing, since it was not your good fortune to be born stupid, you'll have to make the best of it. Inasmuch as you've decided to go exploring—— You decided?—What nonsense am I talking? You have no choice: your destiny was decided in your mother's womb. But since you have the urge, then let no one, nothing, detain you. I repeat, all the dangers and hardships I enumerated so blindly are facts. But in true Errorian fashion I told you only half the truth."

"Let's hear the whole truth. I can stand anything as long as it's the truth."

"You sweet young thing, the truth is the one thing which most people can never stand! But I think you may prove to be an exception. Know then that to explore the dark continent of Africa is but a boy scout's pastime compared with the exploration of Nithking; pioneering in early America was but child's play, and the white Alps of Europe so much heaped-up meringue." Sophistica sighed and sank back against the pillows as though the mere memory of it made her swoon. Then she laughed. "Damme, if I don't get drunk on my own words!

"Ah, yes," she resumed, "make a journey through Nithking, for, as I said to you ten years ago, it is the most glorious journey that earth affords to man. Perhaps you will scale the dazzling peak of Manu Mission; be lured ashore at the Siren Islands; and your quest for Certitude may carry you to the summit of the highest mountain in the world. It is Great Ghaulot; and that is the abode of the human gods whose laughter renders them immortal! I, as a seasoned Nithkinger, know, however, how futile is advice to the young explorer, but one word of counsel I must offer."

"Oh, it all sounds so glorious! But you want me to be careful, I suppose, as my mother invariably cautions me, but I don't intend——"

"Ah, no, child, you do your hedonistic aunt an injustice. My counsel is: Do *not* be careful. Be wise and rush in where fools fear to tread. Heed no voice except your own—not even mine. Let your——"

"Let my conscience be my guide, you mean?"

"A second injustice to a good pagan like myself, but no matter. No, little Puritan, let your desire be your guide: deny yourself nothing. Throw yourself into this expedition with a whole heart—half measures are for puny people. Abandon yourself recklessly to the passion of living, for it is the grand passion, and all others are but feeders of it. Be the grand amoureuse of life—for you receive from life, your lover, only what you give him. And the best lovers reside in Nithking, of course."

"Lovers, Auntie?"

"Figuratively, darling, figuratively! That's your chief defect (other than being a Christian, which is a blot on your scutcheon you will remove, I trust)—you have no sense of humor. That, doubtless, is because you are happy, the true source of humor being not joy but sorrow. Humor will develop rapidly, however, after you have suffered sufficiently—to which little matter Nithking and your own thin skin will attend, I doubt not."

Rising, she moved restlessly back and forth across the floor as she expatiated further upon Nithking. "Welcome everything that crosses your path: hardship, deprivation, illness, loneliness, disillusion, even acute suffering, pain, and despair. Envelop them, make them enlarge your mind; make them enrich your nature so that out of their fertile soil will grow the rare flowers of tolerance and pity and humor—and the rarest flower of all— human understanding."

The young Tellectina sat motionless under the spell cast by the words of the older Tellectina: words whose full meaning she too would some day come to understand.

"Leave no mountain of Nithking unscaled, no sea uncharted. If you return from this trip alive, even though maimed and scarred, you will possess a living memory of adventure of which neither illness, nor old age, nor poverty, nor pain can deprive you—only death has that power and privilege. And if you die during your adventure, well—" and here she shrugged her beautiful white shoulders—"sometimes the gods are kind."

"Die, Auntie! But I shall not die! I shall travel all over the world and find all the lovely things I seek! I'm *sure* of it! I'm eager to fight, I long to try my strength. All will be gloriously happy, I know. I must be off at once, early tomorrow morning. Good-bye, and don't worry about me; I'm afraid of nothing."

"I know you're not afraid. That's why I worry." Sophistica sighed and sat down suddenly. It was as if an inner light had been extinguished. "That such a brave adventurous spirit should be housed in such a fragile feminine body! Here, my dear, is a little farewell gift." She extended a wallet to the girl.

"Oh, Auntie, you really are too good! But I want to work and be independent; it isn't really necessary, but——"

"Accept it to please me."

"Of course, Aunt Sophie, and I do appreciate it a thousand times over." Quickly and impulsively she kissed the older woman.

"And this," Sophistica said, indicating a book which she had carefully concealed in a large carton of cigarettes, "is my latest effort which I should like to present to you to read on your trip. It is, as you see, *The Chastity Myth Exposed,* but I shall not give it to you yet—twenty being the age when we like serious tragic books. No one, says my present husband (my second, you know), no one who is under thirty can appreciate satire. And whatever you do, don't marry a weak man—or a strong one, either—both are impossible as husbands."

"Oh, I don't intend to marry for years yet. I want to live first."

"Well, darling, marriage is hardly an interment. But as to your adventure, remember my commandments, child, and keep them wholly. Demand everything from life and you shall receive much; ask nothing and you shall receive even less. When life stabs you in the back—as she assuredly will—laugh in her face; wrestle with the old bitch, fight to the finish, show her she has chosen a worthy opponent. And after she defeats you (and she defeats us all) she may, woman-like, reward you with a kiss or an unexpected favor; or, of course, she may stab you in a new place—be prepared for either. But never take her blows lying down: give blow for blow. Not, of course, that you can ever touch her: she's an agile old tart; but it keeps your manhood up, so to speak!

"But why on earth do I preach to you—of all people? It's just that words intoxicate me. Forgive me. And if and when you return——"

"Return!" Tellectina looked horrified. "I never intend to set foot inside Smug Harbor again as long as I live!"

Sophistica smiled. "Of course not, dear darling young thing. But when you return I shall be waiting for you with open arms. And in the meantime, if you ever need me, you have only to call. It may, however, be necessary for you to call quite loudly, for I invariably choose both my writing room and my boudoir with *very* thick walls!"

The young girl threw a puzzled glance at the older woman, then, thanking her again for the money, rose and made her departure quickly. And early on the ensuing morning, Tellectina set out, despite the formidable silence of her father and the frantic protestations of her hysterical mother.

Blindly but hopefully she struck out across country, only to discover that the Land of Err was completely cut off from the rest of the world by a dense forest of half-grown thruts which were so dwarfed, twisted, and misshapen as to be painful to behold. Although obviously in a state of arrested development, they were astonishingly hardy and tough, obstinately resisting her efforts to cut her way through them.

It was a great surprise to Tellectina to discover how much a girl who had known nothing but the most sheltered and easy life could enjoy the exercise of her ingenuity and strength. The struggle through these thruts caused her to realize that it was this Half-grown Forest which gave the name of Halfish to the language of the inhabitants of Err. Every night as she rolled herself up in her blankets, she would dream of some beautiful country free of dwarfed thruts where the sun shone always and living was an endless delight. Each day the young pioneer's exhilaration increased as she forced her way farther through the thick tangled undergrowth with determined and obstinate head bent low.

Suddenly one morning she collided with some very hard object. Recoiling, Tellectina rubbed her bruised forehead; then, on examination, discovered a stone wall concealed by vines and shrubbery. Unlike the usual vertical wall, it was curiously curved inward like a sea wall, as if designed to keep people in rather than out. A premonition that she was on the verge of a new and thrilling adventure seized her. With feverish eagerness she began to tear away the vines and moss in order to decipher the half-visible words chiseled in that ancient weather-beaten wall:

THE GREAT WALL OF ERR

THE DIVIDING LINE BETWEEN THAT LAND
AND
NITHKING, THE FORBIDDEN COUNTRY

Tellectina stood breathless and motionless, in her excitement scarcely taking time to read the inscription in smaller letters below:

> *Any inhabitant who leaves this country will be forced to pay a heavy penalty and to forfeit his citizenship in the Land of Err.*

Tingling with joyous anticipation, Tellectina attempted to visualize what might lie behind that formidable wall: anything —everything, perhaps!

For a long time she stood poised on tiptoe, uncertain and fearful; then resolution impelled her forward. "No, half measures are for puny people: it's whole heart or none for me!"

Her young self-confidence apparently lent her miraculous strength, for after retreating a few paces she bounded forward and at one flying leap cleared the top of the wall. Picking herself up out of the deep sand on the other side, she was amazed to see a vast trackless desert as far as the eye could reach.

"Is this the country about which my aunt became so rhapsodic, about which that pilot at Rote Hill became so agitated? Is it for this that I made my mother weep and my father disinherit me?"

Puzzled, frightened, and yet curiously alive, she stood there uncertain as to which way to go. Then, the thrill of the adventure returning with redoubled force, the amateur explorer started recklessly and confidently across the burning sands. An advance of only a few paces had been made, however, when without the slightest warning a band of outlaws who had been crouching behind the dunes awaiting an unwary traveler attacked her. They rushed upon the defenseless girl, tore off the pack of supplies strapped to her back, rifled her pockets, and tore her clothes in their mad search for food.

Tellectina struck out fiercely in every direction, but it was one frail girl against a score of ruffians. They rolled her in the sand until she begged for mercy, devoured all her supplies, but continued to demand swernas and seedd, foods which Tellectina did not possess. Sitting on their haunches, they formed a circle about her, glaring at the disheveled girl like a pack of hungry wolves ready to spring. As the bruised and frightened explorer knelt helpless in the sand, each outlaw in turn began to badger her, loosening such a volley of angry questions at her that she could only look from one to the other in a state of stupefaction.

"We're political outcasts," one of them said, "brutally driven out of Err. What are you? Are you a member of the conservative Errorian party or a radical Noequist?"

"If you're one of them, we'll torture you, we'll destroy you!"

"Do you speak Reasonese or Halfish?"

"I—I—a little Reasonese," she faltered.

"Then prove it!"

Another Noequist sneered, however. "We'll discover soon enough what she is. Answer these questions: Do you believe in war?"

"No. I—I believe that men's—er—minds were given them to be used to—to settle——"

But another outlaw was tearing at her now very soiled shirt. "Answer my question first. Don't you know the Eighth Commandment is wrong? Why should a person declare his nation to be the best when it was only an accident of birth which placed him on that plot of ground? Answer or I'll——" He made a threatening gesture.

"Yes, yes, perhaps. I mean, patriotism is a misplaced——"

But a giant Noequist was making an attack from the rear, shouting, "What right has any man to rule over any other man? Should not every human being have the same freedom, the laborer, the servant, the Negro, and even the woman? Are not all Errorian officials ignorant and unscrupulous? Isn't their system of education a farce, and aren't their newspapers corrupt?"

"Why, yes, I realize now—but I hadn't thought, I——" the girl was stammering when another powerful Noequist struck her cruelly right between the eyes.

"Isn't it high time you began to think, young woman? We'll wake up your brains, if you have any. Tell me this: Why should some people be allowed to become overrich through luck or dishonesty while others suffer and die from poverty through no fault of their own? Why shouldn't wealth be distributed more evenly? Have you no social consciousness? Can't you see that the whole world is reeking with injustice, suffering, and crime? Can you stand by and do and say nothing? What sort of a cold selfish animal are you?"

"But—but," the obstinate girl protested, "I didn't cause the evils of the world. Why am I responsible for the crimes—or even the lives—of other people?"

"What, don't you know it is the duty of the intellectuals to better the world for those who are not equally well endowed?"

"My heart is wrung with pity for all human suffering. And I want to help. But why is it my duty? Why shouldn't every person spend all her energy improving her own condition?"

"Have you no heart, no sense of justice? Are you totally devoid of the milk of human kindness?"

"Yes, no, I mean, I *do* want to alleviate the misery of the human race, but how? I am so confused: you all talk at once. I can't think coherently. Wait, wait, for heaven's sake!"

Tellectina's head reeled. Overwhelmed, she sank into the sand only to have a woman exile, whom she had not previously noticed, lift her to a sitting position with a vicious tug of her hair. The girl cried out in pain and anger, but the woman merely bent over her, shouting frantically in her ear one question after the other.

"Why do you suppose I was banished from Err? Because I went about boldly inquiring of all: Why shouldn't women be as free to dispose of their sex as men have always been? And how can there be any love which is not free? Why should any human beings—even women—be forced to obey laws in the making of which they take no part? And why not free them from the slavery to house, husband, and child? If you don't answer these questions properly, young woman, I'll know you're an Errorian, and I shall torment you until——"

At this point, however, the largest Noequist of them all, a great gaunt emaciated man with burning eyes, thrust the woman Noequist, who was herself an amazon, roughly aside and, shaking Tellectina by the arm, demanded: "Answer *my* question first! Isn't the Church built on hypocrisy? Do the pious not profess spirituality and actually worship materialism? Are not the psalm-singers the most intolerant and inhuman in daily practise? Do the churchgoers ever do unto others as they would have others do unto them? Is the spirit of Christliness, gentleness, and brotherly love ever found in the churches except in saccharin words? Does the Church ever show pity or compassion toward illegitimate children or toward any poor woman who has 'gone wrong'? Answer all these questions in Reasonese at once and find us some swernas and seedd or we'll devour you! You can't go another step into Nithking until all these outcast Noequists have been satisfied!"

"I'll answer all your questions if you'll only give me time to think. You've taken all the food I have; but if you'll give me the opportunity to put my wits to work, I'll find swernas for you—and even seedd, perhaps."

Looking frantically about her, she espied the canteen of wine

which had rolled off to one side unnoticed. Rising with difficulty, she stumbled toward it and dragging it into the circle
said: "Here, you Noequists, drink this!" She passed it around,
each allowing the other only one swallow. "I—oh, I will help
you, I swear it! It enrages me to think that people who speak
such perfect Reasonese as you do should be cast out of Err!"

"Yes, we were beaten and spat upon and thrown over this
wall to starve here in this great Dotbu Desert."

"It's an outrage! But you needn't have attacked me so violently: you almost finished me off! Here, give me a drink too,
I'm parched!" Turning the bottle up, she drained it to the last
drop.

The wine came from the Semsianic vineyards which are
famous for producing the most potent wines in existence, whose
intoxicating properties are of a peculiar variety. One draught
was sufficient—it went immediately and violently to the girl's
head as well as to that of all the others, working a radical
change both in Tellectina's appearance and demeanor.

When she looked up, her young eyes were shining with the
unnatural brilliance of one beholding a vision. Like Joan of
Arc, this quiet gentle girl felt herself being mysteriously transformed into a fearless, almost fanatical leader of a band of
churlish men.

Seizing a rough club, she brandished it above her head and,
rising unsteadily, cried aloud to them, "Come! Come back with
me to the Land of Err, to Smug Harbor! Did they not cast
you out? Then let them answer for it! Anyone has a right to
be a member of the Noequist party—it's a noble undertaking.
You are infinitely superior to the rulers of Err. Your ideas are
right and theirs are wrong. Follow me! We will raze that
ancient stupid land to the ground!"

She staggered forward too intoxicated to notice that she was
not going toward Err but away from it and deeper into the
Dotbu Desert. Light-headed from hunger and wine, the outlaws
followed, dancing and pirouetting about her in drunken delight.
Then, stopping abruptly, their leader pointed to a spectacle

which had suddenly loomed up before her eyes. Was that not Smug Harbor in the middle distance, sleeping peacefully? Standing motionless in the sand Tellectina and her outlaws beheld a mirage that was indeed miraculous, for they saw themselves make an attack upon the capital city of Err. They saw themselves swarming over the city walls and in one mighty rush crash down upon all the houses of oligarchical government; beat upon the walls with their improvised battering rams with such terrific blows that, defenseless against such well-aimed and unexpected attacks, all the established structures of Err tottered and fell. They saw themselves marching up the main street of Smug Harbor over the débris, shouting victoriously, "Long live democracy! Long live the radical Noequists and Tellectina, our leader!"

In the excess of her enthusiasm the young rebel would have deemed herself a traitor to a noble cause if she had lifted a hand to save her own family. She saw them escape, however, after being severely wounded. Tellectina could see herself seized by this strange new madness, drunk with triumph, standing in the midst of the débris of fallen and ruined houses, of fleeing citizens, of the dead and the dying, shouting with glee:

"Raze it to the ground! If it's old it's useless! If it's old it's wrong! If the people of Err cannot defend themselves against these noble Noequists, then let them perish!"

The destruction of Smug Harbor continued until no two stones of the old city could be seen standing one upon the other. Then gradually the spectacle faded away. Tellectina shook herself, blinked, and looked about her, uncertain whether her attack upon the ancient city had been a mirage or a reality. Observing the ragged Noequists behind her, however, she concluded that it had actually occurred and consequently cried out to them in exultation:

"There, are you not satisfied now?"

"No, no!" came from a score of throats. "We are drunk, we have razed Smug Harbor and the Land of Err to the ground;

but food—food that men can live by! We want swernas and seedd. Wine is not enough!"

Their young leader stood aghast—sick with fright. Had she not destroyed everything in the known inhabited world? Where could food be found? Were the swernas and seedd for which they clamored so persistently to be found in this unknown Land of Nithking somewhere ahead of her? If only she could conduct them out of this barren desert of Dotbu all would be well. Leaning heavily on her now lowered club, she thought quickly, recovered her lost courage as best she could, banded them together again, and rushed forward into the desert.

The most aggressive and importunate of all the exiles was Awr, who incessantly tormented her both with his demand for food and his endless questions as he followed at her heels across the parched sands. "If men ceased to desire excessive wealth, wouldn't war end?" he reiterated.

"Oh, leave me in peace. I'll answer all your questions when I find food for you!" Tellectina retorted, straining her eyes in every direction for an oasis.

One morning the woman outcast returned with good news from a little reconnoitering of her own; whereupon the two women hastened together to a grove of palm trees clustered behind some immense sand dunes and there came upon a small blue house built in that rectangular biblioesque style peculiar to the houses of Nithking. To the owner of this small blue structure Tellectina promptly announced that this poor woman Noequist craved some swernas and seedd, although she herself was uncertain as to what they were. At the man's bidding there immediately appeared at the entrance a young woman whom he introduced as Sister Carrie.

His own name of Theodore Dreiser was printed on the door of his dwelling. Tellectina looked at it again and said, "I have heard of both of you before and am very glad to actually meet you. I am just a young explorer named Tellectina Christian. Is Carrie married, Mr. Dreiser, or does she earn her living some other way?"

The traveler peered inquisitively through the doorway; and when he informed her that Carrie was paid for being a "mistress," both Tellectina and her companion stared at the man in bewilderment. " 'Mistress'—what does that mean?"

Curiosity impelled her to go farther when invited inside by Dreiser; and once within Sister Carrie's house the little Puritan listened with avidity and consternation while Mr. Dreiser explained Carrie's mode of life in detail and at great length. Tellectina's eyes were wide and frightened. At once repelled and attracted, she advanced cautiously like a cat. The woman Noequist, however, refused to accept any food, declaring that everything in Sister Carrie's house had a monetary stench: at which statement Dreiser seemed to shrug his shoulders indifferently. Feeling bewildered and quite guilty the visitors were issuing from the rear exit when they were met by the whole group of outlaws creeping stealthily from behind the dunes.

Tellectina turned beseechingly to her host. "Oh, Mr. Dreiser, can't you help me feed these ravenous Noequists?"

The man, however, merely shook his head and murmured that he could offer them neither swernas nor seedd, but that they might be sustained somewhat by a concoction of his which he called *Hey-rub-a-dub-dub*. They all sampled this mixture at once, and although it had a pleasant taste it merely served to increase their appetites.

Once more the young explorer appealed to him. "But surely you can direct me as to the way out of this terrible desert? I'm lost in doubt: you're a seasoned explorer, whereas I'm but an inexperienced traveler and a woman, besides. I feel confident that if only once I could get out of this desert I could find Mt. Certitude where there is said to be an abundance of food for all Noequists, radical or otherwise. I beg of you, do direct me to Certitude!"

Turning pained and bewildered eyes on her, Dreiser reminded her of the fact that he *lived* in the very heart of Dotbu.

"Well," she said, "honesty compels me to say that I am disappointed in you; but doubt loves company as well as misery, therefore it is consoling to discover that I am not subnormal to have become lost in Dotbu." And thanking him politely for his *Hey-rub-a-dub-dub*, she departed.

Day after day they wandered across the ever shifting sands. Sometimes at night after pitching camp, Tellectina was unable to sleep owing to the noise of the restless Noequists, who slept little, night or day. The soft haunting sound of feet padding across the sands disturbed her even more, and often she would hear the howling of the Parides jackals which caused her blood to run cold with terror. She would lie awake for hours planning ways of escape from this fearful desert. There was nothing to help her except her own wits; but with the coming of dawn her self-confidence and courage invariably returned.

After she had lain awake unusually long one night, she arose and awakened Awr and all the other outcasts. "Listen," she said, "I have had a vision. I have seen ahead of us the Ideal State. It is just behind those dunes, and I shall lead you to it soon. I see a group of grave men in conference together. They are the representatives of every nation in the world and are assembled to settle all disputes amicably, intelligently, and justly. War in that world no longer exists, and patriotism is an evil of the past. No graft, or selfishness, or capitalism, or privilege, or abuse of power is to be seen there. We shall soon be moving toward it! But wait!"

She summoned to her side the exiled Noequist who was most importunate next to Awr. It was he who had been driven out of the Land of Err for asking questions about democracy. Eagerly she pointed out all the advantages in which he would be most interested. "Ahead of us is the world as it ought to be: where democracy is practiced and is not merely a pretty fiction which exists only in the speeches of senators. See, everybody is free and equal; there is no individual ownership of property; everything that is used in common is owned and operated by the government. And observe those benign white-bearded men: they are the government, they dispense justice and wisdom.

That is the kind of government which should be superimposed on people for their own good. The masses of humanity don't hold the ideas they possess because they originated them; they have caught them like a contagious disease from the group in which they live. Consequently, the way to solve all the problems of the world is to impose on the human race a good and just government."

She then called all the other Noequists nearer. "Isn't it clear to you that the first requirement for the ideal state is the loosening of all the bonds that constrict man, the bonds of matrimony, religion, family, tradition, 'morality' so-called, patriotism, and class distinction?"

All the outcasts listened avidly while their leader, with a beatific smile on her face, continued. "I see in the ideal state before you that there are no churches, no organized religions of any kind, but that everybody actually practices every day the precepts of Jesus and does unto others as he would have others do unto him; that everyone really loves his neighbor as himself; that there is universal brotherhood and no poverty; that there is no family and no home; but that children and parents are friends only if congenial, and that children are brought up by the state by trained experts. And I see that women are thus freed at last to work and become men's equals in every way. Listen," she exclaimed to the woman Noequist, "it isn't very clear to me just now, but I can see vaguely that all sex in that world is kept beautiful, and there is no disease nor prostitution nor illegitimate children; no legal bonds of matrimony, only those of affection; and I can easily see that all the women are voting. I can't discover just what the new system of education is, but I'm certain it's very different from ours, and the press is used only to dispense news, not to mold public opinion."

And in this shining new world Tellectina could see no old and ugly women cast off by their lovers for younger and more beautiful women; no jealousy, no heartache, no outraged desire for homes and privacy; no mothers fighting to retain their own children, no innate and ineradicable stupidity, weakness, and malevolence which would wreck the smooth running of the perfect social machine.

As they moved toward it, however, and gained the top of the dunes there was no state in view, Ideal or otherwise. The Noequists complained bitterly, but Tellectina reassured them. "But it must exist somewhere, this Utopia, else I could not have seen a vision of it. It may be the Certitude we are seeking. It is surely not merely a chimera. Have patience, for we shall gradually work toward it." Thus the hungry Noequists were forced to be satisfied with the vision of what was to come instead of the food they craved.

Years later, when Tellectina looked back over the Dotbu Desert, she realized that she had but wandered at random through it and missed the several opposing camps of Karl Marx, Adam Smith, Ricardo, John Stuart Mill, and other professional guides who might have been of invaluable assistance to her. Unaware of their existence, however, she struggled on with no guide but her own wits and instincts.

The hungry troop marched bravely on until they stumbled upon a great pile of boxes half buried in the sand, containing strange foods which they eagerly and hopefully sampled. To their extreme disappointment they not only derived no nourishment from them but found them painfully dry and quite indigestible for their young stomachs, and concluded that some other travelers who had gone before had likewise discovered these foods to be impalatable and simply dumped them there in the middle of the desert. Yet the cases were plainly marked: each one asserting that within was nourishment suited particularly to explorers of Nithking. Examining them again, Tellectina carefully read the labels; all had been put up by persons whose names, however, were for the most part foreign to the little Errorian, such as Kant, Spinoza, Descartes, and Hume.

After many days had passed, a terrific sandstorm arose. The sand cut across their faces unmercifully, blinding them, filling them with the dreadful conviction that they would be compelled to spend the remainder of their lives wandering about uncertainly in this awful waste land. Finally, however, the storm subsided yet failed to reveal an oasis; but it did reveal a new and painful condition—that of excessive thirst. The heat became horrific, their throats grew parched, and their tongues black and swollen. But where could they obtain water? Where? The situation was growing desperate when Tellectina spied an exceedingly verdant oasis. Running forward hysterically, she was overjoyed to find a man standing there as though actually awaiting her arrival. The swollen condition of her tongue necessitated communication by gestures.

Having recognized the outlaws as the same Noequists who had formerly attacked him, the stranger immediately understood the situation and offered the girl assistance. As quick as a flash, he lifted an old blue weather-stained magazine lying on the ground beside him, which the explorer recalled long afterward was the *English Review,* and dexterously fashioned a cup of it. With a flourish of his right hand, he revealed a spring of clear crystal water bubbling up before their astonished eyes. Quickly dipping it up and refreshing Tellectina first, he hastened to each thirsty Noequist, assuring them that he was fully cognizant of the hardships they had undergone, and could easily surmise the cause of their banishment from Err.

" 'The world,' " he said, " 'is suffering today from the . . . age-long accumulations of its unveracities.' "

At this all the Noequists shouted with one voice, "Did I not tell you that, Tellectina? Did I not tell you that?"

Then the man continued: " 'It has never been "organized" . . . in view of the collective needs of its constituent elements. . . . Boots are not made that human beings may be shod but that dividends may accrue; restaurants are not run to feed you but to produce dividends.' "

The waters he dispensed went to their heads like strong wine, and every word he uttered increased their fervor. Growing jubilant, they clamored for more of his intoxicants, both of which he supplied with equal proficiency.

" 'Meddlesome . . . explorers have dug around the founda-

tions of society and found them to be hollow. . . . It is all sentimental nonsense to say that truth wins; on the contrary, lies
are never put down.'"

"Oh, you speak the most lucid Reasonese I have ever heard in
my life! It positively intoxicates me! Who are you? Who are
you?" the girl exclaimed in her passionate young voice.

On being informed that he was Robert Briffault, she and her
band commenced to dance madly about him in a circle, laughing, shouting, singing his praises and those of the crystal fountain in the sand. The young enthusiast was carried away by her
zeal, but as they had one more round of drinks, Briffault warned
her that the journey through Nithking would prove far more
formidable than she imagined, and that no one could accomplish it who feared to face the truth.

"'The difficulties of refraining from unveracities . . . have
grown to be . . . a task calling for almost superhuman heroic
courage . . . only to be faced with girded loins and hearts of
treble brass. . . . "The truth for an hour" would mean the
uttering of things almost unmentionable.'"

The young explorer's eyes glowed with renewed ardor. "Ah,
yes, yes! And these Noequists are all representatives of truth,
and I have striven to answer them truthfully. We are not afraid!
'The truth for an hour,' you say? No, the truth for all time—
now and forever!"

With his final words Briffault proffered the girl the last of this
remarkable catalytic water, assuring her that the Land of Err
was doomed to destruction and that she was headed in the right
direction to find a new and better country. "'The future must
be an aristocracy . . . of believable thought. To breed such an
aristocracy is the highest task to which in this hour of Nemesis
we can hopefully set our hands.'"

Like drunken crusaders they set off again with redoubled zeal.
Their intoxication alone was sufficient to carry them along for
days. Eventually, however, when their exultation began to wane,
hunger and fatigue returned with increased force, and they
dragged their feet wearily across the merciless, burning sands.

For days they struggled on hopelessly—lost—lost in Great Dotbu.

Their leader had stopped and was scanning the horizon with desperate eyes when she suddenly beheld a moving black speck in the distance. She waited fearfully, uncertain whether it represented help or was merely the outrider of some marauding band. As the rider overtook them, however, he dismounted quickly and presented Tellectina with a letter which the distraught girl, too astonished to speak, read hastily.

DEAR TELLECTINA:

I thought I heard a voice crying in the wilderness, "Come over into Nithking and help us!" I was visiting friends on Ghaulot, where the atmosphere is so clear one can see to the very ends of the earth, and I looked out, and lo, what did I see? My darling little Tellectina lost in Dotbu.

And since I, unfortunately, still seem to you to be a part of your family, I thought a stranger might be of more assistance to you. This, therefore, is to introduce Mr. James Harvey Robinson, who can lead you out of Dotbu, I'm sure, as he is a seasoned explorer of Nithking. In fact, I am familiar with no guide book giving such explicit directions for crossing over from Err to Nithking than his *Mind in the Making,* as he called it. I regret that he neglected to write it before you left Err.

And now that you've turned your scornful young back on Err, remember that no matter how beautiful the mirages are that lure you on, you should never allow yourself to lose sight of your Motherland altogether. At least keep her memory fresh, for she is a jealous, despotic, and vindictive old woman—impregnable even against the most violent and radical Noequists and intoxicated young Tellectinas.

Enjoy your trip through Nithking thoroughly, but remember that those who forget Err entirely live to regret it. And I hope Mr. Robinson gives you a lift.

Always your loving and interested,

SOPHISTICA.

After reading such an enigmatic letter the girl felt obscurely resentful toward her prototype, who less than a year ago had urged her to be wise and rush in where fools feared to tread and was now cautioning her to be careful. So great was her relief at the sudden appearance of a rescuer, however, that for the time being she dismissed the letter from her mind.

She gave one long searching glance at the man and his sturdy desert pony of the roan Koobish breed; and with the knowledge that she was safe, the tension relaxed, and she would have collapsed had not her companion supported her. Seated behind him, the explorer was borne by the swift little pony almost out of Dotbu. While resting on the large oasis to which Robinson had carried her, she discovered that all the Noequists had followed them. Without the necessity of an explanation, Robinson appeared to comprehend the entire situation perfectly. And yet he fed only Tellectina, offering nothing to the outlaws as she had hoped.

Despite its hardships, he thoroughly approved of her attempt to explore the Forbidden Country, adding that the inhabitants of Err invariably cast out Noequists when they upset their established beliefs. " 'Few of us take the pains to study the origin of our cherished convictions, . . . but find ourselves filled with an illicit passion for them when anyone proposes to rob us of their companionship.' "

"Oh, yes," Tellectina agreed, "I certainly noticed that when I made that attack on Err with my outlaws. But why do people hold such stupid convictions?"

" 'As we grow up, we simply adopt the ideas presented to us in regard to such matters as religion, family relations, property, business, our country, and the state. . . . They are persistently whispered in our ears by the group in which we live.' "

"I—I, that's exactly what I was guilty of in Smug Harbor!" the girl stammered.

The man nodded and continued. " 'The fact that an idea is ancient and that it has been widely received is no argument in its favor, but should immediately suggest the necessity of carefully testing it as a probable instance of rationalization. And——' "

Tellectina turned to him with increasing excitement. "Oh, you have indeed rescued me, for I was hopelessly lost. I had begun to doubt my own faculties and was merely moving in circles. And you have not only given me strength but self-confidence, as well." Although she looked at him with passionate gratitude in her eyes, she nevertheless rose and thus cut short his reply.

In fact, Robinson had a great deal more to say, but the excited girl had already received from him all the help she needed at the moment; consequently he remained politely silent and quietly disappeared. Tellectina sat for a long time absorbed in thought, then commenced a feverish search all over the oasis for swernas and seedd, finding a quantity of the former but none whatever of the latter. She was amazed that by her own efforts she was able to gather sufficient food to pacify the Noequists for a short while, with the exception of the one woman outlaw who had vanished suddenly and mysteriously.

As Tellectina apportioned the food she had found, all her courage and joy returned twofold and her young voice rang out with confidence. "Ah yes, Err is a land reeking with stupidity and injustice; therefore I must search until I find another country, where there is justice and liberty and equality for all; then I shall send for you. If it does not exist, I shall assist in the creation of an ideal state, even if it requires a lifetime. But I believe it can be created on Mt. Certitude, for which I must continue to seek." She rose. "There, I have fed all you hungry outlaws to the best of my present ability, so leave me in peace for a little while at least." Glancing over their heads she inquired, "But where is that woman Noequist? I feel compelled to feed her, for, being a woman myself, I consider that I am more responsible for her fate than for any of yours. And to tell the truth, I am more interested in her too. Ah, there she is on the very edge of the desert. I must follow her."

After assuring herself that all the other outlaws had fallen into a light slumber, Tellectina escaped from these tormenting

Noequists with vast relief, and running across what remained of the Dotbu Desert came out onto a pleasant veldt. Although she pursued the woman Noequist as rapidly as possible, the explorer soon lost sight of her. After traversing the veldt, however, she was abruptly arrested by a portentous sight. On realizing where the woman Noequist had gone, the girl wondered if she possessed the courage to follow her, and stood amazed, murmuring to herself, "I don't yet understand why Nithking is called the Forbidden Country, but it is now only too apparent that it is a forbidding country."

CHAPTER V

HOW THE YOUNG EXPLORER WAS CAPTURED BY CANNIBALS IN THE
JUNGLE, SWAM AGAINST THE CURRENT OF THE SACRED RIVER,
PUBLI COPINION; AND FOUNDED THE COLONY OF NEW CHIMERA

THERE CONFRONTING the young explorer was a formidable green wall: a jungle—thick, impenetrable, sinister, and alluring. Overwhelmed by a sense of her own insignificance and utter impotence, the girl stood motionless. Suddenly, however, she was again seized by that insatiable inquisitiveness, the cause of her lust for adventure, and the impetus which had originally prompted her to leave the dull safety of Err. Obstacles and the unknown merely served to increase it, causing her blood to race and her eyes to dance. Although never in her whole twenty years had she even seen a jungle, the intrepid tenderfoot felt supreme confidence in her strength and sense of direction.

There were no trails to be seen anywhere, and the tangled undergrowth—apparently undisturbed for centuries—rendered progress slow and difficult. Even the brilliance of a tropical sun was unable to penetrate this jungle: the light dwindled to a strange green dimness, and everywhere in the darker shadows, rotting wood gave off a weird phosphorescent glow.

Totally unaware of her danger, the inexperienced explorer resolutely worked her way through the jungle until at length there appeared a muddy evil-smelling river, sprawled on the banks of which was an extensive settlement of pygmies. When questioned in a sign language, the natives replied in a dialect of

Halfish, informing their inquisitor that this was the sacred river in which the spirit of their chief god, Publi Copinion, abided. All along the banks the pygmies could be seen making continuous sacrifices to the great river. The white woman attempted to convince them that it was stupid to worship such a fickle god, that if they would break with tradition and move to higher ground they might develop into men and women of larger stature. The pygmies, however, threatened her with their darts poisoned with Nartso-tiva until she was forced to flee.

Tellectina had lost her way in the dense greenness when suddenly the mysterious woman Noequist once more confronted her. At her shrill savage cry, scores of amazons in full war regalia appeared, leaping from behind the trees with lifted spears. Their onrush was so sudden and violent that all effort at self-defense was futile. As the white woman was thrown to the ground, a sickening thought reeled through her head: perhaps this woman Noequist was the spy for some neighboring tribe of head-hunters which had sent her out in the desert to watch for white travelers.

Before she was fully aware of what had befallen her the captive was dragged off to a near-by cannibal village and bound to a stake. As the cannibals began to circle about her in a mad drunken dance, they tormented her by pricking and prodding her with the points of their spears. The savage shouts and ceaseless maddening throb of the native drums gradually paralyzed her ability to think.

All was a fearful confusion through which the captive noticed that their glistening spears were curiously shaped after the fashion of the white man's question mark and decorated with tufts of human hair. Realizing the fate of former victims, Tellectina felt all hope desert her; and closing her eyes in sick despair she hung limply on the ropes that bound her. Then, without warning, all sound and movement abruptly ceased. The prisoner opened her eyes to see all the warriors falling face downward in the dust at the approach of a strange procession which was headed by a beautiful young woman bearing aloft a tray with a human skull on it. The white woman moaned aloud, fearing that her own would be the next to ornament it.

The tray bearer was evidently their high priestess; and the ancient and highly decorated female following her, the chief of their tribe. The latter bore an especially large spear in the shape of a question mark which was apparently the extraordinary symbol of these extraordinary head-hunters. The captive inquired of the spy, who had originally revealed her whereabouts to the cannibals, as to the nature of this tribal religion. She replied that their goddess was Frewo and their priestess, Frelo. After translating these names into Reasonese, Tellectina promptly begged permission to also be allowed to kneel in worship of both. This it was which saved the captive's life, for she was released instantly and permitted to join the procession.

With her arms still bound, Tellectina was conducted to the rear of a crude temple made of Ophe bamboo and strewn with innumerable shiw-mats. On the altar lay a horrible pile of skulls, all of which—judging by their size—appeared to be those of the female sex. Behind this stood the figure of their goddess whose noble proportions called forth a gasp of admiration from the astonished white woman.

As the preliminaries of the ceremonies got under way, Tellectina realized with amazed relief that the language of these cannibals was not only easy to comprehend but was, in fact, merely a corruption of Reasonese. On conversing in whispers with the spy sitting beside her, she was informed that this tribe of women was not native to the jungle but had merely been hardened by long exposure to hardships and the fierceness of the tropical sun. They had come originally from a country called Err whence, so legend had it, their ancestresses had been expelled because of their religious beliefs nearly two thousand years ago. They had been wandering about in Nithking ever since, where necessity had obliged them to resort to the consumption of human flesh, though their preference was for a diet of swernas and seedd.

As the high priestess reverently placed her latest acquisition on the top of the pile of skulls, the spy further explained to

Tellectina that the name of their chief and leader was Quma. "And mine," she continued, "is Woqu. I joined the outlawed Noequists but I am really a spy for this tribe of amazons."

"Oh," Tellectina responded, again translating their dialect into Reasonese, "what fascinating names! Do you think it possible to persuade your noble chief to grant me a hearing before she—" here the prisoner shuddered—"I mean, I might be able to find some ripe swernas and an abundance of fine seedd for you."

The spy turned happy and incredulous eyes on the stranger. "Yes, I'll arrange it later; but first you must admire all the chief warriors. As they approach the altar I shall name them for you."

As a succession of these fine amazonian creatures presented themselves, they quaffed a strong draft of native wine which Tellectina learned afterwards was similar to that from the Semsianic vineyards. As each knelt, first to receive the blessing of the high priestess and then to kiss the feet of their goddess, they radiated such intense religious fervor that even the white woman began to be stirred. Tellectina listened carefully to their names. Each seemed more commendable than her predecessor: there were Equi and Vomo and a husky, surly-looking warrior called Eco, and a rather graceful woman known as Sub; there were Sin and Cooco and many more who passed before the altar of Frewo to make their obeisance. The last two, however, Tellectina considered particularly beautiful: the twins, Sexu and Sexu.

Surely this was not a primitive, savage religion at all, but a simple, natural one, infinitely more civilized and embodying more truth and beauty than any she had ever encountered before in her life, putting to shame the Casuistry under which she had been brought up in Smug Harbor. The young explorer longed to turn native and live forever with these splendid radiant people of nature.

Their religious fervor was becoming contagious. Tellectina's eyes also began to shine with an unnatural brilliance. Reflecting that half measures were for puny people and that it was whole heart or none for her, she suddenly burst her bonds and rushed up to the altar to throw herself at the feet of the goddess. The priestess, however, barred her progress with an outstretched arm.

"You can't approach Her except through me. Kneel."

Impulsively the young zealot caught up the ends of the narrow girdle of the priestess, exclaiming, "Ah, yes, I gladly kneel and worship you too, for in my language your name signifies Free Love!" Then, rising, she looked out over the faces of the other devotees. Not in all Err have I seen creatures of such beauty, such radiant health, and majesty of carriage. It is because you endeavor to emulate your goddess, Freewoman!"

Facing the altar again, she gazed enraptured at the statue. "To you, O goddess, O Frewo, O Freewoman, I dedicate my services! Henceforth I shall serve you faithfully even unto death!"

Sinking to her knees, she kissed the feet of the stone image; then, leaping to her feet, stood on the steps of the altar and spoke to the amazons in her passionate young voice. "All these years you have been lost—but it looks as if God Himself has sent me to help you! These warriors and erstwhile cannibals I shall turn into missionaries. We shall go forth into all the earth and preach the gospel of the Freewoman.

"Pass before me, noble amazons, and I shall tell you what your names mean in Reasonese. First your chief, Quma, and your courageous young spy, Woqu. Both have done well, but not always will you be led by Questionmark and Womanquestion. Ah, and there are those noble warriors whose names in Reasonese signify Equalrights and Voluntary Motherhood; and Sexu and Sexu, those inseparable twin sisters of equal beauty, whose names when translated are Sexualunion and Sexualpurity. Ah, but do see, Frewo, the strongest of all your servitors, Eco and Cooco, who will fight to the death for women's economic independence and the ideal coöperative community where you yourself would receive the worship due you. And last comes the two most beautiful of the natives, Sub and Sin— for does not Freewoman need to be served by sublimation and a single standard?

"Ah, your names are music to my ears—and in Reasonese they sound even better! Follow me! I can and will lead you to a utopia, to a land flowing with swernas and seedd; to a land where women can live in perfect freedom, perfect equality, and perfect love. I have seen it often in a vision that comes to me in my dreams. It is New Chimera. But I hope you continue to attack other women as you did me until you convert them also to your religion."

Catching up another cup of wine, Tellectina drank it off at one draft. Her eyes shone with that singular light common to all religious mania: her serious young face was aglow with ardor, her body trembled with excitement.

Facing the worshipers once more, she cried, "Rise up, noble amazons, leave your spears behind! No longer will the question mark be your symbol. Rise up! Bring your goddess Frewo with you—we will build her a bigger and better temple in Chimera! Come, follow Tellectina!"

Bearing aloft the shining statue on its pedestal, they marched out of the temple like crusaders in a holy cause and on toward the river, Publi Copinion. The expression of the chieftainess was decidedly skeptical, but she followed nevertheless.

Urging them on, Tellectina said, "I'm sure Chimera can't be far from here; but I think the quickest way is to go upstream rather than through this almost impenetrable jungle. Wait here on the bank until I engage a canoe large enough to carry the thirteen of us and inquire about directions. After we are settled in our new colony we shall send for the remainder of the tribe."

When the stranger made her requests in the pygmy village, the natives fell back horrified. "But no one ever goes against the current! It would make the god angry, and he would destroy you! The banks are white with the skeletons of those who have attempted it."

The white woman merely laughed. "I intend to go up river, sacred or profane."

Continuing her search through the village, she finally encountered an ancient witch doctor who could speak Reasonese. He stood in front of his hut going through the ceremony of sacrifice to the local god with great elaborateness. On completing the rites and facing about, he proved to be a rather weather-beaten white man who was merely dressed in the weird native costume. The girl explained her predicament.

When the man attempted to dissuade her, she pleaded with him again and again. "But why? Surely you do not believe that this river is a god!"

"Believe? Why, my dear child——"

"Child? I'm twenty!" Tellectina corrected him.

The man smiled indulgently. "My dear young lady, I believe in nothing but peace and comfort and my own thoughts."

"But I don't want peace and comfort: I want to find Chimera, for only there dwell justice and freedom and truth."

"Out of the mouths of babes!"

"You talk nonsense! I see that you won't assist or direct me, so I shall swim against the current. I'm not afraid of Publi Copinion!" the young girl exclaimed scornfully.

"You are courting certain danger. This river may not be sacred to you, but it possesses too many of the attributes of a god. It's omnipotent, omnipresent, and revengeful."

"But this pygmy religion is so stupid!"

"Ah, but in stupidity there is strength. My dear lovely young thing, I should have no respect for you if you *did* heed my very wise advice. The courage of one's convictions is an admirable thing—even though the convictions are wrong. The banks of this river are white with human skeletons: you may be destroyed. And it is not possible to go beyond its reach, either: it floods the entire country."

"I am not afraid!"

"I wasn't afraid either—once. But it is not a matter of fear but rather a matter of payment."

"Oh, I'm wasting my time!" the girl exclaimed and turned to go.

To the group of head-hunters who had awaited her return impatiently she announced in disgust, "All the people hereabout are cowards! They've never heard of New Chimera, and they're afraid even to assist us in going against the current. But none of you are worshipers of Publi Copinion, thank heaven! Bring your statue, now, and in we all go—we'll swim!"

They all plunged boldly in and started swimming against the turbulent stream, pulling the statue after them. The sting of the angry waters only increased their efforts, and the sound of their defiant young laughter rang out above the noise of the torrent.

After a while, however, they all showed unmistakable signs of weariness and fear. As they cried aloud for help, the river lashed more ferociously against the statue of Frewo. Trembling with fright, the women commenced to jabber in a mixture of Halfish and Reasonese that they could interpret the angry voice of the river and it said, "You anger me—you are disobeying my commandments! Woman's place is at home; women are inferior to men. Physical chastity (of women) is priceless, and all sex is obscene! I am a god of vengeance—if you try to be free women I shall punish you!"

Tellectina's followers were afraid to go farther, but she shouted encouragement to them above the roar. "For shame! Courage! Publi Copinion never speaks the truth! If we can only combat the force of his current long enough we'll reach the utopia we seek!" But it was not long before exhaustion caused her to cling to the jungle creepers along the banks. While resting, she again heard the padding of those invisible feet which were pursuing her through the jungle; but plunging into the water to drown the sound, she pretended not to have heard it.

The fate of her followers was at its most precarious when, rounding the bend of the river, they sighted a huge blue outrigger canoe of curious rectangular shape with her blunt bow pointed upstream. With a cry of relief Tellectina swam toward it, noticing as she did so that its name, *Woman*, was painted in gold letters on the side.

In the canoe sat a small dark woman who was directing the native crew, while on the bank stood a river trader. Before the spent swimmer could climb out of the water, he commenced to bombard her with his high-pressure sales talk. When he guaranteed that she would convey Tellectina to the land of woman's freedom—for only two dollars—the weary young explorer listened entranced to the shrewd little trader. Madelaine Marx explained that she was a worshiper of Frewo herself and a servitor of Frelo. Even all the warriors were welcomed by the little Frenchwoman.

Too deeply moved to speak, the explorer extracted her waterproof purse and paid the trader, then stepped into the canoe with reverent feet—awed by the presence of one possessing both the courage and skill to go against this treacherous current and one who, furthermore, was acquainted with the location of the fair land of woman's freedom. All the bedraggled tribe slipped respectfully into their places, feeling that their lives had been saved. They pushed off, but the canoe had not gone far before it sprang a leak in several places. To this, however, Tellectina deliberately closed her eyes. Suddenly there loomed ahead of them the gigantic and almost inescapable rock known as the Mar-it-al, which stood in the very center of Publi Copinion. Running head on against it, the canoe instantly began to fill with muddy water and to go swirling downstream so rapidly that Tellectina commanded all the natives to dive into the river again.

With furious disgust they gave the boat a vigorous push that sent it spinning even more dizzily down river. Disappointed and discouraged, the swimmers moved on more slowly for a time until their leader realized that if food and assistance were not forthcoming soon they would all either drown from weakness or be washed downstream and so out into the ocean. Certain that the sea would eventually carry her back to the shores of Err, Tellectina preferred death on the spot.

The presence of several white people on the river, however, indicated the possible existence of others. Bidding her companions rest on the bank among the bleached bones of less fortunate explorers, Tellectina went into the jungle to reconnoiter. To her vast relief, she soon came upon a broad trail. After having followed it a little way, she suddenly beheld a sight so staggering that her heart leapt into her throat. It was as if a dream had come true in genuine Arabian Nights' fashion: there confronting her—with its gold roofs glistening in the tropical sun—lay a fabulous city.

"Incredible Nithking!" she cried. "Land of endless surprises!"

Weak from fatigue and hunger but strengthened by hope, she stumbled forward until she fell half fainting onto the steps of the first palace, which was constructed in that rectangular biblioesque style peculiar to the houses of Nithking. Looking through the door which a page had opened for her, she felt as if transported by magic from a primitive world of hardships to a world of luxury and refinement. Beautiful ladies and elegant lords in pleasant conversation could be heard within. Three of the famous men Tellectina recognized from pictures she had seen of them long ago: the Duke of Wellington, Chateaubriand, and Benjamin Constant.

Convinced that she and her followers were saved, the explorer rushed back to the river and led all her starving headhunters to this mansion. She was conducted to the mistress of the house by a man who had introduced himself as Herriot. Immediately Tellectina related the story of their sad plight, confident that this woman, who was capable of attracting the greatest men of her day, possessed both the desire and the ability to assist worthy young explorers of Nithking.

The exquisitely beautiful woman discoursed at length—of fancy ball gowns, and public adulation of her beauty—her conversation never rising above society gossip. To all this Tellectina sat listening in growing misery. "Oh," she finally interrupted, "but you have answered none of my questions! Monsieur Herriot says that you are very powerful, Madame Récamier.

Your fame has spread even over into Err. But aren't you interested in women's problems—in women's freedom and equality? Can't you give us some kind of sustenance and then direct us to New Chimera?"

Shrugging her beautiful white shoulders, their hostess admitted that she was not clever, suggesting, however, that perhaps her friend Madame de Staël might be of some assistance. Sick with disappointment, the young explorer turned her back on the beautiful and virginal Madame Récamier but nevertheless ran immediately to the house of Madame de Staël near by, where she was admitted by a page and introduced by Gribble, the major-domo. The very virginity of Récamier had convinced Tellectina that she could have been neither very intelligent nor very rich—emotionally. Grouped about the famous writer, however, was her lover, Constant, and Talleyrand, Lord Byron, and the Duke of Wellington. A brilliant salon, a brilliant woman, fearless, intellectual, and openly amorous—was it not natural to expect everything from her? Yet only a few crumbs from her tea table and some words of encouragement she offered the explorer's party. Never having heard of this land they sought, she was naturally unable to give them directions for finding it, but assured them that they would enjoy listening to her daughter, Corinne.

In the heart of this City of Women Corinne was found seated in the public forum, extemporizing, playing a harp, composing poetry—worshiped by the literary and æsthetic public. Tellectina promised her proselytes that thus would they too pass their days in the land of woman's freedom.

Next they sought assistance—in vain—from the Comtesse de Noailles and Marie Bashkirtseff. Then they visited a famous Frenchwoman who proved to be a philosopher as well as a grand amoureuse, with great feminine charm and beauty. Here, at last, thought Tellectina, is the woman we have been seeking. When informed, however, of Ninon de Lenclos' promiscuity and her means of livelihood the little Errorian covered her face in shame, running from the house weeping and moaning, "No, no, the Freewoman we worship does not permit promiscuity nor the bartering of sex for money either out of marriage or in it!"

Before leaving the French Quarter she determined to make one more attempt. And when George Sand urged her to make a religion of love, asserting that she too had dreamed of an ideal community and was constantly plagued by a dual personality, Tellectina was elated beyond words. She and her poor starving followers enjoyed a feast they had long awaited, finding much encouragement but still unable to obtain directions.

Feeling quite refreshed, however, the exploring party turned its steps hopefully toward the section of the city occupied by the English. On hearing of a highly intellectual writer who had lived fifteen years with a man without being married to him, Tellectina hastened to the house of this admirable woman. After a short visit, however, she departed in great disappointment: George Eliot had lived in a free union not because it was an ideal to her but merely because George Henry Lewes was unable to obtain a divorce.

When some passer-by related the story of the Brownings to Tellectina, she lamented deeply that they had terminated such a lovely idyl with the commonplaceness of marriage. On inquiring if there were no emancipated women in this city from that country which prided itself on being "the sweet land of liberty," otherwise known as America, she was laughed at unmercifully. Nevertheless, she searched until she found two small obscure houses in which there resided the Puritan, Margaret Fuller, and the circus rider, Adah Isaacs Mencken.

The majority of the passers-by laughed when the girl made inquiries in her earnest young voice. One kind Englishman, though, assured her that the one person in the world best fitted to help her was Mary Wollstonecraft. Having experienced so many disappointments, and having perceived that the beautiful women were devoid of intellect, and the intellectual ones of charm (with the exception of Ninon de Lenclos); and having obtained directions and assistance from none of them, Tellectina concluded that in all the City of Famous Women there were none who were true worshipers of either Freewoman or Freelove, and all were consequently outside the fold of the saved.

Although she admired, respected, and envied these women for their courage in taking lovers, their motive was not commendable, being a desire for pleasure rather than an assertion of freedom. Omitting the one woman prepared to direct them, the expedition departed.

"But do not be discouraged," Tellectina assured them as they retraced their steps to the river. "Some day, somewhere, we shall find the place we seek."

Secretly, however, despair was already causing their leader to flounder about aimlessly in the river when a river barge drew near. After her brief explanation, its occupant introduced himself as Edward Carpenter and bade her get in. The grateful girl lifted the brown canvas covering (often used on such conveyances) and settled herself in comfortably. Warning her that no such community as she sought existed, he nevertheless offered to carry her up river—it being his conviction that it was the Tellectinas of the world who possessed the courage and vision to create an ideal place where love might come of age.

After a rather incoherent endeavor to explain her still unformulated conceptions of an ideal community where people went naked and lived and loved in perfect freedom, the young zealot sat at Edward Carpenter's feet, listening as though he were some great prophet. For, as usual, to hear her own chaotic and vague young thoughts nicely arranged in neat sentences caused her to consider the speaker the most marvellous and admirable person she had ever met.

" 'A healthy delight in and cultivation of the body and all its natural functions, and a determination to keep them pure and beautiful, open and sane and free, will have to become a recognized part of national life.' "

"Oh, yes, yes, people have lost all respect for their bodies—thanks to the Puritans," Tellectina exclaimed heatedly.

" 'Let every woman whose heart bleeds for the suffering of her sex hasten to declare herself and to constitute herself, as far as she possibly can, a free woman. Let her accept the term with all the odium that belongs to it; let her insist on her right to speak, dress, think, act, and above all to use her sex, as she deems best; let her face the scorn and ridicule; let her "lose her own life" if she likes.' "

That unearthly light common to all religious mania began to glow in the young girl's eyes. "Lose my life," she whispered, "yes, that's it." Then, lifting a beatific countenance, she proclaimed in a defiant voice, "If I am drowned, destroyed, by the power and treachery of Publi Copinion—I do not care! My heart bleeds for the injustices done to my sex! I'll gladly sacrifice my life in an effort to have justice done to women and love!"

They soon came to a point beyond which Carpenter said it was impossible for him to take his passengers. Tellectina observed the rapids ahead, but he had kindled her zeal to such a pitch that no obstacle had the power to deter her now. The young girl's effort to express her gratitude to him resulted only in a few happy tears. After she and her followers had disembarked, they all stood watching the brown barge; fearing for its fate as it was carried back downstream, hoping, however, that it would bring up other young explorers.

The contact with Edward Carpenter imparted such strong impetus to their swimming that they soon arrived at a suitable clearing where the ground was high enough to be safe from the inundations of the river—so Tellectina thought. At once they set to work like true pioneers, felling trees and cutting underbrush until they were able to construct rude huts of Norancegi bamboo and Zest leaves, which provided temporary shelter. The somewhat battered and mud-stained statue of Frewo was set up in a hastily erected temple and garlanded with flaming passion flowers and lilies intertwined in equal proportion.

During the excavations for her permanent home, Tellectina's improvised spade struck the feet of a buried statue. On being unearthed it proved to be very ancient and very curious. While setting it upright, she was astonished to see coming toward her two more explorers whom Carpenter had evidently brought up river. After exchanging greetings and explanations with the women, the young men dropped their kits and circumambulated this extraordinary statue many times in great perplexity.

"Oh," concluded the dark young man laughing significantly, "it must be Janus. A Roman remain left here no doubt by soldiers on the march through this country long ago."

"No," contended the fair young man, "it's too primitive to be Roman. See, it has two bodies as well as two faces. And look," he brushed the earth from its base, "their names are carved on it, 'Seva-Doxnel.' "

"Well," the first youth responded laughing, "you're the scholar of this group, you should decipher its meaning. My only interpretation is that the worship of Siamese twins like that would be damned awkward!" And with this remark he sought other amusement.

His companion, continuing to converse with Tellectina, concluded, "Whatever its name or origin, it possesses great beauty."

The girl agreed, lamenting the fact that it had lain so long neglected. After introducing himself as Nesse, the dark youth informed Tellectina that his companion's name was Ray Niviso and that the latter had induced him to depart from Err, not only to search for a land of woman's freedom, but also for a place to establish an ideal coöperative community.

Tellectina soon discovered that Ray Niviso's fluency in Reasonese so far excelled her own that she could only deem it a privilege to become his pupil. And thereafter she endeavored to imitate his messianic accent to the best of her ability. For hours each day they sat beneath the shade of a opia nut tree, equally intoxicated with each other's conversation and with their own; while every evening he would play his own compositions on the violin which he had with great difficulty brought from Err. Then at night, as Tellectina unrolled her mat to sleep, she would sigh happily and murmur:

"Ah, at last, at last! This is what I've been seeking all my life! This mental companionship alone is worth all the hardships I've had to undergo!"

One morning while weaving fresh garlands for Frewo, they commenced to lay elaborate plans for the simple life. Together, they said, they would establish an ideal colony where everyone was free and equal; where there were no rules or laws except those of the inner man; where there was no possessing of property but everything was shared and shared alike; where everyone would be above jealousy, and where the human body would be respected and kept beautiful and all inhabitants would walk in proud nakedness. Here in New Chimera all unions would be free, the community bearing the expenses of motherhood and the burden of rearing the child. Reasonese would be the only language spoken, and Halfish a past crime to be forgotten as speedily as possible. Art and philosophy would flourish in this atmosphere and be tended with such loving care that their blossoms would astound the poor people of Err. And in Chimera lovers would lie on a bed of wild violets under the trees, bathe nude in moonlit pools, and dance their natural spontaneous dances in the woods. Tellectina was absolutely ecstatic: was not this her goal? Was not this Certitude?

In the meanwhile, Nesse, having scouted around, had collected a group of explorers who had either been lost or washed ashore by Publi Copinion. It was not long before an entire village of thatched huts sprang into existence in the very heart of the jungle. Every evening after work, Tellectina and Ray Niviso (although not his real name, he was called such by his friends, he confided) had gradually fallen into the habit of meeting at the statue to renew their attempt to unravel its meaning.

One lovely moonlight night, when the pale ceromna seemed to drip with sweetness, Tellectina was annoyed and astounded to see Femina suddenly and mysteriously glide onto the scene, fulfilling her threat made some nine months before.

Concealing herself behind her sister, Femina inquired in a whisper, "What is his name?"

"It's a secret; but he confided in me and declares it is 'Olev,' " Tellectina replied.

"I don't believe it," her sister returned. "But I'll wait and see. We shall be obliged to call him Olev the Second; though I presume he thinks he's Olev the First—they always do."

Femina immediately began to make eyes at Olev the Second in such a way that he promptly forgot Tellectina's presence; but the latter subsequently remonstrated with her sister as they unrolled their mats that night. "Femina, you're so frivolous and silly! This is my affair, anyway—why didn't you stay away?"

Femina laughed. "Because I felt irresistibly drawn to the scene of your endeavor. Remember, it is a curse put on us at birth to share any man in which the other becomes seriously interested. Besides, you couldn't have held him without me."

"Don't be ridiculous! But what have you been doing since I last saw you in Rote Hill?"

"Oh, amusing myself with men who would bore you," Femina replied as she turned over and yawned like a lithe, luxurious cat.

In the days that followed Tellectina more than once accused Olev of caring more for her sister than for herself: to which he invariably replied, "Oh, no, you do me a discredit. But of course I do think Femina pretty and charming, any man would. It's Tellectina and her fine mind that I love, however; she's far superior."

Sighing happily, the girl would murmur, "At last, then, I have found a man who cares more for intellect than for feminine smiles and smirks!"

One morning what suddenly seemed a very obvious fact dawned on Olev and Tellectina: the statue of the gods Seva-Doxnel, which they had unearthed from its ignominious grave, could be the symbol of nothing other than love and sex. For, said they, who knew nothing of either, are not love and sex twin gods, forever inseparable, omnipresent, omnipotent, and even omniscient? As they refurbished the discarded idols, they put their heads together to consider the style of temple most suitable for such important gods. The discussion continued far into the night. What could be better, contended the young man, than to imitate glorious nature herself in the design? The young girl, never in her life having even seen the natural formations he referred to, agreed with a beatific smile illuminating her face.

After studying the natural formations with a sort of religious awe, they laid down the groundwork of the temple, employing both the Gothic and Pelvic arches seen everywhere in nature and performing with solemn reverence all things which the situation required—even the unmentionable ones. The center column, designed by the young man, antedated even the Gothic —going back to the Early Phallic. Olev, however, experienced great difficulty in its erection: a matter which would have been interpreted as an evil omen by any save a novice. But the girl was too inexperienced in the proper erections of such architectural members to evince any surprise.

Above the altar was placed the refurbished statue of Seva-Doxnel, while in an oval niche below and to the right they introduced another statue, of a mother and child. For a consultation of Olev's authoritative books on the origin of religions revealed that Sanger and Carpenter and Stockham agreed that undoubtedly the goddess Magnition, or Karreza, as some devotees called her (but by the heterodox known as Restraint) gave birth to Sublimation. It was, of course, an immaculate conception. And this Son, like His predecessor, was also destined to become greater than His mother.

It was necessary, however, to excommunicate Nesse at once for his blasphemy. He laughed at the ritual in honor of Magnition, asserting that he failed to see how any strong healthy man could be expected to go through with it, declaring he had indisputable proof that Magnition gave birth not to Sublimation but to nervous disorders.

Frewo was similarly enshrined in a niche to the left. Before this statue Frelo was to officiate at the union of the men and women of New Chimera. One night, as Tellectina and Olev were strolling through the moonlit woods, he proposed that they be initiated together into the religion of Seva-Doxnel and thus unite their lives forever. The girl consented, saying, "But only on *one* condition, that we be united by the high priestess Frelo."

"Well, if you really wish it. I admire her myself, but some people might think that marriage——"

"Marriage! Don't mention that abominable old-fashioned word! And we are above what other people think or say. I worship Frelo almost as much as I do Frewo. First we'll be *verbally* united by Frelo, but then shouldn't the Great Mystery come——"

"Oh yes, that should come much later!" the young man agreed hastily. "We must prepare ourselves for it. I'm thirty, but I've been waiting to be initiated with the woman I love. I've kept myself pure all these years in anticipation of that great day. Why, it seemed to pollute me even to touch a woman until I met you. I've never so much as kissed a woman before in my life."

The girl turned incredulous eyes on him. "Really? Is that possible? I thought all men considered it their prerogative to indulge in sex and—— But no, I guess your abstinence is proof that you are all the purer and more worthy to worship Seva-Doxnel. I'm twenty-one, and I know almost nothing about the great gods we revere so much—except theoretically. And my sister Femina is almost as abysmally ignorant as I. You must unite with her too, you know. Do you object to living with two women?"

"Oh, I prefer it. You and your sister are like two halves of a perfect whole." And so it was agreed.

Although the villagers had been eager to perform all the ceremonies befitting the five gods of the temple, they had restrained themselves until the example should be set by their two leaders. Olev and Tellectina, however, wishing to arrive at the appropriate spiritual state before being initiated into the Great Mystery, refrained from entering the temple, preparing themselves religiously by studying the gospel according to Kraft-Ebing and August Forel. Their unfamiliarity with the terms rendered the scriptures very difficult to comprehend.

Their research brought them closer and closer together until finally they felt themselves to be ready. One day at high noon a tom-tom summoned all the villagers to the temple where Frelo united Tellectina and Olev the Second for life in the holy bonds of freedom. They vowed to make their union as nearly perfect as possible, to build a house in pure Idyllic style, to make Reasonese their only language, and to speak it in impromptu verse.

Femina, however, was mysteriously absent from this ceremony, but Tellectina was so elated at being the first woman united to a man by Frelo that she temporarily forgot the very existence of her sister. All the other couples followed suit, for legal marriage barred people from living in Chimera. Tellectina and Olev immediately began to build a long-house adjacent to the temple. When completed, Femina reluctantly consented to live with them. Inasmuch as the sisters resembled each other very closely and seldom appeared in public together, few people ever realized that Olev was living with two women. It was their very difference which delighted him, though.

The men of the colony admired Olev's mate when she was Femina but not when she was Tellectina: the latter rarely showed herself to women, but one look at the former was sufficient to engender deep hatred in most other females, a fact which both pained and puzzled Tellectina but seemed to amuse Femina excessively.

For several weeks after they moved into their new home, Olev the Second would read aloud to Tellectina after supper each evening. They would sit far into the night conversing ecstatically about poetry, beauty, love, the art of living, and the alter ego—while Femina sulked in the corner. Each time she would timidly run her hand through Olev's long blond hair and whisper, "Kiss me," he would kiss her perfunctorily and say, "No, not yet, we are not spiritual enough."

For this overt action Tellectina would reprimand her sister in an undertone. "Certainly not, Femina, you are too earthly, you can't understand our feelings."

"No, I certainly can't!" the other would mutter inaudibly, and going to bed would lie awake pondering on the cause of her unhappiness.

Several months passed in this way. Their intellectual companionship delighted Tellectina but irritated Femina, who, though not moved by the religious impulse, was moved by another. Moreover, she felt an intense curiosity concerning the ceremony in honor of Seva-Doxnel. Knowledge that every other virgin in Chimera had long since been initiated into the Great Mystery caused Femina instinctively to conceal the fact that she was still a virgin and consequently unconsecrated and unholy.

One day, beset by an inexplicable discontent, Femina led her sister into the woods where they could talk in private. "Now, Tina, you must listen to me! I'm not happy. I want to be loved. These mental and so-called spiritual unions may satisfy you but they don't me. You who are so intellectual seem to forget that I am the personification of all that's feminine. And I'd respect Olev a damned sight more if he'd catch me up in his arms like a real man and make me his without all this nonsense about being initiated into a mystery in a temple!"

"Oh, Femina, what about our fine ideal of being spiritually united before we unite physically?"

"All damned nonsense! And I tell you there's something queer about our marriage that I don't understand!"

"*Union!* Don't lower it by calling it marriage. That word is absolutely taboo in Chimera—you know that."

"And I know it's time our—our union was consummated or—or, oh, Tina, I didn't want a virgin man. I'd respect him infinitely more if he had had experience—it's unnatural for a man to be so 'good.' A man thirty years old and never been kissed —there's something wrong somewhere. I don't know what it is—but, oh, Tina, you got me into all this mess, and I'm not happy! I'm not happy, I tell you!" Wringing her hands in great agitation, she began to pace up and down the path.

Tellectina was genuinely upset, also. "Don't cry, please, please. I'll see what can be done."

Fearful of seeming unspiritual, Tellectina intimated Femina's feelings to Olev as best she could with gestures. He understood, however, and they began to prepare for the great event. It was not long before they, who were familiar only with the outward forms, felt moved to perform the ceremony with something approaching fervor.

The temple was thrown open: the bowed head of the priest was anointed with oil in private, after which initial rite he rose slowly and prepared to make his entrance. And as the priest entered, Femina, in obedience to a custom immemorial for virgins, made the blood sacrifice to the great god Seva-Doxnel. There followed the secret initiation which it is forbidden to record, after which the man poured his libations over the altar and withdrew. Tellectina, who had witnessed but participated very slightly in the sacred rites, eagerly interrogated Femina as to the nature of her sensations during her initiation into the Great Mystery.

"Oh," her sister whispered while still in the prostrate position required by the ceremony, "I—I was frightened and amazed and—and rather disgusted!"

"Oh, don't say that, Femina, that's sacrilegious!"

"But, Tina, do you suppose that this is all there is to it? I never was so disappointed in my life! I had anticipated a gorgeous orgy! But that high priest doesn't arouse me at all— he—why, he merely gives me a pain!"

"Don't worry, the scriptures say that it's like that at first for the novice; but as the ritual is repeated the worshiper's ardor increases, especially if the priest rises to a sufficient emotional height to fill her with his own great warmth."

Each time the ceremony was performed, however, the two young votaries were secretly distressed because the high priest who had been ordained to fill this office failed to look the part for his high position. Beauty was a necessary attribute of any object worthy of worship, Tellectina felt instinctively. And from no angle was the priest attractive, nor in any position. Furthermore, he seemed unable to stand entirely erect during the ceremony and therefore failed to command the proper reverence from either of the two women. The location of the temple itself soon proved to be a disturbing factor—there was really nothing about it, when examined with cool critical eyes, that was æsthetic or conducive to veneration.

After a few months had passed, Femina's religious inclinations waned. One sleepless night she confided to her sister lying beside her that she agreed with Nesse: Magnitation gave birth not to Sublimation but to nervous disorders, sleeplessness, and bad tempers.

"Oh, Femina, it's blasphemous to talk that way. I won't listen!" Turning over, she actually prayed for sleep, but the ceremony in the temple had agitated her nerves to such an extent that she lay awake far into the night listening to Olev snore unromantically.

Surprises in New Chimera never ceased. The lovers discovered that when they disported themselves on the bed of wild violets which Tellectina had so artistically arranged under the trees the leaves tickled them and the stems irritated their skin; and invariably they awoke the next morning with bad colds. And when they went dancing gayly down to swim nude in the pool, all the snakes in the vicinity likewise chose moonlight nights for this sport; consequently the creatures were soon left to enjoy it without the interference of human beings. Although nudity was one of the tenets of their new religion, Tellectina admitted privately that it would have been a decided kindness to their fellow beings if many of the villagers had covered themselves with any sort of garment, however unæsthetic; especially the older women with sagging breasts, and the men with great paunches and spindle legs.

It was Femina, though, who was the chief lawbreaker of this

ideal community. It seemed an absolute impossibility for her to refrain from coquetting with the other men of the village, let Tellectina reprimand her as she would. On several occasions Olev became so jealous that he and Femina actually degraded themselves by quarreling in Halfish. But the greatest disillusionment of all was brought about by the fact that the mere struggle for existence precluded the possibility of any intellectual life. Expecting to study in the mornings, work in the afternoons, and engage in brilliant conversations in the evenings, they had sent over into Err for all their books. By the time the food was gathered, cooked, and eaten three times a day, however; the dishes washed as many times, the water brought from the spring a half-dozen times, the beds made and the bedclothes laundered, the house cleaned, and the gardens cultivated—the day was over. And when night came, physical fatigue prevented them from accomplishing anything more intellectual than falling asleep immediately after the evening meal. The two sisters loathed all their domestic chores with intense violence, yet when desperation drove Tellectina to seek diversion by writing up her travels in Nithking in her diary, she was aghast to find that Olev resented her desire to do creative work of any variety.

One afternoon, as Tellectina was lifting their heavy earthen dishes into the dishpan, rebellion flared up in her; and gazing out the window at the beautiful and indifferent palm trees waving high above her head, she protested vigorously:

"Was it for this that I braved the dangers of Publi Copinion? I am no better than a servant girl, and Olev lives the life of an ignorant jungle native: gathering food, eating, copulating, and sleeping—nothing more. Where are all our fine dreams? Hours of reading, talking, writing, and composing music? I hate dishes and houses and beds, hate it—hate it! I was not born to be a domestic slut—I am Tellectina!"

Yet she saw no possible avenue of escape; the employment of servants was against the rules of the ideal community—even if they could have afforded them, which they could not. Discontent ran like an undercurrent through all the life of New

Chimera, but no action was taken until after the spring rains set in. Publi Copinion suddenly overflowed its banks, inundating much of New Chimera, carrying off a number of the inhabitants, drowning others, and doing untold damage to the unsubstantial houses of the coöperative colony. It was then that someone surreptitiously removed the statues of the Mother, Magnitation, and the Son, Sublimation, from the temple; but with one accord the entire community affected not to notice their absence. All about the temple a strange poisonous vine sprang up in uncontrollable profusion. Every time it touched Tellectina or Femina it produced such a painful rash that her worship of Seva-Doxnel waned apace.

After Olev and the two sisters had been united about six months, Tellectina awakened one morning to find Femina sitting on the edge of the bed patting her abdomen and talking to an invisible person.

"There, you little rascal, move your feet! You're pressing on your mother's ribs too hard and it hurts—move, I say!" And Femina rubbed the upper part of her abdomen vigorously.

Tellectina was almost speechless. "But, Femina, you told me you were furious because you were having a child at twenty-two, and now——"

"Ah, yes, that was at first. But now that I can feel him move —I, oh, Tina, I love him so! Feel his little head—here: isn't it adorably sweet? I love carrying him, I feel so complete, so fulfilled, so content! Oh, I'm happy, happy as never before!"

Tellectina felt the small head and buttocks beneath her sister's fair white belly. "Yes, but why couldn't nature have devised a more esthetic method of birth? You look hideously deformed. I wasn't ready for you to have a child: you should have consulted me. Birth is certainly a mysteriously wonderful process, and yet I think it is quite ludicrous, too."

"Bah, I don't care what you think—I'm happy! I wonder why Olev was so abnormally anxious to have a child. It's an unnatural sort of obsession with him because he doesn't really love children at all—I've watched him with them. It's very mystifying, but, anyway, I'm happy now!"

Again she stroked her rounded white belly and touched her full breasts wonderingly while Tellectina looked on in amazement and murmured, "And you experience all these emotions over which I have no control whatever! It's all quite bewildering to find instinct so much stronger than the mind."

Although at the birth of the child Tellectina was forcibly ejected from the room, she was able to hear Femina's agonized screams—and she hated all nature with a fierce savage intensity.

A few days later, when she leaned over the bed she was amazed to observe the radiance of Femina's face when she played with the ugly little piece of red flesh, astounded at the delighted noises that flowed from her sister's lips and at the expression of utter content in her eyes when the infant suckled her breast. "And so the processes of nature go on quite well without help or hindrance from the mind and will of the individual. It makes a Tellectina feel humble and insignificant for the first time in her life!"

Thus Tellectina was reflecting when an uproar outside the house caused her to leave the room in order to investigate its cause. She was confronted by all the inhabitants of New Chimera swarming about her doorway. Standing on the top step, she gazed at them in consternation.

One woman moved forward and spoke to her in Halfish. "Tellectina, we've brought a priest from Err to marry you. Now that you have a child you should be legally married for its sake."

Tellectina was so taken aback she was speechless.

Then a man spoke: "Oh, yes, we know this free love business is a grand theory, and if you want to bring disgrace on *yourself*—that's all right. But you have no right to bring it on a helpless child!"

White with anger Tellectina opened her lips, but no words issued forth.

"We knew you'd be angry, therefore we didn't tell you; but

we have nearly all been secretly married by this priest some time ago and——"

Suddenly the enraged girl found her voice. "You traitors! You couldn't endure your freedom, could you? You've forsaken your ideal and fallen so low as to marry! You've reverted to type and begun to speak Halfish among yourselves! And oh, heaven, you've disgraced yourselves: you're wearing fig leaves!" She covered her eyes and moaned.

A confusion of angry voices arose. "Well, you'd better get married, or you'll regret it!"

"We're giving you fair warning!"

A man behind her whispered, "Maybe—maybe it would be wise."

Turning, she beheld Olev. Then her eyes dilated with the intensity of her emotion. "What! Betray our ideals! Deny our child the greatest heritage of freedom any child ever had bequeathed to it! A thousand times, no! A thousand times more important is it now to be free! I'm proud—proud, can't you understand that? I'd be ashamed to marry—I'm above the laws of mankind! Marriage is all right for cowards—but you, you Chimerians, oh what have you done to yourselves? All the opportunity and effort and beauty thrown away!" Supporting herself against the column of the porch, she wept despairingly.

The mob, however, was not listening: it was departing with laughter and jeers. Blinded by tears, Tellectina went indoors; and approaching the child's crib, stood staring down on the small sleeping form with a face in which fierce yearning was mingled with pained uncertainty.

As time went on Olev and Tellectina were awakened more and more frequently at night by the sound of missiles being thrown at their house. The village enmity finally became very annoying; for although Tellectina reveled in the martyrdom of being snubbed in the streets, it was highly inconvenient to be refused the communal breadfruit and bananas and other foods for which Olev had arranged to exchange lessons in musical composition and Reasonese. And when Femina refused to relinquish her baby to the custody of the community child's house to be reared, Tellectina's attempts to persuade her of the wisdom of it were only half-hearted.

It was not long, however, before the baby, who had from the first been small and undeveloped, sickened and died. Although Femina's grief seemed to Tellectina very unreasonable, it was nevertheless quite terrible to witness. Day after day she would find her sister weeping at the child's grave.

"But, Femina, since the child would never have been strong and well, it's unkind of you to wish him to live. It's pure selfishness, and if you really loved him you would——"

Femina turned on her like an angry lioness. "Why was it sickly? You killed it! You chose a sickly man—all brains and no body! A pale poetic blond—thin and nervous—not a drop of red blood in his body! That's why my child died—that's why it was weak and sickly. That man you chose has the soul of a woman: his la-di-da ways make me sick! I hate you and your damned intellect, and I hate Olev and his spiritual tommyrot! And his name isn't 'Olev'—he doesn't even know the meaning of the word love. He's nothing on earth but a visionary —impractical, incorrigible, and utterly impossible!"

"Oh, Femina, how ghastly, how monstrous! How can you!"

"How can I? Because I see the truth, and I have the courage to speak it and you haven't! And every day his cold wet kisses nauseate me more and more! I loathe him, I tell you! He has become so repulsive to me that every time he comes over into my bed, my flesh positively creeps! He has no more passion than a cold wet sponge—no more than a—a serpent!"

"Oh, Femina, this is terrible! Such treachery—such——"

"Yes, it is terrible, because it's true."

"But he's so brilliant, so erudite, a famous scholar and artist! He's so—so spiritual and idealistic—so wonderfully mystical! Oh, he wants to save the whole world!"

"Well, he'd better try to save his own wife first! Oh, Tina, Tina, I don't understand what's the matter: all I know is that if Olev ever touches me again, I'll—I'll kill him! I swear it, I'll kill him! Those long white hands, those thin arms and cold wet lips—they have no more lovingness in them, no more passion than—— You *know* there's never been a complete union! I read some of your books, and they explain—— Oh, Tina, why didn't you marry a real man? He's more feminine than I am, even, before heaven he is! Oh, Tina, help me, help me, I'm so miserable, so miserable! I wish I were dead—dead—dead!" Sobbing bitterly Femina fell prostrate across her child's grave.

Even Tellectina began to weep. "Poor Olev, poor Femina! Oh, yes, I've felt all the time that something was the matter— but what is it?—what is it? If we only knew!"

The two women sat rocking back and forth in abject misery until suddenly Tellectina was arrested by the sound of approaching footsteps. Although unable to see anyone, she heard two voices: one low and deep and the other so high-pitched that she mistook it for that of a woman. A distinctly audible note of tenderness convinced her that they were lovers. But as Tellectina listened a strange fear crept over her. Rising cautiously in order not to crackle the twigs under her feet, she parted the foliage and discovered two men—an older one with his back to Tellectina and a younger one facing her.

Horror stricken, she whispered to Femina, "Look!"

Her sister rose, and as they stood there, they beheld the tall blond youth flashing coquettish eyes at the older man and dropping them as coyly as any woman. It was Olev.

He turned just in time to realize that he had been observed. After one horrified glance, Femina had fled through the woods; while Tellectina, frozen with abhorrence, stood motionless, listening to Femina's dying footsteps, aware that she was powerless to stay her flight, aware that Olev had lost Femina forever.

Stumbling blindly home, Tellectina threw herself on her bed shaken by great dry sobs. She was too sick, frightened, and shocked to cry—horror seemed to have frozen her tears at their source. Repeatedly the girl murmured, "It isn't possible! It isn't possible! Such things can't happen! Such men don't exist!—No, no, it isn't possible—but it's true! Oh, God, I wish I were dead!"

Suddenly a slight tremor ran over the earth: the house began to shake. Olev came rushing in the door, shouting something to her which was indistinguishable; for before he was able to reach her, the foundations of their house crumbled under them, and the walls collapsed upon them. . . .

Long afterward, when Tellectina regained consciousness, she felt the weight of mountains on her. Struggling desperately she managed to lift the end of a stone block off her chest; then, working her way up through the débris of wood and stone, stared dazedly about her. Projecting from beneath a stone there appeared a man's arm and hand, crushed and bleeding. Dragging her own bruised and bleeding body over the wreckage, she rolled the heavy slab aside. The man was breathing, but he lay prostrate, unable to rise, and Tellectina lacked sufficient strength to help him. For hours they remained there helpless among the ruins of their home. Finally crawling toward his wife, Olev lay clasping her feet desperately against his breast.

In a stricken voice he murmured, "Oh, what has happened? And where—where is Femina?"

"I don't know."

"Will she return soon?"

"I don't know."

"Something tells me—— Oh, why did she run away?"

"I don't know."

"You—oh, you won't desert me too, Tellectina, will you?"

There was no reply.

"Oh, answer me, my dear, my love, my life! You *are* my life! Without you, I couldn't live—I wouldn't want to live!"

"Please don't, please!" Tellectina's body was racked by great deep sobs.

"I don't know what made our house collapse," the man said, "but I'll build you a larger, a more beautiful one."

"I don't know either, there seems to have been an earthquake. I'm so—so confused, so bewildered and dazed, I can't think clearly."

"But you won't leave me—oh, promise! You don't know, you don't understand, how terrible and tragic my life has been. I thought, you see, when I married you that everything would be all right. I was reborn when I met you: I wanted nothing but to devote my whole life to making you happy and building a fine home to house our love in!"

Overcome by pity, Tellectina sat with her hands covering her eyes, mumbling, "Poor Olev, poor Olev," but opened them just in time to see the man lift one hand with that strange feminine gesture which had irritated her so inexplicably on numerous occasions. A deep-seated antipathy rose and checked the tears on her lids.

That gesture! It was the symbol of all that had antagonized her every woman's instinct: it hardened her heart against him. Then once more pity rushed in to melt it, prompting her to reflect, "Oh, but he can't prevent it; he doesn't wish to be effeminate. Oh, that's the tragedy: he can't do anything about it!"

Soon some of the villagers came to stare at the disaster, saying with intense satisfaction, "We told you so: serves you right. All free love has a curse of some kind over it." A few friends, however, assisted the two wounded people to extract themselves from the wreckage.

Tellectina bound up Olev's wounds as best she could and for several days they crept painfully about, neither able to sleep nor eat. Each night the man scarcely dared touch the woman beside him, but hungrily kept one of her hands imprisoned in his, moaning over and over again, "If you leave me, if you fail me now, I'll kill myself! I'll kill myself!"

Tellectina's heart would stand still with terror while within herself she was saying, "What right have I to kill a man? No, no, I'll stay. It's a kind of spiritual murder, anyway. I've made my bed, as the old adage says, so I must lie in it!" Yet with the coming of daylight after a long sleepless night she would think, "But let me look the facts squarely in the face: did I make it or did he? Or did my parents, because they brought me up in such criminal ignorance of sex? No, they, poor things, are not to blame: it's this whole damnable Puritanical system that we all live under which causes these tragedies. If I—if Femina—had had experience, this could never have happened. It would have been better if Femina had allowed men to kiss her: then she would have suspected some deficiency in the beginning. Oh, God, the crimes committed in the name of purity! Where is God that He permits all these things to occur when people are innocent? No, I'll leave Olev. Surely a young girl is not to blame for her own ignorance. Besides, people can't marry with their minds alone, as we did—it's doomed to failure."

The young girl was torn between going and staying. "Oh, I don't know what to do! I want to do the right thing. Have I the right to leave him? Did our tacit agreement mean that I have promised to live with him all the rest of my life, no matter what he does? Must I do it, no matter how he fails to carry out his side of the contract? Am I morally bound to him, or does his original deception now automatically release me? I want to be fair and just, but was he fair to me in the beginning?"

One morning about dawn, Olev found her leaning against a tree sobbing bitterly, hysterically. "Oh, Olev, Olev, why did you do it? You must have known all the time, and I didn't. You took unfair advantage of my youth and ignorance. I—oh, it's so terribly painful for both of us! Our relationship has been almost wholly mental: I was so attracted by your brilliant mind, and that is still unchanged, but——"

At once hope leapt into the man's voice. "Then can't we still —still——"

"I, Tellectina, still care for you: I alone might be able to live happily with you. But there's Femina to be considered: she has left you forever."

Dropping to the ground, he clasped her frantically about the knees. "Oh, give me another chance! I'll build up my health, I'll get stronger, and then——"

Tellectina put her hand on his beautiful blond hair. "Oh, poor Olev, poor Olev, I'm so dreadfully sorry; but don't you see,

Femina and I are really the same person, although we appear
to most people as two different girls. And we do actually live
separate and independent lives except in cases of men whom
we both take seriously."

"But I was in hopes that—that——"

"I know, Olev. I see it all now a little too clearly. You married me in hopes that it would cure you."

"Well, three different doctors advised me."

"The criminals!" the girl exclaimed angrily. "But, no, they
were just poor ignorant fools, I suppose. And the only reason
on earth that you wanted a child was to prove to the world that
you were really a man! Have you no consideration for the
child? What sort of heritage could you give it? Have you no
consideration for the woman whom you chose to cure you?
Oh, Olev, Olev, it's all too ghastly!" The woman shuddered and
drew away.

The man buried his face in his hands. "Oh, but I was desperate, desperate! I wanted to be like everybody else. You'll
never, never know what men like me suffer!"

"But is that any reason why you should deliberately make
other people suffer? You didn't feel the slightest real passion
for Femina at any time: it was all pretense, I realize now. We
were both deceived. Oh, I'm sick, sick! I wish to God I were
dead! All our beautiful dreams! We aimed so high and have
fallen so low!"

Olev commenced to sob long, deep, heart-rending sobs. Tellectina gathered the man in her arms as if he were a baby and
sitting on the ground gently rocked him back and forth. It
was the first time she had ever seen a man weep, and it un-
nerved her completely. But the man sobbed too long: involuntarily the woman grew disgusted with his weakness and,
pushing him from her, rose. Suddenly Femina flashed past, casting a look of mingled pity and horror at the sobbing man such
as she might have given a wounded monster, and, catching Tellectina's hand, forcibly drew her sister after her without a word.
Looking back as they ran, Tellectina beheld Olev lying prostrate

in the grass—a picture that was to haunt her for years to come. She likewise observed that the few remaining villagers were engaged in a violent civil war and were destroying with their own hands the community they had built up.

As the two sisters fled from the ruined colony of New Chimera their feet caught in a vine which flung them headlong to the ground. It was of the same species that had sprung up about the temple. The already painful rash which had been tormenting them for some time increased tenfold.

Finally the two fugitives realized with a shock that they were lost. The sun disappeared. A great darkness descended upon the earth for forty days and forty nights. The two wanderers moved aimlessly, hopelessly through the eternal night of the Black Forest of Simery, living on a meager supply of cessneray roots and berries. They were tripped up by the tangle of tropical vegetation and thrown to the earth more than once; were struck in the face with heavy branches of trees; stumbled into stagnant swamps which stank to heaven; trembled with fear at the sound of hundreds of invisible beasts which infested the jungle; and eventually became so numb with pain that no new pain could affect them.

There was one question which Tellectina reiterated daily: "Is it possible that all my ideas of love and marriage and sex and life and God can be wrong? Where—oh, where is God that He allows such unjust things to happen to people who have done no wrong? God, where are you? . . . God is dead. Everything is black, it is the end of the world! But it is better to die than to live always in this Black Simery. Oh, God, how can you justify what you've done to me, to poor Olev? Is it my fault that I was ignorant? Is it his fault that he was born that way —half woman? Didn't *you* make him that way, God? You must have an explanation of everything you do; but how do you justify these injustices, God? Answer me that!"

But the great darkness gave forth no response save the ghostly padding of ghostly feet which drew closer and closer every day. Something—some invisible animal was relentlessly pursuing her, of that she now had no doubt: the same thing which had been pursuing her ever since she had leapt over the wall into Nithking two years ago.

She struggled on but was constantly being tripped up by a vine which seemed to cover every inch of the ground. It was the same poisonous vine she had encountered so often before, but now, not only did her whole body smart painfully, but the poison had even affected her eyes. And once a dead limb from a Parides tree fell upon Tellectina, fastening her to the earth for three days and three nights. On calling to Femina she received no answer. Thrusting out her hand she came in contact with the small round berries which Tellectina recognized by their odor as the Scei Dui. Her one desire being to escape her misery, she hastily consumed several handfuls of the poisonous berries only to be made violently ill. She loathed herself for lacking the courage to take a sufficient quantity actually to kill her, loathed herself for her desire to live in a treacherous world of eternal darkness. Involuntarily, however, she rose and stumbled on; till, finally discerning a faint glimmer of light, she moved painfully but hopefully toward it, despising herself for her hope, and feeling puzzled by the thin golden thread of joy that ran through all her blackest misery.

CHAPTER VI

TELLECTINA GROPED her way toward the faint point
of light until eventually she emerged from the Black Forest
of Simery. It was not until she beheld again the once familiar
world that she realized the great change which her eyes had
undergone. It enabled her to see with startling clarity now:
every defect in the landscape was painfully visible, every barren spot, every worm-eaten flower, every dead and gaunt limb,
every tree trunk and hillside that had been blasted by the cruel
lightning.

"So this is what the earth is really like: drab and hideous, relieved only by occasional spots of beauty! It is just as Aunt
Sophistica predicted years ago: the poison from the Sillidinous
vines has indeed removed the protective film from my eyes. Oh,
I wish it were possible to retain it, even if it did endow everything in life with artificial beauty! But, no, I wish to see everything as it really is. The truth at any cost!" In fact, to her further
consternation, she even found herself again deriving a sort of
bitter and perverse pleasure from her own misery and painful
clarity of vision.

Slowly, aimlessly, she wandered on across the veldt until a
familiar sound arrested her in her tracks. Standing motionless,
holding her breath, she listened with strained intensity. Yes,
there it was again—that haunting ghostly padding of pursuing
feet. A sick, inexplicable fear ran over her like a chill. "Oh,

they've never been this near before! Two years they've haunted me! Dear God, why can't they leave me alone? Why must I be pursued like a criminal?"

Intermittently her pursuers had been faintly audible though never visible. But now fearfully, reluctantly, as though hypnotized against her will, the girl glanced back over her shoulder. There, some distance behind her, was an incredible sight—a sight which evoked a sense of guilt even surpassing that of fear. Two enormous white hounds, unlike any other she had ever beheld in her life, were running straight toward her.

"Oh, I recognize you!" Tellectina exclaimed. "Appearances can't deceive me! You wouldn't descend to earth in your own form, of course, but you send these hounds of heaven as your earthly symbols to pursue and torment me! I know who you are, Godsson and Onegod. But oh, what can I do? How can I escape? I can't outrun you—oh, I am lost, lost!" she moaned.

Quivering in every limb, she stood for a long minute rooted to the ground by fear; then turning, fled as fast as her feet would carry her—anywhere—everywhere, to escape her pursuers. She ran across the veldt, rushed recklessly through the underbrush and on into the woods, leapt streams, stumbled on the rocks, fell, rose, and fled on again blindly—not knowing where she went and not caring. Night came, and in desperation the fugitive, torn, bruised, and exhausted, climbed into the arms of a great broad-limbed fanecedi tree and lay close against it like a squirrel, staring down at the two ghostly figures below circling about her in the ghostly dark.

No sun announced the coming of day, only a chill wan light. Having made her breakfast on the ripe Pur Poses hanging above her head, she formulated her plans. While the two figures below appeared to be sleeping she would attempt to throw them off the scent by passing from the limbs of one tree to those of another. The exigencies of the situation lent her new cunning; and having swung cautiously from one swaying limb to another, she dropped softly to the carpet of dead leaves which covered the ground.

Relieved at even this brief respite, she breathed again in peace. No sooner had she arrived at the conclusion that they had lost the scent forever, and was striding confidently along, wondering what new adventure this exciting land of Nithking held in store for her, when there came the sound again—not of two hounds but of one. That soft padding noise was unmistakably produced by the smaller but much fleeter animal, Godsson. With swift light steps Tellectina resumed her flight.

Insidiously, a thick white fog crept over the face of the earth, and the girl became hopelessly lost. The farther she went, the denser grew the dismal chilling fog; until, seized by panic, she ran about in circles hither and thither, maddened by the incessant beat of those relentless feet. Forced to stop for breath, she placed her hands over her ears, but it was impossible to shut out the soft, uncanny rhythm of those approaching footsteps.

Leaning weakly against a tree she moaned, "Are you as merciless as a bloodhound that searches out fugitives from the laws of Err? And am I a criminal that I must be hunted down thus? Is it then such a crime to doubt? But is Tellectina a meek rabbit to be terrified by a mere pursuing hound? Or can she be as sly as a fox and outwit him? Oh, I myself do not know!"

She plodded wearily on until she stumbled against a rock. Remaining where she had fallen, she laid her burning forehead on the cool damp stone, with a sigh. "Oh, that is the *real* trouble: I *know* nothing! I think, I feel, I doubt, I pray, I fear, I hope, I tremble—but I *know* nothing for a certainty. Least of all am I sure of which way to go to escape Godsson. . . . But why do I wish to escape him? Even that I do not know. Oh, if only I could find Certitude; then surely this maddening pursuit would cease. But I doubt if I ever attain such a great height; nor do I know which way to seek this famous mountain that is said to offer sanctuary to travelers in Nithking. I can't see for this miserable fog. I've completely lost my way in this terrible country! Oh, dear God, why don't you show me the way?"

She lifted her head. "If I weren't endeavoring to run away

from you, Godsson, you would not pursue me. I flee because I doubt your divine origin and for that I must be punished. And yet no one else in the entire world holds such heretical notions, as far as I am aware. Who am I to doubt what all men believe? Why can't I join the cult of J. C.? Why can't I believe in him, worship him as a deity—and live in peace as others do? Oh, why, why am I as I am? Why am I—I?"

Beating the rock angrily with her fists she burst into tears of exasperation. As the footsteps came nearer, she turned; and at the sound of her defiant young voice coming through the mist Godsson paused.

"Stop, O hound of heaven! Hear me, for I am Tellectina! I am not an emotional, illogical woman whom you can frighten into hysteria and—and hymns! Come closer. If you are an earthly symbol of something divine, then I want to see you more clearly."

The figure, however, did not move and through the mist it seemed to the overwrought and imaginative girl to assume a startling resemblance to a man's pale face above nebulous white robes. "Now, Godsson, if you're divine, as everybody asserts, then I must follow your teachings. But your teachings don't work—I've tried them. Yet if they are divinely inspired, they must be right; and if they're right, they ought to work. Where lies the difficulty? Why don't they work? Answer me that!

There was a long ominous silence.

Suddenly the young girl clasped her hands in passionate entreaty. "Oh, dear Christ, I want to believe in you, I want to be good and just and gentle and forgiving. And I have forgiven my enemies; but when I do unto others who are vicious and stupid as I would have them do unto me, they merely consider me a weakling and a fool and treat me accordingly—and that sort of treatment I most emphatically cannot permit. If I practise your precepts, people—life—will destroy me. Destroy me, do you hear? I *must* fight constantly merely in self-defense."

Dropping her head on her arms, the girl sobbed bitterly. Then at length she flung it up in defiance. "Oh, Jesus, I cannot feel humble—even when I try. I come of an old aristocratic line, and my deepest nature demands that I keep people in their proper and subordinate place. I did not make myself this way. It is not that I think, it is that I *feel,* that no man lives who is my superior—neither kings nor potentates! My instinct is to rule—not to obey—but to rule with justice. Why, why, is humility a more beautiful thing than pride? It seems to me that what humanity needs is more pride—not more humility."

She lifted her tear-stained face in supplication. "And yet—and yet my heart is invariably wrung with pity even for my enemies who do me wrong. It's all intermingled with my anger. Oh, it's all so confused! And there's something queer about this Christliness that I don't understand."

There being no response of any kind, Tellectina sighed heavily and, rising, started slowly through the woods. The instant she attempted to flee from Godsson, however, he resumed the chase. Frantically the fugitive redoubled her speed, determined to outdistance him once for all. Thus Tellectina passed through a forest wherein she "saw many things not salutary to notice." But finally, her strength spent and her breath coming in painful gasps, she was forced to slacken her pace. Emerging from the densest part of the woods, she came suddenly upon a little clearing where a woodman had set a trap. Hoping it might be of service to her, she hastened into the small brown cottage near by, which was built in that rectangular biblioesque style peculiar to the houses of Nithking. To the stranger who met her in the entrance she explained breathlessly, "I've lost my way. I'm being pursued by a relentless hound of heaven. Merely because I can't believe as others do, Godsson is sent to follow me across the face of Nithking. Oh, how can I escape him? Help me, please, I beg of you!"

The man led her gently toward the designer of the trap, informing her of his pursuit by a similar hound of heaven when he was just about her age, explaining how by use of his reasoning powers Renan had been able to construct an infallible trap for Godsson.

"But," the trembling girl asked, "you mean that a divinity like Jesus can be rendered powerless by a human being? Because Godsson is Jesus' representative and so is divine, isn't he?"

" 'I mean,' " said Renan's friend, after he had introduced the girl to the quiet thoughtful man seated in a large comfortable chair, " 'that as Jesus was born while his parents were living in lawful wedlock, . . . and as his father, Joseph, was well known as a . . . respectable mechanic, . . . Renan fails to discover anything miraculous in the birth of the child Jesus.' "

"And that is—is historical fact!" The young girl was dumbfounded for a moment. "Facts! that's what I want, that's what I've never been able to obtain anywhere in Err!"

Renan took up the discussion in a quiet, sweet voice, discussing the proven facts of the life of Jesus, explaining the actions of the men who had recorded his life. " 'Luke softens the passages which had become embarrassing on account of a more exalted idea of the divinity of Christ; he exaggerates the marvelous; . . . he interprets the documents according to his own ideas.' "

"You—you dare to say this! You are not afraid of being struck dead for such blasphemy!" she exclaimed reverting unconsciously to Casuistry.

Shaking his head in the negative, Renan continued in a slow but confident voice, " 'Sometimes they reasoned thus: "The Messiah ought to do such a thing: now Jesus is the Messiah; therefore, Jesus has done such a thing." ' "

"Oh, I see, I see! that is good human psychology which I can believe. But I *can't* believe in a Messiah, try as I will, because it is neither sensible nor logical. Explain more to me, though, more, please! The truth, that's what I long for!" the incredulous and excited girl cried, sinking to a footstool at Renan's feet.

" 'The man who is a stranger to all idea of physical law and who believes that by prayer he can alter the path of the clouds, can arrest disease, and even death, finds nothing extraordinary in miracle, inasmuch as the whole course of things is for him the result of the free-will of the Divinity. This intellectual condition was always that of Jesus.'"

Tellectina leapt up joyfully and began to pace the room, her eyes burning with excitement. "Ah, yes, yes, you wonderful man, you explain everything! What you mean is that poor dear Jesus was simply uneducated and ignorant or he couldn't have believed such things! Why, even little I know more about clouds and disease than Jesus did. Even a little science contradicts the ideas prevalent in those unenlightened days!"

As she seated herself reverently on the footstool again, the man resumed his argument: "'Paradise would, in fact, have been brought to earth if the ideas of the young Master had not far transcended that level of ordinary goodness which the human race has found it hitherto impossible to pass.'"

All the obstinacy indicated by the square firm jaw of the young explorer suddenly asserted itself. "But are meekness and humility the noblest qualities possible to man?"

Renan ignored her interruption. "'Jesus prohibited divorce and all swearing. . . . He held voluptuous desire to be as criminal as adultery.'"

The girl frowned and blinked her eyes thoughtfully for a moment. "But, no, none of these things are inherently wrong: it depends entirely on circumstance. I can imagine circumstances under which marriage would be twice as criminal as either divorce or adultery could ever be! No, Jesus was wrong—as narrow as the people of Smug Harbor on these subjects. Perhaps he was not highly sexed, and sex was no problem to him personally. No, no, I cannot love—or even respect—the man who started Puritanism, the curse of the world for so many generations, and the brunt of which has always been borne by women! I suppose, of course, that Jesus did originate Puritanism—certainly he gave it an impetus which has lasted nearly two thousand years."

Suddenly she leapt to her feet. "Oh, why, why have I not seen these truths for myself? You say 'A single error proves that a church is not infallible; one weak part proves that a book is not a revealed one.' How obvious—even a fool wouldn't try to refute that!" Stopping, she gazed at him with glowing eyes.

"Ah, Renan, Renan, you wonderful person! Your fearlessness, your sweet calm honesty! What you say is so easy to be·lieve. You speak in Reasonese, logically, of credible things whereas the Church in Err taught me about Jesus only in Halfish. Come quickly, please, and show me how your trap works. I must be rid of this famous hound of heaven once and for all!"

The man shook his white head, implying that she was impatient, that there was much more he wished to tell her; but Tellectina caught his hand and urged him hurriedly out-of-doors. The instant the fugitive appeared, Godsson rushed toward her again; but she hastened to the far side of the trap, looking imploringly at Renan to save her. He, however, resumed his discourse quite calmly.

"'There are those who make Jesus a sage, a philosopher, a patriot, a good man, a moralist, or a saint. He is neither or any of these. He was a——' "

He paused, and as Godsson leapt toward them Renan uttered the single word "charmer," at which moment the trap suddenly sprang, mysteriously and automatically. The hound of heaven now lay pinned to the earth. The young girl stood trembling, waiting breathlessly for Renan and herself to be struck dead where they stood for daring so blasphemous an act.

When no bolt fell from the blue, she fearfully crept forward to peer in relief and incredulity at the entrapped creature. There lay the hound of heaven which had not only haunted her dreams from the time she was born but had actually pursued her for months on end—not dead but helpless, harmless, and pitiful at her feet, gazing up at her with dumb reproachful eyes. It was sad to behold one who had been so formidable now so impotent.

Overwhelmed, she closed her eyes and swayed unsteadily, then murmured, "Is it possible that I am free of him at last? Ah, poor Jesus, your misplaced humility, your superhuman self-denial are false ideals, after all. And no more do I need to be harassed by the idea of the divinity of Jesus, the little Hebrew carpenter. Yes, J. C. remains a rather wonderful but foolish man, a religious fanatic. And I thought for a long time that I was the only human being in the world who doubted his divinity!" Transferring her gaze to Renan, she looked at his kind, intelligent face with unspeakable gratitude shining from her eyes. Then, sighing, she brought herself out from under the spell of sadness.

"I feel like a man with a club foot who has dragged his burden after him all his life, who on looking down one day suddenly sees that it has miraculously vanished. The relief is wonderful, but I miss it too." Again and again she thanked her rescuer and was preparing to depart when Renan suggested that they dispose of Godsson more decorously.

"No, no, no, I can't wait. I must fly on. I have yet to explore Nithking and find Certitude. Instinct tells me that I can travel much faster now that I am not pursued by this hound of heaven. I have no words with which to thank you; for you have not only saved my life but my sanity. Surely you understand— you——" Emotion choked her voice but, smiling at him, at the trap, and at his brown cottage, she turned and sped away through the woods with light buoyant steps.

Almost before she was aware of it, Tellectina was at the top of a hill. Halting abruptly, she listened intently for the sound of footsteps: there was not a sound anywhere except the wind singing through the trees. Lifting her young arms exultantly she laughed in the very face of heaven. "Ah, I am free, free at last! I am happier than I have been since I entered this strange country of Nithking. What a marvelous piece of luck to have encountered Ernest Renan just at the right time. Still, perhaps I would in time have been able to rid myself of Godsson by my own efforts. Renan only hastened and simplified the process."

Days and weeks passed in pleasant aimless wandering. Life seemed very sweet. Never had the scenery about her appeared so enchanting. One day, through her singing, however, a familiar sound crept in; whereupon, she merely sang all the louder to drown it. That night, when she curled herself up in her blankets, the noise became so distinct that Tellectina broke out in a cold perspiration. Lying motionless, she strained her ears but was almost deafened by the violent pounding of her own heart.

"Oh, God, surely not again!" She laid her ear against the earth to catch the faint rhythmical beat. "It is—it's those feet again. But Godsson can never trouble me any more: so what can it be? The tread is heavier and slower. That's it, I know: it must be Onegod this time. He's larger and probably possesses far more endurance. Oh, must I be pursued like a criminal for the rest of my life?"

There was no moon, and although the night was a thick velvet blackness, Tellectina rose and slashed her way recklessly through the woods. Morning found her bruised and bleeding, lost in an interminable gloomy valley overshadowed by gigantic purple mountains. For months she wandered in this valley of chill shadows where the sun never shone, subsisting chiefly on wild Hopes berries, of which she found an abundance. The ghostly feet never ceased to follow her, being sometimes near and sometimes afar.

Seized by an angry despair one day, she seated herself on a rock, determined to meet Onegod face to face. As the footsteps approached she muttered defiantly to herself, "Is thought then such a crime? For what is doubting but thinking? If there is a God up there attentive to our happiness, then where were you, God, when you allowed me through well-meaning ignorance to form that disastrous union in New Chimera and become lost for all those horrible months, so unhappy that I tried to commit suicide? And certainly my unhappiness is not unique: I have seen misery on every side of me every day of my life. Have you been just to mankind or even half fair?"

The girl's brows drew together thoughtfully. "If you created mankind, aren't you responsible for it? If you're not, who is? You can't hold man responsible for his own innate weakness!"

Reasoning thus, Tellectina nevertheless felt a nameless fear clutching her heart. The hound of heaven had by this time caught up with the fugitive and was circling round and round her, closing in upon the frightened girl slowly but certainly.

She sat swaying to and fro, moaning, "Oh, why, why, don't you help me, Lord? Why torture me this way? Answer some of my intelligent questions intelligently! Speak to me! Speak to me in Reasonese for once! Have mercy—deliver me from this insistent pursuer who will surely tear me to pieces soon!" Overcome by fear, anger, and despair, Tellectina buried her head in the bend of her arm; and with every nerve tense she awaited destruction. . . .

As it failed to overtake her, however, she relaxed and looked about her. The mists had risen to reveal an unexpected and very welcome sight: a brown cottage constructed in that rectangular biblioesque style peculiar to the houses of Nithking. Hoping to hide herself from Onegod at least temporarily, the fugitive advanced, opened the door, and after peering in was irresistibly drawn farther. The plain exterior certainly belied the rich and exotic interior. At once Tellectina was greeted by the most beautiful and extraordinary women, most of whom spoke only Halfish, however, and two exceedingly attractive men—one of whom was named Jurgen and both of whom discoursed merrily in Reasonese on a variety of subjects—none of which, however, included the danger of the hounds of heaven.

Unaccustomed to Reasonese spoken with such a humorous accent, the young Errorian was not able to understand all that was said. While laughing rather feebly at all the provocative masculine statements, she was secretly wondering if Femina's repartee would ever be equal to such an occasion. Although the entertainment was unique and delightful, the young explorer was at that moment not seeking amusement but a means of escape from Onegod; consequently, she was on the point of departing from this delightful house when the host spoke five words which caused her to follow him without a question. Leading her through a special passage, he quickly conducted her to the top of a mountain. On glancing back fearfully, the girl ascertained that the hound of heaven was still following her—at a safe distance, however.

Tellectina and her companion stood on a great bald crag far above the timber line, commanding a magnificent view of the world below. Such a pleasant intoxication pervaded all the young girl's senses that she was convinced this was the greatest height to which she had ever ascended. When the man bade her look down to the left, she descried a great valley filled with such black and venomous smoke that it seemed to have been belched up from the infernal regions themselves. By a slight movement of his right hand the man did that which caused the awe-stricken girl to wonder if he were a sorcerer or a magician or some sort of god in human form—as he apparently possessed power over the elements. For suddenly all the swirling smoke in the distant valley below rolled away, revealing to the girl's incredulous gaze—hell, itself! Staring as though hypnotized, Tellectina beheld gigantic flames leaping up in every direction; old Grandfather Satan sitting in a tall chair of black marble; innumerable little devils carrying fuel laboriously; and everywhere the misery and writhing of the condemned men and women. And as she listened, the explorer heard the small devils conversing with the same handsome debonair young man whom she had met in the brown cottage and who, in his turn, was now saying, " 'But wherefore is this place called the Hell of my fathers?' "

" 'Because your forefathers builded it in dreams,' they told him, 'out of the pride which led them to believe that what they did was of sufficient importance to merit punishment.' "

Tellectina Christian gasped, then she laughed nervously. "But—but, aren't you afraid?" she said to the man beside her. "How do they dare to talk that way?"

Her companion smilingly reminded her that he was James Branch Cabell and the debonair young man below, Jurgen. Then he pointed out Jurgen's father, Coth, who "stood conscientiously in the midst of the largest and hottest flame he had been able to imagine, and rebuked the outworn devils who were tormenting him, because the tortures they inflicted were not adequate to the wickedness of Coth." At this sight the little Puritan laughed feebly, for she was trembling violently.

Then, leaning forward, the young Casuist gazed intently down into hell. For a long time she stood motionless, remembering, reliving, all the hours of fear she had endured as a child in Smug Harbor, reliving even the terror of hell which her ancestors had felt for nineteen hundred years. Was it possible that all their self-torture had been unnecessary, futile, and meaningless? Suddenly Cabell made a pass with his right hand again, and before her astonished eyes, the flames died down, the brimstone disappeared, the smoke vanished into thin air, and all the wailing and gnashing of teeth ceased.

Overwhelmed, the girl swayed slightly. With another wave of his hand Cabell swept Satan and all his devils out of existence. Tellectina closed her eyes and on opening them once more saw that hell itself had faded away, evaporated into nothingness like an evil dream. Where the hell of her fathers had been there was now nothing more startling than the tops of very green trees far below, waving nonchalantly in the sunlight.

Delighted, yet still incredulous and frightened, Tellectina murmured, "So—there really is—no hell!" Then she laughed joyously. "Has not Cabell shown me that hell is an illusion built by the conceit of our fathers? And can one deny what one has seen with one's own eyes?"

Her young laughter rang out defiantly and, mingling with the deep mellow laughter of the man beside her, it echoed and reëchoed until it reverberated like thunder through all the mountains. This strange rumbling sound caused the hound of heaven to tremble violently.

And when Tellectina realized the power that human beings could exercise over Onegod she exclaimed, "Ah, never again shall I be afraid of him! Nor shall I ever fear hell again. How grateful I am to you, sir, for having taught me to laugh at our fathers' hell! And I see that if mankind took itself less seriously it would be far happier."

Willingly, eagerly, the excited girl followed her guide up another and even higher peak of the same range. She noticed, however, that Onegod had resumed his chase though exhibiting none of his former energy. After they had passed through a thick mist, the man bade her look down into another valley. It was filled with great billowy white clouds.

She now witnessed a bit of thaumaturgy which was even more staggering than the disappearance of hell. This extraordinary man apparently possessed unlimited power over the elements; for at the same gesture of his right hand the clouds dispersed, revealing to the young explorer a sight from which she would have turned away her eyes except that she no longer retained control over her own faculties. Cabell had removed the very roof of heaven itself, exposing to the Casuist's dazzled gaze: cherubs, and angels with golden harps and long white robes, and even the great Lord God himself, seated "upon a throne, beside a sea of crystal. A rainbow, made high and narrow like a window frame, so as to fit the throne, formed an archway in which He sat." It was the very Casuistical heaven about which she had heard all her life. It seemed exceedingly odd—and rather terrifying and dangerous—that she should have ascended to so great a height as actually to be able to look down on heaven.

Stricken with wonder, fear, and joy, Tellectina listened to the voices of God and the young man who was standing before him. It was Jurgen, and he was saying, " 'I fear You, . . . and, yes, I love You: and yet I cannot believe. Why could You not let me believe, where so many believed? Or else, why could You not let me deride, as the remainder derided so noisily? O God, why could You not let me have faith?' "

And Jurgen's words were Tellectina's thoughts.

Then she listened breathlessly while God related the story of his own creation. There was brought before Koshchei, "who made things as they are, . . . a decent little bent gray woman" in an old gray shawl. Her name was Steinvor, and she "did not believe in things as they are." And so in order to please her

Koshchei ordered Earth to be brought to him. " 'This was done and Koshchei looked over the planet, and found a Bible. Koshchei opened the Bible, and read the Revelation of St. John the Divine. . . . Then Koshchei smiled and created Heaven about Steinvor and her illusions, and he made Heaven just such a place as was described in the book. . . . And Me also Koshchei created at that time,' " God concluded.

Standing there, breathless and motionless, the young girl whispered, "You mean—you mean, that there is some one above —above God! That heaven is merely the delusion of an old woman!"

Suddenly all the young Puritan's childhood fears, hopes, illusions, beliefs, prayers, and questions surged up through her, flared up in one great final leap—guttered and died out like a candle flame.

Closing her eyes, she waited for the fatal and inevitable blow. "I shall be destroyed! My own destruction I have brought on my head by doubting, by fleeing from Onegod!"

She waited. The earth shook. She knew that for this blasphemy—all the more dangerous for being true—Cabell would be struck to the earth by a bolt from the blue and she with him for believing his heresy. . . . But as God wreaked no vengeance on them, the trembling girl dared once more to open her eyes.

There was no longer any heaven—merely a sea of white clouds floating indifferently across the valley below. With one gesture Cabell had wiped the earth clean of heaven forever. The young girl began to tremble violently. "Have I not with my own ears heard God say that he himself is but the illusion of an old woman? Have I not with my own eyes seen that heaven is nothing but a delusion of old women? And who can deny what she has seen with her own eyes? Oh, but it is terrible —terrible! I have lost Christ—and now I have lost heaven and hell and even God! No, no, it is too much! I can't bear it, I can't bear it!" Tellectina Christian began to sob bitterly, covering her eyes to shut out the unbearable spectacle of nothingness and space.

The man waited patiently until the young woman's excessive emotion should subside. When she heard Cabell's voice again, however, she felt herself once more falling resistlessly under the hypnotic spell of his words. Walking unsteadily, she followed him as though in a daze till she came to a certain high place. As she went over it she noticed "many things not salutary to record"; but on reaching the end of this high place, the over-wrought girl—exhausted by the intense emotional strain she had undergone—greeted his next revelation with apparent calm. The great height rendered the visibility so extraordinary that they were able to see an incredible distance. To the south Cabell pointed out a group of ancient Egyptian ruins that had been temples long ago, where men earnestly worshiped goats and crocodiles and hawks and cats and hippopotami. These holy places were now fallen into decay and overlaid with the dust of centuries. Then looking farther toward the east, Tellectina saw evidences that the men in India had once built temples in honor of monkeys and tigers and, neglecting them, had soon turned to newer gods. Below the great mountain on which they stood lay also the relics of other religions—Greek and Roman. Lastly the man called her especial attention to the more recently erected temples of "a tribal god come out of Israel."

As the young woman was gazing upon these familiar structures with new eyes, there suddenly appeared beside her a small brown man whom Cabell introduced as Janicot. The newcomer spoke of many things saying in conclusion: "'And I know not how many thousands of other beautiful and holy deities have had their dole of worship and neglect and oblivion. . . . You think with awed reverence of your Jahveh. . . . Yet you should remember, too, that to me, who saw but yesterday your Jahveh's start in life as a local storm-god upon Sinai, he is just the latest of many thousands of adversaries whom I have seen triumph and pass while I have stood patient under all temporary annoyances.'"

And even as he talked, dust began to settle on the temples of Jahveh, on the figure of a mother holding a child. and that of a man nailed on a cross. Tellectina saw the beginning of the end of the Casuistry often miscalled Christianity, saw that fashions in religions change as do all other fashions, and that the religion to which she had once fastened all her faith was doomed to pass away.

The girl shook her head sadly, "So I see, there is no *one* true god. There are, and have been, many gods, and each will pass or has already passed into oblivion. Why did I not see all this for myself years ago? I have studied history blindly—absolutely blindly. And the Casuistic god to whom I kneeled by my bed as a child—that person from whom I begged mercy when in pain and asked strength when in difficulty and whom I thanked when happy—that one to whom I showed my inmost mind and secret thoughts—the only one with whom I shared my intensest yearnings and from whom I expected assistance when everything and everybody else (including myself and my own courage) failed—he is no more—because he never was. I have prayed to an illusion. The great Lord God on whom I relied was but a shadow without substance—the mere projection of a weak human need.

"Ah, yes, I have lost my God, and the loss is irreparable! When life becomes insupportable is there then no help for a human being?—no greater power to lean on? No, man has no support but himself—man is alone in the world. That is a terrible thought, and yet there is compensation. For no longer need I fear a vengeful Father who will punish me for sins he created me weak enough to commit. The fear, the torture, the bewilderment in the face of so many incongruities—all that too is ended now. I am a free person for the first time in my life! The folly, the futility, the puerility, and absurdity of the whole conception is all so apparent to me now! What can anyone, who views it from this vantage point in Nithking, do except laugh at Casuistry, at Onegod, and at one's self!"

Both the men standing beside Tellectina were laughing—each in his own particular way. And for the first time the girl laughed with some semblance of confidence and humor. Glancing over her shoulder, she perceived that the great hound of heaven lay prostrate—motionless—and harmless. "Evidently human laughter resounding all about Onegod like thunder finally overcame him. And never, never again can he pursue me as if I were a criminal!"

Tellectina stood there equally overwhelmed by the amazing spectacles Cabell had shown her and the enormity of her gratitude toward him. With great effort she restrained herself, murmuring inwardly, "Remember, Tellectina, you are nearly twenty-three now and must not weep even on wise men's hands as you once did." She could only gaze at her rescuer with unutterable things in her eyes. When Cabell offered to show her still more, the girl refused, for she was still trembling.

"I—I can't endure any more revelations yet, please, please! You have rendered me three immeasurably valuable services already. And though you have saved me from being tormented almost to the point of insanity by the hound of heaven, nevertheless—well, does a patient who has just been operated on by a skilled surgeon ask for more the same day? My gratitude is boundless, but have mercy: I can't endure any more now!"

It was not the nature of her companion to insist. Turning suddenly away from Cabell, confident that he would understand the abruptness of her departure, she walked slowly down the mountain past the dead Onegod; and past the brown cottage, glancing at it with affectionate eyes—feeling strangely weary, pervaded not with happiness so much as a sensation of intense relief.

"No," she reflected, "I have not yet found Mt. Certitude but such mountain climbing as I've been engaged in recently should put me in training for it later. So I must continue my quest for Certitude—which surely can't be far distant now."

Entering a thick wood she journeyed along in an empty kind of peace for many weeks. To her dismay the uncanny silence sometimes begot a perverse regret for the loss of those pursuing feet. One morning, however, a too familiar sound suddenly took her breath away. Summoning all her courage, she looked back and was aghast to discover that Onegod had now been replaced by the largest of all the three hounds of heaven. Her first reaction being that of utter desperation, she involuntarily fell to her knees.

"O God—(but my God is dead!)—ah, but I must, I must, pray to someone—something! Ah, God, I might have survived two pursuits—but three! This is too much for human endurance! And I am only a woman, remember, a weak woman; and I journey alone through this perilous country of Nithking!"

As the sound drew dangerously near, she rose to her feet; and then it was that a challenging note entered her voice. "Of course I know that *the* God is dead, the Christian God; but is there then a greater, more powerful, more admirable God—a sort of all-pervasive spirit beyond all creeds? And merely because I am not sure about him, is it necessary for him to dispatch this great relentless hound whose name must be Godidea, I presume, to dog my footsteps all over Nithking?" She flung up her head. "Well, let him!"

Stretching her lithe young limbs, she filled her lungs with air. "We'll see which is the better runner! These two and a half years in Nithking have toughened me and sharpened my wits! I am stronger and fleeter since the pursuit of Godsson and Onegod. I rejoice in my strength: this chase begins to thrill me! Come on, Godidea, and see if Tellectina is afraid!"

Tightening her knapsack, she commenced to run at an even pace. "This bids fair to be a long race, beside which the other two were mere child's play. I fear it's really a matter of life and death this time, for after all one must believe in some sort of a God to continue living at all, mustn't one? And yet——"

The young explorer raced through gloomy valleys, climbed snow-covered mountains, touching volcanoes both dormant and active, and was nearly drowned twice, but she maintained a good pace except at night. Then it was that the footsteps drew terrifyingly near, frequently forcing her to resume her flight in the darkness. The farther she ran, however, the fleeter she became; until the realization dawned on her one day that

for some time past the footsteps of Godidea had been audible
only at intervals. Was it possible for her to outdistance him and
leave him behind forever? This was her hope.

One warm night Tellectina had no more than arranged a
bed of leaves and lain down to sleep when an unaccountable
restlessness seized upon her. Never had her mind been so
restless and alert—it forced her body into wakefulness. Rising,
she slowly walked on, her mind surging with inchoate thoughts.
Never had the countryside appeared so beautiful as it did this
moonlight night. Did not the trees wave to her in fraternal
fashion? And even the clouds hung lower than usual as they
drifted idly across the face of the moon. And was not the
friendliness of the night an invitation to all those shy thoughts
which feared the laughing eyes of the sun?

The wind ceased abruptly: an uncanny silence fell over the
earth. Tellectina stopped dead in her tracks—waiting for she
knew not what. Unheedingly she had walked to the summit
of a high hill. She stood there without moving, staring fixedly
up into the clouds as if by the very intensity of her gaze to
pierce that white curtain, to penetrate to the awful mystery that
lay beyond them. The premonition of some impending evil
caused her to tremble. An unnatural silence enveloped everything, grew suffocating, oppressive, beyond endurance. With a
wild cry she strove to fling off the evil spell.

"Oh, what is it, what is it? What do I sense in this mysterious
night? Is there someone—something—up there behind those
clouds who's—that's—interested in my personal welfare—that
will assist me in my pursuit of happiness? Is there, I say? What
is the meaning of it all? What is this thing we call life? Why,
oh, why do we struggle on—on, toward what? All my desires,
my dreams—what, why, are they? Toward, what? What is this
power to which I find myself still praying involuntarily? Oh,
what—what *is* the meaning of life?"

In an agony of suspense she waited for an answer, straining
forward toward the invisible presence she felt stirring in the
night. "The answer! Oh, there must be an answer or I couldn't

go on! There must be a meaning—no one could live if life were meaningless!"

Suddenly the night grew dark; a violent wind sprang up. It lashed the frail young girl as though to rend her soul and mind from her body; and just as abruptly an uncanny calm ensued. She sensed the presence of a living thing there in the silent darkness before her. The cold sweat of terror broke out on her forehead; the pounding of her heart was deafening. She waited breathlessly for she knew not what.

Finally those clouds which had obscured the moon passed. There, coiled up in the path directly in front of her, was an enormous serpent with its head raised to strike. The explorer recognized the species as that of the Mean Ingless, the deadliest cobra known to man, but one to whose existence she had not given credence when travelers in Nithking wrote of their encounters with it. It glistened so horribly in the moonlight that the young girl stood petrified with terror. Closing her eyes, she swayed slightly. . . . Surely this was death come at last.

After the first paralyzing effect of fear passed, however, defiance asserted itself. "So this is the answer to my question! But it's not fair! I don't deserve to be killed by this poisonous serpent! I believe life has a meaning, but I don't know what it is! If it were meaningless, that alone would destroy one!"

She glanced back along the path, moved by the hope that for once Godidea might assist her. Surely the hound of heaven could protect her from this deadly creature. That poor creature, however, trembling in every limb, was shrinking back in fear. Now too paralyzed with fright even to defend herself when the serpent struck, she felt everything go black, and fell heavily to the ground.

When the horrid coldness glided over her body and the poisonous fangs were piercing her flesh, Godidea leapt forward ferociously. Caught beneath the two contending foes, the girl was helpless. Over her prostrate body the terrible struggle ensued. Her brain reeled insanely; the blood seemed to congeal in her veins. Unable to move, she lay, torn and bleeding, uncertain whether she were dead or alive. For long interminable hours the Mean Ingless and Godidea fought to possess the girl and to destroy each other. An eternity of agony passed, and then, by a superhuman effort, Tellectina summoned sufficient strength to crawl out from under them. But she lacked the courage to wait and witness the awful outcome of this struggle. Sick from the poison of Mean Ingless, and weak from the loss of blood, the young girl crept away to hide herself in the darkness.

The following morning she awakened just where she had fallen from exhaustion the night before. Stiff and sore, she examined her bruises and wounds, amazed that the poison of the cobra had not killed her. On glancing about, she was aghast to find that she had only run about in circles all night: there beside her lay the hound licking its wounds, while on the other side of her the mangled serpent was creeping painfully away.

"So neither of you won! I can't but feel grateful to Godidea for once—he saved my life. If this is the species of serpent, however, which infests Nithking, I fear I shall never live to come out of this country alive!"

The injury received from Mean Ingless had reduced Godidea's strength appreciably, and this enabled the fugitive as a consequence to walk more slowly and thoughtfully than heretofore. While strolling down a gently sloping hill one afternoon absorbed in the problem presented by the Godidea Tellectina failed to notice where she was going. Suddenly she stumbled and plunged precipitously into a great evil-smelling slough. Floundering helplessly about in the mire she protested vigorously:

"So this is what Godidea has driven me into! What mud, what filth, what a stench! And I sink deeper and deeper all the time! But how can I extricate myself? How different from the Slough of Despond which Bunyan's Christian fell into! It should be simple for a Christian to find a way out of any difficulty—there are always plenty of Casuists near to help him.

But I am no longer a Christian, I fear, I am merely Tellectina—
and alone."

Ceasing her futile struggles, she remained absolutely motionless, thinking intently and considering the possibilities of a
rescue. Finally she laughed confidently as if some splendid idea
had occurred to her. She began to shout for help, calling again
and again until the echo of her cry was taken up by the mountains and reëchoed. Then she waited with a smile of assurance
on her face.

Eventually a stream of people commenced to pour over the
hillside, and they were without exception lame, halt, or blind.
In their futile attempt to pull her out, their own suffering was
so apparent that it merely increased Tellectina's own. After
thinking rapidly, the desperate girl dispatched a number of
messengers into Err, bidding them say, "Come over into Nithking and help us." But as she waited she laughed skeptically
and reflected, "Can any good come out of Err?"

It was not long, however, before another stream of people
appeared. The messengers had brought their own kind back
with them: there were thousands of lame, halt, and blind. Catching the rope which they threw to her, Tellectina fastened it
securely about her body. But by the time they had contrived to
pull her out on dry land on the opposite side of the morass,
she was sorely cut and bleeding profusely. Tellectina felt keenly
resentful toward the scheme of things because the only people
able to rescue a person from the Slough of Despond into which
Godidea ran her were the unfortunate of the earth. The heavenly
pursuer had been dismayed by their presence but oddly enough
neither molested nor frightened them. They, Tellectina concluded in astonishment, were blissfully unaware of his identity.

While the explorer stood there wet and chilled, endeavoring
vainly to remove all the mud from her clothing, the hound of
heaven started toward the far side of the slough. Quickly everyone who had come in response to Tellectina's call now voluntarily lined up so that they touched shoulder to shoulder. This
human wall soon stretched for many miles. The fugitive sought

safety behind it, for the hound of heaven was unable to get through it or under it or over it. As she watched him running with grim determination along it, however, she realized that eventually he would get around it.

Feeling that she was master of the situation at last, Tellectina laughed and despatched still other messengers into Err, instructing them to request only two kinds of people to come: first, those who had suffered through no fault of their own from the benevolence of the Creator in the form of floods, droughts, earthquakes, storms, hurricanes, wild animals, plagues of insects, and disease; from their own innate kindness and gullible natures, from unattainable dreams, unfulfilled desires, or unrequited love. These came in thousands and tens of thousands. Then, like a triumphant general, Tellectina stood on a hilltop to direct them to their places in this great human barricade. Next were summoned that multitude of human beings, the reason for whose existence had often sorely puzzled Tellectina, and whom she now realized were merely separate units of the Great Wall of Evil which should be collected to form an insurmountable barrier and thus arrest the progress of Godidea. She laughed when she saw that their number was legion, inasmuch as it included:

All Christians, Jews, Buddhists, and Brahmans;
All Mohammedans and pseudo-occultists;
All prohibitionists, patriots, and other politicians;
All ugly people who aren't interesting,
Interesting people who aren't well-bred,
Well-bred people who aren't intelligent,
Intelligent people who aren't kind,
Kind people who aren't amusing,
And amusing people who are cruel;
Supercilious dowagers—all bosom and no brains;
High-pressure salesmen,
Peroxide blondes and other gold-diggers;
Men with vigorous minds and impotent bodies;

Men with flabby hands, flabby faces, and furtive eyes;
And women with masculine voices, masculine clothes, and
furtive eyes;
Large men who hold small dogs on long leashes while they
piss in public;
And fat females who cuddle and coddle pop-eyed Pekingese
and pusillanimous poodles;
Wholesome novelists of sweetness and light;
Pseudo-artists with soiled linen and unkempt hair who think
genius can't flourish except in dirt and disorder;
Cocksure Babbitts and all other "homoboobiens";
All those deaf to discord—but especially women with shrill
voices;
Men who undress women with their eyes in public;
Fat Jews with features like misplaced genital organs;
Seducers of women who wouldn't marry any girl who
wasn't a virgin;
Beautiful women with soft hands and hard hearts;
The narrow-minded, thin-lipped, hard-hearted, and self-
righteous;
The stupid and ignorant and other bores;
Cowards before the stern face of truth, and "heroes" before
the stern face of duty;
All pious, pusillanimous, persecutors of pleasant pagans;
and others too numerous to name.

The end of the line was now far out of sight. And after some
time had elapsed, hordes and droves of them returned from the
opposite direction, assuring Tellectina that the Great Wall of
Evil already encircled the entire world. And as they closed up
the circle she saw to her amazement that there were thousands
of stupid and ignorant to spare. Having once again slipped
through the last opening, she found herself on the outside of
this wall just in time to see Godidea come running back—
baffled and defeated—to fall dead at her feet.

"So," Tellectina cried trumphantly, "I am safe from the great hound of heaven henceforth and forever! The Great Wall of Evil forms an impassable barrier to Godidea! From this point on travelers in Nithking can advance without fear of pursuit." With pity in her eyes and an ironical smile on her lips, she thanked her rescuers, who seemed to be unaware of the inestimable service they had rendered her.

Turning her back on the Great Wall, she raised her arms exultantly to the sky. "Ah, I am free, gloriously free at last of the three hounds of heaven—and there are no more! Godsson is harmless, Onegod died of fright at the sound of human laughter, and Godidea was destroyed in his attempt to get around the Wall of Evil. To have rid one's self of the three hounds of heaven should enable the young explorer to advance into Nithking with greater rapidity and ease."

The triumphant young explorer marched on with a fine swinging stride, singing lustily at the top of her happy young voice. It was not long, however, before she found herself in the midst of a great barren plain. Everywhere there was empty space—nothingness—just earth and sky—and Tellectina!

"Ah," the girl moaned, "there's no one—nothing—in all this great universe that I can turn to now for help. There is nothing to guide me, help me, give me courage, except myself. But how can one pull one's self up by one's own boot straps? No, no, it is impossible! Now I have no religion, no God, no Christ to love or pray to or to help me in time of distress! Now that I have no religion to live by, I must find a philosophy to support me. Yet how can I find a philosophy till I attain Certitude? And where in heaven's name is this great mountain? I don't even know which way to turn to seek it!"

Suddenly despair caused her to sink heavily to the ground. "Ah, why did I ever leave Err? Who am I to explore a vast unknown continent alone? What egotism, what misplaced confidence! I have given up everything in life, and now I have nothing. I'm utterly alone in the world—and lost in a barren wasteland! How fortunate, how comfortable, oh, how wise, are those who stay safely at home! The loneliness, that is the most terrible of all things in Nithking! I could bear *anything* if I only had a companion. Oh, God, the loneliness of this world— but there's not any God any more! There's only loneliness— and myself!"

Sighing wearily, she rose and trudged on, concentrating her gaze upon her feet in order to shut out the awful vastness of earth and sky and space; consequently she was unaware of the surprise which awaited her on the other side of the hill whose summit she had now attained. As she paused for breath, a sight which made her heart leap with joy greeted her astonished eyes. There before her was a small fertile plot of ground projecting out from the mainland of Nithking proper, a cape. And nestling among the trees could be seen what was undoubtedly a white settlement composed of many houses built oddly enough in the Errorian style and clustering about a large imposing structure in their midst.

Instantly the young explorer reproved herself. "I should be ashamed to feel so overjoyed at the sight of an Errorian village, doubtless inhabited entirely by Errorians even though it has been established right on the edge of Nithking. But I long so desperately for a little rest and comfort and human companionship." Her own words shocked her. "No, no, I must continue my search for Mt. Certitude and not rest by the wayside. I shall make a detour and avoid that settlement altogether."

Redoubling her speed, Tellectina hastened on—making directly for the little colony.

CHAPTER VII

ADVENTURES IN CAPE COVERTURE; HOW TELLECTINA FELL VIC-
TIM TO TROPICAL FEVER AND ENCOUNTERED OLEV THE THIRD

"TURN YOUR BACK! I'm coming out!" an excited feminine voice shouted.

The man on the bank suddenly wheeled about, but at sight
of a nude girl rising from the water commenced a polite with-
drawal into the jungle.

"Sorry to have shocked you," the girl's voice continued from
behind a screen of dense vines, "but it was the crocodiles."

At the word crocodiles the footsteps returned. By this time
Tellectina had clad herself in the few garments whose scantiness
was warranted by the excessive tropical heat.

"Where?" the tall man clothed in white and wearing a pith
helmet demanded as he turned searching eyes up the river
without so much as a glance at the girl beside him.

"Down river," she said. "I presume I didn't look sufficiently
appetizing: they've returned to their siestas in the sun."

"Silly child, coming out here to bathe within fifty yards of
those brutes!"

"I'm not a child!"

"All women are children," the man said in a tone of one who
indulgently reiterates a worn truism.

Tellectina laughed, feeling both pleased and displeased simultaneously.

"Don't you know they have no respect for youth and beauty!"
the stranger continued.

"But they have for my revolver," the girl announced confidently, motioning toward an automatic lying on the ground beside her large sun hat.

"Do you really know how to use it?"

"What a masculine question! I was obliged to learn after I came to the Cape. But, by the way, whatever you do, don't mention the fact to a soul that I went in swimming without any clothes on. Because I'd lose my position."

"So you endanger your position as well as your life!"

"But what on earth is the relation of one's way of swimming to one's work? I have a right to do as I damned please about personal matters!"

"The right, but"—the man shrugged—"seldom the opportunity."

"I suppose I might at least introduce myself, since I'm the older resident. I'm Tellectina Femina Christian—and it's almost as difficult to live up to the first name as to live down the last! As to the middle name—the less said about her the better. You, I suspect, are the new scientist—bacteriologist, isn't it?— who was coming out to study the yellow fever."

The man bowed with mock solemnity. "Your humble servant, madam. And allow me to present myself." He offered her a rather moist card which read "Mr. Elam Domitann."

"How do you do," the girl said. "Everybody has heard about you, though. This is a very small colony, here on the Cape. The government, as you probably know, has recently established a small college for the children of the colonists, and I am the English teacher there. I've only been here a month myself. Before that I was——"

Tellectina paused on noticing that her companion was gazing at the jungle on the opposite bank of the river with an unmistakable air of boredom. She bit her lip resentfully, studied the deep lines in the man's interesting face, the gray at his temples, and his small impersonal eyes.

Her companion had transferred his interest from the girl to

the mountain whose top was visible in the distance. "That's the extinct volcano I've heard about, old Cynosure," he said.

"Yes, that's what newcomers invariably call it. But its proper name is really Sinecure, because——"

"That's ridiculous. The name is self-explanatory. It's only too obvious that it is the cynosure of all eyes. Sinecure is an ecclesiastical term."

"Exactly, and this mountain was named by an old priest who evidently had a sense of humor. Old people who remember him say that he was very charming but very lazy—that's why he thought of the name. So I'm fairly certain it's spelled with and 'S' and not a 'C.' "

The man laughed indulgently. "The ignorance of the female mind! It would be great sport to walk up there some day before the sun gets too hot. It isn't more than five miles to the top."

"Oh, yes, it's every bit of ten because——"

"Nonsense!"

"Because I have climbed it twice. Have you been up it yet?"

"I don't need to walk it to know how far it is. I can estimate distance within a fraction of a mile. I'll wager you five dollars it's not more than five miles! Women are such poor walkers that all distances seem twice as long to them." Again he laughed confidently.

The girl looked at the man intently for a long minute; then she too laughed indulgently. "Have it your own way."

This strange, vehement, and self-confident male left the young woman rather breathless. She was still staring at him in amazement when a gesture of his hand, impatiently brushing away a swarm of gnats, showed her the time on his wrist watch.

"Oh, heavens, I shall be late to dinner at my precious boarding house! That damned old Miss Thanedorn refuses to serve after seven. You're staying at our one and only little inn down near the wharf where the river boats come in, aren't you, Mr. Domitann?"

Amused surprise flashed over the man's face. "And has the

news also been broadcast as to the kind of underclothes I wear?"

Tellectina laughed. "That will come next."

"The devil fly away with all busybodies!"

"If you have any influence in that quarter, I wish to heaven you'd exert it. I'm so disappointed in the Cape. Although there are a great many research workers, naturalists, and chemists stationed here—and writers too—there should be a tolerant scientific spirit about the place."

"Oh, I suspect there is," Mr. Domitann interposed, "one of intense research into other people's affairs. But to hell with all the old women of both sexes! Come and dine with me at my modest little inn tomorrow evening—say that I may have the honor!"

"That *would* be exciting, seeing that all the other males in the colony are thoroughly married. Most men bring their wives out here." She looked at him with eyebrows raised significantly.

"No, er—ah, I'm—I'm not married any more. Though I have two grown daughters." Turning abruptly he picked up her revolver and hat, and they started to stroll back toward the settlement.

Finally Tellectina broke the silence. "I'm not either—any more."

"Oh, so you have been incarcerated too?"

"No, I don't believe in marriage."

The man looked at her with real interest for the first time.

"I certainly do not!" The young woman exclaimed with conviction. "What right has anything or anybody—the state—and least of all that putrid institution known as the Church, to interfere with one's purely private and personal life! If people can't be bound by affection they should not allow any law to bind them. The whole idea is hideous and intolerable. I, for one, shall never marry—never wear a ring to advertise to the world that I'm bought and paid for—nor shall I ever use a man's name. Isn't a woman a separate entity just the same as a man?"

The man smiled. "Well, she does get excited, doesn't she?

It's fortunate for you, my dear little thing, that the man to whom you happen to reveal your heterodoxy is—as he is. You might be—ah—well, misunderstood."

"But, dammit, every word I say is true! I had just as soon shout it from the housetops!"

"The truth is the last thing one can shout from the house-tops."

"I'm not a coward!"

"Cowardice and discretion are two words often confused. I gather that this flowerlike face is merely a deceptive camou-flage. No man expects a woman to engage in an ardent explo-ration of Nithking but evidently you have been doing just that. You intrigue me immensely. Come to dine *this* evening—now, this minute, and tell me about your adventures. Most pretty women, you know, consider that they've generously discharged their duty to mankind by presenting a pretty face."

Till three in the morning Tellectina and Elam Domitann sat at a small table by the window of the inn dallying with their liqueurs and cigarettes and talking. The young girl promptly sketched a word picture of her complete life, omitting nothing of importance except the reason for leaving Olev the Second. The man conversed wittily, cynically, learnedly—divulging nothing of his personal life save in one brief reference to his extreme fondness for his two daughters (whom his divorced wife refused to allow him to see) and the difficulty of supplying his three dependents with as many funds as they demanded. He praised Tellectina's valor in exploring Nithking, assuring her that there was sufficient forbidden territory both without and within the Cape to occupy them both for years.

And in the days that followed they made many delightful excursions together into various interesting sections of Nithking. Tellectina was in her glory. A fearless adventurer and intel-lectual companion was the very thing she longed for most in the world. As to the discrepancy in their ages, she merely re-joiced in it: men of her own age bored her. Domitann was forty and she was twenty-three. How often had she dreamed of a man who had read and thought and traveled through Nithking as extensively as this man. The only drawback, however, was her inability to understand all that he said owing to the decidedly humorous accent with which he spoke Reasonese. The seasoned explorer constituted an excellent guide for the amateur. And although the daring of some of his expeditions rather frightened the young woman, she followed him as far as her courage permitted.

During their daily walks there was no conceivable subject which they did not discuss, Elam insisting that their concord was extraordinary. On matters about which they disagreed Tellectina argued with passionate conviction, all the more violent when uncertainty forced her to convince herself as well as her opponent. On such occasions the man never lost his temper but generally laughed and changed the subject. Tellectina resented the implication that she was a child and not worthy of serious consideration and every point on which they disagreed she remembered vividly; and after returning to her little room at the Thanedorn boarding house would lie awake for hours turning over and over in her mind every word he had uttered. However incredible his ideas appeared, she felt that whatever Elam Domitann said was nothing less than gospel.

They discussed woman suffrage—which he thought a ridiculous fanfare but of which Tellectina was at this time an ardent advocate—in theory: in practice she was indifferent. They agreed that war was a savage custom which should have become obsolete along with bows and arrows. He launched into long, enthusiastic rhapsodies about his work at the laboratory where he spent the better part of every day and the best part of the night. In order to familiarize herself with the technical terms which he employed constantly and of which her lack of understanding seemed to annoy him, Tellectina borrowed a book from Elam's assistant, a young man with whom he lived at the inn. And she nearly blinded herself in her endeavor to read all the novels and biographies that Elam ordered sent out to her from Err in every week's post.

Both her vitality and ardor, however, seemed inexhaustible. Often she came to him from her own day's work radiant with enthusiasm.

"Do you really enjoy it?" he asked incredulously one evening, as they sat down to dinner at the inn.

"Oh, I love it!" Tellectina exclaimed.

"That's very odd for a woman."

"But, Elam, you love your work passionately, even if it doesn't afford proper remuneration. Is a person incapable of loving her work merely because she happens to be a woman? I get very tired standing up all day, of course, but I cherish the independence that work gives me. I would loathe teaching anything else in the world except English, however. I get a thrill out of the smallest tail of the smallest comma!"

"But you waste your precious youth and energy on such nincompoops!"

"But a few of them are alive. They are college seniors, after all, and think how marvelous if I can help to awaken in them a response to the stimuli of ideas—of words! It will give them a source of joy for the remainder of their lives."

"You are so touchingly optimistic about these little insects we call human."

"What about you, sir? Don't you spend your life sweating in the laboratory over some serum that will save these same little insects from dying of yellow fever?"

"That's not why I do it. I'll confess, if you promise never to betray me. I don't give a goddamn about saving humanity—the world would be a very nice place if all the human vermin were killed off. I do research work because it affords me more pleasure than anything else on earth!"

"Wicked, wicked man—that's why I teach a lot of dull-witted youths, too, I suspect. Really, we women are improving."

"Impossible!"

"From any other man that might be taken as a compliment."

"Ah, she is nimble-witted!"

"But the sex has never had half a chance till now. From the

beginning of time woman has played whatever rôle man cast her for. She has never been allowed to be herself."

"What is her real self like?" The man inquired waggishly.

"Nobody knows. She's never had the opportunity to find out."

Elam laughed. "Like the chameleon—eh? With one leg on tradition and one on modernism, to which color do you think she'll turn?"

His levity, however, could not divert her serious intent. "I don't imagine she is so very different from men, fundamentally."

"Let's hope some difference always remains!"

"You—and your naughty mind! But it's a fact: woman is exactly what man has made her through the ages—so he ought to be satisfied. But is he? He is not!"

"The cynic might say that the nature of the material determined the result."

"No," Tellectina continued earnestly, "man bungled his handling of her and blames her because he turned out a bad job."

"What! do women also admit that it's a bad job?"

"You devil!" The girl flashed him a fond smile, then resumed her serious air. "Certainly. So henceforth women are going to take a hand in the matter themselves."

"More power to them!"

"Well, till now you men as fathers and husbands have had almost complete power over women—but you have abused that power abominably, and now woman rebels against you!"

"How soon will the revolution start?"

"I know you don't take it seriously. But you will some day, and you won't like it, either."

"A good scrap is always to be relished—all my ancestors were fighting men. What kind of ammunition does the enemy expect to use? A mere helpless male should be prepared. Is not forewarned, forearmed?"

"Ammunition? Well—er—money chiefly, I suspect."

"Of course, I admire a woman who supports herself, but it's difficult for a mere dense male to see why, when a woman can remain snugly and safely at home and let men do battle with the world for her, she doesn't appreciate it and let well enough alone."

"Because it is not well enough. How would you like to ask your father, say, for every cent of money you spent and account for it to boot, like an untrustworthy child, Mr. Elam Domitann?"

"In your very commendable eagerness to do women justice, Miss Tellectina Christian, you seem to forget that since the beginning of the human race the majority of women have been supported and protected and loved and even worshiped by some men. Men often sacrificed career, home, even life, for them."

"And you seem to forget, mister, that since the beginning of the race the majority of women have been kept in a forced state of arrested development by men. You treated her as either a drudge or a toy for your pleasure. At best you treated her as a child."

"There are worse things than being treated as a child, my dear."

"And better things. But the things men have denied women in the past make the modern woman see red!"

"Men have never denied women the things they wanted most: love, children, marriage, homes, and protection," the man stated quietly.

"And what price did you make them pay for it? They paid with their self-respect, and that of men too, make no mistake about that; with subservience; suppression of their own individuality."

"So all the millions of henpecked husbands in the world are proof of nothing—not even of the fact that innumerable women have never suffered from suppression of any kind."

"You know those are in the minority—I'm talking about women as a whole. In your blessed overrated Greece even, you denied wives every right on earth except to bear children and to wait on their husbands. At one time you denied her the opportunity even to learn to read and write. You always denied her the right to her own body and even the custody of her own children, till recently, as well as the right to the use of her own patrimony."

The man laughed. "Hell! if women disliked all this so damned much, why the devil didn't they rebel long ago?"

"Why don't servants defy their masters? Why doesn't a small, dependent nation rebel? Why do the Jews hate the whole world? Why does the day laborer hate the capitalist? Because they feel that their race has been unjustly treated for several centuries too long! Women would have rebelled long ago if they had had the power."

"Power? What king has ever had more power than Cleopatra, Queen Elizabeth, Queen Victoria, Catherine of Russia, and the many all-powerful mistresses of the many kings? Why didn't these women rebel and do something to free their poor downtrodden sex? That's a question I've always wanted some woman to answer for me."

For a moment Tellectina was at a loss. Then she said, "Do men in power usually help their fellow men? They do not! What have most kings done but add to their own wealth and possessions and personal aggrandizement? No, most of the benefits of man have come about by accident, force of circumstance, and through intellectual rebels like Voltaire, Emerson, Luther, Ingersoll, and Mencken—rebels whose ideas leaven the whole of the social dough until it changes. And during the machine age material benefits have accrued through the byproducts of some inventor's pleasure."

Again the man laughed. "Honestly, if you weren't so damned pretty and so bewitchingly feminine (which I realize now is the basest sort of camouflage!) and so adorably coquettish, if your eyes didn't sparkle so alluringly, I might be better able to attend to your noble lecture."

"No, if I had flat feet and wore nose glasses you wouldn't attend to me at all; you wouldn't even invite me out to dinner!"

"Damned right I wouldn't!" Elam agreed chuckling.

Tellectina laughed too. "You simply won't take me seriously. You are so damned male and so damned sure of your eminence that you look down from your throne indulgently at the amusing cavortings of that quaint little animal known as woman."

His laughter more than confirmed it, but his words were, "You do us both an injustice, for I sincerely admire your perorations. A woman who thinks at all is such a novelty to a man that——"

"That he likes to put her up like a performing bear," the girl interpolated, "and see her go through her stunts."

"Why, my dear little thing, you're surely not bitter, are you? You certainly can't ever have had any grounds for complaint. Men must have swarmed about you like a drove of bees about the sweetest flower in the whole garden."

"It's not myself I'm concerned about, it's the whole race of women, it's all downtrodden peoples. I want to see equality for everybody."

"But you have told me repeatedly that you dislike women, that they bore you and——"

"But justice! Justice is the keynote of my character. Any and all injustice, even abstract injustice, makes my blood boil."

"If boiling blood can cleanse the world of injustice, well enough," the man agreed. "And theoretically you may be right about everything, but as long as the world is composed of weaker and stronger human beings, just so long will there be injustice. And whatever my intellect may coolly say, tradition is too strong in my bones. I'm afraid I still believe in the divine right of the aristocrat."

"And the divine right of the male?" Tellectina added.

Elam Domitann repudiated the charge with a smile of deprecation. "And one would be astounded to hear this tall, graceful patrician who is very obviously an aristocrat herself, pleading so eloquently for democracy, if one did not recall that it is a phase through which youth often must pass. One remembers Shelley."

"But," the girl objected, "the more fortunate one has been in one's own heritage, the more reason for helping those less fortunate."

"Are they less fortunate? 'He that increaseth knowledge increaseth sorrow.' Most people are clods, my dear, and barring actual physical discomfort, the duller the man the happier. Ah, well, perhaps you are a born crusader, little Tina."

"A polite way of putting it—born reformer, you mean. But don't the stupidity and injustice and suffering in the world incense you? How can you stand by and——"

"And laugh?"

"Yes, you laugh at absolutely everything."

"Laughter, my little solemn-serious, is the best weapon with which to protect ourselves from life. Where in adversity and disillusion some men take to drugs, others to liquor, or women, or gambling, I have taken to laughter. It is less wearing on the system and infinitely less expensive. Being too intelligent to be always serious, you too will learn to laugh some day. Though you exhibit a taint of the messianic, you possess unlimited potentialities. After a long and arduous journey through Nithking you too will, I doubt not, arrive at the highest mountain in the world."

"But I feel too—too passionately about things, about everything—to laugh at anything."

"Youth, my dear, blessed adorable youth."

"I'm not so very young, I'm twenty-three."

"Sweet one," the man said, and smiled and patted her hand. Tellectina withdrew it petulantly. "And you're so adorable when you pout, and your eyes are like stars when you get angry, and the dimples play hide-and-seek about your thin petal-like lips while they're making such serious sonorous statements."

"Oh, I hate you!" the girl exclaimed, and confirmed it by smiling directly into his eyes. "And probably all the time a woman is talking about high-and-mighty matters the man is sitting there thinking how nice it would be to kiss her."

"Are you a mind reader?"

"Oh, men are incorrigible!"

"Does that matter as long as they find women adorable?"

"Not to the men," Tellectina said, tossing her head.

"Nor to most women," Elam Domitann added.

"I know it—dammit!"

"Then why attempt to develop an intelligence in women which they don't want—and wouldn't know how to use if they had it?"

The woman cast her eyes to heaven in supplication. "Didn't I say that men are incorrigible?"

Just then a servant brought in Elam's mail, which had arrived on the Saturday evening boat. The letters he tucked in his pocket, and opening the roll containing the months-old copy of *Punch,* handed it to Tellectina.

"There, my dear, amuse yourself with that."

"But don't you want to see it first or read your letters?"

"And deprive myself of your charming companionship? I'll smoke and watch you enjoy *Punch:* you can read aloud to me what most amuses you. It delights me to watch your sense of humor bubble."

And every week thereafter Elam insisted on Tellectina's seeing *Punch* first: a fact which later there was occasion to remember.

It was Domitann's habit early each Sunday morning, before the sun became too hot, to take a long walk up to the top of the only near-by mountain, Sinecure, the extinct volcano. When she accompanied him, the girl listened entranced to his brilliant and witty conversation. His familiarity with all conceivable subjects surpassed anything she had ever known. They conversed only in Reasonese, and Tellectina's young blood danced in her veins as she struggled excitedly with the intricacies of that difficult language. She was blissfully happy, for was not this the sort of life she had longed for and dreamed of? Oh, if only this perfect intellectual companionship would continue indefinitely!

Not many weeks had passed, however, before complications arose. One morning after Tellectina had spent a restless night (as she invariably did when the moon was full) her walk with Elam was completely spoiled. They had just started swinging gayly along the trail when, to Tellectina's shame and annoyance, Femina suddenly appeared out of the jungle with flowers twined in her hair, around her neck, and even in her shoes. At her approach the man stopped in pleased astonishment. Femina came dancing forward and playfully placed a large acacia blossom behind the man's very dignified ear.

"Well, and who is this delightful creature?" he asked.

With a coquettish toss of the head, Femina replied, "Oh, I'm Femina, Tellectina's better half, you know! Haven't you seen me peeping out from behind her skirts lately?" And thrusting her sister aside she usurped Tellectina's place at Elam's side. The gay intruder promptly commenced to monopolize the conversation with laughing assurance. Shame spread over Tellectina's face when she noticed to what light and personal subjects the other girl diverted it. Being somewhat accustomed to her sister's frivolous manner, however, Tellectina was not so amazed by her actions; but the astounding reaction of this man who had spoken such admirable Reasonese to her only a moment before disconcerted her. Completely ignored, Tellectina soon fell behind.

Slackening their pace, the three of them strolled leisurely along the shady trail that wound through the dense woods. As the morning wore on the man seemed to forget his work and to forget Tellectina's presence altogether. Gradually she grew discouraged and lingered far behind watching the other two walking gayly along ahead of her, Femina cocking her head this way and that, laughing merrily at nothing, and flashing mischievous glances at the man who had never once taken his eyes off her impudent laughing face.

"The same old story," Tellectina murmured to the indifferent jungle. "Smiles and smirks, I call it—for that is all it amounts to. And yet every male we've ever met succumbs to that sort of effervescent froth!" She smiled in puzzled indulgence over this inexplicable sister of hers. Then a little sob caught in her throat. "But how *can* an intellectual man prefer her with her smiles and smirks to me with my Reasonese? It's an awful reflection on men, that's what it is!"

Finally they started home, and Tellectina followed; but before emerging from the privacy of the woods the man lifted Femina's hand and kissed it. As he did so Tellectina suddenly caught a fleeting glimpse of a man behind Elam, one who, she was later to learn, was his manservant. Then, touching the flower in her hair, Elam said, "Do you know, Femina, that you are like a flower yourself—a very delicate slender flower with a very radiant face—and that I love all beautiful things?"

But almost instantly the tender light in his eyes died out and he was again the detached, cool, impersonal man of the world that Tellectina had always seen.

Femina, having entered Tellectina's room as if she belonged there, stood with her sister at the window watching Elam as he walked away. "Well," she said triumphantly, "see what I've done for you, little Tina! The poor man's in love. It only required one day for me to accomplish what you, with all your brilliant intellect, failed to accomplish in a whole month!"

"Don't be an idiot, he's not in love with either one of us. He loves us as a man loves a—a flower or any beautiful object, as he put it. How could such a wise, mature, famous, great scientist love a mere slip of a girl like me—or you?"

"He is interested in you, but he loves me."

"Oh, Femina, I wish to heaven you hadn't come! I was perfectly content as things were. His intellectual companionship, our excursions in Nithking, our long hours of reading together, and our marvelous conversations—I want nothing else."

"Well, you little fool, you couldn't have kept those very long —without my artful assistance. Besides, it was good sport: he was difficult to catch. I had to perform nearly my whole repertoire of tricks—whereas two smiles are enough to ensnare most men I have met: you know, one on the lips saying 'go,' and one in the eyes saying 'come.'"

"You—you cold-blooded creature! And such egotism! But there's something queer about men I don't understand—why do they invariably succumb to a little flirting?"

Femina laughed her provocative little laugh and proceeded to ensconce herself in her sister's bedroom with impudent assurance. And thereafter, when Tellectina was at school teaching every day, Femina slept. It was not only because they looked so much alike, but because they so seldom appeared in public at the same time, that few people beside Elam were aware of the existence of two women. The man seemed attracted to them both and talked to them alternately; but, as the weeks flew by, Femina monopolized Elam with increasing confidence. It was Tellectina, however, who invariably sat with him when he read aloud, at which time Femina would retire to a far corner of the room to sulk.

The sisters had no more than agreed that they were happier than they had ever been before in their entire lives when misfortune befell them. Each one contracted a mysterious tropical malady—Femina's attack being the more severe, however. Although people on every side of her were known to contract the tropical fever, designated by the scientists as walking pectoralitis, which Elam had once laughingly explained was merely a febrile, though often infectious, but never fatal, disease characterized by pallor, palsy, and pectoral disturbances and transmitted generally by the hands, the lips, or other external organs— it never occurred to Tellectina that either she or her sister might become infected by such germs. Their symptoms, being entirely different from those she had observed in any other disease they had ever contracted, continued to mystify her. Femina grew paler each day, lost her appetite, and trembled all over in the most unaccountable fashion at times—particularly when in Elam's presence.

Despite this strange illness, or because of it, Femina seemed to alternate between acute suffering and excessive happiness. Tellectina was amazed that Domitann, the great scientist, failed to detect anything abnormal in Femina's condition. Each morning when he met her at their rendezvous under a flowering mimosa tree he would exclaim: "You look radiant, Femina! Gloriously radiant!"

And the girl's invariable answer to that was to look more radiant than ever; her eyes sparkled with an unnatural brilliance; her smiles flashed over the man like spring sunlight; her laughter overflowed as spontaneously as the rapturous caroling of birds; even her flesh took on a luminous quality, and her very hair shone with new lustre. Her step was buoyant, her whole body felt light, her blood sang a thousand wordless songs in her veins. As the man and girl strolled along the well-worn path Femina felt the air take on a soft golden quality; vaguely she was aware that at their approach flowers burst into bloom on every side, and that the earth was filled with the happy trills of birds; yet all the while she seemed to see nothing but the face of the man beside her, heard nothing save the accents of his voice.

One morning Elam declared a holiday from his research work. The little party of three climbed to the top of the old volcano which both girls now also inaccurately called "Cynosure," in order to preserve peace. After standing on a small plateau of clinkers, gazing into the fathomless crater—locally known as Lovers' Grave—and gayly recommending it to each other as an ideal place to commit suicide, they lugged a lava rock down under the trees and spread their simple lunch; after which the man, being very tired, laid his head in Femina's lap while Tellectina read aloud to him.

He was soon asleep, and as they kept watch over him Femina smiled indulgently but Tellectina was a trifle annoyed. On awakening Elam exclaimed, "Oh, forgive me, Tina, but your voice is like the soft murmur of a brook. The fact that it could lull a weary man to sleep is really a great tribute."

Femina glowed with pleasure at the compliment to her sister, while Tellectina smiled and thought, "Yes, the eternal male —with his grand excuses!"

Finally they rose and retraced their steps in leisurely fashion, Tellectina being neglected, as usual. A few large raindrops fell upon the broad leaves above their heads, but no one was aware of them. Femina and Elam strolled along arm in arm, laughing hilariously at nothing. The rain grew heavier. They walked along as though it were the balmiest of spring days, while the rain soaked their clothes and ran in rivulets over the brims of their hats. The man's coat flew open unheeded in the violent tropical wind. The sky grew black with ominous storm clouds; the rain descended in great silver sheets: still the man and woman strolled on oblivious of everything but the sunshine radiating from their own hearts.

Suddenly Femina's foot caught fast in its track. Slipping her foot out of the shoe buried in the mud, she stood on one leg and, looking up at the avalanche of water descending mercilessly on every side, laughed merrily. "Why, look, Elam, it's raining!"

The man looked about him in surprise. "Bless my soul, so it is."

Fishing out the wet shoe from the bog, he hoisted it gayly on a stick. Femina continued to wave it like a banner over his shoulder as he carried her in his arms down the mountain side. Their laughter mingled with the thunder which they, however, failed to hear.

After this memorable episode, their days passed like seconds. Every trip to the mountain top or into the jungle was a glorious adventure; every simple meal which they shared was as gay as an elaborate banquet; every small misfortune that befell them was a decidedly amusing comedy. In every decision left to her, Femina strove to foresee the man's wish and make that her own.

The inexorable day arrived, however, when Domitann perfected the serum and was therefore due to return to Err. At their last luncheon at his inn he laughed in a strained voice, saying, "But you won't miss me as I shall miss you. Because even though I lack the right to do so, I love you."

Both sisters smiled and replied in concert, "Of course I shall miss you, I am very fond of you, as you very well know."

Later, when he came to the house to bid them farewell, Elam stood motionless in the door of the girl's bedroom looking into Femina's eyes but saying nothing.

The man too seemed to have contracted tropical fever: his face was strangely pale, his eyes burned into Femina's like two black coals, and his hands trembled. Suddenly, dropping his precious parcels to the floor, he caught her fiercely in his arms. Femina's fever mounted instantly—uncontrollably. Growing so delirious that she was unaware of her own actions, the girl bared her left breast to him, pressing his hand upon it again and again. His fingers closed convulsively over it, and thereupon both girls closed their eyes. . . .

And then it was that an absolutely incredible thing occurred —a horrible, unspeakably cruel thing. Neither one of the girls ever knew how it happened. But suddenly Tellectina's blood was curdled by the sound of an unearthly, inhuman cry of agony. Instantly opening her eyes, she was greeted by a sight which struck her dumb with horror. She stood staring wide-eyed at it—at Femina's heart wrenched from her breast, suspended before Tellectina's very eyes—dripping with blood— bloody threads depending from it—bloody cords connecting it with her body. Femina had fainted and slipped to the floor. The man had gone. Racked with such excruciating pain that she was not even able to cry for help, convinced that Femina was dead, Tellectina also lost consciousness and slipped to the floor beside her sister. . . .

It seemed a long eternity before she was awakened by the sound of Femina's voice calling frantically, "Wait! Wait!"

Looking dazedly about her, Tellectina saw that Femina's heart had been mysteriously replaced in her breast and that she was pressing her hand over the wound as she rose and rushed blindly from the room. Following her out of the door, Tellectina descried Elam a few paces down the road stumbling uncertainly along like a sick man.

"Oh, wait, wait, for God's sake!" Femina cried. "I didn't recognize you, I didn't recognize you! I didn't even know who you were till now! Why didn't you tell me your real name was Olev? Only Olev could have the strength, could have the cruelty, to tear out a human heart!"

The man's white face was so stricken with pain, his mouth so twisted with suffering that Tellectina realized that he too must be delirious and a hapless victim of the same tropical fever. With a sob he caught Femina in his arms murmuring, "Oh, my love, my love!"

Unable to believe her own eyes, Femina happily sought to reassure herself of Olev's reality by running her hands over his face and figure, sobbing and laughing hysterically. "Oh, my love, my love, I've been waiting for you all my life—looking for you—searching the face of every man I met! And yet I didn't recognize you when I saw you! But why, why, must I have my heart torn out by the roots in order to discover your identity? Don't you see that to part from you is to have my heart literally wrenched out of my breast—is to die!"

The man strained her to him hungrily, kissed her eyes, her lips, her hair, drank her tears, murmuring, "Oh, my dear, my sweet, my beloved, don't cry, don't cry!"

Tellectina, who had lingered behind, caught up with them, saying, "Yes, yes, I've heard you described a thousand times. I was sure I'd recognize Olev the minute I saw him! How strange that all these months I never once suspected who you were. Oh, do wait—wait—for God's sake!"

Supporting a girl with each arm, the man led them to a grassy bank and sat down—then dropping his head between his hands, murmured, "God in heaven, is a man to have no sunshine in his life, no beauty, no tenderness—must he go on forever grinding out money—money—money for others! I have no right to your love, I shall never be in a position to marry again, and yet I can't give you up! But it's so unfair to you—the discrepancy in our ages, the incessant demands on my time and money, and yet——" He buried his face in Femina's breast. "Oh, I love you, I love you—so intensely! I need you, so desperately, so desperately—you can't understand. Oh, damn God for making life such a hell!"

Femina held him fast in her arms, forgetting her own pain in an effort to soothe his. It was not long before the warm tropical night descended on them, and when Olev laid Femina back on the grassy bank his fever took quite a different form. His delirium increased steadily, and he showed very plainly that he desired Femina to quiet it. Consequently the girl, though afraid, and amazed at herself, "did that which seemed expected." . . .

While the man slept peacefully in her arms, Femina lay looking up at the stars responding in a whisper to the questions of the ever curious Tellectina who lay beside her. "No, no, it was rather painful to me, but it makes me very happy to be able to do something for *him!*"

"But it's wrong, Femina!" Tellectina remonstrated.

"But I love him, and love makes everything right. Besides, nothing that Olev does can ever be wrong!"

"We'll have to call him Olev the Third."

"Oh, no," Femina protested, "he is the one and only real Olev, the only man in the world who deserves the name. A woman often *thinks* she loves when she doesn't, but when she does love, God knows there's no doubt in her heart!" She pressed her hand again over the wound in her breast.

And Tellectina murmured wonderingly, *"So this is love!* This pain, this agony, this wrenching out of one's heart! No, no, no, I won't allow any other human being to torture you so, Femina; to have the power of life and death over you or me! Come away, we'll leave this man at once!"

Femina smiled pityingly on Tellectina. "And have my heart torn out again? Oh, no."

"But love, oh, it's a disease—it's a fever you can't control! It's a trap—you can't stay and you can't go—either way it's agony.

It's not fair! It's not fair! And I had always thought that love meant happiness!"

The next morning they, or rather Tellectina, discussed the situation with Olev as calmly as it was possible under the circumstances. Olev had already decided to postpone his trip to Err. Tellectina again aired her opinions on marriage, declaring that she considered herself above it, explaining her theories about the ideal union of men and women; asserting that if intimacy were wrong the night before marriage, it was wrong the night after marriage, and that it was love which made it right, not a few words mumbled over one's head. She scoffed at wives, saying, "Wives! those are the people who nag nice men, tell them to wear their rubbers and not to stay out too late at night or to spend too much money on books! I know the breed! God forbid that I should ever sink so low! No wifery for me!"

"Was there ever in the world a woman like you?" the man exclaimed. "But marriage laws were designed primarily for the protection of women, dear, not of men. I feel that I shouldn't accept your generosity. After all, it's the man who must always do the thinking for both."

"Isn't that rather an insult to my intelligence?"

"That's what I say to myself: if it were anyone else in the world but you I would say 'no,' for the woman's own sake. But you are so intelligent and yet—and yet, you are so young too— so utterly unsophisticated—so ignorant of the world. Think of the scandal if it becomes known! And it's the woman who always bears the brunt of all such things!"

"It's nobody's damned business but ours! And shouldn't one be willing to suffer a little for the sake of love? I don't do things that I think are wrong—I'd just as soon shout it from the housetops!"

"Well, for God's sake, don't! We must be very, very cautious."

"I hate lying, I'm willing to suffer for woman's freedom and independence—they are my sworn ideals. You don't seem to understand that, Olev!"

"Yes, yes, darling, I do; but you don't understand the world as well as I do. You must keep our—our intimacy an absolute secret. Promise me."

Tellectina looked very earnest and was silent for a long time. "All right, I promise, although I prefer to tell people. I'm proud of it—proud of having the courage of my convictions."

Elam smiled and kissed her. "Well, it requires two women to accomplish all that! And I've found the intellectual and feminine combined, so I'm a lucky devil. But such women are as rare as snowstorms—on the equator."

"They shouldn't be. I shall continue with my work and you with yours. And since romance and love can thrive best without the disillusionment of daily life under the same roof, we can live separately just as we do now. I certainly don't intend to use any of your hard-earned money, sweet dear."

Femina remained ominously silent all this while. But there ensued a period of such happiness as Tellectina never dreamed existed on earth. Suddenly she saw the world with new eyes. Never had it appeared so beautiful: everyone seemed intent on exhibiting to her his hitherto concealed goodness. The only fly in the ointment was that she neglected her work—but she was too happy to care. Femina looked radiant but ate almost nothing.

After several months of ecstatic happiness Olev announced it was no longer possible to postpone his journey back to Err, as he had received official orders to give a résumé of his yellow fever experiments at government headquarters.

While standing on the bank after Elam had boarded the river boat, Tellectina and Femina both made a brave effort not to cry in his presence. He promised to return just as soon as possible —in a few weeks, he hoped, adding as he leaned over the rail and gazed into Femina's eyes, "Being here with you is the greatest happiness I've ever known in my entire life. Surely you are convinced of that by now."

Unable to speak because of the painful constriction in her throat, Femina managed a wry little smile. Until the boat rounded the last curve in the river and passed out of sight she waved steadily to him, although his figure was blurred by her tears.

A week passed and yet no letter arrived. The spring rains had begun in earnest. It rained every day after Olev's departure. Such gloomy weather was depressing enough, but Tellectina finally became seriously concerned about Femina's health, which she persisted in endangering even further by walking up and down the length of the garden heedless of the rain and mud.

Going to the window one afternoon, Tellectina called and beckoned to her. "Femina, what *is* the matter with you?"

Her sister flung down the large orchid she had been twirling in her hand disconsolately. "Nothing. Everything. I don't know. All the zest is gone from life. I—I—oh, life is so futile—I wish to God I were dead!"

"But you should try to occupy yourself with something. Come in. You might at least mend some of Olev's clothes which he left with us. It'll prevent your being so restless and discontented."

Femina entered sullenly, seated herself at the west window, but immediately arose. "Oh no, I can't sit still two seconds!"

Finally Femina's sick condition also affected her sister, who found herself constantly murmuring, "If we understood the malady we could apply a remedy, but it's all so mysterious. It's not a complication of pectoralitis I'm certain of that much, anyway."

On the tenth morning Tellectina was awakened by low gurgles of laughter escaping from Femina's lips as she danced around her sister's bed.

"What *is* the matter with you, you blessed idiot? Have you completely lost your mind?" But Tellectina's indulgent tone belied her words. "What have you hidden inside your dress that you keep your hand pressed to your breast so carefully?"

Femina drew out a crumpled letter and waved it triumphantly in the air.

"What does he say, Femina, that makes you so happy?" The only reply was a low gurgle in the throat, and as Femina kissed the letter repeatedly on both sides Tellectina noticed that it had not even been opened. "Let's open it, silly, and see what he says."

Together they read and reread it.

When Femina carefully placed the envelope inside her dress against her bare breast her sister exclaimed, "How foolish!" but that night when Femina was not looking Tellectina stealthily stole it, slipping the letter underneath her own pillow to sleep with her hand touching it all night. It was almost as comforting as the touch of her beloved's hand.

Olev's absence lengthened into three months owing to the fact that he was unable to procure sufficient funds for the return journey. The government declined to advance him any more funds than it had already advanced him, and he steadily refused Tellectina's repeated offer of her own little savings. Though separated by thousands of miles, the lovers felt closer together than when under the same roof.

"His invisible presence is more real than his physical presence," Tellectina frequently observed.

Every minute of the day the sisters conversed aloud with him; they were never alone—Olev was in their room every day and walked beside them through the garden in the cool of the evening.

Late one afternoon Tellectina came unexpectedly on her sister reading from a collection of small slips of paper. "What have you there? Why, it looks like a jewel box. I didn't know you had any jewels. Who on earth gave them to you?"

Femina flushed but said nothing, and hastily locking the box, held it jealously against her breast.

"I won't steal your jewels, foolish female. I merely want to see them."

Unlocking the jewel box the girl shyly held out some worn slips of paper with Olev's handwriting on them.

"Why, Femina, you've cut these out of my letters!"

"Only the parts intended for *me*," the other maintained stoutly. "I care nothing for the philosophy and wit and all that Reasonese that amuses you so much. It bores me; but these—

ah, these are the most precious possessions I have in the whole wide world."

Examining one after another of them written in Olev's small but vigorous masculine handwriting, Tellectina commenced reading them aloud:

" 'All the sunshine, all the wholesome merriment went out of my life when I said good-bye to you, dearest beloved.

" 'Your sweet soul is like the pearl the fisherman finds at long last—the perfect and pure of his dreams—after having brought up tons of seed pearls.' "

Smiling tenderly, she shook her head slowly, then continued reading:

" 'Tonight I am confused—destroyed by the most desperate depression. The thing has me as though a black devil gripped my shoulder, leaned upon me—and its fetid breath suffocated me. I want you and your very being.

" 'I think of you always, dear lovely, of your perfect loveliness—a loveliness of mind and of soul that is even greater than that of person—and could one say more?' "

A sob caught in Tellectina's throat, but she went on eagerly.

" 'I love you, and I admire you and I respect you equally, I think—for one cannot be without the other: they are the three graces of attraction.

" 'Devotedly, ever constantly and loving, Olev.

" 'We are very much—almost wholly alike—except for a difference in age and sex. I "feel" you all the time. Separation from you would be equal to losing an eye—oh, stupid!—much worse than that! but the "feeling" of loss would be the same.

" 'Dear lovely, you did not know that last night we (WE) read together for five hours! I read aloud to you from first to last the life of Lady Hamilton by Morehouse. For last evening, fretful and bored, I cast aside my work. And I said to myself, said I, "I will sit me down and I will imagine She is Here—and I will read this aloud to her, and my soul will be comforted." And it was so.' "

"Oh, Olev, Olev!" Tellectina murmured and, dropping to her knees, buried her face in Femina's lap. After a while she lifted her head and continued to read:

" 'My dear, my most dear, it is stupid, it will make you laugh —but this it is—that if several days pass without a letter from you—I am miserable—desolate to a point of utter death.

" 'Good-night sweet fragrant flower of my life—fragrant equally in mind and body. I love you back, oh, so strenuously!

" 'Oh, I cannot—do not wish to, conceive of life without you.' "

Both sisters were weeping softly now, consequently they were unable to read aloud, but took up every slip to the very last one in the jewel box. And it was Tellectina this time who entwined her arms about Femina.

"Tonight, sweet beloved, the desire, the frantic longing to speak with you—touch your hand—be with you—was so great that in my 'loneliness' and desperation, I went down to the depot and boarded the train which went toward you—though I had not the fare.

"The devotion of a fine soul to any object of his or her love or admiration or worship *never* 'wavers'—never dies—never is sullied or affected by *anything* or any person or circumstance.

"And then I think, at what time in the years to come will I lose *Her?* I ask the gods and they smile—poor fool! For, of course, by the very nature of things 'lose' you I must! But let's not think of it. All one's philosophy is of no avail in certain crises!

"Why in the name of all that we consider Sense—is it made by Circumstance and Condition in a wholly Destructive and Stupid world impossible for me to see and speak with you when of all things I desire most and to the utter oblivion of all else in creation to go to you and to REST."

"Ah, my poor love, if only I could save him from all this!" Femina murmured.

"Do you know that your letters to me—my letters to you— are my ONLY opportunities of mental diversion and relaxation—and of 'life' above the daily and apparently interminable grind of the money-machine!

"There is no word from you lately—but I am stupid and no doubt bore you by my heart's desire to KNOW by the very sight of your sweet handwriting that you are at least safe and well. Wisdom? Dearest lovely, let us thank the gods we must always be 'stupid' in some things and Ever where the affections are REALLY placed.

"Remember I am permanent—fixed—unchanging and unchangeable—always at your service. Wherever you may be or wherever I may be, you have but to call and I will come. Sometimes in the years to come that knowledge may be a comfort to you."

Putting forth her hand, Tellectina groped blindly for her sister's hand; the tears blurred her sight. The two women embraced each other so closely that they seemed to fuse into one woman, and it was in one voice that they murmured softly, "Please, God, make me worthy of him!"

They remained thus, motionless, till the moonlight came in the window and found them there.

The following day there was great commotion when a letter arrived announcing that Olev would return early on the morning of June the first, which would be Wednesday. On Monday, Tellectina witnessed a sight which even she, who at times was so close to her sister that they appeared as one person, felt she had no right to witness. For should a human eye ever intrude on the sacred privacy of a devotee at her worship? To her logical mind, the whole episode seemed incredible until illuminated the next day by another incident which was nothing short of a genuine miracle.

On opening their bedroom door on Tuesday morning in search of her sister, Tellectina was arrested by the extraordinary scene before her. Femina was stroking a rough ragged old coat of Olev's which she kept hanging in her closet; then burying her face in it, she sobbed as if her heart would break. Finally she bared her left breast and pressed the rough material to it convulsively until the touch of his garment stilled her sobbing.

When Tellectina at last summoned the courage to enter, her sister was sitting calmly by the window with a strange enigmatic smile on her lips.

"I was just thinking, Tellectina, how wonderful it would be if sometime he should be very ill—almost dying—and we had no money or food, and I had to go out and prostitute myself to some awful man to secure food and medicine to save Olev's life."

Tellectina paused, dumfounded. Pulling herself together with an effort, she endeavored to say in a casual voice, "Well, I only know one thing: and that is, that love is a disease which simultaneously unbalances people's minds and ennobles their characters."

As usual Femina ignored her sister's remarks and continued to gaze out the west window across the garden in the direction from which Olev was to return.

On the third morning she awakened Tellectina before sunrise. She ran about the room with light dancing feet, filling it with flowers, singing as she worked. When everything was in readiness, she sat down by the west window to wait. Tellectina could not bear to look at that face, radiant with happy anticipation. At first there was an enraptured smile on her lips. But as she waited—and waited, the smile gradually faded. She ran down to the dock a dozen times during the morning to peer hopefully down the river, the boat being unusually late. The morning dragged by, noon came; and still Olev had not arrived.

When the boat finally came in and there was no Olev on it, Tellectina soothed Femina with the suggestion that he might be taking a special boat from the army post and might arrive later. Femina, however, began to feel so faint that she was obliged to return to her room and lie down. Every time there were footsteps on the road she would start up trembling joyously—only to sink back again in disappointment.

"Oh, waiting, waiting!" Femina exclaimed. "What does a woman ever do in life but wait! What in God's name *can* a woman do but wait! We spend our lives waiting for love; and then, when love comes, we spend the rest of it waiting for the beloved! Oh, the wretched misery of being a woman!"

"Yes, a man can at least act: he can go forth and find his beloved."

"I know now, Tina, that he'll never come. He doesn't love me any more, or he would have allowed nothing to prevent his coming when he promised. He loves some other woman."

"O you of little faith, for shame! He's been delayed unavoidably. I'm certain he's as eager to see you as you are to have him come."

Femina rose and began to pace the floor like a caged animal, only to throw herself on the bed again, sobbing violently. "I don't care whether he ever comes or not, now—it's too late. I —I—oh, I'm so miserable, I wish—— Oh, listen, Tina!" She started up. "I hear his footsteps! There, wasn't that his voice calling me?"

They both sat motionless—listening breathlessly. There was not a sound. Femina lay back on the pillows, white and still, waiting in aching silence, too disconsolate to stir even when footsteps echoed on the road periodically.

Desperately Tellectina endeavored to rescue her own reason from complete submergence by the great waves of desolation that surged over her repeatedly. "But explain it, Femina, try to analyze it! What is it? What hurts you?"

"Oh, everything, everything! I ache all over. Every inch of my body throbs and aches like a breaking heart! Every time those footsteps go by—oh, I tell you—every step I've heard this day is imprinted here—here!" She struck her breast with clenched hands. "Oh, I shall die—I know it! There's no use for him to come now, I shall be dead." She turned her face to the wall while Tellectina sank down beside her, overwhelmed by despair.

Finally, at dusk, Olev appeared and had sunk into the first chair inside the door before they were aware of his presence. He sat there without speaking, spent and dusty, breathing heavily, as though he had had a long walk overland. It was then that Tellectina witnessed the first of two miracles.

Without a word the sick girl ran to him and kneeling beside his chair pressed her cheek against the sleeve of his coat and remained thus for a long time, motionless, saying within herself, " 'If I may but touch his garment, I shall be whole.' " Then, like the sick woman who touched the hem of Christ's garment and was healed, Femina arose healed and was made whole from that hour. No word was uttered, but quickly piling the pillows high on the couch Femina led the exhausted man to it. Gently she lifted his dusty feet, and then, leaning against the pillows, she opened her arms, and the weary man sank onto her breast with a sigh of relief. Not a word had been spoken since his entrance into the room. The man lay with closed eyes, while the woman slowly and gently stroked his hair.

Finally Olev began to speak in short broken sentences, in a low voice as if talking to himself; recounting all his experiences in Err; telling of the chicanery, the hypocrisy, and the graft he had encountered on every side; of the constant, terrific, and inevitably losing fight of the man handicapped by breeding, honesty, and indifference to money. He also spoke bitterly of the cruelty of being allowed only fifteen minutes to see his two daughters. Both sisters listened, but neither spoke nor moved: instinct warned them not to break the spell. The weary, disillusioned man unburdened himself; unshed tears stood in his eyes. And all the time Femina was softly weeping behind him, taking every precaution to prevent his seeing her tears.

As soon as the recital ceased, the man relaxed, fumbled blindly for her breast, pulled down her dress, and kissing her only once, sighed contentedly, and promptly fell asleep like a tired child with the tip of her breast still in his half-open mouth. With his head pillowed there, he slumbered peacefully, while Femina's desire for a child by this man whom she loved so desperately rose and swept through her with such hot consuming waves of yearning that her whole being ached unbearably. Her arms grew numb with his weight, but she remained motionless, fearful only that the warm tears falling on the beloved face on her breast might waken him. Afterwards she informed Tellectina that these were the happiest moments of her entire life; and that she could feel such tenderness surging up through her heart—through her breast—that it must have overflowed like warm milk, bathing and healing him; that she longed poignantly to nourish him with her love, her tenderness, her very blood and soul, if need be; that the conviction came to her that the only perfect happiness for her would be to sacrifice herself—her life—that her beloved might live more abundantly.

After having slept a few minutes, the man awakened, sat up briskly, and laughed joyously. "Oh, I feel splendid now! I'm a new man and as ravenous as a wolf. Beware that I don't devour you, sweet darling! Come, let's have quantities and quantities of dinner, shall us? Aren't you starving too?"

Hastily Femina brushed away the tears. The spell was broken. "Yes, yes," she faltered, "I'm—I'm hungry too. Do let's." And she managed to laugh as she rose unsteadily on benumbed limbs.

Tellectina was so dumfounded to see two people cured of illness and fatigue and misery by a mere touch of the beloved one that she stood gazing at them as though hypnotized, murmuring inwardly, "So miracles are possible, after all!"

As they departed for dinner, she concluded that the form of jungle fever of which these two were victims was beyond human analysis and composed of unearthly elements. Almost immediately after dinner, however, Olev's fever assumed another and more violent form, as it frequently had at night. As usual Tellectina was unable to be of any assistance to him whatsoever. It was Femina's name he constantly murmured as he lay tossing on her bed with his temperature rising steadily. The latter wrestled bravely with him until finally he lay as harmless as a lamb, as though all the strength had suddenly gone out of him. As on countless other nights, Tellectina sat by the bedside watching the man who slept contentedly, and the woman who lay beside him, bruised and nervously overwrought and staring wide-eyed at the ceiling. (She was also puzzled at this time by the brief appearance of Passino, Olev's servant, who was proving himself to be an absolute sluggard.) The pleasure which her sister apparently derived from the sacrifice of both her comfort and sleep was astounding. Tellectina was wondering how long Femina could continue such sacrifice when her speculations were interrupted by the sound of a woman's voice softly chanting in the darkness:

"When my love lies sleeping and I beside him—sleepless; oh, that is the hour of my eyes' delight! Like two starveling bees they rove stealthily over each dear feature of his face, culling superabundant sweetness to sustain them through the long winter of his absence. Too proud to look my fill while my love lies waking, I abandon my shy young soul to my ardent eyes."

There was a slight pause and then the song was resumed: "When my love lies sleeping and I beside him—sleepless; oh, that is the hour of my heart's delight! Like a miraculous fountain in the sands where no fountain ever was before, tenderness comes welling up, comes swelling up, within my heart; till, surcharged, it breaks its narrow bounds and flows over and about my love, soothing and healing him while he slumbers! The sweet excess of love brings inexplicable tears to mingle with the flood of ineffable tenderness flowing over my love."

This little song of Femina was chanted in a voice that was like the murmuring of bees. A pleasant sad drowsiness overcame Tellectina, and she drifted into sleep; while Femina, lying sleepless beside her lover, sank deeper and deeper into her sweet voluptuous sorrow which had not yet broken through her new-found happiness.

As soon as trouble did start, however, it rained upon the lovers thick and fast. Late one night Tellectina, in great perturbation, came to Olev's room at the little inn. After hastily sending his assistant out on some ostensible errand, he took her in his arms; but the girl was too excited and angry to remain still for long.

"Oh, Olev, Olev, I've been thrown out! That damned old landlady, Miss Thanedorn, found out about our—about us, and turned me out of her silly old boarding house!"

"The old hell-cat! How dare she! I'll——"

"Oh, she dared all right! And the names she called me aren't even in the dictionary! Said she wouldn't have a—a harlot—in her——"

Bursting into uncontrollable tears, Tellectina fell heavily against Olev's shoulder.

"The God-damned old bitch!" he exclaimed savagely. "Excuse me, darling, but—the infamy, the—— Oh, I'll attend to her!" The man rose and began to pace the floor in extreme agitation.

Bitterness crept into the girl's voice. "You can't attend to her. There's absolutely nothing you can do: that's the worst of it all —we are powerless against all the landladies in the whole world."

Suddenly Olev wheeled toward her. "I'm a beast to have got you into all this trouble. The only kind thing I can do is never to see you again."

The girl looked at him through narrowed eyes, thinking to herself, "The only kind thing you can do is to make me marry you tomorrow!" Aloud she said, "Oh, it doesn't really matter. Such people have the power to inconvenience one, that's all. I was a bit upset by the suddenness and vileness of her attack. When I came home from school this afternoon I found all my possessions packed and my luggage thrown in a heap by the gate—but outside, outside her garden, mind you. When I handed her the key to my bedroom door she drew back as if it were polluted. That angered me so much I flung it to the floor and told her she was an evil-minded, damnable old maid with a mind like a sewer; that I loved you; and that, yes, I did sleep with you and I didn't care if the whole world knew it! And that, besides, what I did was none of her damned business anyway! At that she commenced to cry, and I, like a soft-hearted fool, felt sorry for her; so I said nothing more but marched away with my head in the air. But she wouldn't even allow her house-man to carry my bags over to Mrs. Jones': I had to carry all those heavy bags over there myself, one at a time."

"Oh, you poor darling, why didn't you call on me? But, no, that would only have spread the news all the more. Oh, I am a brute to have ever allowed you to start this thing!"

"Well, I didn't mind being thrown out of my living quarters so much: what really concerned me was that she might tell the president of the college, and I'd lose my position."

"She wouldn't stoop to such a low—— Oh, Gawd, the things women do to women!"

"It's nothing," Tellectina reflected in bitter silence, "compared to the things men do to women!" To Olev, however, she said, "Oh, she assured me she'd stop at nothing; that she considered it her Christian duty to protect the innocent youth of the college from my immoral influence, and also other respectable landladies who were trying to make an *honest* living; and that she couldn't afford to give her own house a bad reputation."

"Sweet God!"

"She said she had already started the rumor that Miss Tel-

lectina Christian was always delinquent about paying her rent
and that anybody who took me in should ask for the money in
advance. And you remember how I always made a point of paying promptly every month? Oh, Lord, look at that clock, it's
midnight! I must fly, or I shall endanger my reputation even
more!" Olev kissed her tenderly and besought her not to worry.

But for the remainder of the night the girl lay on her bed
sobbing; tormented by thoughts the ignobleness of which served
only to torment her all the more.

Although Tellectina weathered this storm, she realized when
the wives of the faculty gradually one by one ceased to invite
her to their teas and dinner parties that she was under suspicion
and surveillance. That they knew nothing definite was also evi-
dent, inasmuch as they continued to nod coolly to her on the
street.

She pretended to find the situation vastly entertaining, saying to Olev at one of their clandestine meetings in the woods,
"They all bored me to extinction, anyway. It was only out of
policy that I didn't refuse their invitations too often. As you
know, I pleaded the excuse of work as often as possible. But the
inconsistent thing is—they continue to invite you, yet knowing
perfectly all the while that if there is a man—you are he! I am
certainly seen very seldom with any other male. It's so unfair
to lay all the blame on the woman!"

"It's damnably rotten and unjust," Olev agreed. "But society
is organized that way. And the maintenance of my position
forces me to attend their inane functions even yet. After all, the
laboratories are governmental too. But, come, let's forget all
the old cats and take a holiday! I hear that the scenery over at
the army post on the other side of old Cynosure is lovely. Let's
go there during your Easter vacation. We can just about make a
good tramp there and back in two weeks. Thank God, you love
cross-country tramping even in the jungle—though the mountain will be cool enough at night. I can carry most of the supplies: you will only have a light pack. We'll take books and

have a glorious time, leaving all the old local devils to stew in their own juice!"

The first part of their trip was a great success. They both enjoyed sleeping in the open, cooking over a wood fire, and wandering over the beautiful country at random. They laughed and loved—after Femina belatedly joined them—like sixteen-year-old children, until they arrived at the army post. The proprietor of the only inn there, however, refused to give them a room together on the grounds that his was a respectable hostelry and that he did not believe they were married since the woman wore no wedding ring and they both lacked the married air. Duty and decency obliged him to give them separate rooms.

Olev was so enraged he was on the point of exploding when Tellectina laughed and said, "Oh, never mind, two rooms will be a grand luxury!"

The man fumed for hours over this unpleasant incident, while Tellectina laughed as though she considered it the most delectable of jests. Later, when Femina slipped quietly into Tellectina's room, however, she saw to it that her sister's amusement changed into resentment toward Olev.

On their return to Cape Coverture, Olev read an account in the month-old paper from Err of his elder daughter's marriage. His very touching silence prompted Tellectina to invent an excuse in order to leave him alone immediately after the dinner of which he had eaten nothing whatever. With a strange distrait air he bade her good-bye at the door of her new lodgings.

No sooner had his footsteps died away than Femina appeared from nowhere, flung herself onto the bed, and began to sob violently. "Oh, yes, I saw everything, and *his* feelings are the only ones that matter! The one obvious thing does not occur to him. He is very upset because his darling little daughter, of whom he has seen almost nothing for ten years, should have married without his helpful presence! But the fact that her marriage frees him from her support so that now he is in a position for the first time to marry me—the woman he loves so unselfishly, with so much consideration—the woman he says he would go through hell fires to get—oh, no, *that* never once enters the back end of the brain of this brilliant scientist!"

"Oh," Tellectina exclaimed, "you terrible creature! You know I said I did not want to marry him, that I did not believe in the institution of marriage at all because——"

"Any man with an ounce of brains ought to know perfectly well that no woman means it when she says she doesn't believe in marriage! He's a fool; he shouldn't listen to your nonsense. He should force you to marry him!"

"Oh, Femina, Femina, I'm ashamed of you! But don't cry this way, you know these hysterical attacks always make you sick! It's becoming a habit."

"And whose fault is it? And whose fault is it if I cry and worry and take vile medicine and wreck my health every month? What on earth would happen if I did have an illegitimate child?"

"But, Femina, Olev says you are silly to worry, that there's absolutely no danger."

"Worry? What does the man know about worry? Why, when I'm late, the fear haunts me till at times I think I shall go insane! I hope I do cry till I make myself sick, I hope I die! It would serve him right. And I *would* die for all the effort he'd make to save me. If I were his wife, everything would be different. But I'm nothing, merely his—his mis——"

Instantly Tellectina's hand flew to her sister's mouth. "Don't you *dare* use such a word!"

"Well, then—his what? I have no name, no position, no claim, no rights, no anything—but misery and ostracism! And if his daughters—or even his divorced wife, the mother of his children, as he always calls her—and I were sick at the same time—he'd rush to them—not to me! And I want to come first!"

"But, Femina, you're his—his beloved, his real mate, his true wife, oh, his more than wife—in the finest and fullest sense of the word!"

Femina flung off her sister's comforting hands. "Words! Empty words! To hell with you, Tellectina, and all your damn-fool ideals about freedom! I want love and security. I want to occupy first place in his life. I want permanence and marriage and all that goes with marriage. And I want a child by him—legally. Oh, I would never have got into all this mess if it hadn't been for Tellectina, the mighty intellectual, and all her false idealism!"

"Why, Femina, what a low, ordinary female you are! You are a constant disappointment to me. And my ideas about marriage and woman's freedom are beautiful and right even if they don't work!"

"But, Tellectina, there seems to be some magic—especially to men—about that little word 'wife'! If a woman isn't married and gives a man her love and faith and sympathy and tenderness, if she places her whole life and happiness in his hands—what does she receive in return? The dominant male type takes all he can get and then grinds her heart under his heel. He not only wants to have his cake and eat it too, but wants her to serve it to him on bended knee. No, by God, a woman can't afford to be generous with any man! No man appreciates it—and that is a lesson I shall never forget!"

"Oh, Femina, how can you be so disloyal to such a marvelous man as Olev!"

"Because I'm honest, dammit! You're so blinded by your fine ideas of what people *ought* to be that you can't see what they really are. I've snapped my fingers in the face of every man I've ever known before in my life—with what result? They loved me twice as much for it! Men thrive on pain. They love only the women who are unkind to them!"

"Oh, I won't listen! I'm mortified for you, Femina!"

"Go on, be as mortified as you like, but remember that to men there is some magic about that silly little word 'wife.' And a man can swear he loves a woman till he's blue in the face, but there's only one proof—and that's marriage!" Horrified, Tellectina rushed from the room while Femina fell back on the bed sobbing.

Tellectina, however, consistently restrained Femina from even intimating her feelings to Olev. He remarked, however, that even Tellectina's gayety appeared forced nowadays and inquired why her face was so sad when in repose. To which the girl invariably replied, "It is simply your imagination," and redoubled her efforts to seem happy.

To the final blow, however, she succumbed completely. The president of the college summoned her to his office, where the sad-faced old gentleman reluctantly informed her that the multiplicity of the complaints coming to him compelled him to take action, or perhaps lose his own position, which he could ill afford considering the large family he had to put through college. He dismissed Tellectina from the faculty with tears in his eyes, urging her not to forfeit the love of Olev but either to marry him or be more discreet in the future.

This catastrophe succeeded in breaking down all her gallant defense. She lay in bed and sobbed until a high fever rendered her unable to meet Olev for dinner at the inn as she had promised. He rushed to the house only to receive word from the landlady that Tellectina was too ill to see him. Being Elam Domitann, he promptly entered, and sitting on the edge of her bed, stroked Tellectina's hand and talked endlessly. The girl lay silent and lifeless, with her face to the wall. After the man had delivered himself of violent fulminations against the president, the entire faculty, and particularly their wives, all the landladies and innkeepers of the world, fate and life, custom and tradition and bigotry and presumptuous Puritans, he finally said, "I'm a brute—we'd better be married soon. In fact, here's a letter from my mother concerning her forthcoming visit. It might be advisable to attend to it before her arrival: any open irregularity might upset her."

There was no response from the sick-bed except a faint faraway voice saying, "I'm very tired. Will you please go away now."

The man departed with a distinctly bewildered and somewhat offended expression on his face. At the door he said, "But of course you will marry me, won't you, darling? Say 'yes'—you don't want me to be in suspense all night, do you? That would be cruel of you."

As soon as the front door closed Femina burst into the room laughing hysterically. "It's cruel for us to keep him in suspense all night, but it's not at all cruel for him to keep me in suspense for a year! Our liaison might upset his mother, but that it might upset me or cause you to be turned out of house and home and job means nothing! I loathe the man. I wouldn't marry him if he were the last male on earth! He can go straight to hell for all I care! I never intend to speak to him again as long as I live!" For once Tellectina was too ill to confute Femina in any way.

When Olev called early the next morning with an enormous bouquet of flowers Femina flung them on the floor but Tellectina rose silently and went out to breakfast with him.

As she dallied with the untasted food on her plate the girl spoke without lifting her eyes. "Of course, you know, Olev, I don't really believe in marriage as an institution. I think a man and woman should be held together by nothing but love."

"You're quite right, darling. It's not that we need external bonds. We know after all these tests that our love is a thing which will endure for a lifetime. You are the perfect woman, you have everything: breeding, beauty, brains—charm, humor, tenderness, and fineness of character—you satisfy a man's every need—and his needs are many, as you know." He smiled significantly at her—disarmingly, as was his way. "It's not for that I think it advisable to have a legal ceremony. It's only to save you—for, of course, the world permits a man to do as he pleases —to save you, the woman, from unnecessary unpleasantness." To herself Tellectina added, "And to save your mother."

"Come," he continued, "one little woman can't defy the whole world alone. We'll have the simplest possible ceremony under our beautiful mimosa tree—our morning rendezvous where we first fell in love."

"But, Olev, you don't understand. It means that I'm failing in one of the chief ideals of my whole life. I should hate myself for compromising just for practical reasons. I don't object to suffering calumny for an ideal. I consider that we *are* married—profoundly and beautifully. For *this* is the real marriage: this love, understanding, sympathy, tenderness, respect—oh, we feel bound to each other by a hundred subtle ties far stronger than any mere law! Therefore it seems—well—wrong to sully it, and yet——"

While she hesitated, the words of the hurt and angry Femina resounded again in her ear. There was no denying that what her sister said was true. . . . And so they were married.

Tellectina asked Olev if he objected to marrying two women, to which he replied that one would have been only half a wife. The girl laughed, knowing full well that frequently he was unaware of which one was confronting him. But since Tellectina and Femina seldom evinced the desire to appear at the same time, except when the sisters were quite alone, it rendered this seemingly insurmountable difficulty a fairly simple matter.

It was decided that they should go to live in a charming little house surrounded by a beautiful garden, offered to them by a young widow who had been brought out to Coverture as a bride.

All of them, however, were too happy at the time to notice or care that although the sluggard Passino followed Olev into the new home, he very soon fell into a profound slumber and seldom put in an appearance at all thereafter.

During the first few weeks of marriage they were deliriously happy, having fallen in love with each other all over again and more violently than ever. As their fever mounted steadily, Tellectina and Femina went about in an absolute daze: putting salt in their coffee and sugar on their eggs, counting every hour till Olev should come home from work in the afternoons. Several times he came home unexpectedly to lunch, declaring himself unable to wait until dinner time to see her. Not infrequently the consumption of dinner required hours, impeded as it was by Femina's sitting upon Olev's knee; and often they would awaken at midnight to find their half-eaten dinner cold upon the table; this they considered such a huge joke on someone that it invariably sent them off into gales of hilarious laughter.

Time passed like a delirious dream of happiness during which all unpleasant things were disposed of by the very simple process of ignoring them. After a few weeks had passed, however, Tellectina emerged from her daze and became cognizant once more of what was going on around her.

One afternoon, after taking a short stroll, they seated themselves on the river bank; whereupon Olev, extracting the new copy of *Punch* from his pocket, began to peruse it in complete silence. The wife blinked at the man incredulously, then continued to sit opposite her husband, twiddling her thumbs and thinking her thoughts. This unprecedented incident, however, was repeated many times thereafter.

While Tellectina was preparing dinner that same evening Olev called out, "Can I help?"

She had no sooner replied, "No, thanks," than the man strolled into the kitchen.

"What on earth are you trying to do, cut your finger off? Give me that thing! I've never yet seen a woman who knew how to open a tin can properly, and it's as simple as a, b, c. Watch now, I'll show you."

He pressed down on the can firmly with the left hand and had it open in no time. "There you are!—But—but what the devil!"

"Oh, my dear, you've hurt yourself! You pressed too hard on the cut edge with your left hand. Here, let me put some disinfectant on it!"

"Get away with your silly medicines! It's nothing! If you'd had a decently sharp can opener it wouldn't have happened!"

The woman stared at him in amazement, opened her mouth, but said nothing, placing her hand over her lips instead. The man stalked majestically out of the kitchen. Then the wife removed her hand, and the smile broadened as she patiently fished out the drop of blood from the peach syrup in the top of the can. And the young bride had many such surprises in store for her.

The following morning she said to her husband, "When you go for your morning walk will you please bring me some of those lovely mimosas? The Joneses are coming to dine this evening, and I'd like a bouquet for the table."

"What! pick flowers for the Joneses and have a backache all the rest of the day?—No, thank you!"

"But—but, Olev, you used to bring them to me every week before we were married!"

"That's different."

Tellectina's chin trembled, and something tugged the corners of it down in spite of herself. "I guess it is different—and so are you. Oh, it's so terrible to see a lover change into a husband!" She rushed from the room in tears.

The man's voice came after her. "I haven't changed. I'll always be your lover. . . . There, don't, don't! Oh, you women, you're always crying over imaginary things!"

"Imaginary! I couldn't imagine such a harsh tone of voice in a bridegroom of two months!" Tellectina muttered as she flung herself onto the bed. And her silent enumeration of the countless "imaginary" things her husband had done to hurt her only provoked more tears. The list appalled even Tellectina, and although aware that he was nursing many resentments against her, she was convinced that her offenses could not approach his. A sort of seething undercurrent could gradually be felt flowing beneath the pleasant stream of their daily lives. It gathered momentum steadily until one day it broke through the surface, all the more forceful for having been held in check for six months.

As Tellectina came in the door one afternoon the sole greeting accorded her by her husband, as he glared up over his newspaper, was, "You're late."

"I know, and I'm sorry, darling. But I'll have dinner ready in no time. Don't be cross with me—I have good news! Guess what."

The man did not lift his eyes from his newspaper. "I don"t know!"

"You don't show much enthusiasm, I must say. I've been offered a position! That's why I was late. I met President Lindky on the street, and he was such a darling. He said he had never had such a good English instructor in all the thirty years of his presidency as I was; and that the antagonism at college had died down since I married—enough, anyway, that with his support I could teach there again this term. Isn't that wonderful?"

"I don't see anything very wonderful about that!"

"Oh, Olev, it's terribly wonderful! Because you know, dear, it has been straining you quite a lot to make enough since we married; and you've had to deprive yourself of things you wanted, as well as I. And now I can add to the income, and we can both live more comfortably."

"I was not aware that our life was uncomfortable."

"Oh, no, dear, I don't mean that—I mean we could have a few of the luxuries of life if I went back to work. And a maid."

"I'm quite content without luxuries and a maid."

"Oh, those are only minor issues. The real truth is, Olev, I *want* to go back to work. I've been wanting to for months— ever since the novelty of running a house wore off. I'm bored doing nothing all day long but rearranging chairs and planning dinner menus. In fact, I never wished to stop work even when we married, but I didn't imagine I could ever obtain another position as long as your work kept you on the Cape."

"I'm sorry that your marriage with me has bored you. And, of course, as a mere male I may be very dense; but I completely fail to comprehend why any woman who has a nice comfortable home wants to stand up all day in a schoolroom ramming syntax down the throats of half-wits! I should think any woman would welcome the opportunity to live a leisurely life with plenty of time to read and play the piano and amuse herself— or do whatever she likes."

"That's exactly what I *do* want: an opportunity to do what I

like! And I don't want to be amused: I want to do some kind
of constructive work, something of permanent value."

"I should think making a happy home a thing of permanent
value. And it could be a constructive thing if the wife weren't
more interested in herself than anything else."

"Thanks for the compliment. But, as it happens, you are infinitely more interested in yourself than anything else—even the
happiness of your wife. And I'll have you know that I'm not
just your appendage nor just a part of you. I'm a separate
entity. And keeping your house, cooking your meals, darning
your socks, and humoring your moods, to say nothing of picking up your soiled underwear and washing the dirty ring out
of your bathtub, somehow fails to fill my life satisfactorily."

"But you do many pleasant things and——"

"But nothing worth while—nothing permanent. God knows
there's nothing permanent in meals and socks. I tell you, the
day has passed when women can express themselves solely
through husbands and children and houses!"

"Oh, this modern-woman balderdash makes me sick!"

"There—there—you've admitted it! At last the truth is out!
You want women to be subordinate! Your mind still thinks in
the medieval age. 'You don't want a real person—you want a
bowl of jelly that you can press into your particular mold.' Well,
that would be nice for you but unspeakable for me. You say
before marriage that you admire intellect in a woman, but
afterward you resent it. And before marriage the man wants to
do the adoring, but afterward he certainly expects her to do all
the adoring. And you want to have all the brains—you want
to be the cock of the walk. The woman is to be treated as a
moron—not even to be trusted with money."

"But," the man remonstrated, "I don't understand you. Never
in all the months we've been married have I ever refused to
give you a cent you asked for!"

"Asked for! Asked for! That's the rub!" his wife exclaimed.
"That I *had* to ask for it. You refused even to give me an allowance. I presume morons aren't to be trusted. Well, now I'll tell

you the truth: women don't want to work primarily because of the work. No, but because once they've had a taste of financial independence it is too sweet ever to relinquish. I see now that it's only with financial independence that she can ever attain any other kind. As long as a woman permits a man to support her, it's in the very nature of the bargain that she must pay in return for that support by subservience to him, by allowing him to dominate her. And I don't like to be dominated a bit more than you do."

The man was growing angry too. "The trouble with you, young woman, is that you've got too damned much individuality and you're so afraid you aren't going to give expression to it that you're perfectly willing to wreck our marriage for its sweet sake! All you need is some children, and you'd stop all this nonsense about 'freedom.'"

"And I suppose it's my fault that we can't afford to have children!"

The man winced as if she had flicked him with a whip. "You modern women are too self-centered: that's the whole trouble with you. That's why you are failures as wives."

"But of course all men are perfect: the very personifications of unselfishness, that's why they have always been such notable successes as husbands!"

"Well, if a man let a woman's hands steer the ship, she'd be sure to wreck them both."

"Whereas, if he steers the marital ship the result is a blissfully happy and peaceful marriage—like this!" the woman retorted.

"And it would be happy if you would listen to sense," her husband persisted.

"You mean, if I'd listen to you, Sir Oracle! Of course, it would be a very happy and peaceful marriage if I'd lie down and be your doormat—happy, that is, for you! You think you are infallible—for the very excellent reason that you are a man."

The man picked up his newspaper with an air of finality.

"Well, I think you are very inconsiderate of me in wishing to return to work."

"Incon—— My God!" The woman laughed. "Male psychology is the eighth wonder of the world!"

"You have only thought of your own pleasure, you haven't stopped to think what a fool a husband looks and feels when his wife advertises to the world that he can't support her adequately. You haven't stopped to consider how I shall feel when I come home from work all tired out and find no wife. You haven't stopped to consider how I shall be obliged to sit at home alone on those evenings when you go to some damned school whirligig the way you used to do before we were married. And when you do stay at home for an evening, do you think I am going to enjoy the society of a tired, cross wife? The man may come home tired and cross sometimes after a hard day's work earning bread for *her*, but you haven't stopped to consider——"

"And I see there are a few more things I haven't stopped to consider," his wife said, interrupting him. "I haven't stopped to consider that my husband doesn't care a tinker's damn how bored I am or whether I am happy or not. I haven't stopped to consider that I have married an utterly selfish unreasonable man who thinks he can tyrannize over a woman just because she is so unfortunate as to be his wife. And I'll tell you another thing I haven't stopped to consider, and that is, that you are fifty years behind the times and that your idea of making a woman subservient is—is—unbearable! I've endured quite a lot these last six months that you are blissfully unaware of! Being married to you has certainly been no bed of roses!"

"Well, since we're exchanging compliments, my dear wife, I might say that being married to a headstrong woman, such as my wife has proved herself to be on closer acquaintance, has hardly been like embracing lilies of the valley, either. There can't be two masters in one house, and the sooner you learn that the better. And you never make allowances for the fact that, after all, the breadwinner is entitled to some rights. Your sense of appreciation is hardly your strongest characteristic. But I won't have my wife going out to work every day, and that settles it!"

Lifting his paper, the man shook it violently and glared at one spot without moving his eyes.

"Well, you *have* settled it, and in fine fashion too! For I'll have you know, my dear husband, I'm not dependent on you for love or money or anything else. I wouldn't take a cent of your old money if I starved to death! I can take quite as good care of myself as you can. I'm through with you and all your damnable domineering! So—good-bye!"

Catching up her hat and purse again, she made for the door. Her husband rose from his chair but did not move. With her hand on the latch of the screen door Tellectina paused: such a sick sensation invaded her that she felt overpowered. She turned, and on beholding the stricken face of the crushed figure standing in the center of the room—the man who was usually so straight and self-confident—she felt her heart melt within her and with a sob flung her purse to the floor and rushed to her husband with open arms.

He held her fiercely to him, murmuring brokenly, "We are such damned fools!"

Smiling through her tears Tellectina said, "But I'm the damnedest!"

"The damneder, you mean. Miss Teacher-of-English mustn't use the superlative for the comparative."

They laughed sheepishly like two guilty children; then, catching her up in his arms, Olev bore her to the next room. . . .

Late the following morning Tellectina put her hand to her head wondering what made it so uncomfortable, to find that she was still wearing her hat. Laughter escaped her lips involuntarily. Olev awoke at once. "What—what the——"

"My hat! I slept in it all night, and look! most of my clothes too! And—and, why, Olev, we didn't have any dinner at all last night! Oh, wasn't it glorious!"

"You're a divine creature! I didn't know any woman could be so—so divinely passionate."

"I didn't either; it was the first—I mean the best time for me."

"Which only goes to prove that most of it is psychological."

"But not all—not all," Tellectina said with significant emphasis which her husband failed to notice.

"It was almost worth quarreling to have such a heavenly—er—reunion! But you will let me take that job, won't you?—because I've already signed the contract."

"You little devil—of course I will." And he kissed her again.

Tellectina believed Olev was really reconciled to her return to work, but his strange sullen moods of the ensuing months finally proved that he had capitulated rather than lose her. The secret feeling of umbrage still persisted and rankled.

The long evenings when Olev left Tellectina alone while he remained at the laboratory working overtime were particularly propitious for resentful brooding on her part; but those during which he left her alone to spend a few hours with his men friends were even more so.

After glaring at her book with unseeing eyes for half an hour one night, she finally gave voice to her feelings.

"Yes, when I'm unavoidably kept late at my work that's terrible—it always annoys him. But if he stays late of his own volition, that is all right. I'm supposed to overlook that and greet him with a smile. And is it my fault that women are so stupid I can't spend my evening with them? And when I endeavored to fill up a few of my lonely evenings with an old man friend didn't he storm like a Comanche Indian? Being a single woman had its difficulties, but being a successful wife requires the tact of a diplomat and the patience of an archangel! But I know a solution. I'll start working on my travel diary again. I have enough material for a dozen books right under my hand, for no adventure in Nithking could furnish more surprises or knowledge of life than marriage. In fact, to explore the male mind and personality in the realm of matrimony is a far more hazardous and startling undertaking than cutting one's way through impenetrable jungles. I do love Olev, but he is so —so difficult—so obstinate. Still, I'm sure he'll be proud of me when he sees what an intelligent record of Nithking I've been keeping."

Thereafter she occupied her lonely hours with writing, and when her husband inquired if she had had a nice time reading while he was away, she invariably smiled and answered, "Yes."

The accounts of the older and more seasoned explorers of the Forbidden Country, whom Olev was constantly inviting to visit them, acted as a stimulus to the young woman; albeit the humorous accents with which some of them spoke Reasonese made it impossible for her to understand even half of what they said. Olev introduced Tellectina to an endless stream of men, famous for their explorations of Nithking, but those to whom he was most hospitable were: Cabell and Mencken, Villon and Voltaire, Richard Garnett, Aristophanes and Ovid, Boccaccio and Rabelais.

One night, after a particularly stimulating tale told by Voltaire, Tellectina decided to reveal her great secret to Olev. Relishing in anticipation his great delight at her confession, she nevertheless approached his work table rather shyly. She exhibited the notebook of her travels in Nithking, pointing out that she was keeping it in Reasonese and outlining to him her treasured plans for a future travel book with philosophical undertones.

Flipping through several pages, the man gave them a cursory glance, then said, "Very nice, very nice," and, returning it, buried himself in his chemistry book again.

Too stunned to speak, Tellectina mechanically took the notebooks. She stood there motionless, as stung by his indifference and masculine resentment as though he had flicked her in the face with a whip. As soon as the pain and shock of it lessened she turned slowly and walked into the next room, muttering fiercely under her breath, "Just because I'm a woman the man doesn't want me to do any creative work! Oh, how *can* such a generous nature be so petty! Well, some day I'll show him if it's the last thing I ever do!"

She patted the little waterproof notebook fondly. Her love for Olev was so great, however, that she forgave him—for the time being. Moreover, the daily discoveries of many new and unpleasant characteristics in herself tended to equalize her resentment toward her husband. In fact, Tellectina's proudest boast—that she and Femina did not act like the ordinary wife—was endangered more frequently each day. She was aghast to discover herself actually nagging her husband to wear his overshoes one rainy day, at which he flared up angrily and stalked out of the house—without the overshoes.

After a very merry dinner that evening, during which overshoes were not mentioned, Olev had settled down to work on some chemical formulæ when he was interrupted by Femina who, on passing behind his chair on her way to bed, tweaked his nose playfully and ran off laughing mischievously. After her departure Tellectina entered and curled up in a big chair across the room to darn her husband's socks. Her eyes constantly strayed, however, to the man bowed over the papers and books piled high in front of him. Her eyes caressed the figure lovingly till suddenly she crushed her hand over her left breast to still the pain there. "Oh, love is so sweet, it hurts! Oh, God grant that nothing ever comes to take him away from me!"

At midnight she besought him to stop work. He replied that it was impossible. At two Tellectina awakened from a troubled sleep, made Olev some tea, and again pleaded with him to go to bed. "But, darling, if you ruin your health entirely, then you will have defeated your own purpose."

When the man finally glanced up with a tired harassed look she exclaimed, "Oh, Olev, Olev, you look like a ghost! This can't go on many more nights. You've been losing sleep for months."

Her husband made no reply but continued his rapid writing. Suddenly Tellectina dropped to her knees at Olev's side, "Oh, my love, my love, you don't understand. I'm so afraid—so afraid that you'll make yourself ill *permanently*—so afraid that you might—" she whispered it—"that I might lose you forever! Oh, I try to act intelligently for your sake, but—— That's what's behind a woman's scolding—nagging, if you want to call it that! For the first time in my life I understand the eternal wife's worry. I'm just a wife too, like any other woman. Illness and death—they are the spectres that may rob her of her happiness. It's fear—fear—and love—fear that her heart will be broken; fear that she'll be left alone in the world; that her whole future life will be ruined—and mine would be ruined irremediably if —if I lost—you!"

"Ah, beloved little woman, you distress yourself unnecessarily. Come—you must get your sleep." Lifting her in his arms, he carried her back to bed and, sitting beside her, soothed her with gentle words. With a promise to stop soon he returned to his desk but worked on until dawn.

Tellectina never ceased to be amazed at the way in which marriage moved forward in cycles of happiness and misery. About three o'clock one morning she was awakened by the mutterings of Femina, who was pacing up and down the floor of the living room. Slipping out of bed, Tellectina went in to her sister.

"What on earth is the matter, Femina?"

"I can't sleep! I haven't slept a wink all night."

"What's happened?"

"Oh, just the usual thing!" she responded in a bitter tone. "And I'm pretty damned sick of it, too!"

"You mean Olev had another nocturnal attack?"

"Yes, and more violent than usual!"

"How is he now?"

"Oh, *he* is all right. He's sleeping like a baby now—he always does. I'm the one that suffers when his fever takes this delirious form. Oh, my nerves are on ragged edge. I'm sore and bruised all over. He frightens me when his fever mounts so high and he gets so hot and all bathed in perspiration, and he becomes so violent he hurts me. I'm just a nervous wreck after I get him quieted down! At first the primitive female in me loved his disregard for me, and I loved him so much I thought whatever he did was right, but now——"

She clenched her fists and ground her teeth. "Now I've come to hate him for it!"

"No, no, Femina!" Tellectina gasped in horror. "You love him, I love him, no matter what he does. You cannot hate your husband whom you love better than your own life."

"But I do hate him—at times—so you've got to speak to him about it, Tellectina. I can't endure it any longer."

"But—but, you know how much courage it requires to criticize an Elam Domitann about anything. He gets up on his dignity at once. However, it would be unfair to him as well as to you—to remain silently critical. I am sure he doesn't know——"

"Doesn't know! Well, he ought to! He's so much older and wiser and more experienced in everything than we are. After all, he must have been subject to these delirious fevers long before he met me. He must have called upon a good many other women to quiet him. He was certainly married once before."

"But, Femina, it's a fever that affects all husbands. I remember hearing Mother and her married friends complain, saying that when delirious all men were beasts and that wives simply had to submit. So I suppose nature intended it to be this way. Apparently it's always unpleasant for the woman, but even if it is a natural law, it's damned unfair to the woman, and I rebel against it. Perhaps we should consult a doctor and see if we've been using the best methods."

"Doctor, nothing!" Femina said in disgust. "There is only one thing the matter, and that is the absence of Passino. Passino is supposed to be the servant of Olev and should help me attend him at such times. I have reason to know that the sluggard is simply asleep near here somewhere. Although I do not know the full powers of Passino, I am sufficiently well acquainted with him from other days to realize that he is what we need now. And if Olev would only see to it that Passino helped me quiet him during these nocturnal spasms, it would not be nearly so wearing on me. Olev blames me for being irritable when he is the cause of it all. God, I never dreamed that any human being on earth could be as selfish as a male!"

"Yet," said Tellectina, "I took it for granted that Passino and his master were inseparable. I never dreamed that they could or would exist separately."

She was seriously perturbed and consequently promised to speak to Olev. The very next night, when he seated himself on the edge of the bed, Tellectina put her arms about her husband and in faltering tones informed him of Femina's difficulty. He replied in rather pained surprise that he was not aware of Passino's absence.

"That's exactly why I am telling you, sweetheart. But it's your duty to awaken him from his prolonged lethargy, not hers."

"If my nocturnal attacks, as she calls them, annoy her so much, we can sleep separately."

"Now, darling, don't be ridiculous. Listen, and I'll tell you what Femina thinks is the quickest way to arouse Passino." And thereupon she informed him of that which it is not lawful to record.

The next morning, after Olev had gone to work, Tellectina returned to Femina, who was still in bed.

"Well?"

"Oh, Tina, it was worse than ever. He tried to follow your instructions but did it so consciously, so grudgingly—like a martyr—that—oh, it's all hopeless, he's not going to change his way of doing anything—even if the world should come to an end. No matter how agitated he has made me he never makes the slightest effort to restrain himself once his fever has begun to mount, or to do anything to quiet me so I can sleep. Oh, it's hopeless—there's nothing to do but endure it, I suppose, since I love him." She began to sob.

"You call it 'love'!" Tellectina retorted. "I tell you that to any detached intelligent person you are simply the victim of an attack of tropical fever. You aren't normal, and you can't imagine how ridiculous and absurd your actions appear to me, how void of logic and sense. Is it logical to allow *one* person to hold your life's happiness in his hands? Is it fair to yourself to permit any other human being to endanger your health? Is it sensible that another's frown should make you weep and his smile make you happy! It's illogical and preposterous that our happiness should in any way depend on one man when there are hundreds of other nice men in the world. Why not take one of them?"

Femina laughed pityingly at her sister, as if her question were too foolish to answer. As time went on, however, Femina became more restless and discontented. One morning Tellectina studied her sister's face in the mirror before which she was petulantly putting up her long black hair.

"What exactly *is* the matter with you, Femina? Has your fever abated so much?"

"I don't know—all I know is that I'd like to be worshiped myself sometimes."

"Oh, you've been worshiped by too many men—you're spoiled. But I'm thankful to find at least one person who is himself worthy of worship. That's why we love him so much probably: because he doesn't worship us."

The flicker of a smile passed over Femina's lips. "Well, Olev the Third is the first man I've ever met in my entire life whom I couldn't twist around my little finger."

"Yes, but there's such a thing as carrying male dominance too far. I don't object—in fact, I prefer my husband to have a stronger personality than I have and to be my superior generally; but he abuses his power too much. The female says she wants a mate strong enough to dominate her and at the same time one weak enough for her to dominate; while the intellectual woman desires an equally impossible duality in her husband! Oh, is there no solution to the marriage problem for an intelligent woman! It's all so confused and confusing! Marriage is so different from what I had expected."

"And yet, Tina, with all his great scientific mind, Olev doesn't make the slightest effort either to diagnose or cure any ailment we may have—psychological or physical. And he winces at criticism like a spoiled child. In fact how such a mature, intellectual, brilliant man can spend so much of his time behaving like an obstinate little twelve-year-old boy is beyond my comprehension!

"Oh, yes, Tellectina always tries to find excuses for him," Femina mocked. "But when he hurts me, I don't feel that he's a little boy—I hate him!"

"Oh, Femina, surely a woman can't hate the man she loves!"

The other woman laughed unpleasantly. "Hate is a mild word. Why, I swear it, at moments when Olev has done something to wound my feeling, I have only one impulse in the world—and that is to kill him!"

Tellectina drew back. "Oh, you—you savage! Kill the person you love best in the world?—the person whose death would kill you? It doesn't make sense."

Femina merely laughed.

"Oh," Tellectina sighed, "is there no logic in love—or marriage either? One always hears that love and hate are very closely related, and yet one believes nothing until personal experience proves its reality."

"When a woman is hurt, as no one has the power to hurt her except the man she loves, the impulse to strike back is stronger than any other impulse in the world—it's primitive and irresistible. It frightens even me. At moments I hate the man I love with a sort of exquisite agony."

"Oh, Femina, this is terrible, and your emotions are so strong you act on them before I can speak to you."

"But if I give expression to them I feel better at once."

"Yes, it astounds me that you never seem to love him so much as just after you've called him all the worst names in your very unladylike vocabulary."

Femina smiled. "Marriage is like that. But I wish I knew some really vile words."

"Oh, you sicken me," her sister said. "Perhaps, however,

Freud was right after all. But what is this deep dark uncontrollable antagonism that arises between a man and woman who are married?"

"I have certainly never felt it before toward any man I've known. Perhaps I've never before loved any man enough to hate him," Femina said.

Then suddenly her eyes closed to the narrow slits of the inscrutable feline. "And he should be more demonstrative. But I know ways of making him show his love."

The voice grew remote and enigmatic. "Oh, yes, he seems like a curious plant, this taciturn lover of mine; like a plant that charmed me strangely as a child—one whose leaves gave forth no fragrance till crushed and bruised by a heedless hand. And I? I shall bruise the lordly heart of this silent lover of mine between my careless fingers, with slow deliberation, with sure divination, until his voice so cold and confident grows warm and falters with aching tenderness; till he looks at me reproachful, with love lying wounded in his eyes; till his indifferent hands, bewildered, seek me swiftly like a tortured thing." She smiled mockingly. "Ah yes! For you, O man, are but a child forever, and I am eternally old and wise. I know ways, cunning ways. I have power, subtle power—else why am I a woman, O man?" Rising and arching her back, Femina glided away with a slow sinuous movement. Recoiling as though from a serpent, Tellectina shuddered and fled in the opposite direction.

And when she later saw Femina put her threat into practice, Tellectina looked on in horrified fascination—lacking the power either to speak or prevent it.

The happiness of their married life continued to fluctuate like the sea: first they were happy, then they were unhappy. As the months passed, however, the waves of ecstasy did not carry them so high, nor were the depths of misery so abysmally low. Gradually they came to accept each other's shortcomings till a calmness, a deep content, unlike anything Tellectina had ever experienced before in her whole life, pervaded her being. Sometimes, when her husband spoke, his thought was so like her own that she would look up at him startled, wondering whether it was he or she who had uttered their common thought, wondering if they were actually two separate people or only two separate parts of the same person. He seemed at times to be as much a part of her as her own arms or her own limbs.

Almost two years had passed—two full ripe years—enriched by shared suffering as well as shared happiness, when one memorable night all the young wife's happiness seemed to concentrate itself into a few brief moments; all the sweetness of marriage seemed to rise like an essence.

As they sat in their small library after dinner, Tellectina lifted her eyes, letting them rest lovingly on the man across the room; then looked at the walls composed of varicolored books, at the vases of gay tropical flowers, and back again at the figure in the little pool of light. Her eyes caressed her husband lingeringly. Such a sweet sadness stole through her that its poignancy pierced her heart and brought a mist of tears to blur her sight. And a slow sweet song of marriage sang like the murmurings of a brook through the woman's heart:

"This is marriage: this end of long waiting, this balm that heals years of yearning, this peace that goes down to the depth of being and quiets the troubled waters of the soul.

"Does not his man's mind encompass my mind? Does not my woman's tenderness cover him like a cloak?

"Oh, the sweetness, the completeness of sleeping in a man's arms! The reassuring touch of his dear warm body against mine, his arms about me to guard me from the dangers of the world.

"Man is strong, and swiftly I seek his protection. Man is but a child, and I am woman, the eternal mother. My breasts are soft for his weary head and his troubled spirit.

"Marriage is a refuge from the storms of misfortune, the cold winds of life.

"The two threads of our lives are interwoven inextricably into a newer and subtler pattern.

"It is a mighty chord of music, and the days of our lives move to the sound of that harmony.

"We are like two trees transplanted side by side, separate to the eye, but in the dark underground of our beings grown together forever in a strange dual oneness.

"This is marriage: this warm glow at the center of my being, at the core of my universe.

"All emptiness is filled, all hunger is fed, all seeking, all questing is ended: we look inward, not outward.

"We have discovered the old secret beauty that lies hidden in those two homely words—'marriage' and 'home.'

"That abused and bitter word 'wife' blossoms anew in the warmth of true marriage, shedding a strange new fragrance.

"That much-maligned word 'husband' comes to mean lover and friend and more: the breath of my body, the beat of my heart, my love and my life.

"The great love that men dream of—that women weep for— I have known. If he dies tonight, I have enjoyed the ultimate happiness of human life. I am a woman loved and loving, enriched—completed.

"And this is marriage."

Feeling her eyes upon him, the man lifted his head and gave the woman such a long, penetrating look of tenderness that it suddenly bereft her of breath. She dropped her own hastily— it was impossible to look at a human soul completely bared.

Like one in a trance, the woman murmured, "Beyond this I want nothing! Beyond this I want nothing! Ah, it is too good to be true, it is too good to last!"

Her words proved ironically prophetic, for it was only a few days later that their harmonious routine was suddenly threatened by the declaration of civil war between two of the states of Err.

As soon as it appeared in the newspapers, Tellectina denounced it in no uncertain terms; but she was later to recall that Olev had remained ominously silent on the subject. One day he came home with a strange, determined look on his white face.

His wife ran to him at once. "What, what is it? Are you ill? Have you lost your position? Is it your mother? Oh, tell me, what is it, Olev?"

He did not look at her, but sat down heavily in his reading chair. "I've signed up. A boat goes down river early tomorrow to meet the troopship from the army post. The first volunteers from Coverture are going on her."

His wife stared at him speechless, swayed slightly, closed her eyes for a sickening moment, then placed her hands on his shoulders. "Say it isn't true. Oh, my dear, it *can't* be! You said you didn't believe in war! You can't . . . you wouldn't leave . . . *me*. Oh, why didn't you tell me before you signed up?"

"Because I knew you'd object," her husband replied.

Tellectina argued, pleaded with him, repeated everything he had ever said against war, but the man only sat stolidly on, staring at the floor. Finally she rose from her knees and with a hopeless air walked into the next room and fell across the bed. But she was not able to cry, and there was a terrible sickening weight in the very pit of her stomach.

Olev entered and, sitting on the edge of the bed, stroked her hair. "But don't you see that it's a question of loyalty, of honor? It's as if a man's mother were in danger—he doesn't stop to think, he simply leaps to her defense."

"But your country is not in danger—you know that. When Mr. Clearsea returned from Err last week he proved to us that it is merely a matter of politics and graft. It is not a cause worthy of a fine man's life and sacrifice. Stop and think, Olev, for God's sake!"

"It is not a matter one thinks about. One's feelings, one's traditions, go deeper than all the logic in the world."

"But it's only a petty civil war."

"But the land that gave me birth, that to which I owe all that I am, which has given me all my opportunities, needs me; I have accepted everything at her hands—am I then going to refuse to reciprocate when she needs me?"

"Sentimental nonsense! You have paid already, you are paying back the state every day of your life for all she does for you —in both your work and in actual money, too. After all, what are taxes?"

"It's time to get my things together," he said quietly. "I've arranged everything at the laboratory so my assistant can carry on. I wanted the last night free for you."

"But your daughters and your first wife—what will become of them if—if——"

"Both girls are married now, and Emma can live with them till I come back. The war won't last long, we'll be back in a few months. Come, aren't you going to help me pack, sweetheart?"

"No," Tellectina said dully. "If you loved me you could not go."

" 'I could not love thee, dear, so much,
    Lov'd I not honor——' "

"Please spare me that, Olev. Honor is just a pretty word. Honor has nothing to do with this war or any other. You are simply a slave to a savage tradition, that's all. If all men faced the truth and refused to go out and get killed to fatten some politician's purse there would never be any war—anywhere."

Without a word Olev began to pack.

The whole town was seething with excitement. People began to run in and out of the house—women were crying; they looked resentfully at Tellectina when she replied that she was not proud of her husband for being one of the first volunteers but thoroughly ashamed of him for being swayed by emotion instead of thought.

That night Tellectina and Femina both lay awake all night while Olev got a little fitful sleep with his head resting on Femina's breast. They rose early to catch the boat, Femina accompanying Olev, but Tellectina remaining obstinately behind.

The wives and children were allowed to accompany their men on the boat down to the fork of the river where the troopship was to await them.

Femina felt curiously numb all over. They made almost the whole trip without speaking. Olev was as dumb as she was. Only one thing did he say to her as she clung to him when they said good-bye, "In love there is no death," and made her repeat it. Her lips moved, but no sound came forth.

The women and children waved to the figures on the departing ship as long as it was in sight. Several women chided Femina as they passed her saying, "Send him away with a smile."

Femina glared with fierce hatred at these babbling women but stood like a person tongue-tied. Not till the troopship turned a bend in the river and Olev was completely lost to view did Femina find the relief of tears. She sobbed hysterically—aloud—holding so tightly to the rail that her knuckles were white with the strain. The tears rolled down her face onto her dress and wet her hands, but she made no effort to dry them. Women stopped and spoke consoling words to her, but she was deaf to them.

Finally, out of sheer exhaustion she dropped to a bench, still sobbing quietly. When she looked around her no one else was crying except a few very young women. Femina glared in horror at the fat matrons sitting placidly around her talking to their neighbors about their children's malaria and new recipes for salads. "What," Femina muttered fiercely to herself, "have they no hearts under those fat bosoms of theirs?"

Days . . . weeks . . . months passed, while Femina waited. Tellectina had fallen into a motionless stupor. One day official notice came that Olev had been killed in action. But Femina continued to await his return just as before. It seemed very odd to receive letters from him no longer, but it was as if he had gone away on an even longer trip. The idea that she would never see him again was beyond her comprehension. He became more vividly alive to her dead than he had ever been while alive. She was more acutely aware of him now than she had been while he resided under the same roof with her. "In love there is no death." Now she understood what Olev had meant.

His image was so deeply imprinted on her mind and so constantly before her eyes that she had to stare twice at every man she passed in the streets to assure herself that he was not Olev.

Weeks passed, and still Femina awaited the return of the man she loved. She went about her daily tasks automatically, with the curious sensation that she was a hollow shell, and with an uncanny sense of unreality, as though she were not really present at all, and as if she were watching a stranger go through certain motions. There was no beauty anywhere in the world; when she looked at the sunsets she had once thought so glorious, she wondered how anything so stupid as a conglomeration of colors smeared on the sky could mean anything to anybody. And the tropical flowers appeared as ridiculous splotches of futile color. The world was gray and empty.

"Oh, it's the emptiness, the loneliness, the eternal waiting that I can't stand! Oh, why, why doesn't he come back to me? I've waited so long; I've tried to be so patient; please—please, send him back to me now. The desolation—the desolation will destroy me—what can I do? I'm so helpless, so helpless!"

Periodically the realization of his death would suddenly pierce her like a knife, and each time she felt as if it temporarily unbalanced her mind.

At other times she would grow rebellious, declaring, "It isn't true! Such things are impossible. It's too monstrous—such undeserved cruelties do not happen!"

She wandered about the house gazing at his empty clothes hanging in the closet, at his motionless walking sticks, at the empty chair at his desk.

Femina's fever seemed to increase steadily: she became delirious, she started up a hundred times at the fancied sound of his voice, at the sound of his footsteps on the veranda, at the sight of his beloved pale face floating through every room in the house. Finally a dumb sort of anguish took complete possession of her, and she hardly ate or slept.

"The terrible thing," Tellectina said, "is my helplessness. Nothing I can do will ever alter the situation one iota. In the face of death a human being is so impotent—oh, the knowledge of one's impotence, of the inexorableness of death—that is the hardest thing to bear! All one's rebellion—grief—longing, will never bring the dead back to life—all, everything, is futile! But where is all that quick joyous movement, all that gay laughter that was Olev? Where has it gone, I say? It maddens me not to be able to find it again!"

These words so engulfed Femina in misery that finally despair impelled her that night to go out of the house and up to the top of the mountain near Lovers' Grave where she had so often gone with Olev. She lay with her face to the ground near the old crater, pleading with Tellectina to send her over the edge to a welcome death. Tellectina hesitated—and hated herself for her hesitation.

"But why don't I do it, why?" she asked herself. "I think a person has a perfect right to take her own life if she sees fit. And we, I, see fit—I wish to die. It isn't that I'm afraid to live—it's simply that I have no desire to live any longer. What sort of a world is this, what sort of life force is it that without reason cuts off a man in the prime of his life! I don't want to live in this kind of a world which has neither rhyme nor reason!"

And still she hesitated. A faint glimmer of hope burned steadily in the innermost recesses of her being and cried aloud for life. While Femina lay numb and motionless, Tellectina stood aloof—detached, watching the other's suffering. "Oh, but is it possible that I revel in the luxury of sorrow? Can't I even give myself up wholly to grief?"

Tellectina surreptitiously extracted a notebook in which she recorded her discoveries in Nithking. Attached to it was a small yellow container; and though despising herself for employing it at such a time, Tellectina applied this drug in the prescribed manner and for a while forgot that sorrow existed in the world anywhere. . . .

Femina, meanwhile, was sleeping profoundly, as she invariably did when her sister resorted to the little gray powder in the cylindrical yellow container. In fact they had both lain on the edge of Lovers' Grave all night. The climax of their grief had been passed when dawn came.

Although the pectoralitis fever was in her blood forever, it had grown sufficiently dormant for Tellectina's old wanderlust to return. Rising slowly, she gazed down the road on the other side of the mountain—vast tracks of unexplored Nithking lured her on. Femina, however, remained behind; and the last Tellectina saw of her, she was lying there at the edge of the crater. The latter packed her kit and departed from Coverture before any of the other inhabitants were astir.

Coming finally to the grasslands, she encountered an unused road which she involuntarily followed. During the day she trudged on without stopping, but at night the loneliness seemed almost unbearable until she realized that she had been inwardly conversing with Olev for some time just as though he had actually been present. "Ah, yes, he lives within me forever! I carry his image in my heart, and I shall never be alone again. And I never really knew what love was until I lost it. And now when in doubt all I need to say is—not as I said as a child, 'What would Jesus do?' but—'What would Olev do?' He will henceforth accompany me wherever I go, for 'in love there is no death.'"

And placing her hand on her heart she looked down and was not at all surprised to see a red mark resembling a small face there on the under side of her left breast. "Ah," she murmured ecstatically, "a stigma!"

This knowledge seemed to bring her a great feeling of relief: she felt free of her grief in a sense, for she was carrying it in her heart forever. Her eagerness to find Certitude, which a happy marriage had kept quiescent for two years and grief obliterated, now reasserted itself more forcibly than ever. "I may have learned more in those two years of marriage to Olev, however, than I would have in exploring Nithking proper."

The two years' siege of walking pectoralitis had left her nerves in that strange, abnormally alert condition in which the more violent forms of tropical fever invariably leave high-strung people. As a consequence she was more keenly alive than she had ever been before in her entire life—a condition which made her next experience almost inevitable. As the dim road brought her to the edge of the Great Jungle of Otherpeoplesideas, she felt a tremendous thrill at the prospect of the exciting adventure which now lay before her.

CHAPTER VIII

RUSHING FORWARD, the young explorer boldly plunged into the jungle on confident feet. Almost immediately, however, the brilliant sunshine which had lighted her way heretofore changed into a wan greenish light. Tellectina groped her way through the veritable maze, confused by the very prodigality of nature. Monkeys chattered on every side, laughing at her bewilderment, so at home were they in this jungle of Otherpeoplesideas.

Hot, weary, and confused, the explorer finally sank to the ground to rest and, looking up, contemplated the vast green walls which rose on every side. "All my life I have heard of this jungle, but I never realized until necessity forced me through it that it was so extensive and so formidable. It is surely logical to assume, however, that Certitude lies at the other end of this jungle—its name implies as much, it seems to me. But wouldn't the surest and quickest, and certainly the easiest, way to reach this Mt. Certitude be to follow the paths made by others? Because I doubt if I have the strength, even if I possess the knowledge and experience, to blaze a trail of my own.

"Now, wouldn't the wisest procedure be to seek the trails made by the most famous explorers of Nithking the world has ever produced? Why, of course, and it is generally conceded that the greatest expeditions through these regions were made by the ancient Greeks. If they prove too difficult to follow, however, I can investigate others; for the German and English have made great names as explorers."

After locating these world-famous trails the young woman found to her disappointment that she was unable to follow them without great discomfort to herself; consequently she returned to her starting point and sought others less intricate and exhausting.

The numerousness and diversity of the trails was in itself a further confusion. They all appeared to go in different directions. In fact, on every side of the jungle tree trunks bore the names of explorers and the dates of their expeditions carved into the wood.

Tellectina decided to be guided by the names of those who had made the most recent expeditions through Nithking, hoping that modern methods would render traveling less strenuous for an amateur explorer.

First she chose the trail blazed by the Rolland and Christophe Expedition, following it to the very end; but she was puzzled and disappointed when it failed to bring her to Certitude. Intersecting this at right angles, however, appeared another broad path marked, "Nietzsche and the Nihilist Party." So the young explorer followed in Nietzsche's footsteps for some time but the ruthlessness with which he had cut down everything that stood in his way made her turn aside.

It was with relief that she espied a narrow but well-trodden trail made by the Lewis and Babbitt Expedition of '22. She followed this until it led her into another path which bore the sign, "The Mencken Expedition," which she pursued with ease and delight for some time.

Gradually, however, the realization was forced on her that every path was crossed by a dozen others, many of which seemed actually to go around in circles. She followed first one and then another, but some of the trails led the trusting young explorer into terrible marotily swamps, while others were alive with bodtu leeches which sucked the blood away, and daily her exertions bathed her in an excess of perspiration. The hot dank humidity grew hourly more oppressive as she penetrated deeper into the forest. At every step there were sinister vines to entangle her feet which invariably left their Sillidinous poison. Disheartened and weary she stumbled on, still confident, however, that somewhere ahead lay Mt. Certitude. Finally, overcome by exhaustion and fear, she lost her footing and fell headlong to the ground.

Lying there she moaned in despair, "Oh, I'm lost—lost in this terrible, treacherous jungle of Otherpeoplesideas! and I'd rather be dead than to be obliged to stay here wandering about aimlessly forever. I waste my time and strength following first one trail and then another simply because I am not sure which is the best one. That is the whole trouble, I am not sure of anything. I think, I feel, I wonder, but I never *know*. Oh, what torture to be young and uncertain! If I only had some strong man in whom I had complete confidence to guide me toward Certitude! But I am only a weak woman and an amateur explorer struggling through Nithking alone! I'd prefer to be a hundred years old and worn out with experience if I could just once in life be sure of something! If only Olev were here—Oh, why did life take my love away from me! He might have conducted me to Mt. Certitude if I had had sense enough to take advantage of the opportunity while he was alive. He surely knew its location. I wonder what Olev would do if he were lost in the jungle of Otherpeoplesideas? Which trail do you suppose he would follow?"

Opening her shirt, she gazed fondly at the stigma still on her left breast. "Why, he'd follow no man—he'd blaze his own trail—of that I'm positive." She paused and said scornfully, "Will the day never come when I need only say, 'What would Tellectina do?' Set your wits to work, Tellectina Christian—your own instincts ought to guide you aright. You will have to feel your way out of this jungle! The trails blazed by other explorers only confuse you!"

The grim determination of the born explorer reawakened in

her. Rising, she commenced to run in the direction instinct dictated, shielding her eyes with upraised arm. This method almost immediately brought her to rising ground which grew steadily more precipitous.

After having climbed for many hours she experienced a strange sensation: she commenced to feel strangely elated—fearfully, deliciously happy. Apparently the mountain air had gone to her head like champagne. Tellectina climbed on, eager but afraid. Suddenly as she emerged into a clearing there poured over the astounded girl a strange light of unnatural brilliance. This phenomenon seemed ominous—it was unlike any other light she had ever beheld, was infinitely more intense than even the noonday sun of the tropics, yet, oddly enough, it gave light without heat. It was not golden like sunlight, but of a strange, unearthly whiteness. Irresistibly drawn on, however, the girl ascended slowly until, passing beyond the timber line, she came out upon a great acclivity of bald rock where it looked as if all life had been blasted away by this terrifically strong light. But to her amazement all the sky was black except for the one narrow rent through which this uncanny supernatural effulgence poured over the earth.

Even though it might mean death, she was powerless to stay her footsteps but climbed steadily up toward this dazzling brightness, passing a signpost which said, "To Manu Mission." On attaining the peak of the great barren rock the explorer was greeted by the sight of a low structure built in that rectangular biblioesque style peculiar to the houses of Nithking. It was to all appearances very old and had been closed for many years. She was too absorbed at the moment in the extraordinary light suffusing the mountain top to take further notice of the small weather-stained house.

Tellectina stood motionless, waiting for she knew not what. She began to tremble unaccountably and passing her hand over her forehead was amazed to find it cold against her burning face. "It's nothing," she reassured herself. "It's only that I'm tired and overwrought and I forgot to eat anything today. Perhaps I merely imagine this phenomenon of light, or maybe I'm losing my mind for I'm not a mystic—I don't see visions like poor St. Theresa." Yet she continued to stand there powerless against this nameless thing—waiting . . . waiting . . .

She held no belief in the supernatural, but she knew there was something supernatural about this uncanny splendor—all nature holding its breath in an ominous silence—the premonition of some awful wonder about to burst upon her pervading all her being.

Suddenly she saw the rent in the sky widen and the black clouds roll back like a curtain; and for one awful moment she beheld that which was blinding and intolerable for human eyes. For one memorable second she had sudden insight into the very mystery of the universe itself. The girl stood awe-stricken and breathless.

This revelation, however, was only the beginning of the phenomenal experience. Suddenly concentrating itself into one mighty stream a great river of light seemed to loose itself from the very heavens themselves, to pour directly into her young mind: a river of liquid light, to flow steadily and abundantly into her own poor bursting little brain. The grandeur, the resplendency of this divine flood thrilled her almost beyond endurance. Like the saints of old beholding a vision, she swayed in an agony of ecstasy, certain that this was death, and closing her eyes fainted with a bliss that transcended consciousness. . . .

Long afterward, when the young girl regained full consciousness, she lay motionless where she had fallen, filled with wonder, but knowing herself to be in the throes of a strange process —a process of rebirth here on the very peak of the world with none to witness the miracle except herself. She realized now that she too had been "blasted with an excess of light" like the saints of old. She understood at last what St. Theresa had experienced, except that her own mighty revelation was not religious but intellectual.

A great nameless joy surged through all her being. Leaping to her feet, she flung her arms heavenward in exultation, crying in a loud voice, "I am free!—free! Free of the whole world! Free of mankind, free of all the things it says and does. I have emerged from the Great Jungle of Otherpeoplesideas! I have gained the mountain top! I am reborn this day—I begin life again. Henceforth I am a law unto myself because I am free!

"Laws? What are they but words put together by men as ignorant as myself? Customs? Merely the opinions of stupid men. Marriage? Bah!—a mere invention of men, an expedient. Love? Mating? Ah, I see, I see! The light sweeps me clean of the last vestige of my puritanical notions about the uncleanness of sex! How obvious now the rightness of my mating with Olev the Third; for the mating of man and woman is natural and inevitable, above all the laws of men. It is marriage that is artificial! The sex act takes its colors, its values and rightness from one's mind. Morality and marriage have no more relation than morality and buttercups! Ah, the basin of my soul that was stained with the old belief it held is washed clean by this river of light! Let all the world acclaim me immoral—while I—I only laugh! I make my own laws! States and divorce laws? Hah! A little group of little men on *this* little piece of ground say that I can't leave this man unless he does so and so. Nations even? Bah! There are no such things! Here a plot of ground with people on it—there another plot with people on it who are exactly the same except for slight differences!

"Clothing, did I say? Styles? Ha-ha! Was not man *born* naked?

"Fine houses? A piece of stone to crumble in a few years. Jewels? Ho-ho—what fun! Minerals like coal or iron, dug out of the earth and strung around women's necks and called valuable by people!

"People? Utterly blind, incorrigible fools!

"God? Why, He is not a great omnipotent man up there as we were taught as children. He is this—this blinding light— this revelation of truth!

"THERE IS NO GOD!
GOD IS DEAD!
LONG LIVE GOD!"

Tellectina stood transported—arms raised and rapturous countenance radiant with bliss—in motionless ecstasy, while the mighty exultation filled and flooded her whole being. Time was suddenly turned back—space annihilated. For one long divine moment she was an audacious young god.

Did she not soar up suddenly through space in a blaze of glory: trip nimbly down the ages across the roofs of Nineveh and the synagogues of old Jerusalem; touch with impudent feet the sacred temples of China and India; run with dancing steps across the Parthenon and the tombs of Egypt's most ancient and honored kings?

Did she not soar higher and still higher until she swung through space? Did she not climb gleefully from star point to star point; sit with dangling feet in the crescent of the moon; laugh full in the face of the sun; and running across the floor of heaven, tweak Jupiter's nose, tickle Buddha's fat sides, and pull Jehovah's venerable beard? Her impudent young laughter rang through the universe until the very planets seemed to swerve in their courses. For one divine moment she possessed the cosmos and snapped her fingers in the earth's billion-five-hundred-million-year-old face.

Finally the divine afflatus began to ebb from her being and she felt herself sinking slowly to earth again. Still bathed in a bewildered happiness she lay there on the rocky peak of what she took to be Mt. Certitude. Slowly the warm soothing tears began to flow, and she knew she was again mortal and safe on the earth.

After the great relief of tears she lay for a long time without weeping, murmuring brokenly to herself: "What this miraculous thing is that has happened to me I do not quite know yet. I only know that this sense of freedom is the thing I have sought all my life, and I have attained at last to Mt. Certitude. I have escaped from the tortuous jungle of Otherpeoplesideas. I am gloriously free—I *know* that I *know!* For this I have waited and prayed and strained my being; for this I have lived and suffered and doubted and died—in order to be born again! But how strange not to be born until one is twenty-five! All my life I have felt like a little green plant growing and slowly uncurling under the black oppressive earth—pushing with my obstinate little head against the obstinate earth. The earth has cracked at last, and I have shot up into the light of day. Beyond this I know nothing."

She lay there motionless; then suddenly leaping to her feet again, proclaimed her triumphant discovery: "Myself! Ah, that is it—that is the secret of life. I see it now, I understand. Within ourselves are we to look for all things—for truth—for God—for beauty—for guidance—not to men, nor laws, nor books!

"Ah, this freedom, this revelation is the height of human joy—beyond this there can be nothing. This more than compensates for all things hurtful in life that have been or that ever may be. For this I will pay any price demanded—pay with my happiness—with my life even. This gift of mental freedom is priceless! And never, never again shall I descend and mix with the poor miserable rabble! On this mountain top I shall live forever.

"The twisted trails of Otherpeoplesideas are but frail threads I could snap between my fingers. For now I know that I know. I have felt, I have thought, I have said, but not until now have I known! My own thoughts are as near the truth as any man's. I thank God a million times—God, or the great wisdom, or the merry jester, or the unknowable, or the life force, or nothingness and space—whatever it is, I thank it! Henceforth I am alone in the world. Tellectina against the world and unafraid. MYSELF! IT IS ENOUGH!"

The tension, however, became too great—ecstasy too intense became unbearable pain. Overwhelmed and frightened, the overwrought girl fell forward suddenly with her face to the earth, clasping the rock beneath her lest she should be caught up in a cloud of fire like Elijah and translated to some kind of heaven.

Suddenly she lifted her head. "I see, I see! I begin to understand. I know now what the saints of old meant when they had visions and said, 'I saw God.' I too saw God—but my god is Truth. And my revelation was mental—not religious. I have never heard of anyone's having an intellectual revelation in my whole life: it sounds like a contradiction of terms. It's incredible, but it's true, nevertheless, because I have just experienced it."

Quite unaccountably the young woman felt herself impelled forward by an obscure force. She was drawn magnetically toward the small biblioesque house which she had ignored heretofore. The instant she opened the door a serene and confident voice from within began to speak to her in sincere and mellifluous tones. It issued from a dignified and elderly man whom Tellectina vaguely recalled having met years ago at Rote Hill.

"'We have little control over our own thoughts. . . . They catch us up into their heaven. . . . By and by we fall out of that rapture.'"

The girl sank to a low stool—listening incredulously, rendered absolutely dumb by the startling appositiveness of his words.

"'As far as we can recall these ecstasies, we carry away in the ineffaceable memory the result, and all men and all ages confirm it. It is called truth!'"

At this astounding announcement a sort of joyous fear caused the roots of the girl's hair to tingle.

"'To believe your own thought,'" the mellow tones continued, "'to believe that what is true in your private heart is true for all men—that is genius. . . . Tomorrow a stranger will say with masterly good sense precisely what we have thought and felt all the time.'"

"Then I—I'm right to believe my own——" the girl stammered, unable to complete the sentence.

"'And truly it demands something godlike in him who has

cast off the common motives of humanity and has ventured to trust himself for a taskmaster. High be his heart, faithful his will, clear his sight! . . . Nothing can bring you peace but yourself. . . . There is one mind common to all individual men. Every man is an inlet. . . . What Plato has thought, he may think; what a saint has felt, he may feel; what at any time has befallen any man, he can understand.' "

"I—you mean—I am incapable of——"

But the voice went imperturbably on. " 'He must know that he is greater than all the geography and government of the world. . . . He must attain and maintain that lofty sight where facts yield their secret sense!' "

Cold chills began to run over Tellectina's body. She could not speak.

" 'Those men who cannot answer by a superior wisdom these facts or questions of time serve them. . . . But if a man is true to his better instincts, . . . and refuses the dominion of facts, as one that comes of a higher race; . . . then the facts fall aptly . . . into their places; they know their master.' "

"Am I of a higher——? No, no, it is too much to be borne! Dear God, save me!" the young girl murmured, but the man continued:

" 'We are like children who repeat by rote the sentences of tutors, and, as they grow older, of the men of talents; . . . afterwards, when they come into the point of view which those had who uttered the sayings, they understand them and are willing to let the words go; for at any time they can use words as good when the occasion comes.' "

"Oh, please—no more—I can't bear it," she pleaded, but listened with all her being.

" 'I have my own stern claims. . . . It denies the name of duty to many offices that are called duties. But if I can discharge its debts it enables me to dispense with the popular code. If anyone imagines this law is lax, let him keep its commandments one day . . . He acts from himself, tossing the laws, the books, idolatries and customs out of the window.' "

"Yes, that's it—that's it," cried the girl, "when I stood on the peak of Certitude, I tossed away everything!"

" 'The epochs of our lives are not in the visible facts of our choice of a calling, our marriage, our acquisition of an office, and the like, but in a silent thought by the wayside. . . . Every man's words who speaks from that life must sound vain to those who do not dwell in the same thought on their own part. . . . All goes to show that the soul of man is not an organ; . . . is not a faculty, . . . but a *light.*' "

"A light—a river of light that flowed into me—yes—yes! but it wasn't the 'soul,' was it?"

But her interlocutor did not seem to hear her question. " 'With each divine impulse the mind rends the thin rind of the visible and finite, and comes out into eternity, and inspires and expires its air. . . . The soul is the perceiver and the revealer of truth. We know truth when we see it, let sceptic and scoffer say what they choose.' "

"To think that this happened to me, little me! But not 'soul' and 'divine.' I can't believe in those."

" 'We distinguish the announcements of the soul, its manifestations of its own nature, by the term *Revelation.* These are always attended by the emotions of the sublime. For this communication is an influx of the Divine mind into our mind.' "

At these words Tellectina opened her lips, but no sound came forth. The voice went on: " 'Every distinct apprehension of this central commandment agitates men with awe and delight. A thrill passes through all men at the reception of new truth. . . . The nature of these revelations is the same; they are perceptions of the absolute law.' "

" 'Influx of the Divine mind into our mind'? No, no, this is too much!" Overwhelmed, Tellectina suddenly began to sob violently, but the man did not heed her tears.

" 'The growth of the intellect is spontaneous in every expansion. The mind that grows could not predict the times, the means, the mode of that spontaneity. . . . What am I? What has my will done to make me that I am? Nothing. I have been

floated into this thought, this hour, . . . by secret currents of
. . . mind, and my ingenuity and wilfulness have not thwarted,
have not aided to any appreciable degree.' "

The young woman was sobbing from sheer excess of joy.

" 'All our progress is an unfolding, like the vegetable bud.
You have first an instinct, then an opinion, then a knowledge,
as the plant has root, bud and fruit. Trust the instinct, to the
end . . . it shall ripen into truth and you shall know why you
believe.' "

"Yes, I know, didn't I feel like a little green plant always?—
always? Didn't I say: 'I felt, I thought and now I know'?
Now—now I understand this miraculous thing that has happened to me!" the young girl cried.

" 'God offers to every mind its choice between truth and
repose. Take which you please,—you can never have both. . . .
He in whom the love of repose predominates will accept the
first creed, the first philosophy, the first political party he
meets,—most likely his father's. He gets rest, commodity and
reputation.' "

"But—please, there *is* no God—why not call it the life force?"
She looked troubled, but joy instantly returned. "Ah, yes, I'm
beginning to see why I had no repose in Err, why I couldn't
accept my father's creed and philosophies—I longed to pursue
truth. I didn't know myself exactly at that time why I felt so
blind and strong an urge to leave Smug Harbor and explore the
Forbidden Country. My own actions are being clarified for me!"

Patiently the man endured the interruption, then said, " 'He
in whom the love of truth predominates will keep himself
aloof from all moorings. . . . He submits to the inconvenience
of suspense and imperfect opinion, but he is a candidate for
truth, and the other is not.' "

"Oh, yes, the inconvenience of not knowing! All through
Nithking I knew I didn't know—that's why I longed to find
Certitude. All the torture of uncertainty was worth this," she
cried with conviction.

" 'Every man's progress is through a succession of teachers, each of whom seems at the time to have a superlative influence, but it at last gives place to a new. Frankly let him accept it all. . . . Take thankfully all they can give. Exhaust them, wrestle with them, let them not go until their blessing be won, and after a short season the dismay will be overpast, the excess of influence withdrawn, and they will be no longer an alarming meteor but one more bright star shining serenely in your heaven and blending its light with all your day.' "

"I see. All the men I have met in Nithking—I listened to, followed, and abandoned—and that is the way it should be, then? And, some day I'll be mature enough to trust myself above all others?"

The man nodded his assent. " 'The highest merit we ascribe to Moses, Plato, and Milton is that they set at naught books and traditions and spoke not what men, but what *they* thought. A man should learn to detect and watch that gleam of light which flashes across his mind from within, more than the luster of the firmament of lords and sages. Yet he dismisses without notice his thought, because it is his. In every work of genius we recognize our own rejected thoughts.' "

"Yes, yes, I can dare to tell you now that such has been my experience," the girl murmured brokenly.

" 'Nothing is at last sacred but the integrity of your own mind. . . . What I must do is all that concerns me, not what people think.' "

As usual, to hear her own vague and chaotic young thoughts arranged in neat sentences before her caused the girl to consider the speaker the most wonderful person she had ever met. Yet it seemed incredible that this wonderful man was the same Emerson she had disliked so much when she was a schoolgirl. But the limit of the young woman's capacity to feel had been reached. The man continued to talk, but Tellectina did not listen: she sat motionless for hours, as if in a trance, overwhelmed, her whole being radiating joy. . . .

Gradually she passed into a deep and dreamless sleep. She awakened the following day at high noon. She lay quite still in an effort to recapture the rapture of the day before, but it proved impossible.

Tellectina discovered that her whole body was stiff with cold. In spite of the fact that the sun was still excessively brilliant, it gave light without heat. The mountain top was not only cold, it was lonely too; and the air was so rarefied that breathing was difficult. None of these disadvantages had impressed themselves upon her the previous day, however. Advancing cautiously to the edge of the rocky peak on which she stood, she peered down at the earth below, only to recoil in terror. The whole world as she had known it seemed to have crumbled to dust and ashes. Terror struck into her heart. She felt dizzy—she closed her eyes—the earth swayed. Certitude itself began to slip from under her feet.

"Oh," she cried out in fear, "give me something to hold to! But there is nothing to hold to except myself! How can anyone hold to one's self? Everything is reduced to nothingness. And how can one build something from nothingness? Oh, I hadn't realized that if I refused to accept the world and the values of mankind that I must create a whole new world for myself, that nothing would exist until I gave it value! I—oh, I am no God— I can't create order out of chaos. I know that I am free of what other men think but—oh, heavens, I don't know what *I* think about anything! Oh, God, do you mean then that this is not my goal—that this is not Mt. Certitude? that there's a still higher mountain in the world than this?" She looked about her.

"Ah, yes, I see now that this little weather-stained structure which was indeed Manu Mission to me gives this mountain its name. This is not Certitude, this is only Manu Mission. Oh, God," she besought. "Ah, but there is no God, there is only one's self to pray to—one's own inner courage. The journey through Nithking is proving too long and too arduous. It is more than I can bear alone. I see defeat ahead." She clasped her aching head and moaned, "Ah, no, man cannot stand alone —above the world—it is too terrifying!"

She moved toward the door to seek Emerson's aid again, but reeled unsteadily, lost her footing, and, falling forward, began to descend the mountain side at a terrific rate. When she finally came to a stop and picked herself up out of the dust, she was relieved to see on peering far below that all the towns and hills and houses of the world had mysteriously sprung from the dust and ashes into life again, resuming their former appearance; and yet the exceedingly bright light descending from above revealed them with extraordinary clarity. And, furthermore, she saw everything with new eyes, for had she not been reborn?

Slowly she descended the mountain, absorbed in thought. "I must travel farther into Nithking until I come to the place where civilization began: I must see with my own eyes every stage of man's and nature's development, if I am to comprehend the true nature of life. I must go to the very beginnings of the beginnings. I must penetrate beneath all surfaces, beneath all commonplaces, all material things, and I must study invisible causes and effects."

Stopping abruptly in her tracks, she stared at the rocks about her as if she had never seen them before. On picking up a fossil containing the impression of the skeleton of a strange animal, she found that it started such a volley of questions in her mind, it made her poor brain grow hot.

"How old is this fossil? How did the earth begin and why? When did man first appear and why? Why is there evolution? What is the origin of ideas, and when did communication of thought begin? Which is nature's handiwork in the world and which is man's? What is the goal of mankind? of the individual? What is the goal of my life? What mode of life is the most valuable: service to one's fellow man (and if so, why?) or complete self-expression, or the pursuit of knowledge or art? What is the place of art in human life: is it merely some beautiful extraneous thing for the pleasure of the few only? Whither should I turn my energies and why? Whither do I wish to turn them? When did morality and immorality begin among men and why? What is right and wrong? Why is sex immoral, and has it always been so considered by the human race, and if so, why? Why are human beings religious, and what is the origin of the different religions? And why don't all philosophers agree? Are there many truths or is there only one truth? And what is this life force—is it good or bad? Oh, will I ever have all my questions answered? I want to know everything—and I know nothing! I am a new-born infant! Olev the Third might have answered these questions, for surely he had visited Mt. Certitude, where one finds answers to all questions! Oh, why was he taken from me? I failed so miserably to appreciate him while he was alive!"

Suddenly the consciousness of her own impotence made her pause. "But he had great faith in me; he would be disappointed in me if I failed, nor could I ever live with myself if I did not persevere till I reach Certitude. I see now that reason and science are the only reliable guides. Henceforth I must be conducted through Nithking by the scientific guides only—surely they can lead me directly to Certitude."

Fired by new enthusiasm the young explorer hastened on and, coming finally to the sea, ran lightly across the narrow beach behind which rose, in all its lofty magnificence, the great mountain where Tellectina had found Manu Mission. She was for some reason, however, not surprised to see a number of ships anchored there as if awaiting passengers. Many of the captains claimed that their craft were designed for the sole purpose of carrying passengers to Certitude. And all were captained by men who were scientific experts. Tellectina went aboard those owned by Darwin, Huxley, Tyndall, and Faraday; but after a brief inspection the young woman realized that, although their ships were exceedingly sturdy and trustworthy, they would nevertheless subject passengers to endless hardships. Moreover, they insisted on making very long trips and going thoroughly over every inch of the territory which they intended to visit. The young explorer knew that she lacked both the endurance and the time for such scientific expeditions, inasmuch as they would leave a great part of Nithking still untouched.

Concluding that what she needed most at this time was a hasty trip around the world in order to refresh her memory of the things she had read, she looked about her. On seeing the outline of *Sithory,* a large substantial frigate, silhouetted against the sky, she hastened forward and after boarding her discovered to her joy that it was designed to render traveling as easy and pleasant as possible for the inexperienced young explorer. The captain, H. G. Wells, assured her that he could take her around the world in fourteen days.

Tellectina liked his terms; consequently they started at once on their cruise around the world. Only in Nithking were such trips possible, for they not only touched upon all the countries of the earth, but even visited them during different ages. They sailed easily through the Azoic age, the Proterozoic, and the early Paleozoic, and on to the modern. Wells pointed out to her the origin of languages, of thought itself, of writing, of the arts and sciences and religions. He showed her the birth and growth of the use of money, of society, nations, customs, and traditions. Although many of her questions were left unanswered, she continued her sightseeing with Wells every hour of the day and far into the night, until her eyes began to rebel—but her enjoyment was too great to heed this warning. Finally, however, this strain, in conjunction with her nervous excitement and failure to take time to eat properly, caused a high temperature to run up, which automatically ended all sightseeing for some time.

While lying ill on the deck of a homeward-bound hospital ship Tellectina gazed up at a sky so rich and generous a blue that it was almost purple, a pleasant proof that she was in a southern latitude, for never in northern countries were the colors flung on with such a lavish hand. It hung so low she longed to reach up and touch it. As her gaze sank deeper and deeper into the soft luxurious blueness, its beauty melted the very heart in her body, until an inexplicable sadness settled over her like a pall. If only she had someone with whom to share this beauty!

"Oh, Olev, Olev, where are you? Dear heaven, give me back my love! Why did you take him away? Why did you allow him to die? He lives in me forever, and the stigma is on my heart, but—oh, I want his physical, actual presence too. Why did you give me the most wonderful man in the world and then take him away from me without just cause? It's all so senseless, so unfair! I hate you, you beautiful heartless blue sky—you cruel infinite with your inscrutable, implacable indifference!"

Involuntarily Tellectina covered her eyes and began to sob bitterly. Grief rendered her oblivious of the storm gathering swiftly behind her. When the squall struck the boat, she was washed overboard without the captain ever being aware of it. She strove desperately to keep her head above water, but immediately a strong current seized her and swept her away. The water grew steadily warmer, till such a delicious inertia came over the girl that she ceased to struggle, abandoning herself completely to the current, allowing it to carry her where it would. And her premonition that she was drifting toward some new and delightful adventure soon proved to be well founded.

CHAPTER IX

THE DISCOVERY OF THE SEVEN SIREN ISLANDS AND HOW THE
EXPLORER INDULGED IN THE NATIVE ORGIES

THE YOUNG EXPLORER had been floating for some
time in the warm voluptuous water when a seductive
breeze brought her the scent of flowers.

"At last," she sighed with relief, "I must be near land and
safe once more! But I wonder to what strange country I have
drifted!"

It was difficult to believe her own senses when there was
wafted to her the sound of human voices singing in soft irresistible tones. Lifting her head out of the water as far as
possible, she espied a group of verdant islands, and on the
beach of the nearest one, several golden-brown natives beckoning to the swimmer.

"But," Tellectina remonstrated, "it's simply preposterous!
This is a modern world I am living in! There are no such
things as sirens. And yet—well, there is something queer about
all this which I don't quite understand. It's obvious, however,
that I've drifted to the Tropic Seas. But my puritan instinct
warns me that it might be dangerous to listen to those alluring
creatures."

At this moment the tide rose and swept her toward the beach.
With all the art of seductive voice and gesture the sirens lured
her ashore; until before she realized what had happened, Tellectina found herself rising from the waves which actually
emitted an amorous perfume of their own as they curled

voluptuously about her limbs. Before the beauty of these native girls, ranged along the beach to greet her, the white woman stood speechless. Small wonder that she had mistaken them for sirens: their golden-brown skins shone like satin in the tropical sun. Nor did they wear anything to conceal their perfections, of which they seemed as unconscious as children. Garlands of bright tropical flowers, whose heavy fragrance was tantalizing to the extreme, hung about their necks and encircled their dark hair.

There were five of these native girls and one youth. Slowly, they began to dance about Tellectina with a natural sinuous grace impossible to acquire in a lifetime; encircling her neck with flowers; laughing, and singing in a simple dialect of which the white woman was soon able to understand a good many words. Even their voices were music of an unutterable sweetness. On the completion of their slow sinuous dance they seated themselves about the stranger, offering to share with her their jugs of wine from which each native drank with amazing frequency. The presence of a white woman on this island appeared to delight them for some mysterious reason.

Tellectina resisted with great perturbation the temptation to sample their wine, adding nervously, "But such hospitality I've never enjoyed before in my life!"

Whether they understood her Reasonese or not, it amused them vastly. They commenced to dispute clamorously among themselves for the possession of their visitor, each one endeavoring to take her hand; until finally, the strongest one, whose name Tellectina soon learned was Ese, succeeded in leading her triumphantly away. The others, somewhat disconsolate, followed closely behind, however, bearing the wine jars on their shoulders with easy grace. The vegetation on this Siren Island flaunted its luxuriousness shamelessly, while the flowers were so large and vivid in their riotous coloring that the white Errorian felt there was something indecent about them. Although aware of its undeniable beauty, the intrepid explorer who had braved so many perils sensed a mystery about this island that was decidedly disturbing. Vague premonitions of weird terrors as well as monstrous pleasures insinuated themselves into her consciousness.

"Ah, well, perhaps it's only that the Puritan in me mistrusts so much beauty," she murmured. "Nevertheless, I certainly wish I knew where they were leading me. Surely these natives are too beautiful and kindly to be cannibals!"

Ese conducted her captive through the great tropical jungle for some distance, then, stopping abruptly, quaffed a full cup of wine and offered another to Tellectina. The explorer was now too parched with thirst to resist. She raised it to her lips, then closed her eyes, for the very aroma of it caused her to sway slightly; then she too drained it at one draught. The effect was immediate and peculiar: it imparted a new glamour to every object. When Ese pointed out a sleeping pool in the middle distance lying between two hazy blue hills, which threw their dark purple shadows across its face, Tellectina began to tremble unaccountably. Had there ever been a landscape so unbearably beautiful? The wine caused the blood to surge so deliciously through her veins that Tellectina secretly feared it would induce an attack of that mysterious malady to which she had been subject all her life but which she had thought to outgrow with maturity. It appeared to be a form of hysteria, for on certain occasions her smiles and laughter were followed instantly by sadness and even tears: facts she had always endeavored to conceal in order that her abnormality might not be discovered.

The enchanting picture produced by the pool, the hills, and their purple shadows evoked from Tellectina a contented smile, even soft laughter; and then gradually the slow tears began to well up. Embarrassed and annoyed, she blinked them back. Although the sensation was pleasurable, it was also bewildering.

"But, Ese, I notice that you look on these flowers and trees and sunlight—in fact, everything about you on this island—with a sort of—well, a religious spirit. Are you then a sun worshiper?"

"No, on this island we worship the goddess Yeta-Bu. She has no temple on the Isle of Forta Feli, where we are now, but I believe that the flowers, water, trees, shadows—in fact, all the beauties of nature are manifestations of our goddess. And it is my privilege rather than duty as a high priestess of Yeta-Bu to direct your attention to them!"

"Oh, I see, a nature worshiper."

"No, you don't see—but if you follow me you may."

Ese was as tireless in exhibiting the beauties of her island to the white visitor as in keeping her plied with wine. She showed her a native dance in which the girls' bodies moved with a rhythm whose beauty was maddening; flowers whose exotic coloring made Tellectina sigh and long for she knew not what; trees tossed in the summer wind like a woman's hair; the ravishing curve of a young girl's throat; and last of all a village at dusk with the houses silhouetted against the darkening sky and little golden lights dancing with their own images in the water's edge. Each of the innumerable beauties produced in Tellectina a little paroxysm of pleasure followed by a sweet inexplicable melancholy. At length, however, even the natives grew weary, and when they lay down on the leaves to sleep, the white woman willingly did likewise.

The following morning the explorer was awakened by the insidious sound of some native instrument being played in the distance. As she sat up to listen, one of the native girls offered her a generous amount of wine but no food, her appetite for which, however, was gradually lessened by the sweetness of the wine. Tellectina, who was constantly soothing her vanity with the assurance that she was not only capable of being mistress of any situation but that she consciously directed her own life with her mind, found herself completely baffled by these apparently simple creatures. Although she had picked up their dialect with a rapidity that astounded her, their true nature and intent remained unfathomable. The natives, however, appeared to understand their captive with uncanny insight; knowledge of their power over her lending them a disconcerting self-confidence. Their secret amusement seemed to imply that they were enjoying some jest at her expense.

While listening to the plaintive strains, Tellectina sipped her wine slowly in order to savor it the better. Finally she exclaimed, "Oh, your wine is different from Ese's, isn't it?"

"Certainly. I'm Reha, therefore I produce my own particular variety. It is all derived from the same source, however, the same sacred vineyard."

"Sacred? What vineyard is that?" The explorer feared they might be preparing her as a sacrifice to their local deity.

"Why, that of our goddess, Yeta-Bu. I, too, am her high priestess. She is next to the oldest deity in the world, although she has few worshipers nowadays. In fact, some of the foreigners who come here as pilgrims to her shrines inform us that the people who frequent these Siren Islands are the only devotees she has left anywhere."

The wine engendered a mental drowsiness so delicious that it was not conducive to further inquiry into the nature of that goddess. The stranger reclined contentedly on a mat which had been mysteriously unrolled for her, little dreaming into what a tyrant's country she had been lured. As she lay with closed eyes, her cup was refilled so frequently by Reha that Tellectina passed into a strange intoxicated state where languor of limb vied with alertness of the senses, until even the wind sighing through the trees filled her with a sweet sadness, until the laughter of a waterfall near by and the simplest songs of the birds pierced her heart "with a joy that was as keen as pain." When Reha summoned a group of natives to sing to the white woman the plaintive minor tones stirred Tellectina's very bowels.

Half laughing, half crying, she said, "Oh, if I remain in these tropics, I fear I shall become a hopeless drunkard or go completely mad or both. That I'm a little mad already I am fully convinced; for who but a mad person would weep as I did just now at the sound of mere human voices singing? But I am so enamored of your wine, Reha and Ese, that whatever fate awaits me here—departure is impossible!"

When Tellectina attempted to rise unsteadily to a sitting position, two of the smaller girls assisted her, one of whom murmured, "Ah, now it's my turn. Do taste some of this delicious papaya," and, breaking it open, offered Tellectina half of the fruit. Its luscious golden flesh produced a strange effect on the white woman. Closing her eyes momentarily, she passed her hand over her forehead in a dazed way; for there before her appeared an enchanting vision of a tall slender woman in diaphanous saffron draperies rising cool and ethereal from the center of a limpid lake. As the taste of the papaya grew fainter the vision faded, so that Tellectina was obliged to beg the native girl for the other half in order to recall it.

"How strange, and how delicious! I certainly relish your native fruit, even if it is a little—well, a little uncanny. What is your name, may I ask?"

"Why, I should think you would know what it is after that —it is Astte."

"Oh, but you're so—so small! It never occurred to me that you moved in the exalted company of real priestesses!"

Offended, Astte turned her pretty golden back, but immediately, Mllse, the other diminutive native, seized the opportunity to present her offering. "Just because we two happen to be smaller than the others is no reason that we are not important, please remember! We, too, are servitors of Yeta-Bu, though not high priestesses."

As if to prove her contention, she proffered Tellectina some sparkling wine whose aroma was more subtle and alluring than any of the others. As the explorer drank it, Mllse playfully twined some red jasmine through Tellectina's hair, the aphrodisiac scent causing that to happen which the young Puritan considered shocking but delightful. Finally she fell into a troubled slumber.

That afternoon she was awakened by a strangely delicious sensation: someone had been stroking her arm very gently, yet there was no one visible anywhere. All the natives had vanished while she slept. As she lay down again and felt the caress once more the realization dawned on her that it was the touch of her own warm clothing; and that without her knowledge someone had removed her masculine trousers and replaced them with soft diaphanous draperies. To her spontaneous little laugh of pleasure there sounded a masculine echo, yet there was no person visible. As Tellectina ran through the woods searching for him, the soft draperies coiled voluptuously about her limbs. Shivering with delight she caressed them gratefully in turn.

"Oh," exclaimed a seductive male voice, "don't waste them on a mere piece of cloth! If you enjoy those caresses you'd adore mine! For I am Chotu, whom all women love." Turning, Tellectina beheld the head of a handsome youth garlanded with passion flowers. He was thrusting out his laughing face from the midst of a blossoming pink shyfell tree.

He approached her, smiling persuasively and bearing a delicately modeled cup filled with a rare wine. Frightened but curious, the girl seated herself on a moss-covered log and sipped it cautiously. On closing her eyes, the better to taste it, she felt the young man's hands steal softly over her, and she lacked the power to resist his touch. As he passed his hands gently through her hair, a shiver of pleasure ran through her body. He placed his warm moist lips against her throat, pressed them into the soft hollow of her arm, cupped his hot hands tenderly, then convulsively, over her small panting breasts.

"Oh, don't, don't, Chotu! I—I must be intoxicated to allow you! I—it—oh, it *must* be the wine you gave me that causes my blood to race and—and my head to reel so! Oh, go away—go away!" she protested.

But she made no effort to repulse him. When the youth failed to renew his attentions, however, Tellectina, affecting elaborate indifference, arose and wandered down to the beach—amazed at the timidity of the male.

Shading her eyes with her hand she stood peering over at the next island. "I wonder if it's as pleasant there as it is here."

A low musical voice beside her replied immediately, "Why not ask me? I am a high priestess of the temple on that island."

"Oh, it's you, Ese!"

"Yes, and if you'll accompany me—my canoe's beached around there in the cove—I'll be delighted to show you the beauties of the isle of Tni Pa."

Running into the water Ese launched her canoe, which was painted in all the colors of the rainbow, and with a few graceful movements reached the opposite shore. They proceeded through the jungle until a vast stone temple, ancient and moss-covered, almost smothered in the exuberant jungle, came to view. Although extending over a great area, the edifice was constructed in a remarkably plain style. As they passed through the beautifully colored doorway, Ese selected two jugs of sacramental wine from the abundant supply found inside the entrance. At the far end of the temple there was an elaborate altar. Above this stood a heavily veiled statue from which emanated a curious white light of almost blinding intensity.

It awed the white woman to such an extent that she unconsciously spoke in a whisper, "Is that the—the goddess you worship?"

The native, however, was kneeling; and with eyes closed was mumbling inaudibly.

When she arose, the curious traveler repeated her inquiry. "What did you say her name was?"

Ese whispered reverentially, "Yeta-Bu—in our language."

"But why is she veiled?"

The islander cast a condescending glance on the foreigner. "No mortal has ever looked on the face of Yeta-Bu—bare."

"But why not? You see I'm not religious, therefore——"

"Ah," Ese murmured in awed tones, "it would blind her."

"Of course, that's difficult for me to believe because——"

"Then, skeptical Tellectina, I'll prove it to you. For sometimes it is almost more than one can endure to gaze upon the sacrifices made at the altar of Yeta-Bu. Those brought here by the more divinely inspired worshipers have all been hung on the temple wall as permanent votive offerings. Look about you."

The explorer had not been prepared for the astounding sight.

Everywhere were gorgeous murals, tapestries, and paintings which now greeted her eyes. Nor did she realize the great antiquity of this temple until she recognized offerings which must have been left there by the Chinese thousands of years ago.

Ese led the astonished and delighted Tellectina to the south wall and, standing before a certain picture, reverently performed the ritual of drinking the sacramental wine intended to induce the proper religious emotion. It was difficult, however, for the white woman to decide whether the native was very devout or very drunk or both. When she passed the wine to Tellectina and commanded her to drink, the stranger obeyed. Slowly and surely it began to take effect, for, as the white woman gazed at the delicate diaphanous draperies of the painted figures before her; at the sweet curve of the women's thighs and bellies; at the mystery of their melancholy faces, she smiled in unalloyed happiness; yet, as she continued to gaze, a great sadness welled up within her. . . . It was necessary to blink her eyes vigorously in order to restrain the tears.

Setting down the cup which she had unconsciously drained to the last drop, Tellectina said in amazement, "Why, I didn't dream that so many pilgrims came to such an out-of-the-way place as these Siren Islands!"

"Oh, yes," the priestess replied. "They come here to worship, surreptitiously. The cult of Yeta-Bu is a secret one, you know. They have come from every country in the world, China, India, Egypt, England, France, and occasionally someone strays in from that heathen country known as America."

Once more Tellectina gazed at the painting and again was obliged to brush away her tears in annoyance. "Oh, I'm a silly fool! Can't I look at a mere picture or even drink a little wine without having one of those hysterical spasms? Ese, who left this offering I've been examining?"

"I don't know, some nice old man, I presume. Few women worship Yeta-Bu."

"You mean you don't even know his name?"

"And I mean, also, that I don't care what his name is."

"But, Ese, what is the picture called?"

"I don't know. What earthly difference do labels make? I enjoy looking at it. If a picture or any other votive offering arouses religious emotions in me—if it never ceases to thrill me —*that* is the only thing that matters."

"What an extraordinary person you are, Ese! So gifted in some directions but utterly lacking in intellectual curiosity. You are a sensuous person only, I can see that—and this is a purely pagan religion, I fear. Now, I am Tellectina, and I like to know the name of the offering I look at as well as that of the donor." Stepping nearer, she read the inscription underneath the painting. "Why, there it is written on it as plain as day: 'Allegory Representing Early Spring, by Botticelli'!"

But the pretty native merely laughed and shrugged her beautiful naked shoulders. "Ah, Tellectina, look at this one! Did you ever see such wonderful sweeping curves in your life?" With her forefinger she traced an outline of the nude figure in the air. "Ah, divine Yeta-Bu, only for your sake are such gifts created and placed here!" she murmured softly and, moving forward, caressed the painted figure as if it were alive.

Tellectina stood before this beautiful oblation transfixed—except for the sipping of the wine which she lifted constantly and almost unconsciously to her lips. Continual drinking was such an inviolable custom on these islands that no one was ever without a cup at her lips. As Ese drew her away to the next one she glanced at the inscription below this canvas which read, "Venus, by Velasquez."

"But why have you turned that large picture to the wall, Ese?"

"Because it makes me sick." She turned it around but instantly closed her eyes and grew pale. "Oh, Tellectina, it nauseates me. Excuse me, I—I think I'm going to——" Ese hastened out into the clearing behind the temple.

On her return Tellectina exclaimed, "But do you realize the name of the person who left this offering? It is Gauguin. Didn't you know he is famous and——"

"I know that his trees are deformed and his women bulbous and that it sickens me to look at them. But see, see!" She then began pointing out one painting after the other, crying rapturously, "But look here and here and over there at those heavenly creations! The divine colors, the inspired lines!"

Tellectina's malady, which was invariably increased by the native wine, steadily grew more pronounced as she passed from Corot's landscapes to Whistler's nocturnes, and Watteau's Embarkation for Cytherea; from Titian's Venus of Urbino to Courbet's Woman with a Parrot and to Da Vinci's exquisite Head of a Young Woman, and countless others.

Trembling and laughing, Tellectina suddenly sank down weakly to the temple floor. "I—I can't look at any more now. Let us—let us speak of something else, please—please, until I can recover my balance." Ese urged more wine on her, but she severely rejected it. "I see that you have a great many pictures which bear famous names turned with their faces to the wall. You're an independent young devil, Ese, you don't even display the accustomed reverence."

"But I am Ese, and I revere only those things that arouse a genuine religious emotion in me personally, that move *me*— thrill *me!*"

"Thrills! Thrills! You sensuous people live for nothing but thrills. Yours is the most extraordinary religion I have ever heard of."

"You speak of thrills in a derogatory manner, like a Puritan. You know we have a strict law forbidding the landing of Puritans on any of these Siren Islands. If, by chance, one comes ashore, she is first tortured, then thrown into the sea to drown. I believe, however, that you have the making in you of a good convert to Yeta-Bu, judging not by your speech or actions but by your reactions. Oh, Tellectina, I can show you how to live a life of constant pleasure as a devotee to Yeta-Bu!" Moving nearer, Ese caressed the white woman seductively, rubbing against her like a purring feline and tempting her with more wine.

The Puritan drew away, confused by the strange admixture of pleasure and fear in her own person. "I'm not sure it's—it's right to be intoxicated all the time the way you want me to be, Ese. I admire Yeta-Bu exceedingly, but the light radiating from her hurts my eyes."

"Ah, but you could grow accustomed to it."

"Yes, I—I suppose so. It's all very mystifying, but this wine and worship of Yeta-Bu increases an old malady of mine which has troubled me all my life."

Ese was not listening, she was preparing to kneel. "Kneel!" she commanded, gently forcing Tellectina to her knees.

The white woman soon sprang up again. "But—but I am Tellectina! I kneel to no one! I remain aloof, detached, critical, and alone always."

When Ese merely smiled in amusement, Tellectina drew herself up with offended dignity. "Besides, I wish to see how Yeta-Bu is worshiped on all the other Siren Islands—I intend to miss nothing as I travel through this strange unpredictable country of Nithking."

Ese departed from the temple with reluctance, but her enthusiasm returned as they launched another one of her canoes, constructed of some beautiful white material which, she explained, was indigenous to the Isle of Tru-Sce-Plu. They pointed it in the direction of the third Siren Island. The temple here, of which Ese was also high priestess, resembled that on Tni Pa, except that the votive offerings left by the pilgrims at the shrine of Yeta-Bu on Tru-Sce-Plu were without exception all statues carved from the native white marble or cast in bronze. The sacramental wine in this temple was plentiful, also, though not as potent as that on the Isle of Tni Pa. Tellectina experienced a rather violent attack of her old malady while standing in front of a certain caryatid whose serene poise completely unpoised her. The sculptured draperies flowed down in soft ripples like water. When Ese next led Tellectina up to the Nike of Samothrace, the white woman laughed as though feeling the wind through her own draperies, and then that same old feeling of sadness

stole over her—it seemed absolutely inescapable. While standing before a beautiful bronze statue of a woman and babe which
had the words, "Bacchante, by MacMonnies," under it, Tellectina felt a thousand little waves of laughter go rippling through
her entire being.

"But," Ese exclaimed rapturously, "see my wonderful Discus
Thrower. Does not that circle cause a sensation of absolute satisfaction in you?"

"Yes, but it would have been twice as lovely if it had been a
woman's figure. I have little use for women as a rule, but
physically they are certainly more beautiful than men even at
their Greek best. No, the greatest beauty of men does not lie in
their bodies as it does with women."

Ese, however, was oblivious of everything but the Discus
Thrower. She lingered before it entranced.

"You know, Ese," the white girl continued, "a perfect work
of art produces the same feeling of accumulated stimulation and
complete satisfaction as——" And here she whispered in the
other girl's ear.

But the native merely laughed, not at all embarrassed.

"I presume," Tellectina concluded, "that all pleasures which
are completed evoke a somewhat similar sensation."

There were a few more statues which produced the same
effect on both the onlookers, but countless others were passed
by with scarcely a glance because Ese declared they did not
seem to her to have been divinely inspired. Several of the most
distorted ones, called "modernistic," forced both girls to hasten
out-of-doors to relieve themselves.

All these experiences left the explorer so weak and overwrought, however, that she was obliged to lie abed in Ese's
house near the temple for several days. The priestess' dwelling
was constructed of shelf bamboo fibers arranged in designs
whose intricacy and delicacy were most admirable.

Immediately on her recovery, Ese urged Tellectina to accompany her to the third and last island on which she served as
high priestess. On the Isle of Bli Du, she explained, there was no

temple to be found but instead there were ruins of architectural fragments, and a few fairly modern buildings, all of which had been built in dedication to Yeta-Bu.

Standing in the very center of the island, Tellectina gazed in fascination at a remarkable structure with hundreds of little spires rushing up into the sky. "But who on earth was ever able to design such—such an overwhelmingly beautiful assemblage of stones and lines and proportion!"

"I don't know! What does that matter? Oh, look, look!" Ese exclaimed, closing her eyes and swaying slightly.

Being still in a hypersensitive and exalted state, Tellectina was absolutely staggered by the sudden impact of the quintessence of perfect form represented by the Gothic arch now confronting her. She too closed her eyes and swayed slightly. After she had passed through this Gothic arch, the sight of a stained-glass window through which an unearthly light streamed, and of the dim cool aisles of stone, caused Tellectina to stand speechless. On emerging from the door once more, she discovered that there was some mysterious quality which emanated from a series of marble steps leading down into a pool of water; and from another flight of steps built along the side of an old wall, topped with a carved balustrade—some inexplicable, troubling quality that shook the onlooker with little spasms of pleasure.

As they passed from one to another of these glorious testimonials of man's worship of the great invisible goddess, Yeta-Bu, Tellectina was equally surprised at the devout expression on the face of the priestess and her own pleasurable sensations. Her concentrated effort to fathom the mystery of her response to certain arrangements of line and mass was interrupted by a song. It came over the water in such seductive tones that the white woman was drawn toward it as resistlessly as though toward a magnet. Emerging quickly from the woods, she beheld another siren beaching her canoe. It was Reha, but as soon as she attempted to lure Tellectina away from Bli Du, Ese, who followed, tugged at the explorer's arm with all her might.

They fought for the possession of the white woman there on

the silver sands until finally Tellectina contrived to escape from the importunate Ese, who submitted but reproached her with her eyes. After expressing profuse gratitude to the priestess and assuring her that she would return soon, Tellectina pushed off with the eager Reha.

Even the splash of the rhythmic paddle in the quiet water was soothing and suggestive of some subtle mystery. The fifth of these tropical bits of green set in the midst of the indigo sea was some distance from the three islands on which Ese was priestess. It was dusk when they arrived. And as they walked single file through the green gloom of the jungle, Reha answered the inquiries of her companion. "Yes, Yeta-Bu is also the goddess of this island, and I am a direct descendant of the first priestess. The office has been in our family from the very beginning."

"Oh, then Yeta-Bu does not demand virgin priestesses?"

"May the great goddess forbid!"

"Why, as a matter of fact, I recall having heard that she actually forbade virgins for reasons I have never quite comprehended. Don't you know, Reha?"

"I wouldn't know, but the reason I wished you to come to the Isle of Cumsi at this time is that some of the worshipers are holding a service in the temple tonight. Although the sacred books have been left there permanently as offerings, I am unable to read them, but I can understand the spoken word. And most foreigners also require interpreters of the language of Cumsi."

They were mounting the steps of a large low building when a sound arrested them. Remaining where they were, they sank to the floor of the porch and imbibed freely of the wine which Reha produced from the shadow of the columns. Sitting in the darkness they listened to the wonderful sacred music which issued from within, the canorous sounds rising and swelling with ecstatic crescendo, then sighing and dying with heart-rending sobs. Both girls laughed a little with pleasure, at first, then began to weep softly in each other's arms, stirred by some unknown sorrow.

"Oh," Tellectina whispered, "I don't understand what is the matter with me! If I lived on the Isle of Cumsi all the time I fear I should be a nervous wreck. And you're right, I do not even understand the meaning of all these sounds which cause such paroxysms of joy and sorrow in me."

"That doesn't matter as long as the sacred music induces the true spirit of devotion in you."

"But I am Tellectina, and it does matter. I like to understand everything. Have you no wise native on any of your islands who can explain the meaning of these sounds to me? What are Wagner and Beethoven trying to convey to us? Is there no one here named Ceve-Peri, as she would be called in your language?"

Reha was offended. "I've given you intense pleasure—isn't that enough? Here, drink some more of this wine and you'll forget all about your silly questions."

Tellectina drank while the music again poured out of the temple. "But wine merely increases this form of hysteria. I fear it's an incurable affliction, and the real truth of the matter is that I'm a little mad—for is not hysteria the beginning of madness?"

While the white woman was in this intoxicated state it was a simple matter for Reha to lead her into the dimly lighted temple and lure her into the sacred orgy. Though it exalted Tellectina to the infinite degree, this pleasure left her prostrate and exhausted on the temple floor.

As soon as she was able to collect her wits the morning afterward, Tellectina ran from the temple on trembling limbs and swam away from this wonderful and terrible Isle of Cumsi as rapidly as the warm voluptuous waters would permit. The intensity of her sensation of both pleasure and pain produced by such orgies was highly enjoyable yet very perturbing to her Puritan soul.

On arriving at the sixth Siren Island, Tellectina was greeted by the largest and most beautiful of all the natives, who ran joyously into the surf to assist her.

An expression of annoyance passed over her face when she noticed that there was another swimmer behind the white woman. "Now, why on earth did you have to come too? I am capable of showing my visitor the beauties of the Isle of O We Tri *alone!* You're eternally interfering, Reha!"

Reha rose dripping from the waves. "My position in O We Tri is equally as important as yours, Ceve-Peri!" And taking the explorer's arm she accompanied her to the temple.

On entering the low structure, Tellectina was surprised to see that although this temple of Yeta-Bu was the largest, it appeared to be the simplest in both exterior and interior decoration. She suspected secret beauties, however, to be concealed behind the mosaics composed of innumerable small rectangles of red, green, and blue which everywhere covered the walls. It was impossible to approach the likeness of the goddess above the altar, for the brilliance emanating from her was more blinding than the noonday sun. Curiosity led the explorer to examine the mosaics, all of which proved to be merely the backs of books. Reverently lifting several from their places, she was delighted to see that they were all written in Reasonese. Evidently pilgrims from every quarter of the earth had come to leave their offerings to Yeta-Bu on the Isle of O We Tri.

And apparently Reha and Ceve-Peri were rival priestesses in this temple, for, decked in resplendent jewels and anointed with fragrant oils, both were now advancing toward her. Simultaneously each removed one of the sacred books preparatory to commencing the ritual. Reha was the more agile, however, for she quickly offered the white woman a cup of the sacramental wine before Ceve-Peri had even poured hers; whereupon the latter, in jealous anger, turned away and left them.

Standing before the image of the goddess with the sacred volume in her hand, Reha began to chant the litany in soft rhythmical tones full of devotional fervor, allowing each syllable to fall slowly into Tellectina's heart like the drops of the attar of roses:

" 'And the silken, sad, uncertain rustling of each purple curtain . . .'

" 'The delight that he takes but in living
Is more than all things that live:
For the world that has all things for giving
Has nothing so goodly to give.' "

The insidious potency of the wine, the subtle puissance of the
religious atmosphere, were beginning to have an effect on the
white woman. Her intention to remain an onlooker at the
strange rites of this strange religion was overwhelmed by her
own deep religious instinct which, though constantly repressed,
had always been very strong within her. The apprehension that
Reha was planning to initiate her into this heathen religion
served to increase her perturbation.

Rejecting the next cup of wine, Tellectina proceeded to sum-
mon the eager Ceve-Peri from the doorway, who immediately
and jealously usurped the place of the other high priestess and,
after quaffing several cups of her own crimson wine, offered the
jar to Tellectina. Then, choosing one of the sacred volumes, she
proceeded with the ritual, reading first a passage from *The Trea-
tise on the Gods,* then from *The Way of All Flesh,* from *Impressions and Comments, Jean Christophe,* and *Jude the
Obscure.*

When the priestess ceased, the white woman was smiling with
pleasure, but almost immediately a puzzled frown appeared between her brows. "But, Ceve-Peri, couldn't you and Reha both
chant in unison? Your voices would blend beautifully, I think.
Surely there must be a few litanies written to Yeta-Bu by the
most divinely inspired of her worshipers which would arouse
the proper religious emotions in both of you simultaneously."

By way of reply, the priestesses lifted four sacred volumes
from the shelves and, opening the first one, commenced to read
aloud from the same page, the golden voices blending in their
beautiful intoning:

"'O Lord, rebuke me not in thine anger, neither chasten me in thy hot displeasure.

"'Have mercy on me, O Lord; for I am weak: O Lord, heal me, for my bones are vexed.

"'My soul is also sore vexed: but thou, O Lord, how long?'

"'Entreat me not to leave thee, or to return from following after thee: for whither thou goest, I will go: and where thou lodgest, I will lodge; thy people shall be my people, and thy God, my God.'

"'I returned, and saw under the sun, that the race is not to the swift, nor the battle to the strong, neither yet bread to the wise, nor yet riches to men of understanding, nor yet favour to men of skill; but time and chance happeneth to them all.'"

While the initiate stood in a state of delicious intoxication approaching rapture, but saddened by a strange sweet melancholy, the two voices resumed their intonation:

"'The man that hath no music in himself,
    Nor is moved with concord of sweet sounds,
    Is fit for treasons, stratagems, and spoils.'

"'Why, let the stricken deer go weep,
        The hart ungalled play;
    For some must watch, while some must sleep:
        So runs the world away.'

        "'To thine own self be true,
    And it must follow, as the night the day,
    Thou canst not then be false to any man.'

"'Tell me where is fancy bred,
    Or in the heart or in the head?'

" 'I must depart into a somber land wherein there is no laughter at all; and where the puzzled dead go wandering futilely through fields of scentless asphodel, and through tall sullen groves of myrtle,—the puzzled quiet dead, who may not even weep as I do now, but can only wonder what it is that they regret.'

" 'But the long low sobbing of the violin, troubling as the vague thoughts begotten by that season wherein summer is not yet perished from the earth, but lingers wanly in the tattered shrines of summer, speaks of what was and what might have been. A blind desire, the same which on warm moonlit nights was used to shake like fever in the veins of a boy whom I remember, is futilely plaguing a gray fellow with the gray wraiths of innumerable old griefs and with small stinging memories of long-dead delights.' "

As the voices died away, Tellectina crushed her hand over her left breast to still her heart, surcharged with a strange new joyousness. Again and again her ecstasy mounted and soared, only to swoon into an inexplicable sorrow. Tellectina, now agitated with delight, sank involuntarily to her knees and listened with bowed head.

" 'I said, "She must be swift and white,
    And subtly warm, and half perverse,
    And sweet like sharp soft fruit to bite,
    And like a snake's love lithe and fierce." ' "

" 'We thank with brief thanksgiving
        Whatever gods may be
    That no life lives for ever,
    That dead men rise up never;
    That even the weariest river
        Winds somewhere safe to sea.'

" 'She is right fair; what hath she done to thee?
   Nay, fair Lord Christ, lift up thine eyes and see;
     Had now thy mother such a lip—like this?
   Thou knowest how sweet a thing it is to me.'

" 'Thou hast conquered, O pale Galilean; the
     world has grown gray from thy breath;
   We have drunken of things Lethean,
     and fed on the fulness of death.'

" 'Though these that were Gods are dead,
     and thou being dead art a God . . .'

" 'Thy kingdom shall pass, Galilean, thy
     dead shall go down to thee dead.'

" 'Thou wert fair in the fearless old fashion,
     And thy limbs are as melodies yet,
   And move to the music of passion
     With lithe and lascivious regret.
   What ailed us, O Gods, to desert you
     For creeds that refuse and restrain?
   Come down and redeem us from virtue,
     Our Lady of Pain.' "

These hymns to Yeta-Bu were more than Tellectina could endure. She knelt in a breathless ecstasy while the blood throbbed
violently through all her body. Paroxysms of pleasure and pain
alternately shook the frail body of the young initiate, until, rapt
in a frenzy of exaltation, she prostrated herself at the foot of the
altar—giving up her Puritan soul to the great goddess Yeta-Bu
in a transport of adoration, silently dedicating herself to the
service and worship of this pagan deity. The final stage of the
initiation into this ancient mystery of the divinity, however, was
now at hand. Opening her eyes, the initiate trembled to see the

two priestesses slowly lifting the veil from the face of the goddess as they chanted:

" 'I am that which began;
    Out of me the years roll:
    Out of me God and man:
    I am equal and whole;
God changes, and man, and the form of them bodily;
    I am the soul.

" 'Before ever land was,
    Before ever the sea,
    Or soft hair of the grass,
    Or fair limbs of the tree,
Or the flesh-colored fruit of my branches, I was,
    and thy soul was in me.

" 'First life on my sources
    First drifted and swam;
    Out of me are the forces
    That save it or damn;
Out of me man and woman, and wild-beast and bird;
    before God was, I am.

" 'Beside or above me
    Nought is there to go;
    Love or unlove me,
    Unknow me or know,
I am that which unloves me and loves; I am stricken,
    and I am the blow.

" 'Canst thou say in thine heart
    Thou hast seen with thine eyes
    With what cunning of art
    Thou wast wrought in what wise,
By what force of what stuff thou wast shapen, and
    shown on my breast to the skies?

    " 'O my sons, O too dutiful
      Toward Gods not of me,
   Was I not enough beautiful?
    Was it hard to be free?
For behold, I am with you, am in you and of you;
   look forth now and see.' "

At the overpowering beauty of these words the young initiate's breathing stopped; life itself was suspended. Was not the face of the goddess unbearable to mortal eyes? Consciousness ebbed and flowed like the sea, till finally her blood began to move, to race, till she burned with a clear gemlike flame. For one awful moment she saw the face of Yeta-Bu—bare; and in an ecstasy of blissful agony, the blinded girl cried aloud and fell at the foot of the altar, fainting with a bliss that transcended consciousness. . . .

Consciousness seemed not lost but suspended as in a shining golden void. Tellectina never knew how long she remained in this state. But when full consciousness returned, the morning sun was shining in her face through a window in the eastern wall.

The instinct of self-preservation impelled her to flee from the temple on trembling limbs without even looking back at the goddess. Racing down to the beach, she flung herself headlong into the cooling sea. The water, which was unusually warm, effected such a cold shock to her feverish body that it brought her somewhat back to normality. But she swam on blindly as though pursued, until she reached the shore of Forta Feli.

Up and down the golden beach she paced, talking aloud—the excited words rushing forth incoherently: "What has happened to me? What have I done? Have I given my life and service to a heathen deity called Yeta-Bu, the goddess of all beauty? Did I give up my soul to her? But I don't believe in a soul! Why did these priestesses initiate me? Why did these sirens lure me to these islands in the first place? And why do people worship this goddess, anyway? Why do these pagan ceremonies produce such strange paroxysms in me? Am I really a convert—or sub-normal or ill or mad or merely drunk?

"I'm no longer a Christian, but I'm still something of a Puritan, for somehow these pagan orgies seem wrong. Yet why is it wrong to enjoy beauty? Is not all beauty natural and good? I resisted the three other priestesses, how came it that Reha and Ceve-Peri initiated me into this mystery without even consulting me? Before I realized what was happening to me I was already in an ecstatic trance.

"Oh, in the name of God—no, in the name of reason, what *are* these Siren Islands that I've discovered? these pagan temples as ancient as the human race itself? these votive offerings whose beauty is so compelling? this wine which intoxicates me so divinely? Oh, there is something queer about beauty that I don't understand! What is this thing that haunts me, maddens me, makes happiness smile through all my being—and then awakens all the sorrows of the world in my poor aching heart?

"How can so little a thing as a perfect human gesture, the subtle tones of a human voice, the curling of a woman's dress about her thighs, a scarlet flower nestling against a girl's dark hair, the lines of a wine jug, the sound and sense of little words—how can these trifles fill and feed me with delight and despair? It is not reasonable—it is inexplicable—it is impossible!

"Why, when I merely look at the curve of a woman's throat, do I feel that all my questions are answered, that my restless seeking for I know not what is stilled? Why—why does a feeling of satisfaction search out the depths of my being and settle there like a dove come home to her nest?

"What *is* this thing called beauty? Why do the human senses lure one into ecstatic orgies? What is this essence which emanates from mere sound and color and line? What are these will-o'-the-wisps which we call 'ideas' that flit through the human head? Why should any or all of these things cause joy to course riotously through our veins—and what is joy? And why should they cause sadness to weigh on our hearts—and what is sadness?

"What—I ask you—is beauty?

"Explain this intoxicating mystery to me!

"For I am Tellectina! I am not content to enjoy my senses—I must also understand them."

As Tellectina was pacing feverishly along the shore of the Isle of Forta Feli, she suddenly beheld a very welcome sight: an elderly man sitting on the trunk of an ancient palm tree, writing in a small book.

Greatly excited, she related to him in incoherent sentences all the strange adventures she had experienced on the six Siren Islands. The man smiled serenely, stating that he understood her condition perfectly, that she was not subnormal at all, but rather abnormally sensitive and an unconscious worshiper of Yeta-Bu.

"But—but," the young woman stammered, "is it—is it not immoral to worship beauty so ardently? While in those temples my whole being was consumed—I burned like a flame!"

The man's reply rendered his young inquisitor speechless: "'To burn always with this hard gemlike flame, to maintain this ecstasy, is success in life. . . . While all melts under our feet, we may well grasp at an exquisite passion, or any contribution to knowledge that seems by a lifted horizon to set the spirit free for a moment, or any stirring of the senses, strange dyes, strange colors, and curious odors, or the work of the artist's hands, or the face of one's friend.'"

"You mean," the girl whispered in awed tones, "you mean—that just to *feel* this ecstasy is—is important?"

Her companion nodded his assent, then continued: "'We are all under sentence of death, but with a sort of indefinite reprieve. . . . Some spend this interval in listlessness, some in high passions, the wisest, . . . in art and song. . . . Of such wisdom, the poetic passion, the desire of beauty, the love of art for its own sake, has most.'"

Both Reha and Ceve-Peri had followed her and now plied her with wine. Laughing with joy, all three began to dance in circles about the quiet figure of the man, who waited patiently till Tellectina's exuberance died down so that he could make himself heard.

" 'Not the fruit of experience, but experience itself, is the end!' "

"Oh, that's it, that's it!" Tellectina exclaimed rapturously; "but the Puritan in me thought everything should be for a purpose—that pleasure was not an end in itself! But who, after all, am I to decide what is beautiful and what is not?"

Raising his hand to stop her volubility, he explained, " 'In æsthetic criticism the first step is . . . to know one's own impression as it really is. . . . What is this song or picture . . . to *me?* . . . Does it give me pleasure, and if so, what sort or degree of pleasure? . . . He who experiences these impressions strongly, and drives directly at the discrimination and analysis of them, has no need to trouble himself with the abstract question what beauty is in itself, or what its exact relation to truth or experience—metaphysical questions, as unprofitable as metaphysical questions elsewhere.' "

The girl leapt to her feet in joy. For invariably, to hear her own chaotic and vague young thoughts nicely arranged in neat sentences caused her to consider the speaker the most marvelous and admirable person she had ever met. "What did you say your name was, you wonderful person?"

He reintroduced himself as Walter Pater.

Laughing and dancing, Tellectina pirouetted about in the sand until the soles of her feet burned. But as usual, after these spasms of pleasure, the tears suddenly welled up. "But why does the thing we call beauty affect human beings at all? And why, oh, why must everything I enjoy most in the world invariably make me weep in the end? It seems a contradiction. There's something queer about all beauty that I don't understand. Is something wrong with me, perhaps?"

Just then a small man with black hair and strange troubled eyes came strolling along the beach and assured the perplexed young girl that nothing was wrong with her. " 'An immortal instinct,' he continued, 'deep within the spirit of man, is a sense

of the Beautiful. Thus when we find ourselves melted into tears
—not through excess of pleasure, but through a certain petulant,
impatient sorrow at our inability to grasp *now,* wholly here on
earth those divine and rapturous joys, of which *through* the
poem, or *through* the music, we attain to but brief and indeter-
minate glimpses.' "

The young man, whom Tellectina had recognized as Edgar
Allan Poe, went off along the beach singing a little poem to
himself, while the girl called her thanks after him. She sat in the
sand at Pater's feet, so absorbed in thought that she was unaware
of his departure or the appearance of a third man dressed in a
flowing Japanese gown.

She was debating aloud, "But this man Swinburne—I feel as
if he voices—I mean, oh, I *want* to *understand!*"

The stranger, after introducing himself as Lafcadio Hearn,
said that he would be glad to explain Swinburne to her. " 'Swinburne, like Shelley, is well born; like Shelley, he has been from
his early days . . . a furious radical; like Shelley, he has always
been an enemy of Christianity; and like Shelley, he has also been
an enemy to conventions and prejudices of every description.' "

Breathlessly, incredulously, the girl whispered, "Oh, but so
am—so have——"

" 'His view of life,' " Hearn continued, " 'is that the essential
thing is to live as excellently as possible, but we must not suppose that excellence is used in the moral sense. Swinburne's idea
of excellence is the idea of completeness. His notions of right
or wrong are not the religious or the social notions of right or
wrong. . . . Swinburne's idea is . . . that man has no god. . . .
He has no divine help, no one to trust except himself.' "

"Ah, maybe that's it! Am I, perhaps, a pagan by nature simply
trying to burst the Puritan mold in which, as a child, my ancestors cast me?"

Hearing another voice near by singing the praises of paganism she stopped to listen. A young Englishman was speaking:
" 'The great split . . . broke life into spirit and matter, heroics
and diabolics, virtue and sin and all the other accursed antitheses.

. . . Being alternately a hero and a sinner is much more sensational than being an integrated man. So as men seem to have the Yellow Press in the blood, like syphilis, they went back on Homer and Apollo; they followed Plato and Euripides. And Plato and Euripides handed them over to the Stoics and the Neo-Platonists. And these in turn handed humanity over to the Christians.' "

"But I—I refuse to be handed over, Mr. Aldous Huxley!" Tellectina announced defiantly.

" 'The resurrection of Apollo,' the man said, 'the Etruscan Apollo. I've been his worshiper and self-appointed priest ever since. Or at any rate, I've tried to be. But it's difficult. . . . You can't get away from the things the God protests against. Because they've become a part of you. Tradition and education have driven them into your very bones. . . . I've got Plato and Jesus in my bones.' "

The girl's face clouded, "Jesus in my bones? Yes, I had Jesus in my bones too, Aldous Huxley—but no more—no more! Now I only have joy and beauty and naturalness—paganism, in other words!"

Again she began to dance joyously along the beach, but paused once more to observe an elderly man reeling drunkenly down toward the water. Hailing her with a leer, he continued to chant strange words, which made Tellectina draw back repelled. There was one thing, he said, however, which startled her into admiration as he staggered off again after just having missed falling into the sea. He was chanting it as he disappeared into the jungle:

" 'Be always drunken. Nothing else matters. . . . If you would not feel the horrible burden of Time weighing on your shoulders and crushing you to the earth, be drunken continually.

" 'Drunken with what? with wine, with poetry, or with virtue, as you will. But be drunken.' "

"Ah, yes, Monsieur Baudelaire," Tellectina called. "I know who you are! And I intend to be drunken the remainder of my life. For I am determined to live always on this marvelous

Island of Forta Feli where I can constantly visit the adjacent islands." She caught up a cup of wine which Ceve-Peri was urging upon her.

"And I shall always be drunken on the wine of beauty and ecstasy!" She drained the cup at one draft. "Half-measures are for puny people! It's whole heart or none for me! This is Certitude—it's a Siren Island, not a mountain, as I had dreamed. And here I shall remain always!" Like a mad Bacchante she began to dance across the whole length of the island.

Finally she sank exhausted on the sands, but her blood was on fire. Extracting a small yellow cylinder which she always kept concealed about her person, she applied the Cianite Vitrgrew drug contained therein in the prescribed manner, until her ecstasy increased twofold. It stimulated her even more than the wine, producing visions of indescribable beauty. While under the influence of this narcotic, her body became insensate; she, as a personality, ceased to exist. She felt like a vessel through which great waves of joy and pure white ecstasy swept—flowing through her, down her right arm and out her finger tips, leaving her empty, but tingling with a joy greater than any she had ever experienced in her entire life.

Recovering slightly, she endeavored to recapture the lovely visions and write them out on paper. She wrote feverishly for hours, until her nerves were in such an agitated state that it was an easy matter for Chotu to lure her and all the drunken natives over to the seventh Siren Island—the only one which Tellectina had not yet visited. As all her senses were abnormally alert, he wisely chose his moment. Every nerve in her body was taut—vibrating like an Æolian harp to every breath of wind, to every word, to the slightest touch.

"Ah," murmured the beautiful youth as he slipped his arm around her waist, "you have no idea of what pleasures await you on the seventh island. It excels all the others."

"Are you the high priest on the seventh island?"

"No," he replied, "but I can lead you to him."

Chotu gently stroked her hair; then he bent her back and

fitted his golden young body against hers until Tellectina almost swooned. Catching her up suddenly in his arms, he bore her to the edge of the water. While they were swimming luxuriously through the warm sea, Chotu again attempted to encircle her waist, but, struggling to free herself, she remonstrated with him, saying, "You befuddle my brain when you touch me. I am Tellectina, and I like to understand everything; so you lead the way, but don't caress me!"

The youth laughed and hurried on to the seventh island, saying, "Later, then, ah, later!"

CHAPTER X

WHEN THEY ARRIVED at the mysterious seventh island, Tellectina rose dripping from the sea, and the very waves curled playfully about her limbs, caressing them in an astonishing but pleasant manner.

Although not far removed from the other six Siren Islands, the seventh presented an arresting variation in its flora. Unnaturally large and brilliant flowers flaunted themselves in suggestive shapes, exuding such seductive sweetness that it almost sickened the young Puritan, accustomed only to chaste odors.

"I feel very apprehensive," Tellectina exclaimed to Chotu. "There's something indecently beautiful about this place. But I must explore it at any cost."

The native youth took her by the hand, whereupon the white woman permitted herself to be drawn into the jungle. He smiled significantly as he glanced over his shoulder at the five native girls who were following silently behind Tellectina—unnoticed by her as yet.

Aware that he was dealing with a Puritan, Chotu kept their destination a secret. Eventually they were confronted by a sight so astounding that Tellectina stopped abruptly in her path. There, buried in the very heart of the jungle, though in a perfect state of preservation, loomed before her a most extraordinary temple. Two beautifully modeled columns of white marble lay recumbent in the deep grass—like the great thighs of some

271

fallen goddess—while beyond them rose a low white dome with a strange Gothic doorway stained a dull red. Above this the temple was ornamented with small twin domes strangely modeled and wonderful to see, the tip of each being faintly dyed with red. Another column, also recumbent, connected the main body of the temple with a small round structure whose entrance was stained a bright crimson.

Having been convinced long since that her religion in Chimera was ridiculous, Tellectina was still irresistibly attracted and yet unaccountably afraid of even the external manifestation of such cults. Cautiously she drew nearer.

Suddenly a girl and youth could be seen approaching the temple. The man, who looked vaguely familiar to Tellectina, had his arm around the girl and was gazing down at her adoringly. When she lifted her face to laugh into his eyes, the moonlight revealed to Tellectina's consternation the face of—Femina. Concealing herself in the shadows Tellectina watched them in amazement. The young man approached the doorway and was in the act of doing that which was requisite before he could pass through the small Gothic entrance when the astounded Tellectina commanded him to stop.

Angrily Femina turned upon the intruder and glared at her through half-closed sullen eyes, then advanced toward her sister with such a slow sinuous movement that Tellectina instinctively recoiled. "This is no place for you!" Femina hissed in a low sibilant whisper.

Tellectina nodded her head sagely and whispered, "I thought as much. You're up to some mischief or you wouldn't be so angry at my finding you! Have you forgotten Olev so soon?"

By way of answer Femina lifted the garland of flowers which covered her bare breasts and disclosed the small pink mark resembling a face underneath the left one.

"Oh, so you, too, have a stigma!" Tellectina exclaimed.

"But of course. Yet one must do something to forget Olev in order to continue living at all. The Ecstatic Mystery performed in the temple helps one forget. But it is a rite for the privileged only. And you're a Puritan, you can't be admitted, so go away at once!"

"Go! I've neglected you too long already, Femina Christian, and I'm responsible for you. I've been so absorbed in my own discoveries this last year, however, that I haven't given you a thought. I've been converted to the pagan religion of Yeta-Bu, and meanwhile I simply let you go your own way—and I might have known that it would be the wrong way. I sensed it the minute I landed on this island. You'd better come away at once!"

"See here, Tina, I'll brook none of your interference from now on! You've tried to dominate me all my life! But now that I've discovered Forta Velo I've come into my own at last. I have become converted to Ecstaticism, which involves many amorous rites beyond your comprehension."

Tellectina disregarded Femina's words, so interested was she in her sister's appearance. "I've never seen you look so blooming—so radiant and young! Have you a new beauty secret?"

At this her antagonism melted suddenly, and Femina laughed that provocative little laugh which especially irritated Tellectina because she was unable to fathom what it concealed. "It *was* a secret, but since the little Puritan has been clever enough to find me she might as well remain and see for herself. You'll be the first Puritan, however, ever initiated into the Mystery of Mysteries; but if you interfere in any way, you'll regret it!"

Tellectina was speechless for a moment, and Femina continued, "There are fourteen absolutely essential preliminary rituals which the priest must perform before he is permitted to enter the temple, and neither the priest nor I, the celebrant, care for a Tellectina as a witness, so conceal yourself as best you can."

Tellectina obeyed, taking care that the priest at least should not be aware of her presence, but watching his every move with wide and fascinated eyes. The initial ceremony seemed to consist of the hierophant touching the celebrant in the prescribed manner.

Then with reverence and exceeding great pride the priest

brought forth the god which it was customary for him to keep always in his possession and guard with his very life if need be. The explorer gazed at this idol in astonishment and amusement. It was being prepared to be introduced into the temple and enshrined on the altar. Femina now lighted the sacred fire all around it.

That the most primitive peoples even in moments of the most devout fervor should worship such a ludicrous object astounded the explorer. To her cool critical eye their idol was far from a work of art. As soon as Femina, apparently a high priestess, lighted the sacred fire, Tellectina saw that the image was composed of some plastic red material evidently indigenous to Forta Velo, which when sufficiently heated, was capable of expanding till the god stood erect like a divine athlete; so lifelike, so strong and muscular, so full-blooded that the turgid veins were actually visible beneath their delicate covering.

Tellectina looked on unmoved, although she conceded it to be the finest representation of a member of the male sex she had ever seen. The instant the fire died down, however, the image collapsed. Tellectina laughed, but Femina's ardor blinded her to the amusing aspects of her god. It was lamentably obvious, Tellectina reflected, that the craftsman who had designed this exceedingly ingenious device valued utility and economy more than beauty, for he had constructed it in such a way as to serve two purposes. When it was not discharging its holy function, it was used as a mere outlet for waste water.

"No," Tellectina protested, "I fail to see wherein this grotesque object is worthy of worship."

"Of course you do," Femina responded dreamily, "that's because you are not acquainted with his divine attributes."

"Well, I confess they are not apparent to the eye."

"Certainly not. You have to feel them. The trouble with you, Tellectina, is that you have never had any real inner life. If only once the spirit of Ecstaci ever entered into you, then——"

"Who?"

"Ecstaci, our God," Femina whispered reverently. "As long

as the priestess keeps the fire burning, he can maintain his erect position for long hours on end. You see, Prolongation is one of his chief attributes, it being absolutely essential, as he must allow his feminine worshipers sufficient time to become aroused to the heights of divine rapture. Although it requires longer to enkindle the women, their emotions are profounder than those of men. And it is his manly uprightness which permits the Ecstatic ceremony to be performed continuously and be prolonged until the female devotees are incited to the most consummate frenzy and cease from sheer exhaustion. Further proof that he is a god is that although he is ready to discharge his holy function at any time and thus bring the orgy to a climax (which is also the signal for its cessation), he exerts truly godlike restraint, and it is for this, likewise, that he is worshiped by countless women and the more intelligent and ardent men."

"But, Femina, love should be the chief attribute of any god! And with that important element lacking in your Ecstaci, I don't believe these orgies can be beautiful. Sensuality seems to me to be his chief attribute; so you'll have to prove to me that these rites have anything beautiful or spiritual in them—otherwise I'll take you away from this immoral island this very night!"

Femina laughed softly. "Wait, ah, wait, little Puritan, until you feel the spirit of Ecstaci move within you."

Tellectina stood gazing at her sister in stupefaction: perhaps she was a little unbalanced to belong to such a cult.

Then the priest performed a strange ceremony which was merely a symbolic pantomime of the final rite. He held erect a miniature torch, a representation of the great symbol of divine fire, called Li-Ngam by the initiated. Next he did that which was customary to prepare Femina to take her part in the ceremony and immersed the Lesser Li-Ngam into the basin of holy water known as the Lesser Yo-Ni which she held up to him. His object was to immerse it as many times as possible without extinguishing the flame. And miraculously enough he was able to perform this strange feat many times. Each time he plunged the torch into the basin with a peculiar rhythmic motion which so stirred the religious emotions of Femina that even Tellectina was moved by it.

And it was at this point that Femina forced on her sister a cup of sacramental wine which Tellectina quaffed against her will and which she realized too late was a powerful aphrodisiac.

Now the priest began the elaborate and intricate rituals necessary before actually entering the temple, many of which Tellectina found it difficult to follow and impossible to understand the significance of. And although her brain reeled in a strange delicious way she forced herself desperately to take note of all that was happening.

Once more Femina added fuel to the sacred flame, and the priest, now breathing heavily with emotion, thrust the idol through the door of the temple while Femina gave a little gasp of agonized joy.

As they advanced down the dim aisle, Femina drew in a deep breath and whispered, "Don't you love the odor of sanctity that pervades the temple?"

Tellectina laughed disdainfully. "Sanctity indeed! Why, it's acrid and pungent! It's very repellent to me!"

Femina drew in another breath. "Ah, I love it! It never fails to stir me strangely! It is used only in the Forta Velo ceremony."

Tellectina looked about her to locate its origin. Lowering her head to the font in front of her she said, "Oh, so it's not incense, it's the holy water!"

"Of course. For days after the ceremony the odor clings to my clothes and skin. I revel in it!"

Tellectina glared at her sister, then followed her down to the altar before which their god was to be enshrined.

Tellectina took it upon herself to make a further examination of this amazing temple. She came upon some sacred books on which were emblazoned the names of some of the famous priestesses of past ages. The record of their devotion was scarcely legible after all these years, but their names alone reassured her. There were Sappho, Cleopatra, Catherine, Ninon, George, and

Margaret, and others of more recent date. But the extreme rarity of priestesses of Ecstaci in the world's history puzzled Tellectina not a little.

Searching further, she discovered a secret cabinet containing the sacred books of Forta Velo written by such inspired men as Ellis, Velde, and Frazer, and there was one—only one, by a woman, whose name was Stopes. Tellectina, however, was not sufficiently familiar with the language of Forta Velo to understand much of them. While she was delving in these volumes, the high priest, who proved to be none other than Femina's handsome companion, came forward and after touching Tellectina in the manner prescribed by the ancient rite, placed to her lips the sacramental wine which was intended to induce the proper religious emotions in the initiate. After having partaken of it, Tellectina realized that it was an aphrodisiac.

After the white Puritan had been initiated into these primary rituals, she was led through several doors of rectangular biblioesque design into a room beyond to witness the main ceremonies. Tellectina stood to one side watching this amazing spectacle breathlessly. All the youths and maidens of the Isle of Forta Velo formed in two long lines facing each other. The girls bore wine jars of peculiar shape, the base being pear-shaped and the neck narrow and elongated. The mouth of this pink clay vessel was stained red. The youths flourished small blunt spears made from the trunk of the Manlig tree in which this island abounded.

In accordance with a primitive custom as old as man a virgin was duly sacrificed by the high priest on the altar of Ecstaci. The maiden's head was severed, and the cessation of blood was regarded as a propitious omen for the ceremonial dance to begin. After the heads of the spears were cut slightly by the medicine men of the tribe, the youths advanced toward the maidens, holding their weapons erect. The girls retreated; then the youths withdrew, and the girls advanced. This was repeated with increasing rapidity in that peculiar rhythm prescribed by Ecstaci. The drums beat louder and louder, and faster and faster—like the throb of a gigantic heart. Finally, in a frenzy of ecstasy the youths plunged their spears into the jars until the red wine spilled like blood over the floor.

These young couples disappeared quickly into the shadows, while their places were taken by two lines of men and women, the latter carrying jars similar to those of the maidens except that they were larger and contained white wine instead of red. When Tellectina observed how inordinately proud of their weapons the men were, it was impossible to restrain her laughter. Some of them were bent out of shape, while others appeared small and harmless; and surprisingly enough, the smallest men often wielded the largest spears and vice versa. She overheard some of the women whispering among themselves, declaring that the real merit of the weapons lay not in their size but in the skill with which their owners handled them. The women religiously performed the customary ceremony of resistance, then permitted the men to plunge their spears to the bottom of the jars of wine and carry them off as partners. Like all primitive religious festivals, this resolved itself into a drunken orgy.

The only objects discernible in the gloom, however, were men and women everywhere in the shadows beyond the columns writhing like tortured animals. Tellectina had thought this a ritual of joy, yet on every side there were moans and cries and even weeping to be heard. Only occasionally were there ripples of warm laughter. She watched for a long time, but the devout were apparently performing the same ceremony over and over again. The aphrodisiac she had drunk combined with the excessive heat and the ceaseless motion of the priest caused her brain to reel uncontrollably.

Suddenly Femina began to moan softly. Then she whispered, "Now, Tellectina, you're to be initiated into the Mystery of Mysteries."

The priest laid his hot hand on Tellectina, and thereupon ensued a terrific struggle; for, though burning with curiosity, Tellectina was nevertheless afraid of being drawn into their drunken orgy. To her consternation she was obliged to fight more violently against Femina than against the man. Suddenly out of the shadows stole Ese, Reha, Mllse, and Astte, led by Chotu, all of whom had followed Tellectina into the temple without her knowledge. To her dismay they at once began to aid and abet the priest in every way, betraying her completely into his hands.

Suddenly the priest bore the idol into the inner sanctum, and Tellectina could but follow. Now the representation of the god was of a size and strength wonderful to see. Desperately Tellectina strove to keep her eyes open and her mind calm, but her lids were heavy and her thoughts rose and fell upon delicious waves of sensation. All was an incredible confusion of strange scents and sights, sucking sounds and soul-stirring sensations. And it seemed that in the presence of Ecstaci, Tellectina and Femina miraculously merged into one being.

By one of those curious and inopportune flashes of memory Tellectina recalled fragments of the words of Apuleius in *The Golden Ass*, concerning his initiation into the mystery of the goddess Isis:

"The priest took my hand and brought me to the most secret and sacred place of the temple. Thou wouldest peradventure demand, thou studious reader, what was said and done there: verily I would like to tell thee if it were lawful for me to tell, thou wouldest know if it were convenient for thee to hear; but both thy ears and my tongue should incur the like pain of rash curiosity. Howbeit I will not long torment thy mind, which peradventure is somewhat religious and given to some devotion; listen therefore, and believe it to be true. Thou shalt understand that I approached near unto hell, even to the gates of Proserpine, and after that I was ravished throughout all the elements, I returned to my proper place: about midnight I saw the sun brightly shine, I saw likewise the gods celestial and the gods infernal, before whom I presented myself and worshiped them. Behold now have I told thee, which although thou hast heard, yet it is necessary that thou conceal it: wherefore this only will

I tell, which may be declared without offense for the understanding of the profane."

Through Tellectina's mind ran a fragmentary rewording of her initiation into the Mystery of Mysteries.

"The initiate sees the priest's eyes glowing with that strange fire betokening his passage into the state of ecstasy, feels his hot panting breath, obeys his command to perform the offertory, lifts the chalice, knows herself to be filled with a maddening joy, feels the divine exaltation move within her, perceives that her ardor mounts and mounts till she writhes with ecstasy, till in a frenzy of exquisite agony, she sinks her nails into the priest's back and buries her teeth in his shoulder as she unites with divine Ecstaci . . . and is sensible of other secret sensations unlawful to be uttered—things forbidden to be known, incommunicable except to the initiate. . . . And at the moment of divine consummation, she passes into oblivion." . . .

It was dawn when Tellectina was awakened by the terrific snoring of the young man beside her. Even that handsome youth was not rendered more attractive by a wide-open mouth and a slack lower jaw. Once more she knew herself to be a separate entity, for beside her lay Femina sleeping like a child—her skin like milk and rose petals, and her vividly crimson lips parted in a smile of utter content. Still in a daze, Tellectina struggled weakly to her feet and departed from the temple.

Emerging into the morning sunlight, she sank weakly to the ground, her mind dazed but lulled by last night's experiences, her thighs throbbing strangely.

She hid her guilty face in her arms. Before she was able to arouse her drugged wits to action, however, Femina and the high priest appeared before her with beatific faces.

"Well, little Puritan," Femina inquired mockingly, "how did you enjoy your initiation into the Mystery of Mysteries?"

Tellectina passed her hand over her eyes in a bewildered fashion. "I'm—I'm confused. I was drunk. I—I swooned away, but—but I'm sure that I don't approve of this sort of paganism."

She drew herself up with a tremendous effort at severe dignity.

"What, did not our divine Ecstaci or the ardor of our wonderful Passino or even *my* transports convert you?"

Tellectina started to her feet at the sound of the priest's name and faced the two shameless ones standing before her. "Ah, so that's this young man's name! High priest indeed! I recognize him now. He is merely a servant. What do you mean, Passino, by leaving your master's house and coming to this island and setting up such a religion? How can you cheapen yourself, Femina, by consorting with a mere servant? For shame! Come, we'll leave this island at once!"

"Servant!" the young man exclaimed. "Passino is a master in Forta Velo!"

"You may be master here," Tellectina scoffed, "but Passino is supposed to be Olev's servant. You traitor! How dared you desert us all those two years we were married to dear Olev! Ah, what would Olev say if he knew that I had succumbed to you!"

"I always sleep when the Olevs aren't clever enough to keep me awake. Why do you pretend to be ignorant of my ways?"

"Well, I'm certainly not ignorant of one point. Femina, you must give up this Passino at once!"

"Give up Passino!" her sister exclaimed. "Oh, Tina, you don't know what you're saying! Remember, he is the hierophant, the earthly representative of the great god Ecstaci. He has aroused in me such exaltations as I never dreamed existed in the whole world, such as I never dreamed any woman capable of!"

She took a step nearer her sister. "Tellectina, don't you understand that I have become a devout pagan; that I have gone native, reverted to nature and all her glorious ways; that Ecstaci is both natural and beautiful; and that I intend to live on this wonderful island henceforth?"

"But this so-called religion—it's—it's beneath——"

"Beneath? Why, it's *above* everything I've ever known as far as pure ecstasy is concerned—even above love. For love is too full of anguish, but Forta Velo lulls anguish to sleep."

The other woman looked incredulous. "What, a woman who knows no anguish! Impossible!"

"No anguish, no irascibility, no nervousness, nor sleeplessness —the specters that haunt most women's lives. Only ecstasy and content do we know here."

"No, no, Femina, all this is too good to be true—judging from what many married women have confided in me."

"Forta Velo has nothing to do with marriage."

"But it should have. And besides, a contented woman is a contradiction of terms."

"Everywhere in the world, it is a contradiction—except in Forta Velo; for no man is permitted on this island unless he swears to make sacrifices to the local deity. Nor can any man become a priest of Ecstaci until he learns to perform the three great rituals, the Sustained, the Erotogenic, and the Climactic. Very few men ever acquire sufficient self-control for the first, as it is a slow protracted ceremony involving sacrifice of their own earthly and animal cravings.

"The second is generally a divine gift even to the novice, but can be acquired by study. For this Erotogenic ceremony is divided into nine parts: the third part of which should be performed in both forward and reverse positions; the fourth, fifth and sixth repeated, first on the left side then on the right; the fifth, however, demanding service of both lips and hands; while the sixth ritual must be performed backward; the seventh with hands only; the eighth kneeling; and the ninth facing forward. The three major rituals are, you see, composed of seventeen minor rites—seventeen being the mystic number required by Ecstaci."

"But they sound too complicated for the minister," Tellectina objected, "though the part of the celebrant seems passive."

"Her chief duty is to respond. But few men ever learn to perform the last and most important ritual at all. Even those who perform the other two major ones perfectly—and thus become priests of Ecstaci—seldom are able, even with years of practice, to perform the third and thereby become high priests. It involves a peculiar rhythm too difficult for most men to master—a sort of frenzied rotary movement, in fact."

"Something like that of the whirling dervish?"

Femina laughed. "Well, covering a much smaller area, of course. And that which incites the worshiper to the supremest frenzy is a continuation of the fourth and fifth ceremonies, simultaneously with the ninth, but that is absolutely beyond the powers of most men."

"I shouldn't think that any man on earth would be willing to go to the trouble of learning all these intricate ceremonies!" Tellectina said.

"Damned few are! And that's why, when they do, the female worshipers confuse dulia with latria (and worship them as divine representatives of Ecstaci). But it is their loss, for not until a man has performed all seventeen ceremonies several times does he realize what transports they can produce in himself as well as in his female devotee."

"So," Tellectina said, "this Ecstaci of the Forta Velo is what you've been discovering while I failed to keep strict surveillance over you! Of course, I realize that all countries have different religions, but this one seems absolutely indecent to me. How does it happen that I have read only the vaguest references to this Ecstaticism? Is it like the ancient pagan religions which——"

"I know nothing and care nothing about other pagan religions. (You know I never like to read anything but love stories.) But I do know that during the third ceremony, when the priest penetrates the holy of holies, performs the rotations, and pours his libations over the altar, that that is the moment when the worshiper reaches such a high pitch of fervor that she feels united with the infinite!"

Tellectina stared at Femina, blinked, and shook herself as if endeavoring to shake off some evil spell. "I don't believe you! I repeat, I don't believe you; and in the second place, you needn't think you can indulge in all sorts of orgies just because you disguise them as a religion!"

"It's not a disguise, you ignoramus! I am a genuine Ecstatica. I was not aware of my own latent powers till Passino led me to Forta Velo."

Tellectina suddenly realized that her usual mocking and unfathomable sister was now in deadly earnest. "Well, Femina, I simply don't understand you."

"You never have, my fine intellectual!"

"But I always maintain that I hold an open mind on all subjects—even the two most controversial ones, religion and morality. Being a creature of the mind only, I realize furthermore, after experiencing both love and marriage, that emotions are subject to quite different laws—if any—from thought. But why didn't Olev the Second or Third initiate you into Ecstaticism and not leave it to a mere servant? How is it possible to be married twice before you discover that you are capable of such intensity of emotion that you must dignify it by the name of religion?"

"Why? Why? I don't know! I don't give a damn about your reasons, but I do know that I almost hate every man I've ever known because they failed to initiate me into this wonderful cult. To think that I might have missed it altogether! What a tragedy—for any woman! If Olev the Third had lived, I might never have known it!"

"Oh, Femina, how can you say such things?"

"Because they're true! Your idealism blinds you to all reality, if it's unpleasant. Olev the Third was a wonderful man, but, like most Elam Domitanns, incapable of being a representative of divine Ecstaci."

"Well," Tellectina said, "I condemn the whole proceedings, please understand that, but I am nevertheless very curious."

"Ah, any woman who has experienced the divine transports that I have could not condemn these rites! Listen, you utterly ignorant intellectual, and I'll attempt to describe the indescribable. For what is to you merely bodily contact with a man is to me communion with the unknown, the unknowable. A woman ceases to be a mere creature of the flesh, she passes through many metamorphoses, in the space of a few minutes—a few hours."

Femina ran her hands caressingly over her own small breasts and slim thighs. "Have you never heard a woman sing the Vaginae? Do you not know that chants are sung continually during the Forbidden Ceremonies? Have you never heard Woman's Song of Ecstasy?"

A strange light came into the young devotee's eyes, and, seized suddenly by intense emotional rapture and lyrical joy, she slowly began to chant:

"I am a flower, full blown—heavy with amorous perfume; a luscious tropical fruit lain long under the Southern sun. I am a bed of lotus blossoms opening wide voluptuous petals under the strong sun of his passion; his eyes and lips and hands a swarm of hungry bees that sip and rifle me of all my honey.

"I am the earth—the parched and hungry earth. When his kisses rain upon me, joy floods the farthermost reaches of my being; every remotest little rivulet is filled and fed, when the tide of feeling rushes inland. I am the earth, wherein all the rivers of all the world fill and rise and rush headlong to the primal sea, when ecstasy moves within me.

"I am a soft couch to man's weariness, the basin wherein he refreshes himself, the fountain wherein he renews his youth; the earth wherein he is buried to rise to new life again. Woman is the shrine wherein man communes with his god.

"And I am a child, an eternal child born into the morning of the world. An innocence lies upon me that a thousand years of kisses could not remove. I am simple and clean and joyous. I mate naturally like the dryads and nymphs—like the butterflies and birds—I am elemental in my instincts and desires. I am pagan pure and simple. I am a daughter of earth made divine by the touch of passion, a high priestess serving the great god Ecstaci."

For a moment the woman paused; then, raising her arms in exultation, continued: "Ah, yes, let me lift up my pæan of praise! Let other women sing of their passion in pale pretty words which say nothing. But I—I am fearless and unafraid! I am proud of my passion—I exult in it! My blood leaps and laughs in my veins! I sing a song of the happy woman, the free, the natural woman! I sing of fulfillment and radiant bloom!"

With radiant face she stood there, her proud head lifted high.

"Man is my lover and my child. I am mistress and mother all in one. With his lips at my breast, I would to God I could nourish him—with my milk, my blood, my flesh—my soul and my life, if need be—anything—everything—to comfort him, the eternal child. I, the eternal mother, yearn to protect him from all hurt and harm.

"Ah, are not love and passion momentarily the same? Is not to awaken a woman's body to awaken her heart and soul? Does not her whole being quiver with joy? Does not the man cease to be a man and become merely Man and she Woman incarnate? Think you that union is a simple thing to a woman: beginning with a kiss and ending in sleep and oblivion, as with a man? Ah, no, woman's body is but the symbol of her inner being. Her spirit takes flight to the infinite when the door of the Yoni is opened at the touch of the Lingam. She hears the music of the spheres and surgings among the stars! Then slowly she sinks to earth again through soft and silent darkness, into peace unutterable.

"All questions answered, all fear and all frettings ended. It is the end and a new beginning, all longing at last quieted. Its sleep but a foretaste of the sleep of death—and peace everlasting."

Then like a true religionist Femina seemed to be passing into orison, for her impassioned voice was almost inaudible.

"To submit, to be subdued, to be a mere nothing—his plaything, to lose myself in him, my master, there is no joy like that! When his face lies close against mine and I breathe in his hot breath, I am but a bit of clay, and he is a god breathing the breath of life into me, and then . . . and at last, in this moment of white heat we become one, my senses no longer able to distinguish my limbs from his limbs, my body from his body, myself from himself—united, irrevocably and forever. The twain shall be one flesh—godlike—hermaphroditic like the original gods of mankind—a divine dual oneness—without beginning and without end—perfect and whole—complete—incomparable —incomprehensible."

The triumphant voice paused; whereupon Passino immediately rushed upon her, but she withheld him with upraised arm. The glow in her eyes changed from that of mystic exaltation to the fire of anger, and she pierced Tellectina with her glance.

"Have you never heard the Special Plea for Puritans? Know you not, O Puritan, that desire, though it spring from the soil, may be made to flower? Were you ever unable to forget the earth in which it had its birth? Though music comes from bits of wood and wire, do you love music the less for that? Have you no ears to hear the symphony, the mighty primordial song that rises from the white body of a woman loved and loving? Must passion always lie on earth a crippled, sordid thing? Can you not lift it on imagination's wing? Is there no beauty, no poetry, in lips meeting lips, distilling slow wine? Have the wings of your imagination been clipped by convention?"

Suddenly she took up the refrain in a low, seductive voice. "O Puritan, when he kissed you—when he thrust both his tongues into both your mouths, did not the wine of your senses quicken even your mind to new life and thought? Could your spirit, housed in a body which trembled with such ecstasy, remain untouched, untroubled, unmoved? By the violent storms in your being was not the very soul loosed for one awful instant from its moorings in the flesh? Did you feel nothing of a striving after the unattainable, after the unknowable? Oh, did you not know perfect beauty for one intensest moment? Did you not soar beyond the limits of human thought and touch infinity? unite with God, dissolve in the universe? return into the womb of time whence you came and whither you long always to return?"

The chanting ceased. Femina stood with her head thrown back, her eyes closed, her face a living replica of St. Theresa immortally caught in marble by Bernini in her transcendent moment of agonized ecstasy.

Tellectina remained on the ground transfixed and helpless. When Passino suddenly rushed upon her, embracing her madly, she fell swooning in his arms. . . .

It was dusk when she awakened and found herself in bed in Femina's house. There was no Passino visible, but beside her lay Femina sleeping with the smile of an innocent and happy child on her face, her cheeks blooming like a wild rose.

Tellectina shook her sister violently. "You also were borne back to the temple by Passino this morning, weren't you? The radiance of your face is proof. But I am ashamed of both of us!"

Her sister merely smiled and, moving luxuriously in the strange pungent fragrance and warmth of the bed, murmured, "The morning after—how sweet it is!"

Guiltily, Tellectina whispered, "What—how—do you feel?"

Femina laughed. "No matter how much our Puritan Tellectina disapproves of a thing, she can never restrain her precious mental curiosity, can she? Have you then never heard the song of the afterglow?"

She smiled a slow introspective smile. "Peace—ah, this blessed peace! I am at peace with myself, with all the world; imperturbable as Buddha, untroubled as a child. Such calm pervades my being that fire nor flood, disease nor death, could disturb me now. If the very universe should suddenly crumble before my eyes, I should only smile. If the millennium should come and I were flung this instant over the edge of the world—hurled into outer space, I should merely laugh!"

Femina rose and walked about the room.

"And over the still dark pool of my content intermittent sunlight dances. Radiant and blooming I am, like a full-blown rose in midsummer, filled with joyous laughter. All the restless body is quieted, all the discordant nerves vibrate no more—all is a sweet, silent harmony. I go singing down the ways of the earth today. I feel magnanimous, generous, patient, and kind. All my dormant virtues which lay shrinking under the acids of denial now burst gloriously into full blossom! And the great and formidable world—ah, see, I weigh it in the palm of my little hand —so! It is to me but a child's plaything. I toss it up and catch it at my will. For I am a woman fulfilled, complete, and whole —in harmony with myself, with life, with my fellow being—in tune with the infinite! Amen!"

Incredulity, bewilderment, admiration, joy, and shame so confused Tellectina that she remained speechless for a long time. Finally she swung her feet out of bed and, sitting on the edge of the couch with her chin in her hand, pondered on this new discovery.

"I—I simply never in the wildest flight of my imagination dreamed that it was—that it could be—like that! Oh, Femina, why didn't you tell me before? I've been so absorbed in my own discoveries I haven't given you a thought."

"I told you I never knew it myself till—till I met Passino. I discovered it quite by accident when Chotu and the other sirens lured me to Forta Velo. I took to it quite naturally, however; for, after all, all our ancestors weren't Puritans—most of them were aristocrats. You say that you have been searching for Certitude, Tina; well, here it is, I have found it for you. Let us live always in Forta Velo!"

"No, I don't believe this is Certitude; but it is the most startling discovery that we've made in all Nithking so far," Tellectina agreed reluctantly.

"More startling certainly than any of the things I have discovered or that you have related to me. Is not the discovery of Ecstaci more pleasurable than the discovery of love or motherhood or the abiding sweetness of marriage? more intense than sudden intellectual freedom or the apperception of beauty as revealed by the five major arts? Is it not more overwhelming than the complete loss of a personal god, of Christ, heaven, and hell—or even the god-idea? Is it not more wonderful than birth or death? more staggering than the discovery of sexual perversion or the true nature of the dominant male or the deep antagonism between the sexes in marriage?"

"I am sure I don't agree with you, Femina, and yet—well, I will concede that no other discovery in all our twenty-six years broke upon us with such suddenness and force. And I wonder why no one, not even Sophistica, ever intimated the ecstatic experiences which a woman could enjoy."

"What I wonder," Femina said resentfully, "is why a woman has to wait so long before she is initiated. Every man should be able to do it."

"Yes, but it's all rather overpowering and confusing. I have just experienced a sort of ecstatic union with the infinite myself on Manu Mission. Intellectual and sexual ecstasy are quite similar except that the former has more of the element of awe and the latter of joy. Of course, you had reported to me the pleasure you derived from being kissed by certain men in certain ways; but in both our marriages you found intimacy either repellent or painful, and now to have discovered a place where sex is regarded as an art and even a religion by the most ardent —oh, it leaves me dazed and bewildered!"

"It leaves me happy and fulfilled," Femina caroled.

"But it's so transient," Tellectina objected.

"It can be repeated."

At these words, however, slowly but inexorably the Puritan taint in Tellectina's blood reasserted itself, began to seethe and boil.

"But it's wrong!" she declared.

"How can anything so beautiful be wrong?"

"I tell you it's immoral!" Tellectina persisted.

"But how can anything which makes a woman feel and look so well be immoral?" Femina countered.

"If you were a married woman, or in love with the man even —this Ecstaticism would be all right, perhaps. But there is nothing between you but affection. No, what it really is—" Tellectina turned on her sister savagely—"it is the lowest form of sensuality!"

Doggedly Femina retorted, "It is the highest form."

"IT IS WRONG!"

Quietly the other woman lifted a defiant chin. "It is divine."

Suddenly Passino appeared at the door. "But, Tellectina, what is the ultimate of any religion except ecstatic union with the infinite? What is the object of asceticism? What is the ecstasy of mysticism? We have it on the best authority that it is 'a state in which the mind is, as it were, freed from or raised above the body; mental exaltation characterized by visions internally initiated.' Wherein does this form of exaltation differ? Don't you know that it was thus that Plotinus 'derived a practical religious system, teaching the devout how to pass into a condition of ecstasy, a foretaste of absorption into the universal mundane soul'? The mysticism of saints is generally nothing but sublimated eroticism."

Tellectina turned fiercely on him: "You can't trick me with any of your specious arguments."

Then Femina commenced to plead: "But, Tina, you say you worship beauty and you have admitted that this is one form of beauty."

The other girl rose and began to pace up and down the room like a trapped but defiant animal. "It's immoral."

"But why? Most of the beauty of the world is transmitted through the senses—that of painting, music, even poetry and nature. Why is one form of pleasure derived through the senses right and another wrong?" Femina demanded.

"Sexual pleasure is—is animal—is purely physical. Other forms of beauty and ecstasy arouse and enrich the spirit and mind!"

"What's so spiritual about that nude you go into raptures about—Velasquez' Venus? How does the sight of a lovely flower improve your mind? What good does a sunset do you?"

"It exalts me, it brings me nearer—nearer——"

"But you don't believe in a god, Tellectina."

"That's right, I don't. Well, then, it fills me with an exalted pleasure."

"So does inter——"

"Oh, Femina, stop torturing me! We must go away so I can think clearly!"

"If it's merely exaltation you're looking for, tell me honestly, Tellectina Christian, has anything else in either your life or mine raised us to the heights we reached at the peak of the Ecstatic ceremony?"

Tellectina maintained a sullen silence.

"You are unworthy of the name of Tellectina unless you answer me with complete honesty. Isn't it the highest, the most intense ecstasy that you have experienced?"

"Yes, but—but it's merely momentary."

"It is not. It affects a woman's whole life and every phase of it indirectly."

"But the ecstasy produced by art is far superior, I feel certain; although I can't perceive the reason just at this moment."

"But this is an art. All the other arts are outside one's self, whereas the art of love makes me into a living poem. Am I not music when skillfully played upon? And do I not make a pretty picture now? And what statue or building is so beautiful in design as the body of a woman? Is not her beautiful white body a veritable temple of ecstasy? Is it a matter for wonder that a woman takes no interest in all man's arts when she has them all latent within her? The art of love is the only art which really interests any genuine woman."

"I won't listen to such blasphemy!" Tellectina declared. "I must think. Never has any problem been so difficult for me! It isn't that passion without love is wrong in the moral sense, perhaps—for immorality and sin are words that do not exist in Reasonese—they are derived from Halfish. It is rather that it is a lie, a form without substance, a mockery of a very beautiful thing. To me a kiss is primarily an outward manifestation of an inner feeling!"

Passino laughed. "Exactly."

"I do not mean a nervous disturbance in the pit of your stomach, stupid one, I mean an inner emotion of affection. It is only natural to kiss people you love and unnatural to kiss those you don't. I will admit, now that I've had time to think it out a little more logically, that it is not a matter of morality but of honesty."

Passino interceded. "But why not passion for passion's sake, pleasure for pleasure's sake? Don't you know that there's little enough pleasure in the world at best? Here you are given as a gracious gift a body capable of divinely pleasurable sensations, and you do nothing about it, and soon you will be old and withered and indifferent to ecstasy, interested only in comfort —is that an intelligent use of a gracious gift?"

"N-no, I don't suppose it is," the girl faltered.

"And is it intelligent to lie awake at night as you do, tortured for hours, trembling, weeping, when I could cure you?"

"N-no, I don't suppose it is."

"Ah, my foolish little Puritan, as soon as your false idealism dies its natural and inevitable death you will welcome me. I shall bide my time. As long as you have Femina for a sister, however, I can reach you through her—though I should like to conquer you too, with your consent."

"That's unfair. Femina is only a weak and passionate female. But I shall never willingly submit unless you come as a servant to love," Tellectina persisted obstinately.

"It should be very obvious to you by now that my so-called master and I seldom visit the same woman at the same time."

"I've noticed that, to my sorrow and disappointment; but then I shall wait until that exceptional time."

"You'll wait an inhibited long time, my pretty Puritan. And if you were older and more experienced you'd realize that any woman is exceedingly fortunate to be visited by either of us at any time. Most poor females go all through life without ever having anything but a poor imitation of us."

"Oh, I don't know what to think!" Tellectina sighed.

The youth smiled at her seductively. "Why think, when it is so pleasant to feel?"

"But I am Tellectina—it is my nature to think. And yet I realize that I have changed a bit since I've known Forta Velo."

"Changed!" Passino exclaimed. "You're in the third stage of your progress now, little Puritan. There are five steps from Puritanism to Paganism, you know."

For the first time in her life Tellectina laughed at herself. "Yes, there was a time when I considered all sex obscene, and then, after great and laborious thought, I concluded that perhaps marriage rendered it moral."

"And then," Femina interposed, "love convinced you that love made passion moral. But I have now come to think that affection justifies passion."

"Well, I don't," Tellectina maintained.

Passino laughed. "Perhaps you will ascend to the fifth step some day, Tellectina, passion for passion's sake."

"Never!"

The youth laughed again. "We shall see what we shall see. This is your first real encounter with Passino, despite one free union and one marriage. Although you have progressed, you are still a Puritan—but what a passionate Puritan!"

Tellectina set her mouth in straight Puritan lines. "Come, Femina, we've cheapened ourselves long enough with this impostor. I refuse to allow sex to be a religion to you."

Passino put out his hand. "Wait. Are you a Tellectina and ignorant of the close connection that there has always been between sex and religion? Have you never read of the Bacchic Mysteries where the ceremonies resolve themselves into drunken orgies in which religion and sex become inseparable? or of the Hindu religions where the worshipers wear phallic symbols around their necks? or of the priestesses who go to their ecstatic death in the inner shrine whose threshold no man is ever allowed to cross? Have you never read of Phallicism, even? If you weren't so ignorant of the history of the human race, of the history of sex and its manifold manifestations, or even of the history of religions, you would not be so shocked at Femina's perfectly natural behavior!"

"But—but——"

"Have you never read of Baal and Aphrodite or of Moloch,

the man's god; or of Sakti, the woman's god—the worship of all of whom entailed the belief that the sexual union of the worshipers in their temples constituted union with their god, that it was but a symbol of something divine, and that, a surrogate being necessary to receive all sacrifices for the gods, it was believed there could be no better one than the high priests or priestesses?"

"I consider all such ideas due to the imagination and lust of primitive peoples. The fact that ancient races confused sex and religion is no alibi for anyone today," Tellectina asserted.

"Primitive? Forms change but not fundamentals. Don't you know that even today religion is for many people either a substitute for sex or merely a disguised outlet for the erotic emotions? Don't you realize that the nun finds solace in the arms of the Heavenly Bridegroom? that hymns are often sublimated love songs for the neurotic old maid?

"Nor has modern religion yet discarded erotic symbols. What is the church spire but a phallic symbol? the wedding ring but a representation of the female generative organ, the leaves carried on Palm Sunday but the emblem of virility, the ark but a classic symbol of the female principle? And even the cross itself is said by many anthropologists to have been originally a symbol of the creative forces in union. And the columns on your churches were formerly designed to represent the male principle."

Tellectina was staring at her informant with wide incredulous eyes, listening in avid fascination.

"You are so ignorant," Passino continued, "of the history and psychology of religion that you are unaware that the very people whom you consider the farthest removed from sex, the saints and mystics, are often the nearest to it—in another guise. Read the diary of St. Theresa—it might well be the diary of some lovesick woman. Read the religious poems of St. John of the Cross, in whom the erotic mysticism of Christianity reached its climax. Even St. Francis of Assisi merely espoused a personification of the female principle which he called Lady Poverty.

Yours—like all Puritanism—is due first to dishonesty and then to ignorance."

Tellectina shrank back speechless and frightened. Femina, however, seized this moment of weakness to mutter in her ear. "You coward! It's because it's so wonderful that you're afraid. You're fleeing from your own passion!"

With great effort Tellectina collected herself, and ignoring everything Passino had said, but by no means forgetting it, she spoke in her severest tones to her sister. "Come, I'm sure that Forta Feli is the Certitude I've been seeking so long. It's not a mountain as I had thought but a marvelous tropical island. We will live there always and visit the other islands where Yeta-Bu is worshiped."

Tellectina caught her by the hand, but Femina resisted, struggling desperately. Passino also employed all his power. In fact, the three fought till they were exhausted; but finally Tellectina, being the strongest, overpowered her two opponents. The real truth of the matter was that they were both a little afraid of the stern intellectual woman.

Bruised and weary, the two women swam back to the Isle of Forta Feli. And during the ensuing months they lived successively on all the other five islands—careful, however, to avoid Forta Velo.

Tellectina attended the ceremonies in honor of the great goddess Yeta-Bu daily, and subsequently developed into one of her most ardent worshipers; went into religious transports continually; was intoxicated and gloriously happy most of the time.

She indulged in repeated orgies in the temples of Tni Pa, Tru-Sce-Plu, O We Tri, and Cumsi, and among the ruins of Bli-Du; but found on O We Tri such a potent form of the *Cianite Vitrgrew* drug that it caused all her other transports to seem superficial. It produced such joyous visions that she feared she might in time become a hopeless addict. At first Femina slept through all Tellectina's orgies, but gradually became more and more restive immediately after each one. One day when her sister had taken an overdose of *Cianite Vitrgrew* and had fallen forward on the table with her head bowed in exhaustion on her manuscript on which she had been working, Femina attacked her sister with violence. Shaking Tellectina, she demanded in angry tones:

"What the seven dying devils do you think I'm made of, anyway, Tellectina Christian? Wood or stone? I've endured all your religious orgies just about as long as I'm able! Do you think I can stand by and see you trembling with a hundred ecstasies, intoxicated, drugged to the point of bliss, and not grow excited myself?"

"Yes, your restlessness has upset me," Tellectina said.

"Haven't you with all your intellect realized that all ecstasies are a matter of nerves, whether produced by religion, art, creative work, beauty, love, drugs or wine, or passion? And don't you know that these raptures awaken desire? that the intense agitation they produce must be quieted by some means? And that the most effective is a Climactic ceremony with Passino?"

"Oh, I—no, I must say I hadn't realized all this! So that explains a matter which has long puzzled me: that is, why the most devout worshipers of Yeta-Bu (who are almost invariably artists) have always been likewise such devout and constant devotees of the Ecstaci of Forta Velo. So that explains that! Femina, as much as I dislike admitting it, you have revealed a great many important truths to me."

"Well, I'd like to reveal another far more important truth to Her Highness: and that is, when a woman is denied the natural and proper emotional outlet too long she feels no reluctance whatever in admitting that she considers her mental guide, her intellectual mentor—a damned fool! Restraint causes her to become irritable, cross, and hypercritical; her disposition grows acidulous; she is dissatisfied with life and everybody in it. She's so nervous she can't sleep at night but has to bite her pillow and drench it with tears."

"It *is* terrible! I hate to see you suffer so much, but a young woman must learn to keep her mind on other matters."

"Why must she?" Femina inquired insolently. "Don't you

know, her whole being yearns painfully, every atom as restless as a million golden moats ceaselessly moving in a ray of sunlight; the very pores of her flesh become as thirsty as a million little hungry mouths, and when the moon is waxing high she is absolutely tortured! But, worst of all, abstinence, restraint,—in other words, the vice of virtue—cause her to grow old and ugly and shriveled!"

"Worst of all! Why, Femina, do you mean——"

"I certainly do mean that it is often a woman's vanity which overrides her moral scruples!"

"But what would the world say, Femina, to a woman who worships this Ecstaci? They would throw mud at her and make her life unbearable."

"The world doesn't need to know."

"But I hate all forms of hypocrisy even when called 'discretion.' And what do men think of you?"

"Yes, that does give me concern at times—for few men are intelligent enough to rid themselves of old prejudices."

"And *I*—I don't approve."

Femina tossed her head impatiently. "I don't give a damn what Tellectina thinks!"

"But I care a great deal what Tellectina thinks of Femina! You can't return to Forta Velo—at least I can prevent that— because I must have time to think all these matters out clearly."

Tellectina rose from her improvised desk, then returned and chucked her manuscript onto it in disgust. "Oh, Femina, you both shock and disgust me, but—" passing her hand over her forehead, she murmured—"but I don't feel very well, either. I think it is a lack of a well-balanced diet, a well-balanced life. A person can't be intoxicated even on the wine of Yeta-Bu all the time and eat nothing but luscious tropical fruits and indulge even in divine orgies and expect to remain in perfect health. As marvelous as these Siren Islands are, I can't afford to ruin my health by living here indefinitely. So the next time a ship goes by we shall hail it. It is extremely disappointing to me, however, that my silly body refuses to allow me to live in a state of continued intoxication; but facts are facts, and no one can gainsay her own indigestion. And this can't be Certitude after all. I must search further, and I'm more eager than ever to locate it since discovering Forta Velo because on Mt. Certitude all these plaguing questions which that amorous island raised will surely be answered."

On sighting a ship which was sailing by one morning, Tellectina dragged Femina down to it and put her aboard. It was not until after they had got under way, however, that she discovered her sister's absence. She concluded that Femina must have swam away and that she would be forced to leave her behind—to what fate Tellectina knew not but guessed only too well. At any cost, however, she herself must resume her search for Certitude for never had she had such a pressing problem on her mind.

Her constant thought day after day as she paced the deck of the sturdy little ship, the *Esse McMoonn*, was, "Am I a coward? Are Femina and Passino right and am I wrong? If all the other pagan religions who have Yeta-Bu for a goddess are right, then why not that of the Ecstaci of Passino, too?"

Her own questions harassed her sleep and wore grooves in her young brain. "Oh, it's hell to be a Puritan—especially a passionate Puritan! But why is one esthetic pleasure lower than another? Why, why? I know the world is against it and men are against it, but that is not what really disturbs me now. Do *I* think it is right? But I can't decide so quickly, I must have time and be away from Passino, for when he touches me just once I cease to think. Oh, it's terrible to have no one to guide me, no one to help me! I simply wander through Nithking at random, following my own poor instincts as best I can, hoping and searching for Certitude always. But I shall find it some day, somewhere, somehow—of that I'm positive."

One uneventful day followed another as the sturdy frigate, *Esse McMoonn,* sailed smoothly along. The plain fare restored Tellectina's impaired health rapidly; but noticing that the ship hugged the shore, and was never willing to brave the high seas the explorer began to wonder if this ship could ever take her to Mt. Certitude. At the first indication of a storm, the little ship put about and sought a safe port. Although a sturdy little craft, her owner did not possess the spirit of adventure. Convinced that, although this might be the common-sense way of doing things, it would never get her where she wanted to go, Tellectina determined to abandon the *Esse McMoonn* and the instant she docked the young explorer set out eagerly on foot again.

CHAPTER XI

WHAT HAPPENED WHEN TELLECTINA MET SOME STROLLING
PLAYERS ON THE HIGHROAD; WHAT SHE SAW BEHIND THE SCENES
OF THE OLD MORALITY PLAY, "THE WORLD'S WORLD"; AND THE
PART SHE PLAYED THEREIN

ALL THE WHILE that the young explorer had been walking over miles of this countryside of pleasantly rolling hills she had been plagued by a dull but deep-seated pain. Finally she was forced to admit that it was a conscience pain produced by her discovery of Femina on the Seventh Siren Isle.

But surely it was not intelligent for a woman to act one way and think just the opposite, to indulge in ecstasy and yet all the while think it immoral. Apparently everybody in the whole wide world considered sexual pleasure wrong (especially those who indulged in it the most), so who was she to doubt? Was it possible that several billion people were wrong and that she, little Tellectina, was right? Well, certainly the question of the morality or immorality of this form of ecstasy must be settled somehow before she could ever know a moment's peace.

As she tramped over the open country she meditated profoundly on this problem until her poor young brain grew hot. Although she met several fellow travelers going in the opposite direction, who made helpful suggestions, she dared not believe them—as yet.

On attaining the summit of a high hill, however, her pain of hunger suddenly obscured all other pains for the time being. To her relief there now appeared a broad highway with sheep and cattle grazing in the meadows on either side. After following the road for some distance the traveler was greeted by an unexpected but very welcome sight.

In the center of the highway there was a wide one-way gate, while beside it rose a worn wooden stile leading over a stone wall on the other side of which appeared an enormous two-story house on wheels. On top of the stile sat an old man peeling an apple with his pocket knife.

Eagerly the weary young traveler inquired of him, "What's that over there?"

"Traveling players," he explained.

"Oh, really? Then it's a portable stage—not a house."

"It's larger than *any* house—got a lot of actors in that troupe. I'm just the doorkeeper."

"I see, and what are they playing?"

"Can't you read?" And here he pointed his knife over his shoulder.

Above the barely legible words "Stage Entrance" was painted the name of the play in large but now faded letters:

"THE WORLD'S WORLD"
GREATEST MORALITY PLAY EVER PRODUCED

"Oh," the girl murmured, "a revival of that old morality play? Why, I've seen that many times back in Err! And read it often too. Odd how the public never tires of it and likes to have it revived every season. I presume the audience approaches from the other direction. I wonder now—I wonder if I could get a part in it?"

The old man looked at her for the first time and shook his head. "That's no place for a young thing like you!"

"Why, I'll soon be twenty-seven. And I have no money left now, so I'm obliged to earn my own living. Besides, it can't be so bad, because I've seen it many times, and——"

"That's just the trouble—you've always been a spectator. It's quite different behind the scenes."

"Oh, but I'm sure it couldn't be very different. I think I know nearly the whole drama by heart. It's the one in which all the characters play the personification of some virtue or vice, I remember: Deception and Truth have a terrible duel, and Truth wins in the end; and the hero is Affluence and the heroine, Purity. Youth falls in love with Innocence, but Sin very seductively endeavors to lead him astray. Each time, however, he invariably returns to his first sweetheart. And the Seven Deadly Sins are hissed off the stage, too. Why, I *know* I could play a part in it. Do you know if the manager is in?"

The old doorkeeper laughed as he crunched his apple ruminatively. "He's never in."

"But—but I want to apply for a position!"

He shrugged and pointed to a small well-worn door beside the stage entrance. "Try in there."

Quickly descending the stile on the other side of the wall, Tellectina entered the manager's office. A stout, ugly man in shirtsleeves looked up from the table at which he was writing.

"Is—is the manager in, please?"

The man laughed harshly. "No!"

"But when will he be in?"

"Don't know. Guess he's too busy to bother with this show." And again he laughed significantly.

"But I want a job."

"What can you do? I'm Kamdinn—assistant manager. I might give you a job." He stared at her lips and breasts, her hips and legs with merciless and lecherous eyes. "Pull up your dress, let's see your legs."

"No," Tellectina faltered. "I don't want that kind of part. But I could play some small rôle. I'd be willing to do anything—almost."

The man made a gesture of dismissal, saying, "No vacancies," and began writing again.

"But at least give me a tryout. I'll be of some value, I'm sure. And I must get work—I haven't a——"

The man's face changed instantly. "You haven't a cent?"

Tellectina tried to laugh gayly. "Not one red cent—and I'm hungry too!"

Leaning across the table the assistant manager chucked her

under the chin with a fat dirty forefinger. "A pretty girl like you shouldn't ever want for money!" He smiled at her ingratiatingly.

Tellectina recoiled involuntarily, but on remembering Femina's advice on the way to handle such men, she turned large innocent eyes on him.

"Then you *will* give me a part, Mr. Kamdinn?"

"What'll you give me?"

"I'll give you an excellent performance of my rôle."

The man looked away and muttered under his breath, "Oh, all right, all right, keep your precious virtue, you hard-boiled little virgin! Step this way—and hurry up about it! I haven't all day to waste on you. Hancce, our director, is out front now. You'll have to play whatever he casts you for. And you'll receive beginner's salary, of course."

Although faint from hunger, Tellectina rehearsed until supper time. She was astounded to discover that although her rôle was advertised on the handbills as one of the leads it was merely a small walk-on part. Hancce had cast her for the rôle of Honesty. She met none of the cast that day other than the small group who appeared in the scene with her and those who sat at her table in the mess tent.

When evening arrived she was amazed at the magnitude of the audience. Great streams of people from the west darkened the white highway, but very few arrived from the east along the road which had brought Tellectina hither. The great crowds stood on the rising slope of the hillside in the open air to watch the performance as the drama took place on a gigantic stage beneath which were countless dressing rooms and property rooms—the whole being mounted on innumerable low wheels. Unlike most portable theaters, this one was open to the air only at the front, inasmuch as quantities of crude scenery were employed at either side.

Although the spectators invariably applauded her appearance loudly, they nevertheless evinced indifference and even annoyance throughout Tellectina's performance. They whispered noisily among themselves, milled restlessly about, crunching apples and peanuts. Gradually the realization came to the amateur that a stipulated share of applause was given to Honesty merely because it was an old tradition among the audiences of *The World's World*. Convinced that she was already thoroughly familiar with the play, Tellectina never stood out in front in the days that followed.

The impossibility of meeting people who were actively exploring Nithking, or at least interested in hearing about her explorations, was a keen disappointment to Tellectina; but she carefully cherished the belief that it was merely a matter of becoming acquainted with more of the actors. After all her lonely years in the sparsely populated Forbidden Country she found it very exciting, however, just to be actually in *The World's World*. It possessed for her all the glamour and lure that distance, romantic books, provincialism, and Puritanism could give the famous spectacle.

After a matinée one day, Tellectina was about to leave the theater to return to her own tent when loud cries issuing from a dressing room near by caused her to dash unceremoniously into what proved to be one of the stars' rooms. A large man, his face crimson with anger and drink, was standing over an old scrubwoman who had been washing the wooden floor. He had evidently struck her with his leather belt, which he now held lifted above his head. Tellectina managed to drag the frightened and feeble old woman out of reach of the strap, but in doing so slipped on the soapy floor and, unable to regain her footing for a moment, could not escape several lashes on her own back.

Cursing violently, the man shouted, "That ought to teach you to mind your own business, you God-damned young upstart!"

With another muttered oath the man ejected the girl roughly from the room, slammed and locked the door behind her. Almost blinded with anger, Tellectina stood motionless for a long moment then rushed off to the manager's office. After listening nonchalantly to her breathless recital, Kamdinn merely shrugged his shoulders and assured her that her imagination was too fertile.

"But—but I saw this with my own eyes!"

"No, no, things like that don't happen in this company. Besides, that man plays the part of Brotherly Love every day— he wouldn't be guilty of such a thing! So forget it!"

"That's all the more reason that—— Oh, but I *saw* it, I tell you! Aren't you going to do anything about it?"

Lifting his eyes for the first time since the girl's entrance, the assistant manager snarled at her like an angry animal. "Yes, I am. I'm going to shut you up! If you don't mind your own business, young woman, you're going to find yourself without a job—and that pretty damn quick!"

Too frightened, too sickened to realize for the moment just what had happened, Tellectina escaped from his office as quickly as possible. Later she related both incidents to the other actresses in her dressing room while they were donning their costumes for the evening performance. They, however, suddenly began to concentrate all their attention on the application of their make-up, merely exclaiming, "How awful! Glad it wasn't us!" leaving Tellectina more puzzled and miserable than ever.

The World's World was so well attended and supported that it was unnecessary for the traveling players to move on. It appeared as though the drama would continue to be enacted daily in the same place—indefinitely. Although she had become sickened by her environment, Tellectina dared not give up her position, as she knew of no other way to earn her bed and board. Gradually, however, such an accumulation of increasingly terrible and puzzling incidents were witnessed by the young amateur behind the scenes that she was inclined to wonder into what kind of a madhouse she had strayed by mistake. Strange incredible things of which she had read, but which she firmly believed occurred only in stories, transpired every week right under her very eyes.

"And it's not as if this were a third-rate audience or burlesque full of the scum of the earth," she reflected: "these stars are all famous high-salaried actors."

Emerging from her dressing room after a Saturday matinée, she beheld a beautiful young actress in the shadow of one of the sets dexterously slipping the watch and wallet from the pockets of an adoring youth while he was tenderly kissing her hair. The man was rather shabbily dressed and the purse quite small. Sickened by the sight, Tellectina turned away for a moment, and when she looked up again they had disappeared.

She hastened out a side exit with the intention of taking a walk in the fresh air of the surrounding woods, in order to shake off the unpleasant effects of the incident, when a large crowd gathered around the stage entrance attracted her attention. A very handsome gray-haired man was standing on the top step selling large yellow ingots which he guaranteed to be genuine gold bricks. Tellectina noticed that most of the purchasers were people who had been in the audience that afternoon. None of the major actors, but a few minor actors and all the stage hands were eagerly yielding up the whole of their long-hoarded savings. He looked such a picture of honesty and his speech was so convincing that Tellectina, who was in desperate need of funds, purchased one with the only five dollars she possessed in the world.

Wrapping it cautiously in her one extra suit of underwear, she concealed it in her tent. Long before a purchaser could be found, however, the gold plating wore off to reveal the lead underneath. Although many were searching for him, the swindler was never to be found in his dressing room, and Kamdinn, merely laughing at their gullibility, refused to take action. In the face of such obvious theft, the indifference of the assistant manager, and her own gullibility, Tellectina's anger was absolutely futile.

An accumulation of incredibly dramatic incidents soon forced the conclusion on the young actress that there was infinitely more drama behind the scenes of *The World's World* than on the stage. She witnessed one unpleasant occurrence after another, many of which, however, were strangely mixed with beauty. One morning she saw an emaciated old actor stoop beneath the steps of the stile to fish a bread crust out of the dust. As he raised it eagerly to his lips, a lean old cur came whining about his legs; whereupon, with a heart-wrenching smile, the old man gave it to the hungry dog. Immediately two sleek well-fed men who had witnessed the little scene gave the old man a kick as they passed by and cried after him, "You old fool!"

Having no money to offer him herself, Tellectina rushed at once to the manager's office determined to ask for an advance on her salary. But with her hand on the door she was arrested by the unmistakable sounds of a struggle within. Suddenly a young boy with disheveled hair came dashing out, followed by two middle-aged men who continued to pluck at his sleeve and urge him to accept a small package. "Here—it's all yours. He'll never know you told us. Come, tell us, don't be a fool! It's a chance in a million for you. You know that information would be worth thousands to us!"

Thrusting them angrily aside the boy fled, but the men pursued him into the woods and so out of Tellectina's sight. This and other episodes which the girl continued to observe as the months went by left her puzzled and unhappy, though they in no way concerned her personally.

After a Saturday night performance Tellectina was walking wearily back to her sleeping quarters when the noise of a drunken party in one of the tents made her pause. A mother could actually be overheard offering her seventeeen-year-old daughter to the highest bidder; and even though done in a spirit of jest, a note of seriousness could be detected beneath it. The horrified young eavesdropper looked frantically about her for someone capable of preventing such atrocities. The realization that there existed no one, and no thing, anywhere on the earth or above it, with such power sent her post-haste to her own tent, there to sink to her cot in despair.

And long before the painful impact of this fact diminished

Tellectina heard a star actor address a sentimental plea to the matinée audience for contributions to a Christmas fund for the poor and needy. With tears in his voice he appealed to them in the name of altruism. His words would have melted a miser's heart. Hundreds of dollars were collected from the moist-eyed, overwrought audience. Later, behind the scenes, Tellectina overheard the assistant manager and several of the stars laughing as they surreptitiously divided the fund among themselves. But the climax to this little drama behind the drama occurred just before the performance that same evening. One of the actors stopped under a dim oil light in the deserted corridor to count his share of the money from the poor fund. Suddenly another man snatched the roll of bills from his hand, and when the owner of it struck the thief to the floor with a blow of his fist, the infuriated offender rose and promptly stabbed the defendant. Then, pocketing the money, he slipped quickly away through the shadows of the dim hallway: unnoticed except by Tellectina, who had witnessed the scene from a distance. Too horrified to move for a long moment, the girl finally recovered her voice and, shouting for help, rushed up to the wounded man.

Kamdinn and two of his assistants responded promptly—looking annoyed, however, rather than horror-stricken. Casting angry glances at the girl and laying his fingers on his lips the assistant manager whispered, "The show must go on! Say nothing!" The two men quietly and surreptitiously whisked the body away, while Kamdinn offered the girl a roll of bills which, outraged, she flung to the floor. Shrugging his shoulders the man picked them up and hurried off as the applause for the opening scene became audible.

Dazed and incredulous the girl stood where the murdered man had fallen, absolutely rooted to the spot, too shocked even to think coherently. "Oh, my God," she moaned, "what sort of a crazy bedlam have I got into? Surely this is all part of some terrible travesty. It can't be real—it's too awful! But which is real and which is unreal? I'm so confused I can't believe my own eyes and ears any more! Surely life isn't like this! If it is, I can't endure it—I must do something!"

Almost in hysterics the agitated girl began pacing up and down the corridor. Then, suddenly running back stage, Tellectina stood in the wings and listened in increasing perplexity to those parts of the play she had been ignoring for months. It was the identical *The World's World* at which she had been a spectator so often in Err and which she had read repeatedly in a variety of versions, and it was given in Halfish, as usual. The audience, which reached back as far as her eye could see, appeared to be enjoying it far more than when she was on the stage. There was one quite astounding thing about this play, however, which she had never noticed before. When the emaciated old actor who had relinquished his precious bread crust to the hungry dog walked on and spoke his lines about the importance of food and money in this world, he was hissed off the stage immediately. He represented one of the Vices, and they shouted his name after him as though it were some shameful epithet, "Improvidence! Improvidence! Take him off! Give him the hook!"

But when a stout overfed man took the center of the stage, soliloquizing at length about the importance of justice and honor; declaring that money was nothing, that love of one's fellow man and service to humanity, especially to the poor and down-trodden, were all that mattered, he was applauded loudly, receiving repeated encores while they clamored for him by name, "Success! Success!" He was so elaborately costumed as the personification of one of the Virtues, and his disguise rendered recognition so difficult, that it was some time before Tellectina realized that he was the swindler who had sold the gold bricks behind the stage months ago. Incredulity and disgust left her absolutely speechless.

Following him, another popular actor emerged from the wings on the other side, likewise richly dressed as one of the Virtues. Acknowledging the noisy acclaim with smiles and bows, he admitted that he was the personification of Brotherly

Love, proclaiming in a voice trembling with exaggerated emotion that "we should all love one another as ourselves— even the poor and lowly." Being skeptical now, Tellectina very quickly recognized him as the man who had struck the poor old charwoman with his leather belt. His make-up so badly disguised the look of cruelty on his face that the girl waited breathlessly till the audience should hiss him off the boards; but when they failed to do so she was dumfounded by the audience even more than by the actor. Peering through a small aperture in the scenery, Tellectina studied their faces intently: the majority wore the expression of credulous gullible children. Only here and there did she discern a skeptical smile.

Scores of actors personifying the various Virtues were parading across the stage: Duty, Patriotism, Altruism, Morality, Justice, Wisdom and Righteousness. Then came several women playing the parts of Purity, Innocence, and Motherly Love. In spite of all the old woman's smirks and tears, Tellectina was able to recognize by her voice the woman who had assumed the rôle of Motherly Love. She was the woman who had sold her daughter to the highest bidder in the drunken revel. Next Purity came simpering shyly before the footlights: the audience rained applause on her, demonstrating undeniably that she was their favorite and the heroine of the play. And yet she was none other than the girl whom Tellectina had seen some weeks ago stealing the watch and wallet from the poor young man who adored her.

Sickened by what she saw, the young amateur leaned weakly against the set, watching the progression of *The World's World* in a kind of horrified fascination. The Vices came on, some in rags, some in silks and satins. Sin, reclining seductively on a couch, tempted Morality, who resisted noisily, drove her off the stage into the privacy of her dressing room, and after a sufficient interval reappeared in a disheveled condition and, flinging the vampire to the floor, reviled her publicly, with great venom and relish. Failure and Folly and Pride followed one after the other. Inefficiency was played by Tellectina's friend, the pale youth who painted such exquisite landscapes in his spare moments outside the theater. Jeers greeted him. No Vice was so vehemently howled down as Inefficiency, even overripe tomatoes and old carrots were thrown at him. When Democracy, one of the Virtues, thrust out his great clumsy foot and tripped up the Vice, Pride, the crowd shouted with joy. As the old man rose with quiet dignity and marched off the stage, Tellectina recalled that after he had conversed with her behind the scenes he had proven himself to be not at all arrogant, but merely one of the most genuinely self-respecting men she had ever had the pleasure of meeting.

Her anger had been seething dangerously for some time—now it threatened to boil over. "My God, if the public only knew how these actors lived behind the scenes, they would reverse the rôles! Not for a second would they tolerate some of them posing as Virtues! And others being cast as Vices! They honestly believe these actors are all cast for the parts for which they have the greatest natural talent, but they ought to know the truth. Someone should inform them. Why, the fool public believes anything it hears and all it sees!"

Just then the audience burst into the loudest applause heard during the entire performance. Peering from behind the wings to see who the favorite of *The World's World* was, Tellectina beheld the man who had murdered his friend for his money stepping down to the footlights to receive the plaudits of the people. They stood on tiptoe shouting his name over and over again, "Affluence! Affluence!" Then abruptly a silence fell on them—they had noticed the bloodstains on his hands. When he observed that this made his admirers slightly uncomfortable, the hero hastily placed his hands behind his back but smiled reassuringly and said:

"Oh, my good friends, don't be alarmed! I was helping an injured man who fell from the top of this tall set while shifting it for my act. That explains both my tardiness and the bloodstains. The poor fellow won't live, I'm afraid," here he pressed a tear from his eye, "but I shall provide amply for his widow and poor unfortunate children. Accidents will happen even in the best regulated theaters, you know. But do not allow this little human tragedy to disturb your kind tender hearts too much."

Although it was not her cue, Tellectina found it impossible to restrain herself any longer. Rushing out on the stage, she pointed an accusing finger at the actor and cried, "He is a murderer! There was no accident, I saw him stab the man with my own eyes! He lies to you, and he is a thief besides. He killed his friend for his money. You should arrest him—not applaud him!" But the accused had already vanished miraculously. "What! you let him walk off the stage unmolested? You don't believe me? But I tell you I saw it all with my own eyes!" the girl protested.

Some of the audience looked bewildered, but most of the people interpreted this as a little surprise comedy and laughed accordingly.

But her earnest young voice rang out again. "Wait! I must tell you something! For heaven's sake, listen to me. I must inform you about facts of which you seem tragically ignorant. Most of the actors playing the parts of Virtues before you are only fit to personify Vices. I have observed them behind the scenes: their private lives are incredibly awful. They are hypocrites and impostors; while those you laugh at as simpletons, I have seen perform beautiful acts when they thought there was no audience to witness or applaud them. Oh, you are like credulous children, you are being grossly deceived by appearances."

There was still a little scattered laughter.

"I am not trying to make you laugh. I was never more serious in my whole life. Listen to me, and I will tell you the truth. Since Hancce, the director of this play, has cast me for the rôle of Honesty, I shall perform my part with a vengeance. Listen, I beg of you. Do you know nothing of human faces? Can't you read people's characters at all? Why do you believe the beautiful lies they tell you about themselves? When really fine characters like the ones you misnamed Improvidence, Inefficiency, and Folly appear before you, how is it that you do not recognize them for what they truly are? You hiss those who should be applauded and applaud those who should be hissed. You are grossly deceived; but let me undeceive you, for your own sakes."

Her passionate young voice was beginning to hold them against their wills. "This play is all topsy-turvy, I do assure you. You are too easily deceived by pretty words and outward disguises. Just because a man elects to pose before you as Altruism, does that mean he is capable of playing the rôle? *You* apparently think so, you raise no question—you accept him! When someone struts before you as the personification of Success, do you never stop to consider how he happened to acquire that part? Do you care nothing if he obtained it by swindling? How can you applaud Affluence who gained his position through theft and murder? How can you admire a woman who wears the guise of Motherly Love and yet sells her own daughter to fatten her own purse? How can you applaud Innocence, who is nothing but the personification of the most abysmal ignorance tricked out in a pretty white dress? Are the rôles that people play on the stage of *The World's World* as important as the lives they actually live every day? No! a thousand times, no!"

The violence and suddenness of her attack had quieted the audience in spite of themselves. Taking advantage of this fact, Tellectina rushed on. "To think that you prefer Affluence as the hero of your so-called Morality play! What about Honor, Intellect, Kindness, and Tolerance? You advertise these as playing leading parts but actually relegate them to minor rôles and allow them to be interpreted by charlatans besides! Don't blame the management—it gives the public what it wants. And to think that your idea of a heroine is merely any female who has retained her maidenhead! Is that the only requirement for Purity? Can you applaud Purity even when the part is acted by a woman who is both malicious and mercenary, as it was today and often is? Your requirement for Purity is entirely physical. Do you care nothing for purity of mind, character, and conduct in a woman? Oh, you poor ignorant children, will you never wake up and use your brains?"

Suddenly coming out from under the spell of her heated diatribe, the audience began to evince angry resentment. The actors, who were peering out from behind the sets, came to life and rushed upon her from behind; while the audience surged down to the stage, shouting, "Take her off! Throw her off! She's insane! She must be immoral herself! She ought to be arrested!"

Missiles were being thrown at the offender when Kamdinn rushed out and angrily dragged Tellectina off. "You God-damned little fool—trying to ruin our show! You're discharged —fired—get out! Get out before I throw you out!"

He thrust her roughly behind the scenes and quickly sent on a comedian to regain the attention of the restless crowd, which gradually subsided and allowed the play to proceed. Trembling with anger, Tellectina nevertheless cautiously concealed herself behind one of the wings in order to watch the remainder of what seemed to her a tragedy. In spite of her exposé, none of the speeches for *The World's World* had been altered one jot and she could scarcely believe her ears when Sentiment appeared and simpered as usual, "Honesty always pays," and the audience applauded earnestly without a shadow of doubt crossing their faces or even the glimmer of a smile— except on the faces of a few.

But Tellectina laughed—for the first time, murmuring, "Yes, pays with her life almost! But what horrible, incredible incongruity is this? Surely it isn't possible that the world *wishes* to be deceived? Is it that they don't believe what I tell them— or that they don't wish to hear the truth? And yet, aren't they obliged to believe me when I expose these actors? Don't they *know* that I'm the personification of Honesty? What on earth do they think *I* gain by discovering and pronouncing unpleasant truths except the satisfaction of having played my part well? Surely human beings want to hear the truth—I certainly do. But, oh, there's something queer about this *World's World* that I simply can't understand!"

But her speculations were interrupted by loud cries for Immorality, in response to which Kamdinn stepped down to the footlights and announced that a new actress would appear in that part; that the management had had great difficulty in procuring her and was delighted to offer her to the public.

"Bring her out!" they shouted. "We want to see Immorality. What's *The World's World* without the spice of Immorality?"

Tellectina shuddered at their cruelty. When sounds of a struggle issued from behind the wings, it visibly whetted the appetite of the audience. Tellectina was distinctly puzzled when she noticed that the most avid of all were the sleek and handsome young Lotharios, lecherous old men, smug fat matrons, and thin rapacious old maids.

"Force her on!" they called. "Make her appear as Immorality whether she wants to or not!"

Between them Hancce and Kamdinn dragged on to the center of the stage a woman whose face was concealed by her upraised arm. Tense with expectancy, the audience rose on tiptoe. Some audibly hissed this new personification of Immorality while those standing in the front rows hurled mud and refuse—a plentiful supply of which they seemed to have brought with them for this high moment. Finally the miserable girl flung up her head with one defiant gesture. At the sight of her face Tellectina was struck dumb. . . . It was Femina.

Tellectina grasped the edge of the set for support. She turned deathly sick in the very pit of her stomach. Too dazed and incredulous to comprehend such an atrocity all at once, she stood there motionless for a long moment. Then suddenly rage shot up through her slender body like a flame, and she sprang to her sister's defense.

"Stop! Stop!" she commanded. "There is some *terrible* mistake! This girl can't play the part of Immorality!" Tellectina stood directly in front of her sister so that to the audience it appeared as though there were now just one girl. "She's not suited to be the personification of any vice!"

For the second time that evening the crowd was surprised into involuntary attention. "Oh, no," the outraged girl continued, "you wouldn't listen to me just now, but this time I'll *force* you to listen, for this girl is my own sister. To appear as Immorality for one minute brands a woman for life; and I won't allow it, I tell you."

This unexpected turn of matters caused tense but restrained excitement. "What do you, the public, know about this girl? Nothing! You've listened to rumors, I presume, and you're avid to believe the worst possible about any woman. You have heard that she was initiated into the Forbidden Mystery. And for this you want to punish her publicly by forcing her to appear in the part of Immorality in *The World's World,* don't you? Well, you're in no position to judge her in any way. I am: I know all about her private life, and that's what should determine the parts people play in public."

Anticipation of lurid details visibly increased her auditors' interest.

"And I pronounce this woman and all others who have possessed the good fortune and the courage to join the Secret Cult of Ecstaci—which you condemn and forbid as immoral— I say, I pronounce such women moral, virtuous, honest, and intelligent. They are far more so than the women who habitually parade before you as the personifications of Morality, Purity, and Virtue!"

There was a little vigorous but isolated applause which the rest of the audience instantly attempted to hiss down.

"I tell you," the girl continued in her earnest young voice, "moral women have been forced to play the part of Immorality long enough, and it's high time a stop was put to it! Don't think I don't realize how dangerous it is for any woman to defend Immorality—I do. But I also realize that some woman must change your erroneous conception of Immorality. It is wrong, absurd, and unjust."

There was a loud rumbling of dissent and protest and a little vigorous applause from scattered listeners.

"I've been thinking about this whole question of Immorality constantly for months and now, thanks to you (and three travelers I met on the way here), my conclusions have suddenly become crystallized. If I had a trace of a pain left in my conscience, if I had a taint of Puritanism left in my blood, your vicious attack on this innocent girl has cleansed me of it completely and forever."

She paused for breath, then hastened on. "I too was once a Puritan, just as most of you are this minute. There is not a thought or emotion about Immorality or Morality which tortures you which has not tortured me. But reason has delivered me from the clutches of Puritanism.

"Furthermore, when you attack my own flesh and blood, as it were, I simply see red! This girl is actually a part of me: she's weaker and more emotional; and I, being the more intellectual, must consequently defend her. You've put the ultimate insult upon both my sister and me—according to your standards, at least. You expose to public ridicule an innocent woman, accusing her of the greatest crime of which you think a woman capable. She has done all that you accuse her of—that I freely admit: but she is not guilty, for the very excellent reason that what she has done is not a crime. I shall prove it to you."

The protests were so loud and numerous that Tellectina was obliged to raise her voice.

"Is it just to convict a person without a hearing? I demand that you stand there and listen to my defense of Immorality whether you want to or not. Millions of women for thousands of years have been miscast in this same rôle. Let me speak for them also. Let us thrash out this ancient, historical, and dangerous matter of Immorality once and for all. We've been beating about the bush for the last three thousand years—don't you think it's about time we brought it out in the open and examined it fearlessly? All I ask is that you listen as intelligently as you are able."

Quickly and quietly Tellectina pushed Femina behind the scenes and before the protests became vocal commenced to talk again. "Why do you believe what you believe? Because you—each individual you, have thought out this matter alone, independently, and logically? No! your beliefs have been inherited from your ancestors along with the color of your eyes. You haven't any reasons: you only have traditions and prejudices."

She now had the unwilling but complete attention of her audience.

"But where did you get your traditions? Have you ever stopped for a single second in your whole lives to examine this Puritan tradition by which you cast hapless women into humiliating rôles?

"When did Immorality first appear upon the human stage? How did it originate? It originated in the Mystery of Ecstaci, but especially the Great Mystery of Sexual Ecstaci. But when, where, and why? I'll tell you. It originated long before the time of Christ, back in the land of the Jews when they were still savages. But why did the human race ever begin to believe that so natural a thing as sex was the source of sin? Sex was always a Great Mystery but how did it become the Forbidden Mystery?

"The records of religions show that the idea of sex and all other pleasures as sin began in the primitive belief that all the pleasurable experiences of human beings created envy in supernatural beings, ghosts, or gods. To prevent the envy and the resultant visitations of wrath, man sought to propitiate these ghostly beings by sacrificing pleasures of all sorts, including sexual indulgence.

"Do you, who consider yourselves civilized, believe in supernatural beings, in ghosts or gods who must be placated by abstinence from pleasure? Haven't you outgrown such savage superstitions? You think you have: but you haven't. But don't you think it's time to discard anything as old as that? Don't you see that our requirements for Morality and Immorality are based on pre-Biblical taboos and superstitions of primitive tribes? Are you willing to use their primitive methods of cooking, eating, and dressing? No, you laugh at such childish, outmoded customs. Then why are you still willing to accept the moral customs of a tribe of savages?"

There were cries of dissent.

"But you are! You do! If you deny it you are merely displaying your ignorance of historical fact. So you'd better keep quiet and listen. These are not my opinions but actual proved and recorded facts, ascertained by anthropologists. Have you ever delved into the Mysteries of human history? Have you ever studied comparative religions and seen the irony of this situation?—for the very religion which persecutes what it calls Immorality most violently is the very one which was of Phallic origin. C. W. Oliver, the great anthropologist, says that most of the Christian religion as we understand and practice it today is of Phallic origin, because the Jewish people had the same rites and gods as the surrounding tribes. Education is what you need, and with it would come tolerance.

"And have you never read that the man who was responsible for the maintenance of the idea of sex as sin and of the inferiority and sinfulness of women was a man who displayed a distinct personal aversion both to sex and women? One who, some authorities deduce, was himself sexually deficient? Why do you allow Paul or any other person or persons in the world to do your thinking for you? And it is only ignorance and cowardice which prevent people from understanding and admitting that the ecstacy of the saints and mystics was merely a sublimated form of eroticism."

The audience was electrified by her blasphemous assertion, but taking advantage of it she rushed on: "Answer me this question. Are there some things in life which are inherently wrong?"

There were shouts of, "Yes, yes, lots of things! Sex, murder, theft!"

"You say 'yes' but I say 'no.' You constantly practice murder, theft, and lying. What is war but murder? What is the appropriation of enemy territory but theft? Or the act of spying for the sake of one's country but lying? In other words circumstances can transform an immoral thing into a moral thing. This proves that nothing is inherently immoral."

"Sex is inherently immoral," an old woman insisted.

"Why?" Tellectina retorted.

"Because it is!" came the determined answer.

"Woman's chief reason for everything, I fear. That's why she's in the backward state she's in today, and you *think* that you think it is always immoral to participate in the Forbidden Ceremony, but you don't. Because don't most of you concede that marriage makes it moral? Then that proves that even you don't think it is intrinsically wrong. Why is the same ceremony immoral when performed outside marriage? Because your fathers and grandfathers thought it was. Is that a reason worthy of adults or children?"

"What's good enough for my father is good enough for me!" one man said with dogged persistence.

"I know it is," Tellectina agreed, "that's exactly what ails the whole world. I wish to heaven I could give you all a copy of *The Mind in the Making*, by James Harvey Robinson; for if you had any minds, that little book would certainly make them. 'The fact that an idea is ancient,' he says, 'and has been widely received is no argument in its favor, but should immediately suggest the necessity of carefully testing it as a probable instance of rationalization.'

"Come, let's get down to basic facts. *When* is any act wrong? Surely an act is wrong only when it wrongs someone. And who, I want to know, is wronged by the performance of a pleasant ceremony by a man and woman? The man? I think you'll admit that it can hardly be said that he is wronged."

There was laughter on the part of the men.

"Who then? The public? In what way are you injured or even remotely concerned? (Of course, I am assuming that there is no child resulting from the ceremony. And there need be very few undesired children now, with the modern knowledge of contraceptives.) For even an ardent devotee like myself admits that whenever there's a child as the result of the aforementioned ceremony the public *is* concerned, for reasons of which we are all aware.

"How, by the wildest stretch of your imagination, can what a woman does with six inches of her anatomy concern you? Do you expect her to consult you, the public, about other private and natural functions like the elimination of water or waste? The idea is preposterous! Then why do you expect her to consult you about an even more private and equally natural function? As long as she does you no injury, nor burdens the public with an uncared-for child, what right have you to interfere?"

She paused, but there was no response.

"It is as obvious to me as the grim expressions on your faces that the woman in question has done neither you nor the man any wrong. There remains then only herself. Answer me this truthfully: Does a woman degrade herself by improving her health, her disposition, and her beauty? by doing that which makes her feel more kind and generous and sympathetic toward the whole human race? by feeling ecstasy flow through all her being? by actually being lifted at moments to a glorious communion with the great life force?"

There was a strange tense silence.

"Tell me another thing: Why is one form of ecstasy more immoral than any other form of pleasure derived through the senses—like eating, drinking, smoking, or listening to music? And solve this problem for me too: If a woman is over twenty-five years old and not happily married, what is she to do?—grow old and wrinkled, irritable and ill?—and even in the end become slightly insane, as most pathetic old maids do? You can't violate the laws of nature without paying for it, you know. Or should a woman be honest and courageous and obey the laws of nature and become a convert to the pagan god Ecstaci? This is a vital problem which confronts every intelligent modern woman, and there is only one intelligent solution to it."

The hundreds of eyes staring at her blinked violently in the highly charged silence that reigned.

"But even if it *were* wrong, how can you defend your injustice of blaming one of the criminals and not the other? In all other instances of partners in crime, *both* are blamed. The idea that it's all right for the man and wrong for the woman won't hold water any more than a sieve if you apply a few pointed reasons to it. If an act is intrinsically immoral for one human being, it is immoral for another human being—that is only logic. If an act is inherently moral for one person it is moral for another person—that is only justice."

The men laughed loudly, while a few women hissed their disapproval.

"The laughter of the men only proves another very important point. Women are beginning to emancipate themselves from Puritanism and enjoy the Mystery of Mysteries: it's the men who linger in the Dark Ages and condemn them for it. It doesn't require long for a woman to realize that the fact that a man pleads for it, wheedles, coaxes, hunts for it, even fights for it, employs strategies, weeps, curses, lies for it, concocts compliments, pursues it for years, jumps at it, even makes love for it, if necessary—all this does not for a moment mean than man approves of a thing—*for the woman*. When a woman consents to perform the Forbidden Ceremony she imputes to the man an intelligence and decency which he practically never possesses. And what sensitive woman is willing to perform any ceremony with any man who is so stupid as to condemn her privately—and even publicly sometimes in her absence—for doing the very thing he besought her to do? So far the human race has produced pitifully few men who are intelligent enough, just and generous enough, to grant to woman the same privilege which they demand—and take—and enjoy, themselves. When will the poor benighted Puritans learn that purity is an active state of mind, not a passive state of the body?"

Judging from the surprised expression of some of the people's faces before her, this idea had never occurred to them.

"Most of you are totally unaware that you are at this minute in the very midst of one of the greatest upheavals in the history of the human drama. Immorality is a rôle the nature of which is changing right under your very eyes. In the near future, no intelligent woman will consent to play the part. It will be relegated solely to those poor creatures who are willing to degrade themselves for the money they can get out of it. It's you Puritans who keep the rôle alive. It's you Puritans who are the cause of the countless infant murders, the girl suicides, the untold suffering of unmarried mothers, parents, and illegitimate children. All these human miseries are caused by you. And who babbles so much about the good of the human race as Puritans do?"

There was no response of any kind.

"And positive benefits would accrue to *The World's World* from a more intelligent conception of Immorality and Morality. Nor is it necessary for you to accept my word for it. Consult some of the greatest people of the world's history and see what they have said. Read Goethe, Balzac, Stendhal. Read the love letters of Héloïse and Abélard—read Edward Carpenter, Ellen Key, Marie Stopes, Margaret Sanger, Van de Velde, Bertrand Russell, Havelock Ellis. Ah, you won't read—you won't think—that's the real trouble."

Anxious and distraught, she looked about her. Some of the audience were laughing and jeering, some protesting angrily, while others were beginning to turn away. Determined to convince them, however, the young enthusiast held up a restraining hand.

"Wait! If you won't listen to me, perhaps you will listen to more authoritative, more famous voices. I see two men in the audience whom I met on my way to your Morality play. Listen to Bertrand Russell. There he is standing right in your midst. He will doubtless tell you that what you need is more education."

The restless audience immediately quieted down at the sound of a man's voice. " 'Everybody who has taken the trouble to study morbid psychology knows that prolonged virginity is extraordinarily harmful to women, so harmful that, in a sane society it would be discouraged.' "

Russell then continued: " 'Men fear thought as they fear nothing else on earth—more than ruin, more even than death. Thought is subversive and revolutionary, destructive and terrible; thought is merciless to privilege, established institutions, and comfortable habits; thought is anarchic and lawless, indifferent to authority, careless of the well-tried wisdom of the ages. Thought looks into the pit of hell and is not afraid. . . . Thought is great and swift and free, the light of the world, and the chief glory of man.' "

"Now listen to another great man," Tellectina said, "Havelock Ellis, who is standing right there in your midst, also—waiting patiently to be heard. That benign-faced man with the flowing white beard."

The dignified man began: " 'Purity cannot be the abolition . . . of sexual manifestations; it must be the wise and beautiful control of them! . . .

" 'It is *more* passion and ever more that we need, . . . if we are to add to the gayety and splendor of life, to the sum of human achievement, to the aspiration of human ecstasy. . . . Sexual pleasure, wisely used, . . . may prove the stimulus and liberator of our finest and most exalted activities. . . . The sexual embrace, worthily understood, can only be compared with music and with prayer.' "

"Ah, don't you see?" Tellectina pleaded. "At its lowest the Forbidden Ceremony should be a physical pleasure and nervous release; and at its highest a divine ecstasy, giving you the mystic sensation (even if you're not a mystic) of union with the infinite. Or have Christianity and your own Puritanism so far cheated you that you have never experienced this great exultation? For no one who has known its sublime beauties could speak ill of it or could for long wish to deny its pleasure and benefit to others."

The young woman looked out over their heads with beatific face and shining eyes, while the audience stared at her with a mixture of feelings—shame and bewilderment, fascination and disapproval.

Then it listened in a puzzled way to the voice of Ellis as he continued, " 'The social claims of women, their economic claims, their political claims, have long been before the world. . . . The erotic claims of women, which are at least as fundamental, are not publicly voiced.' "

Tellectina, unable to restrain herself, interrupted. "Well, it's high time they *were* publicly voiced! Men have been directing women's erotic rôles both in public and private for thousands of years, and a grand failure they've made of it!"

Ellis waited patiently until she ceased and then he resumed his quiet discourse: " 'Until it is generally possible to acquire erotic personality and master the art of loving, the development of the individual man or woman is marred, the acquirement of human happiness and harmony impossible. . . . The woman's whole nature remains ill-developed and unharmonized, and she is incapable of bringing her personality to bear effectively on the problems of society and the world around her. . . . We have to understand that the art of love has nothing to do with vice, and the acquirement of erotic personality nothing to do with sensuality. . . . Her new erotic experience has not only stimulated all her energies but quickened all her sympathies. She feels more mentally alert, more alive to the influence of nature and art. Moreover, . . . a new beauty has come into her face, a new radiancy into her expression, a new force into all her activities! . . . And the play of lovers becomes one with that divine play of creation.' "

The audience, feeling extremely guilty because they had so long allowed themselves to remain under the spell of these blasphemous Reasonese words, of which they had at least understood enough to make them angry, now turned upon their denouncer with doubled fury. Ripples of derision ran through the crowd; excitement increased rapidly until suddenly there rained down on the culprit a great deluge of stones and sticks, mud, refuse, and oaths. A missile struck Tellectina full on the chest. There were shrill catcalls and shouts from every side: "Give her the hook! Throw her off! She's as immoral as the one she's defending!"

And before the miscreant realized what was happening, the audience surged forward, leapt up on the stage, and rushed toward her. The actors themselves got in some telling blows from behind, but those whose hypocrisy had been exposed proved not half so vicious as those whose illusions had been disturbed.

Tellectina rushed back stage and, catching Femina firmly by the hand, dragged her hastily out a rear exit. But the mob followed through the theater, around the theater, over the wall, and down the highway along which Tellectina had so recently come, hurling sticks and stones at the fugitives as they ran. It was not until they saw that an enormous rock thrown by a veritable giant had struck Tellectina's leg and prostrated her so that she was unable to rise again that the pursuers were willing to abandon the attack and return to their Morality play.

After painfully setting the broken bone as best they could and encasing her leg in splints improvised from tree limbs, Tellectina and Femina lay by the roadside nursing their pains and miseries in silence. The former had also fallen into a bed of Sillidinous vines whose poison increased her Hynuppa rash tenfold. Unable to move, she lay without speaking, the quiet broken only by her sobs, while Femina maintained a sullen silence. Finally, however, Tellectina gave vent to her pent-up emotion.

"Oh, it is all too terrible—too incredible! But the worst thing is not this assault on me—from that I shall recover. The worst thing is that human beings are capable of such attacks, of positive malice, deliberate injustice, of such unwarranted cruelty and hatred of honesty! Knowing that these evils exist—even thrive—how can one continue to live in such a world? The injury to me, to my leg, is painful, but the poison Sillidinous into which they forced me tortures me more. Oh, oh," she moaned, "every illusion I ever had about mankind is gone: their cruelty is exceeded only by their stupidity.

"But how can one frail woman, however fiery, save the whole world? educate the world? or even change the basis of morality from sex to social actions? Any effort toward a life of honesty, or harmony, or beauty, is futile. And how can I in future protect myself against the stupidity and malevolence of *The World's World?* Ah, other places and other people must exist somewhere: places where life is not so hideous, people who admire honesty and are unafraid to look at life as it really is. I shall leave *The World's World* behind forever. Surely I can find a few persons worthy of one's complete respect and admiration, people who have attained the greatest height at which it is possible for human beings to live. Such people could certainly be found on Mt. Certitude—and I too shall live there as soon as I can locate it. Ah, yes, I must continue my search, however painful!"

But the very effort to move was so agonizing that, with a low moan of despair and agony, the young explorer sank back instantly into the bed of poison Sillidinous vines.

Femina appeared oblivious of Tellectina's words, even of her presence, in fact. The pain was excruciating when Tellectina attempted once more to move, but fortunately a poor but generous passer-by left the sisters some food and one old blanket. There was a great wound over Femina's left breast which, if it ever did heal, Tellectina feared would leave a hideous scar for life.

Having maintained her sullen silence for days, suddenly one morning Femina turned on her sister with all her long accumulated wrath. "Good God, Tellectina, what a fool you are! What a fool you were to fly in the face of the whole world that way! I could have managed it better myself, played the part once and then continued to live my own life without your exposing us both to all that ridicule and abuse! And what was your reward for your eloquent defense of Immorality? A broken leg and Sillidinous poisoning. And you actually endangered our lives!"

Shocked and disgusted, Tellectina struggled painfully to a sitting position. "And your miserable little life is far more important to you than truth or honesty, I suppose! You're not willing to suffer for your ideals!"

"Well, my little Tellectina, you can't make the world over—you nor all the rest of the intellectual women in the world put together. You told the world to go to hell—and what happened? It didn't—but *you did!*"

Her sister shook her head despairingly. "I know, I know, and yet I was right and they were wrong! Oh, it's not fair! But I won't compromise—I won't be a hypocrite."

Femina interrupted. "Hypocrite? Some call it hypocrisy, others call it discretion; but by either name it's the better part of valor, apparently."

For once Tellectina had no answer ready. Slowly and painfully Femina arose. "I wish you'd championed these fine ideas earlier and not dragged me away from Passino. You have certainly changed radically in the space of one and one half years! But you can rave and rant till you're blue in the face, for all I care. I'm through! I'm tired of Nithking and all its discomforts and your damned foolish ideas and ideals, as it pleases you to call them."

"But, Femina, does woman's freedom mean nothing to you?"

"Freedom? What in God's name does a woman want with freedom? What's she going to do with it when she gets it? Sure, freedom is a grand thing, it leaves a woman free to live alone and eat her heart out in loneliness; it leaves her free to have as many lovers as she wants, and free to find them all disappointing and disillusioning. It leaves her free to come home every night to an empty house, free to eat alone, sleep alone, be sick alone, free to grow old alone, weep alone, and die alone! Sure, freedom is a grand thing! It leaves a woman free to battle with the world alone, work for her own livelihood, free to go through life without protection, free to belong to no one and have no one belong to her. Sure, freedom is a grand thing for a woman!"

"But if she is a man's equal, then——"

"Equality? What do I want with equality? I can get all the things I want without equality. Am I not a woman? Do I not know ways—subtle ways of indirection by which I can obtain all the things I want from a man? To hell with all your freedom and equality and independence! What I want is marriage and a husband to protect me and lean on, a home and security, and—and a baby."

"Marriage!"

"Yes, marriage was the old-fashioned word I used. It's the only life for a woman. And it would be easy enough for me to find a man to suit me if I didn't have to consider your hypercritical intellectual tastes. Oh, why must we live together? Why was that curse laid on us at birth? I wish to God you had never been born Tellectina Christian!"

"Allow me to return the compliment, my *dear* sister! And your gratitude for my defense of you is really touching!" Then the tone of her voice softened. "No, no, Femina, don't get married. Come with me. I'm almost twenty-seven now, and arriving at that age when a person should settle down in her own home with her own philosophy. If you'll only let me direct our lives, I shall lead us both to happiness. I'm sure I shall find Certitude soon. I shall renew my search as soon as ever my leg will allow. Wait and follow me."

By way of answer Femina arose and scanned the western horizon. "Well, this road we're on looks well traveled, so I shall continue along it. But look! Here comes a carriage around the curve of that mountain! What unexpected luck! I shall certainly ride in it, at any cost!"

"But Femina, it's the road the audience of *The World's World* came on—it will surely take you back to Err—you don't want to live there!"

"Humph, I don't care where I live as long as I have love and marriage and security and protection and comfort. Besides, I'm sick of myself. I want to do something for someone else for a change, and as I said before, I'd like to have a child."

"Oh, must you degenerate into a mere female, Femina? But you can't desert your sister Tellectina entirely!"

"Oh, can't I! Try and stop me!"

Femina hailed the ancient carriage, which soon drew up beside her, but the face of the grizzled old cabman was so muffled in his scarf as to be practically invisible. Quickly making arrangements for her journey, the girl climbed in. Tellectina raised a protesting hand, but it was only a half-hearted gesture, for she knew that there was truth in all her sister had said.

Settling herself comfortably in the deep hollowed cushions, Femina waved farewell. "I'll see you in Err!"

"Never!" Tellectina retorted scornfully.

"Never is a long time, so don't make rash promises!"

"Traitor!"

For answer Femina placed her thumb to her nose and waggled it jauntily. While Tellectina sat watching the carriage pass around the curve of the mountain out of sight, a sick feeling of defeat engulfed her.

"Oh, God, what can I do when my own blood turns traitor? My hope of turning Femina into a Tellectina—crumbled to nothing! All my braving of dangers—undergoing the hardships of Nithking—the fearless facing of slander, of death, even—all for nothing! Dear heaven, that's a bitter pill to swallow! But she is Femina, a mere woman, after all, and she *does* need love —I understand that. Whereas I am Tellectina and sufficient unto myself." She looked at the stigma on her left breast. "Yes, Olev is ever present. Never will his image fade from my heart or hers—but still one *does* get lonely. Oh, God, what a world!"

She sighed heavily, shook herself, and, blinking back her tears, drew in a deep breath. "Well, I at least shall not be a deserter. I am Tellectina, and my journey through Nithking is not yet ended!" Lifting her eyes toward the mountain ahead of her she wondered what those white clouds which obscured its top might conceal and determined to settle that question at once.

CHAPTER XII

THE SEARCH FOR MT. CERTITUDE CONTINUED; HOW MENCKEN
SHOWED TELLECTINA HIS VIEW OF THE LAND OF ERR; AND
RASCOE ACTED AS OFFICIAL GUIDE TO THE GREAT MOUNTAIN

"NO, I DO NOT wish to deceive myself, however painful the
discovery of a truth about Tellectina may be!" The young
explorer was sitting at the base of the great mountain talking
aloud to herself, as becomes the habit of people too much alone.
"And I am honestly beginning to fear that I shall never be able
to find Certitude by my own efforts. Complete independence of
all other human beings and traveling alone through Nithking
is not quite as easy as I had anticipated seven years ago, when
I commenced this journey at the overconfident age of twenty.
I would willingly follow some man now if I possessed sufficient
faith in him.

"Perhaps I should search out the houses of some of the great
explorers of Nithking whom I have particularly admired and
discover which ones enjoy the best views. Certainly I should be
competent to judge such matters now, for Nithking is reputed
to improve one's vision. I am exceedingly curious to know who
has attained the highest altitude in Nithking which is habitable
by man and established himself there. It would seem merely
logical to assume that some of the most famous explorers might
reside on this mountain ahead of me. It appears to be the highest I have yet encountered. Although its top is continually
obscured by those amazing ciro-nange clouds. But I shall climb
it if it's the last act of a misspent life!"

Rising, Tellectina began slowly to ascend the steep mountain

332

side with the aid of an improvised walking stick. Neither path nor trail being discernible anywhere, the young explorer was obliged to work her way laboriously through the dense undergrowth. Although the amateur setting of her broken bones, combined with the Sillidinous poison and the exertion of climbing, produced almost unbearable pain, the determined girl ascended steadily without pausing to rest.

In her haste to attain the summit, however, she slipped on some loose stones, bruised herself painfully, and fell into a bed of those same poisonous vines which grew everywhere in Nithking in such profusion. The Sillidinous creepers seemed to curl themselves about her lame leg like serpents, so thoroughly entangling her that the courage to struggle ebbed away and she lay there motionless, nursing her pains of both body and mind.

The explorer had been lying there for some hours, too miserable even to wish to move, when she was startled by a decided tremor of the earth beneath her. To her amazement it was caused, not by an earthquake, as she had feared, but by the mighty thunderous guffaws of human laughter. Struggling to a sitting position, she was frightened and yet relieved by the sight before her. A group of giant men in hunting clothes was approaching on its way up the mountain. Towering high above his companions was a colossal giant, whose Rabelaisian laughter, rolling down the mountain side like peals of Olympian thunder, began to warm the weary explorer's blood to new life.

He was many times the size of an ordinary man, being so enormous that he failed to notice the young woman half buried in the leaves and tangle of vines. Tellectina called aloud to him for assistance, whereupon he glanced about him and, advancing quickly toward her, knelt beside the prostrate girl in order to hear her feeble voice.

In answer to his inquiry as to what had reduced her to this sad condition she briefly related her misadventures in *The World's World,* emphasizing particularly the inescapable Sillidinous vines which produced such terrible Hynuppa rash that it tormented her every waking hour.

Making an impatient gesture, the giant assured her that for Sillidinous poisoning he could do nothing. It was an ailment every explorer contracted in Nithking sooner or later. It was, however, one of the prices paid for the glory of the adventure, and was well worth it.

Tellectina then had the unique experience of having her troubles laughed at. And to the sick girl's own amazement the man's laughter failed to produce the expected resentment and instead acted upon her drooping spirits like a very potent tonic. He bade her cheer up, assuring her that the Hynuppa would grow worse but that eventually one became accustomed to it and even learned to laugh at Sillidinous. He said that the rôle of honesty was always dangerous but often delightful, and that he had treated so many people wounded in similar misadventures that he might be of service to her on that score.

As he worked he talked steadily, condemning her persecutors, declaring vehemently that their acts were the result of Puritanism. " 'The Puritan's utter lack of æsthetic sense, . . . his unmatchable intolerance, his unbreakable belief in his own bleak and narrow ideas, his savage cruelty of attack, his lust for relentless and barbarous persecutions—these things have put an almost unbearable burden upon the exchange of ideas.' "

Then the giant laughed, informing the astounded girl that it was both stupid and foolish of her to launch her attack at such people from any place other than such a vantage point as the top of a mountain like the one on which they now were. He invited her to visit him there while her leg was healing. Tellectina accepted gratefully. His harsh kindness seemed to give her strength. The Gargantuan man swung her lightly up into his arms without more ado and continued his ascent. Though ashamed to discover how relieved she was to have so strong a man do both her acting and her thinking for her, the young woman closed her eyes in contentment.

A few mighty strides brought them to the summit of the mountain where an enormous old castle constructed in that rectangular biblioesque style peculiar to the houses of Nithking, was discernible. The healthy laughter of this Gargantua was so infectious that she laughed in spite of her aches and pains, only to discover that laughter caused them to diminish miraculously.

Her host bore her to a great dining hall where he ordered drinks and refreshments for both his guests and himself. When cakes and wine were set before them on the great table constructed in a series of steps, he angrily ordered his portion away, calling for beer, salad, and cheese. The salad was not to his liking, either; so he went out into the kitchen garden, returning shortly with several gigantic heads of lettuce as large as small trees. As he poured quantities of oil and vinegar over them, Tellectina noticed to her consternation that three priests were crouching under the leaves trembling violently with fear. She, being as dumfounded as they, said nothing; and the next thing she knew they were balanced on the giant's fork, eaten before he noticed them, and washed down with mighty quaffs of strong dark beer.

He lifted several pounds of cheese to his mouth, but suddenly put it down again, made a wry face, and, hastily excusing himself, left the table. It was not long before Tellectina heard a great commotion, and completely oblivious now of her miraculously cured leg, flew to the window, where she witnessed the strangest sight yet beheld in this Nithking, the country of innumerable surprises.

The three priests had so nauseated the giant that he had been forced to rush out-of-doors to relieve himself. Supporting his head in his hands, he stood with his elbows on the garden wall and disgorged three mangled priests, who went swimming giddily downhill in a torrential stream of beer. Nor was this all, for evidently the three priests had merely been spies hiding in his garden to give the signal of attack to their followers. For scores of priests and clerics of every sect, having banded themselves together, had crept up the mountain and stationed themselves just outside the garden walls. They were all now being washed unceremoniously down the mountain side in a river of brown bitter liquid. Tellectina, watching this extraordinary sight from the dining-room window of the castle, found herself laughing heartily for the first time in years, while the giant shook the castle with his uproarious laughter when he noticed how his illness had affected his enemies.

Later that evening after dinner Tellectina withdrew alone to the library while the giant and his merry companions remained about the table telling stories which provoked such Rabelaisian laughter that it tantalized her. Strolling about the enormous library she stopped to examine some of her host's books which, like gayly colored mosaics, decorated the walls to an incredible height on every side; and she too began to laugh as she read aloud their amazing titles:

The Holy Howlers
Pusillanimous Platitudes by Rotarians
The Presidential Cipher
Virginity Per Se
The Gaudy Gorgeous American Scene
The Higher Hooliganism
Homo Boobiens of the Bible Belt
The Delusions of Democracy
The Divine Right of Aristocrats
The Intelligent Minority
Our Annual Production of Messiahs
The Bill of Rights Done to Death
The Asininity of the So-Called Prohibition Law
The Great Camouflage by Comstock
The Common Sense of Women and the Dreams of Men
The Place of the Hymen in Modern Life
The Hemorrhage of the Old Testament
The Sempiternal Cinderella Story Lifted to Cosmic Dimensions
Civilized Man His Own God
The Mewling and Puking of Priests
The Boobocracy of America

There were countless others, but she noticed that all those whose titles she had read were by the same author: a man named Mencken, about whom she determined to ask her host. She thought the men took an unflatteringly long time to join her, consoling herself, however, with the assurance that if she had brought Femina along with her they would not have lingered over their liqueurs half so long.

"Ah, well, men never care for the Tellectinas of the world," she was lamenting when they entered the room and, seating themselves about the light evening fire, apparently set about to prove the injustice of her accusation.

Before the flood of this giant's conversation about Nithking, all thought of her painful leg and poisonous rash receded, for his discourse recalled the thrills of her own recent trip; and as usual, to hear her own chaotic and vague young thoughts nicely arranged in neat sentences caused her to consider the speaker the most marvelous and admirable person she had ever met.

The young explorer sat eagerly on the edge of her chair, her eyes riveted on the face of the gigantic man opposite her. He spoke at length of Err, with audacious honesty and loud and frequent Rabelaisian jests. He revealed that Err was his own native country and that this estate was but a summer home to which he retreated for recreation and pleasure when Err became unbearably suffocating. He praised Nithking and particularly those people who dared explore and write about that strange Forbidden Country, contending that they were the only producers of real literature, of which there was a lamentable insufficiency in Err.

"'Our literature, . . .'" he said, "'is chiefly remarkable for its respectable mediocrity. . . . As if paralyzed by the national fear of ideas, the democratic distrust of whatever strikes beneath the prevailing platitudes, it evades all resolute and honest dealing with what, after all, must be every literature's elementary materials. One is conscious of no brave and noble earnestness in it, of no generalized passion for intellectual and spiritual adventure, of no organized determination to think things out.' "

At the word "adventure," the young woman had suddenly caught her breath and murmured to herself, "Yes, that's it! And the virtues out of which great literatures are born should also be possessed by people, you mean? But that's exactly why I wanted to explore the Land of Nithking—because only in that country was there an opportunity to 'think things out'!"

After her excited murmurings had ceased, her host continued: " 'When one turns to any other national literature . . . one is conscious immediately of a definite attitude toward the primary mysteries of existence, the unsolved and ever-fascinating problems at the bottom of human life, and——' "

But all that immediately followed was lost on Tellectina, for she was arrested by the phrase "definite attitude." Clasping her hands in great perturbation, she rose and paced up and down the long room. "Oh, it is *that* which I seek, a place where I can find a definite philosophy of life! It exists on Mt. Certitude, but I almost despair of ever finding that elusive goal."

Her host waited patiently, then resumed his own discourse on the fiction of Err: " 'It habitually exhibits, not a man of delicate organization in revolt against the inexplicable tragedy of existence, but a man of low sensibilities . . . yielding himself gladly to his environment. . . . The man of reflective habit cannot conceivably take any passionate interest in the conflicts it deals with. . . . His hero is not one who yields and wins but one who resists and fails.' "

The word "fails" chilled Tellectina with a sense of dread. She murmured within herself, "But *I* have resisted. Does he mean that *I* might fail? Oh no, it couldn't be! It's impossible for me to fail in life, because I long so terribly to win! It wouldn't be fair because I'm endeavoring so earnestly to win!"

Apparently her host failed to notice the effect his words were producing on the young explorer. His voice was unperturbed. " 'Where above all is courage, . . . the capacity for independent thinking? It is in . . . men of such high rank as Mark Twain that one finds the best proof of the Puritan influence. He could not get rid of the Puritan incapacity for seeing beauty as a thing in itself, and the full peer of the true and the good.' "

"Ah," Tellectina responded, "but it's so difficult, even if as a child he or she loves it with absolute passion, and even after she has come to worship it with an almost religious fervor. But you—you evidently accomplished the entire journey long ago and can now rest securely in your strong castle here on this mountain top; while I am still a homeless wanderer who is beginning to grow very weary."

His smile appeared to be sympathetic but he resumed his discourse on his native literature: " 'The more a man dreams, the less he believes. A great literature is thus chiefly the product of doubting and inquiring minds in revolt against the immovable certainties of the nation.' "

Tellectina leapt up from her chair with a little cry of triumph. " 'Doubting and inquiring minds'! But that's I—Tellectina! And didn't I revolt against the immovable certainties of the nation of Err? And as to the great literature I may create, I can't say yet, but I am secretly keeping a travel diary of this trip through Nithking!" Turning eagerly to some of his followers, Tellectina inquired again the name of her host and was informed that he was a twentieth-century Rabelais, an extraordinary Gargantuan named Henry Mencken who was famous for his fearless expression of what he was pleased to call his prejudices.

Standing before him with downcast eyes, the earnest young woman suddenly began to inspect her hands minutely, while she said in a low voice, "I admire your prejudices to excess—perhaps because I agree with them. And although I am twenty-seven now, I believe I have so far left no inch of Nithking unexplored, nor would I accept anyone else's opinion or report about any part of it, nor have I arrived at my destination yet—although this mountain may be the place I'm seeking."

Her host assured her that no one could decide that question for her except herself, but if she would be interested in seeing his view of the surrounding country, she might come to the great southwest tower tomorrow; then she could decide if she liked Ghaulot—which was the name of this mountain. Some people considered it too chilly and uncomfortable at that height, so he suggested that she examine the mercury in her bedroom to see if she wished to accompany him.

Early the next morning she examined the mercury, and it stood so high that she dressed hastily and accompanied her host up the long flight of stairs to the tower. Standing beside him, she looked out his castle window and beheld a sight which left her speechless—for this was higher than any mountain she had ever been on. There, spread out below his west window, was the Land of Err, the despised country which Tellectina thought she had left forever, the land which she believed to be hundreds of miles away. The realization that her explorations in Nithking had led her back toward Err filled her with pained bewilderment; the discovery that this great Gargantuan man had chosen to build his fine castle on a mountain which lay on the border line of the detestable Err and the glorious Nithking frightened and puzzled her exceedingly.

To her further consternation, on looking closer she saw that the whole theater of *The World's World* lay in Err, and that she had merely climbed the stile over the wall dividing the two countries and entered from the rear.

These discoveries agitated the young girl till she grew so feverish that the Sillidinous poison appeared in a more virulent form than she had ever experienced heretofore. She leaned against the cool stone window sill, overwhelmed by misery and despair, convinced that life had completely defeated her and that her exploration of Nithking and her quest for Certitude were equally futile.

A sound in the corner of the room aroused her, and, turning, she realized that this was the magazine for Mencken's explosives. She saw him filling a rectangular object with a deadly-looking black liquid. After it was prepared he leaned out the window and hurled it with true Gargantuan strength and gusto high into the air. After some time had elapsed there was a tremendous explosion with violent repercussions all over Err. The girl looked out in amazement and was dumfounded to notice that this bomb had cleared the foggy air of Err to such an extent that she could see for an incredible distance. In hundreds of towns the populace began running hither and thither in impotent anger, gesticulating vindictively in the direction of Mencken's stronghold.

The giant laughed with the glee of a dozen schoolboys. Even his own castle began to shake. And Tellectina laughed too, but had no more than recovered from the effects of the first one when Mencken sent another bomb spinning through the air a little farther to the south. It dispelled the heavy fog that obscured everything below it and revealed to her stupefaction the same city of Smug Harbor which Tellectina thought she had destroyed seven years before with her army of outlawed Noequists. Tellectina rejoiced, however, to see the atmosphere cleared in that city for once. Mencken immediately followed this one with a score of others fearlessly and unerringly aimed at the largest and most important structures of Err—the churches, the governmental structures, the universities, and the press buildings.

From this height the Casuists who poured excitedly out of the churches looked like midgets trying to fight off an invisible enemy in the air. The senators and other governmental officials scuttled guiltily about the streets like frightened mice seeking for hiding places. All the inhabitants of Smug Harbor swarmed out of their houses like thousands of angry ants whose mounds had been violated. But there proved to be what Mencken termed the intelligent minority who were immune from everything except the laughing gas and tear bombs; and these, combined with the antics of the "homo boobiens," caused them to fill the air with such uproarious laughter that even the frightened squeaking and shrieking of those who had been struck could not drown it. Tellectina laughed till her blood began to race through her body with renewed vigor and health.

"Oh, I see now that my method of attacking the Errorians was stupid and futile. Reasonese and logic hurled at them in solemn seriousness are not the proper weapons: your Derisory bombs are far more effective. I am glad I found this mountain. I would have sought Ghaulot before if I had known how invigorating it was. I haven't felt this well for months—for years, in fact!"

Indeed, the former invalid felt so strong and well that she hurled a few small Derisory bombs of her own making. Every day thereafter for several months she witnessed this twentieth-century Gargantua hurling bombs into Err. The majority of the Errorians merely danced frenziedly about in inarticulate rage, but the clergy retaliated with a variety of small Vituperate cannon. Only a few balls, however, were able to carry as high as Mencken's impregnable castle. He ran out on the terrace in high spirits to gather them as specimens for his Schimpflexikon collection, the formation of which was one of his chief hobbies. Tellectina feared for his life as he stooped down to pick them up, but was relieved and amused to see the giant gleefully comb the cannon balls out of his hair with his fingers.

The girl smiled to herself in happy assurance. "Ghaulot renders him immune from all Errorians. And I too shall be immune from their onslaughts some day when I build my own impregnable house."

Anticipation of possessing a house of her own revived all the old restlessness. Mencken was so absorbed in making new bombs that he failed to notice her departure. Racing down the wide steps and out through the gardens, she came to the great lodge gates. Admirable as the Gargantuan's view was, she felt it necessary to see many views before she became an adequate judge of any one. Renewed strength and vitality filled her with eagerness to resume her journey through Nithking. She was peering through the gate wondering what the unexplored part of this Mt. Ghaulot might offer when a man approached her. They soon entered into an animated conversation concerning the giant owner of the castle, during which the stranger said:

" 'That Gargantuan attack upon the habits of the nation . . . has made Mr. Mencken the most powerful personal influence on this whole generation of educated people. . . . The man is bigger than his ideas.' "

"Ah, yes," Tellectina agreed with enthusiasm, "he is a great force, and he certainly deserves a good Boswell."

" 'One feels,' " the man continued, " 'that Mr. Mencken is deeply outraged because he does not live in a world where all men love truth and excellence and honor. . . . He has created a force . . . which has an extraordinarily cleansing and vitalizing effect. . . . His wounds are clean wounds, and they do not fester. I know, because I have fragments of his shellfire in my own skin. The man is admirable.' "

"Yes, for he has made a direct attack on the sacred absurdities of Err with unprecedented violence."

The stranger nodded assent. " 'The Mencken attack is always a frontal attack. . . . He is splendidly and exultantly and contagiously alive. . . . He calls you a swine, and an imbecile, and he increases your will to live!' "

"That's it! Increases your will to live! You appreciate him as few people are capable of doing. What, may I ask, is your name?"

The man introduced himself as Walter Lippmann. And Tellectina knew that she would never forget that name or that calm and confident voice. "It has certainly been a great pleasure to talk with you, but I must return now to Mr. Mencken and express my gratitude not only for his hospitality but for his many cures. He also stimulated my sense of humor, which had almost atrophied from disuse, and that has renewed my health to an incredible degree! He has taught me to laugh at the stupidity and puerilities of the Puritan Errorians. Heretofore, my own seriousness oppressed me terribly."

Bidding good-day to Mr. Lippmann, she went bounding back to the castle; and rushing up to Mencken in the great southwest tower where he still sat making bombs and chuckling to himself, breathlessly attempted to explain what he had done for her—before self-consciousness should reduce her enthusiasm to polite phrases.

When he turned around, she said, "I am far more deeply indebted to you than you can possibly be aware. I'm sure you don't realize at what a crucial moment in my journey through Nithking you arrived. Pain and despair from my misadventures in *The World's World* had absolutely incapacitated me for further progress when you appeared.

"For having carried me up into this invigorating air and renewed my health, my gratitude is boundless. Even though my Sillidinous poison is, if anything, worse, you have given me the courage to endure it good-naturedly. And never again shall I be consumed by a messianic fever to save people from their own puerilities since you've shown me a new and better view of Err. The perspective gained from this height reduces them to their proper proportions. And for the incomparable entertainment you have given I shall always be indebted to you. Yet I can't remain in your house too long, because I have not completed my explorations of Nithking or even of Mt. Ghaulot, and I can never rest in peace until I have covered them both and found the most suitable site for my own house."

The man laughed at her earnest and breathless recital, saying in a kindly indulgent tone that the real trouble with her was that she had too much pity in her blood; that this prevents the formation of sufficient humor to keep one in robust health; and he feared that there was no cure for people like her.

"I know," Tellectina admitted, "but something tells me that I shall be the victim of it all my life." Overcome by sudden shyness at her own frankness, the young woman hastily swung her pack to her back and rushed from the room.

Emerging from the park surrounding the Mencken estate, she resumed her expedition with renewed zest. On exploring the great Mt. Ghaulot, up which the Rabelaisian giant had borne her, however, she was surprised and confused to discover that it did not rise into one great peak but exhibited a vast area of uneven ground more nearly resembling a plateau, rising into mounds and hills of various heights. Ghaulot appeared to be the favorite resort of many great people. The mountain was covered with the estates of the famous, all of whose views were reported to be admirable—a statement which Tellectina refused to accept until she had verified it with her own eyes.

Although Tellectina had met most of the inhabitants at one time or another, it was necessary to renew her acquaintance with them in order to see their views from this particular mountain. It being impossible to determine from a distance which house occupied the highest and most desirable site, and consequently afforded the best view of the two worlds of Err and Nithking, she decided to visit each one and settle that important matter for herself—and the even more important one of selecting a site for her own residence.

The estates of the American colonists who had more recently taken up residence on this mountain being more easily accessible, she called upon them first. There was an estate adjacent to Mencken's whose host proved exceedingly cordial and willing to show the young explorer his unexcelled view down the main streets of some typical towns of Err. It was indeed a clear view and, moreover, he had constructed a remarkable Trisalic searchlight which he played upon them, showing up all their crudities and absurdities in its merciless and penetrating light. It appeared to Tellectina a sight both amusing and pathetic; and an admirable accomplishment on the part of her host, Sinclair Lewis. Whether the inhabitants remained within the bounds of their main streets or dared to venture outside them, all those on whom Mr. Lewis played his spotlight came to a sad end. Although admiring Mr. Lewis' view very much, the young explorer explained that she could not appreciate fully the merits of any one view without seeing others, also; so, thanking him cordially for his hospitality, she departed.

At the next estate she visited, the host requested one of his many delightful guests (whom he seemed to be entertained by rather than entertaining) to show the young traveler the view from her own boudoir window. Tellectina's guide was no less than Helen of Troy herself in all her well-known beauty but hitherto unsuspected wit and wisdom. So admirable and delightful an outlook had her host, John Erskine, given this beautiful Greek woman that the visitor lingered a long time, wishing heartily that she herself possessed a similar view, but tore herself away finally to continue her journey.

The Americans who had attained this mountain were conspicuously few. Hastily she visited others, enjoying the whimsical charm of Christopher Morley's view, and finding the decidedly masculine taste exhibited by Don Marquis' outlook very enlightening.

It was a great mystery but an even greater disappointment to the explorer that so few women maintained residences at this height. The male inhabitants hastened to inform her that the feminine sex had seldom thrived at such an altitude. She learned, however, that Jane Austen and George Eliot had made occasional ascents long ago.

Her delight exceeded all words when Tellectina discovered two American women who, although she understood that they had primarily sought Ghaulot as a temporary retreat from the male sex, had remained and gradually enlarged their grounds and broadened their outlooks. Edna Millay had a delightful view, and down the hillside appeared a smaller but also attractive estate with a similar but somewhat gloomier outlook belonging to Dorothy Parker.

Ellen Glasgow's remarkably fine view of the South was unequaled by that of any other woman. She had withdrawn to a sufficient height to obtain a proper perspective, and at times a brilliant light could be noticed playing over the entire landscape. A somewhat different outlook could be enjoyed from a bit of barren ground lying to one side of her estate, and, though austere, it was broad and splendid.

Edith Wharton's windows opened out on the well-cultivated world of the East, and although admirably aloof from it, her outlook was nevertheless somewhat circumscribed by the conventional high wall which enclosed that small world.

After having renewed her acquaintance with these four American colonists, Tellectina's hopes for the future of the feminine sex, with which she had the keenest sympathy, had risen decidedly. Their ability to climb to such heights when they discovered that a detached view of the world afforded them the most happiness was indeed a good augury. It caused the young explorer to consider establishing her own abode near them. Feeling, however, that no satisfactory conclusions could be arrived at until a traveler had at least obtained a glimpse inside all the most famous rectangular biblioesque dwelling places on Mt. Ghaulot, Tellectina hurried on.

Proceeding to the north, she encountered a group of English colonists whose views were delightful, especially those of Bernard Shaw, E. M. Delafield, Richard Garnett, and Aldous Huxley—although a rather cold biting wind whistled about the Huxley house continually. That of Norman Douglas especially captivated her. In the beginning, however, Tellectina had not considered his view so good; but as soon as he showed it to her in a south wind she realized that its charm was exceptional. Unfortunately her host departed from his high estate as soon as the south wind ceased; but hoping that Douglas would return with another, Tellectina waited impatiently. To her keen disappointment, however, there was only one south wind; consequently she too departed very regretfully—never forgetting, though, the intense pleasure once given her.

Anxious to see if some of the older English residents possessed even superior views, Tellectina hastily surveyed those of Sheridan, Congreve, Gilbert, Samuel Butler, Swift, Fielding, and others whose fine old mansions had withstood the test of time. But none of these outlooks appeared to the critical young explorer to be the best ones which Ghaulot afforded. On searching for the older American residents, she found only one on this entire mountain. It was Mark Twain, but there were too many obstacles which obstructed his view—except when seen from his secret Elizabethan chamber of 1601, which few people, unfortunately, ever had access to or even knew existed.

Ascending another low range of hills, Tellectina was confronted with a series of fine old French châteaux in which she enjoyed the most delightful outlooks shown her by Rabelais, Voltaire, Molière, and France. The first, however, proved to be a little too rough for her feminine tastes; while the second revealed the earth in a brilliant but pitiless light. With her fourth host, however, she lingered a long time. The panorama of both Err and Nithking was most admirable from a particular angle, obtainable only on a small rectangular plot called Penguin Island by its owner, Anatole France.

The skeptical young woman still felt for some obscure inexplicable reason that she had not yet attained the greatest height at which it was possible for man to live in comfort and enjoy in consequence an unexcelled view of the two worlds of Err and Nithking. So, on and on she went, growing weary but never losing hope.

Up in the mountain fastness was situated an old Spanish castle where she reveled in the scenes visible from Cervantes' window. From here she journeyed to another old villa also completely isolated. Although the view offered by its owner, Boccaccio, of the Mounds of Venus and Natural Phallic Formations was both extraordinary and amusing, its chief drawback was that it was restricted to these only.

The older the castles, the more confidence they aroused in Tellectina of finding what she sought: her assumption being that their owners had remained on this mountain all these years because their property possessed the best views. As this seemed only logical, she next hopefully visited a group of old Roman palaces displaying in their interior the early Satrici style at its best. These were owned by Horace, Juvenal, Apuleius, and Ovid. In spite of their fame, however, Tellectina concluded that they were surpassed by an old Greek near by named Aristophanes, who possessed a broad and sweeping view of the entire landscape that was most admirable, delightful, and refreshing. Although the obstinate young woman had almost exhausted the possibilities of Ghaulot, she still was not satisfied.

Standing on a high knoll, the explorer looked about her disconsolately in all directions. "Everyone who has sought Ghaulot lives at such varying levels with such varying views that it is difficult to determine which is the best. I've seen so many, I have become confused. Or perhaps it's my own fault, perhaps my judgment isn't mature enough or my experience sufficient to enable me to decide which is the best even after I've seen them all. It might be advisable for me to consult some authority on the subject at once. There must be many excellent guides to such a famous summer resort as this. In fact, I've often heard them talking, but being over-self-confident, I have never listened to them."

Turning, Tellectina hastened off in the direction in which she heard voices, but on consulting many who claimed to be official guides the young traveler was given a different answer each time. Even some of the residents themselves contended that their own houses were built on the highest ground, and without exception each one defended his view heatedly when it was criticized by one of the guides. And practically all the tourists she met were only too eager to constitute themselves self-appointed guides, assuring her that their information was infallible. The divergence of their opinions, however, as well as that of the official guides, was even wider than that of the residents themselves.

Exasperated, the explorer realized that it was a question which she would have to decide entirely by her own efforts without either help or hindrance. Consequently, one hot August morning she seated herself under a giant oak tree and carefully compared all the views with which she was now familiar.

"Well," she finally concluded, "it seems to me that it all amounts to this: there is something about the view of every resident on this mountain which I honestly admire; but most of them have done one or two things. Either they have built their house on the northern side where the view is unexcelled for clearness but where, in that cold merciless light, even what is ordinarily beautiful appears unlovely; and although those cold cutting winds may be stimulating at first they would be too trying to live in all the time and, besides, they harden people eventually; or, being genial souls, they have sheltered them-selves on the south side and seem unaware that they see both worlds always in the light of a warm golden sunlight which en-hances even the hideous parts of the scene.

"No, no one of these groups has settled on the best site, for surely that is located at the very top of the mountain where one could obtain a comprehensive sweep of the entire landscape both in the merciless northern light and also in the rosy glow of the setting sun."

With slow dogged steps she continued steadily upward, though the ascent proved to be surprisingly difficult. She climbed for days without encountering any human habitation. Finally, hav-ing lost all sense of direction, she sank exhausted in a deep drift of leaves and lay there motionless.

"Oh, I'm so weary and discouraged! Where is this remarka-ble and unsurpassed view of the world for which I'm searching? Why not be satisfied with those I've already seen? Or perhaps there exists no higher point and no better view—it is merely an ideal place which exists only in my own imagination."

The sun having long since disappeared, there was left now only a vast expanse of dirty gray sky. The explorer lay gazing up at it intently. "I wonder, is there really some thing, some power, up there which is interested in—which directs—human welfare—my welfare? Or is it a force of actual malevolence, or merely infinite indifference? It's all very well to laugh at the stupidity of the Errorians as Mencken taught me, but what of my own happiness? I can't laugh at my own misery, can I? What is the thing which controls human living? Don't effort and desire accomplish anything whatever in this world?"

She shuddered at her own thoughts. "Oh, I have tried so hard to attain my goal—to find Certitude! But it looks as if I shall fail. All my hope is ebbing away. My journey through Nithking is proving too long and painful."

Such terrible despair descended on her that she buried her face in her arms and murmured brokenly, "Where, oh, where is this thing I seek? Is my quest for Certitude to continue forever? Not to know—and know that I know, tortures me so! But why, why do I yearn so passionately to build my house on the highest peak in the world? Other women don't. Oh, what a curse to be a Tellectina!" She sighed heavily but nevertheless arose slowly. "I suppose I shall find it if I can only persevere long enough and don't die in the attempt. But if I only had someone to help me, a guide who knew his way about these treacherous mountains."

She climbed on doggedly while the air became more and more rarefied. Suddenly she was arrested by the sight of a signpost directing her to the house of an official guide. Hastening toward it, the weary and discouraged explorer rushed unceremoniously into the house, beseeching the smiling man she encountered there to give her directions on her long and fruitless quest.

At once he began to show her his own views of both Nithking and Err and so comprehensive and superior were they that it proved conclusively to the explorer that here was also a very superior type of guide. For hours they sat and talked while the guide pointed out to her from his windows the abodes of a group of men whom he called, "'Prometheans,'" because they " 'have, like Prometheus, brought fire and warmth to their fellow men. . . . The men and women who have wrought warmth into the bleak terror of man's war against the elements, against his own nature and against the imminence of death, have brought us out of savagery. . . . They have always suffered, and their hearts have been torn out repeatedly by the spectacle of the cruelty men can inflict upon one another in their efforts to survive. But their hearts grow back, for further pluckings, because the belief persists that all the difficulties of life may some day be smoothed away.' "

And from his window could be seen another mountain that looked almost as high to the surprised young woman as Ghaulot, and which was likewise dotted with the estates of other famous people. Evidently this famous and agile guide, Burton Rascoe, was equally at home at either height. For in speaking of Ghaulot, he said, in that ambiguous language of

Nithking, " 'Humor is a solvent for the brine of tears; and in many of those who are articulate the urge and the genius to provoke a chuckle or a smile is as definite and as sublime, as wise and as beautiful, as the urge and the genius to purge the mind by evoking pity and terror.' "

And when he said, " 'One wishes that young children were not starving and that feeble old men innocently abroad on their routine affairs were not shot down by gunmen. One wishes above all that wars might cease, disease be conquered, and that kindness, generosity and magnanimity might universally prevail' "; Tellectina knew that in this house and in this man kindness, generosity, and magnanimity did prevail, and therefore, in her whole-hearted young fashion she gave herself up to his direction; assuming, of course, that he would answer explicitly the question she wanted answered most in the world. But he had a surprise in store for her.

He not only pointed out the abodes on both mountains of nine famous Prometheans from St. Mark through Lucian and up to the American, James Branch Cabell; but also those of another group of thirty people, whom he called "Titans"—from Homer through Sophocles and Montaigne to George Moore. And he also described with humor and wisdom and vigor their respective and varying views to his excited and entranced young auditor. And although he saw the defects in each view, he admired passionately all that was admirable, exhibiting the rarest quality Tellectina had found among the famous in Nithking —a lack of enviousness.

After many gloriously stimulating hours with this remarkable guide, the young explorer felt so much renewed energy and courage that she felt as if she could conquer the world. Consequently, when Rascoe refused politely to point out to her which resident of Ghaulot lived at the greatest height—implying that this was a matter every true explorer of Nithking must find out for himself or even herself—and adding that on this point there was violent disagreement, that after men attained a certain height relativity was a matter of personal opinion, she agreed, knowing that he was correct, but feeling disappointed, never-theless. Thanking him profusely, she rushed out to continue her search. She upbraided herself, however, for lacking the patience to visit personally all the men Rascoe had mentioned and ex-amine their views with her own eyes, but it was in vain for she *was* impatient. But recalling certain things Rascoe had said about a certain resident of Ghaulot she started off gayly in his direction. Soon she was arrested by the presence of an eagle's shadow which produced a strange effect on her. It seemed like a good omen. She followed it until she suddenly encountered an even stranger thing, and, with a premonition that she was on the right track, began to follow the figures of earth unlike anything she had ever seen which she now came upon, and was thus led to a high place. The view obtained through an opening in the leaves filled her with delight.

She stopped, breathless for a moment. "Is it possible that I shall soon be able to view the world from the highest place (or, as that official guide Rascoe, said, what looks to me like the highest place) at which man can live in comfort? Is it possible that Certitude lies ahead? Some instinct tells me that I'm near-ing my goal of a lifetime! Attaining to Manu Mission was won-derful—but this I fear as much as I long for. Ah, no, the human spirit cannot bear to rush into a new-found glory too suddenly! The very fact that the end of my seven years' journey through Nithking may be at hand almost overpowers me!"

With eager yet fearful steps she moved upward again and was overjoyed to see the white roofs of a palace through the treetops. "Ah, I was right! Someone does live on the very top of the mountain!"

She soon came upon a great brown palace and stood knocking at the door which had the figure of a gold stallion "rampant in all his members" outlined in the lower right-hand corner. Her heart began to beat violently from the excitement at her ap-proaching adventure when without warning of any kind an electric storm broke loose. Lightning began playing about her in blinding flashes; thunder resounded throughout all the mountains; then suddenly a bolt directly out of the blackening heavens struck Tellectina to the earth. She lay unconscious.

After the lightning had been swallowed again by the black storm clouds which spat it forth, some tourists from Err who had heard Ghaulot highly praised and had come up to see and scoff, spied Tellectina's prostrate form as they were hurrying through the woods on their way home. At first they pronounced her dead; but one man, on placing his hand beneath her nostril, felt the faint breath being exhaled; whereupon two men formed a pack saddle of their hands and arms and thus carried her down the mountain side, over the border into Err.

Since there was no means of identifying the strange young woman, the two maiden ladies, the Manhu sisters, who had first seen Tellectina, practically adopted her—keeping her in their house, nursing her indefatigably night and day, sparing no expense for famous physicians. The lightning had played a strange trick on her—it had paralyzed Tellectina's body and her every faculty, leaving her mind, however, unimpaired. She lay there blind—deaf—and dumb—while her brain and stomach worked on unhampered as though in an ossified body. She seemed to be a living corpse and yet able to feel pain. Thus she lay helpless for days, cursing the lightning which had failed to kill her but had given her a living death instead. The days, however, she was able to endure—it was at night that the real trouble commenced.

CHAPTER XIII

A FIGHT FOR HER LIFE, AND THE PART PLAYED THEREIN BY THE
MAGIC POWER OF A STRANGE LITTLE PACKAGE CONTAINING
STRAWS AND PRAYER BOOKS

THE PARALYZED GIRL lay helpless—suffering, thinking, eating, and eliminating—nothing more. This continued for days that were to her like interminable years. One night her internal pains reached their acutest point since her terrible accident. Tellectina was lying in her bedroom alone—so she thought —yet that uncanny sensation produced by the presence of another person forced her eyes open. Though gradually having regained the use of her sight and other faculties, she could still see only dimly.

Passing to and fro across the window by the invalid's bed a strange shadow was barely discernible. Premonition of some evil chilled the sick girl's blood, but she hastily assured herself that it was nothing but a cloud floating across the moon.

Every night thereafter, however, the shadow not only returned but lingered longer each time. Despite her determination to ignore it, Tellectina felt her eyes magnetically drawn toward the window. And as this ghostly figure drifted by like a wraith on the wind, it seemed to the invalid that it was beckoning to her with long thin fingers. Instantly she closed her eyes, making an elaborate pretense at not having seen him. His face was in fact rendered invisible by a long gray cowl which appeared to float nebulously about his head.

While asleep at dusk one evening Tellectina was seized by such terrific pain that she awoke suddenly with a cry of agony and found herself looking straight into a hideous face at the foot of her bed. It was that of the gray specter who had crept into her room. Never in her life had she beheld such a fearful sight. With slow noiseless motion the figure advanced inexorably upon her. The girl's eyes closed involuntarily, her brain reeled sickeningly, and she felt consciousness slipping away when suddenly some fierce determination to resist awakened deep within her.

"What!" she muttered fiercely, "you came for me! For me, Tellectina Christian! That is not possible! I refuse to go with you! I defy you! You take other people—but not me—I am Tellectina! Why, I haven't yet accomplished the things I set out to do—the things I was destined to do. I have not yet attained the greatest height possible for man to attain in Nithking—and that is my goal. I have not yet found my own philosophy of life. I have not written all the great books I have planned, nor has Femina known a long sweet marriage. No, I am not ready, I tell you! Go away, go away! I command you! When I have lived fully and done and felt and seen and learned all there is in life—then I shall welcome you—but not till then, no, no!"

But the silent gray figure drew steadily nearer with a slow, inevitable, inexorable movement.

The terrified girl pressed back into her pillow, staring at it wild eyed. "Oh, no, no! You wouldn't take me—I'm so young —so pretty! I'm only twenty-seven—I haven't lived yet! Oh, it's not fair to take me so soon. I've done nothing to deserve death! Mercy, mercy, I beg of you. Please, please, I'll get well some day—I'll live again, I've never really given up hope!"

She felt suffocated as though by a thick gray fog; she gasped desperately for breath. Illness rendered her body helpless, but all the determination and defiance of her young being rose within her. She intended to defy death by the very force of her human will. She steeled herself for the encounter and, closing her eyes, waited, rigid and breathless. . . .

Oblivion had stolen insidiously over her. And the next thing of which the invalid was conscious was opening her eyes and

not being able to see any of the accustomed things about her—
neither the walls of the room nor the bed. Before her there
stretched a dim gray wasteland—illimitable—uninhabitable—a
barren nothingness as far as she could look in every direction.
And then once more she drifted imperceptibly into uncon-
sciousness. . . .

Slowly and gradually the coma lifted, and sensibility returned
with an acute attack of the same excruciating pains that had
awakened her at dusk. Gazing dazedly about her, Tellectina dis-
tinguished vague shapes moving about her bed and heard
faintly familiar voices which sounded very far away. Little fragments of their speech penetrated the gray fog in which she
seemed enveloped.

A woman's voice was saying:

". . . Unconscious when we came into her room to say good-
night." It sounded like the older of the Manhu sisters.

A deep masculine voice responded, "Well, death nearly bore
her off this time, there's no doubt about that."

The invalid heard the voices ebb and flow uncertainly about
her bed, until suddenly a very sharp prick in her arm was followed by a strange sweetness which went stealing through all
her limbs, a sensation more delicious than anything ever experienced before in her whole life—even more pleasurable than an
orgasm, she decided sleepily. As the pain receded she drifted deliciously and voluptuously into oblivion, and in the interminable
hours that followed pain continued to alternate with that seductive forgetfulness which attended the repeated pricking of that
little needle.

Thus days passed until the pain eventually lessened and the
invalid returned to the plane of normal life feeling as though
she had been dragged down into the dark and fathomless abyss
of another world. The long weeks which ensued allowed her
more than ample time in which to speculate on the nature of
her recent experiences. She strained her every faculty in an
effort to comprehend what it would feel like actually and
quietly to follow the mysterious gray specter into that gray land

of nothingness of which she had had so brief a glimpse, or to be snuffed out like a candle submerged in the black agony of a painful death. But it was impossible to realize, even to imagine, complete extension, nothingness—illimitable time and space and infinite silence.

"But why—why do people fight against death so fiercely? Why did I, who had every reason to welcome death? Ah, but death is such an affront to one's ego—the idea of being snuffed out like a mere candle—like that—at one breath! It's so belittling! It's intolerable. Little had I dreamed how strong was the human instinct to live—however painfully. And that seems ignoble—to cling to life when life could only be a miserable imitation of the real thing! It is illogical and unworthy. I am ashamed of my own desire to live. Until now I have evidently gone gayly along through life regarding death as a calamity which befell *others*. Certainly no one values health till she has seen the face of death.

"But why?—why should all this happen to me—now!—now, at the youthful age of twenty-seven? I don't deserve to be killed—or even to be ill! The unfairness of it torments me as much as the illness. I've done nothing to deserve this illness—to say nothing of death! To be punished for committing a crime, yes—that I would endure without complaint. But I have violated none of the rules of life or even of health. Blindly, indiscriminately, life struck out at me in the form of lightning. Such gross injustice—it's incredible—inexplicable! What is wrong with the scheme of the universe that it permits such unjust treatment to an innocent human being? And yet such calamities befall hundreds of other people every day, I suppose. I failed to give the malevolence of nature much thought till it struck home. A whole young life, that might have been of value in many ways, ruined—ruined for no reason at all! It's so unjustifiable. Oh, there's something queer about this life force that I don't understand!"

These thoughts spun around and around inside the invalid's head until they literally wore grooves in it.

All the famous physicians and specialists who had been called in had offered a different diagnosis and a different remedy, each more futile than the preceding. For nearly a whole blank black year Tellectina lay practically motionless and helpless, obsessed by a single idea: to find a means of terminating the life of an active mind in a dead body.

It was now that Tellectina discovered the amazing fact that emotional and mental illnesses merely constituted exciting duels with a sporting opponent whom one could eventually defeat by adroit use of one's wits; but physical illness was a slow crushing by an invisible force which relentlessly and blindly disregarded all rules of all games.

So gradual was the partial recovery of the use of her faculties, so slow and tedious a process did it prove to be, that Tellectina derived no pleasure from it. After this mysterious and formidable paralysis had obliterated one and one half years from her life, she regained the normal use of her oral, ocular, and auditory senses. Although able to move her arms, she was still unable to walk or even sit up in bed; consequently her desire for a quick and painless death increased daily. All the specialists had long since dismissed her case in disgust, but a village doctor, who had been considered too insignificant to be consulted, became so interested in the rumors of the mysterious malady of the mysterious stranger that one morning he called of his own volition. When he deposited his medical bag on the table by her bedside, Tellectina stared in fascination at a small phial therein marked with a skull and crossbones. While the thermometer was in the patient's mouth the doctor stood at one of the windows conversing with the two Manhu sisters in inaudible tones. His examination consisted principally of sitting beside the invalid's bed and asking her questions.

Finally he shook his head sagely. "Just as I expected. I endorse no 'isms,' but your chief trouble now, young lady—whatever it may have been originally—is mental. You do not *will* yourself to recover because you have no desire to live. Your mind has become sicker than your body."

To the invalid's half-hearted protestations the doctor rejoined, "I understand perfectly: you mean it was your body which induced the mental sickness in the first place—true; but it is your mind that is prolonging your bodily illness now. It is indeed a vicious circle. No one can cure you but yourself. It seems unkind to say that, my dear young lady, but it's true."

The two maiden sisters who had been listening at the foot of the bed left the room impatiently. They who had been all sympathy during Tellectina's protracted physical illness suddenly lost patience with her mental and spiritual illness, filling the house with an air of resentment because Tellectina failed to recover. As the days passed, the invalid girl, although understanding their lack of understanding, was none the less hurt and thrown into deeper despair than ever before. And she deepened their gloom by a repeated avowal that she longed for the courage to die by her own hand. Although the initial appearance of the gray specter had filled the girl with defiance and dread, she had gradually become somewhat accustomed to seeing it hover about her windows. And ever since the visit of the village doctor this somber figure had held a phial in his hand. Its fascination for the invalid increased steadily, as she wondered desperately if the pain caused to others by deliberately expediting her journey into the realm of gray oblivion were justifiable.

Overwhelmed by despair, one midnight the sick girl called to him feverishly, "Come, I welcome you! Everyone else, everything else, has failed miserably. Perhaps only you can cure me, after all. Come, I no longer fear you or dread you—I welcome you! My life is unbearable. I am prepared to go with you now!"

With her hand on the phial that had been silently tucked under the edge of her pillow she hesitated. Vividly there flashed across her mind all the glorious dreams and plans for her future; rebellion welled up strong within her, and a fierce longing for life surged through her whole being, but with a quick, bitter determination she lifted the little phial and drank some of it. Then the figure leaned nearer and nearer until she felt his chill breath on her cheek. But as soon as the nausea caused by the poison began to rack her whole body, Tellectina, who thought she longed to die, was amazed at the terrific struggle she once more put up to save her useless and painful life. She thrust the phial back under the pillow. Lying there convulsed by excruciating nausea, she despised herself for lacking the courage to take all the poison as he urged and follow him.

The gray face continued to haunt her window every night, however; but Tellectina had seen the face of death so often now that it no longer frightened her. She felt infinitely weary and dully indifferent to both death and life, steadfastly refusing, however, at all times to divulge the name or whereabouts of her parents, assuring the Manhu sisters that she was an orphan, and assuring herself that to remain silent under the circumstances was the kindest thing she could do for her parents.

When every physical remedy had failed, the older sister ventured to recommend once more that which she had suggested in the first place. Entering the sick-room one evening with her eyes glowing mysteriously she said, "Here, my dear, do try this Holy Guide. It is better than all the medicine in the world. It is the only thing which has given me strength to go through life." Placing the book in the patient's hand, she stole softly from the room.

Tellectina accepted the small black book and, turning it over slowly in her hands, eyed it curiously as though seeing it for the first time in her life.

"I would to God I could find a book—any book—a religion, any religion—or a philosophy, that would ease the burden of living. I even wish I could regain my childhood's faith. Life is too hideous without help of some sort! Reason, science, have failed me—must I then turn to religion? But nothing short of a miracle can save me now from destruction through my own despair!"

Opening the worn black book at random she began to read:

"And I gave my heart to seek and search out by wisdom concerning all things that are done under heaven: . . .

"That which is crooked cannot be made straight: and that which is wanting cannot be numbered. . . .

"For in much wisdom is much grief: and he that increaseth knowledge increaseth sorrow. . . .

"As it happeneth to the fool, so it happeneth even to me; and why was I then more wise? . . .

"And how dieth the wise man? as the fool. . . .

"I returned, and saw under the sun, that the race is not to the swift, nor the battle to the strong, neither yet bread to the wise, nor yet riches to the men of understanding, nor yet favour to men of skill."

Tellectina closed the book hastily. "This is cold comfort. Just to confirm my own miserable thoughts. What profit has my effort to attain knowledge and wisdom afforded me? And was I not struck down even as a fool might have been? Made useless and helpless just when I was nearing my goal? Oh, it's all so damnably unfair! The whole scheme of man's life is wrong —wrong! But what can anyone do about it? Oh, God, what a miserable failure the life of mankind is! Without rhyme or reason. It seems monstrous that no force should exist anywhere that cared anything about man!

"Certainly wise old Solomon was no Casuist. How I envy people like the Manhu sisters their blind, stupid faith. If I had only been born stupid—that is life's greatest blessing!"

She wept with slow despairing sobs until both her fever and Hynuppa increased doubly.

As she lay there in the darkness, the long accumulated flood waters of misery suddenly burst the dam of reserve, and Tellectina commenced to pour out her troubles in a mighty torrent of words, flinging her plaint of disillusion into the face of the indifferent night.

"Ah, don't you see, don't you see? My life is made doubly painful! It is not only the pain of physical illness, nor the atrocious injustice of being incapacitated for proper living by this damnable paralysis—from that I may recover with sufficient patience.

"No, no, there is something worse! I am poisoned—perhaps fatally! That terrible Sillidinous vine which infests all Nithking, and the Hynuppa rash that starts as a mere surface ailment— these have finally poisoned my blood—and that has poisoned my very heart, my very mind!

"Oh, it's so terrible to think that it's my explorations in Nithking which have reduced me to this sad state! Nearly every discovery I made there led me into a veritable bed of those awful vines! To come in contact with Sillidinous vines invariably means to be disillusioned—that is the nature of their poison. My very spirit is sick with it!

"All medicine—all science, has failed me, and religion is not for a Tellectina. But, oh, life, fate, whatever you are, why don't you help me? I can't permit you to defeat me so ignominiously! I can't, I tell you—every drop of my blood rebels against defeat! Yet of what avail is rebellion—or courage or thought!"

An invisible presence seemed to the overwrought girl to be listening with interest, consequently she rushed on: "You see, I expected to find in Nithking such very different things from what I actually did find.

"First there was 'religion.' To learn that the Bible we trusted implicitly as a child is a false guide book, that the man whom we thought our divine saviour was merely a charming orator— merely a religious fanatic; to be shown that the Christian heaven toward which we once looked with longing eyes is but an old woman's illusion and hell merely a conceit of our fathers; that Christianity is but Casuistry and only one of many religions which will, like all others, pass from the earth; that the God to whom we prayed for succor in time of stress is but the projection of a weak human need; that the deity we thought omnipotent and benevolent is neither because he does not exist, and that the monstrous, endless problem of evil precludes forever the existence of any sort of god anywhere—these are the painful discoveries which leave one infected with poison—but these I can survive.

"Even to learn that love does not mean happiness but anguish, that even the happiest marriage is full of pain and disillusionment, that love does not beget love but that cruelty often does, that love is not necessarily accompanied by passion, and passion seldom by love—these are discoveries which can be and have been sustained by me with equanimity.

"And men! To be taught as girls that men are the lords of creation; that all men are virile, strong, and independent, in every sense women's superior, only to have intimacy or marriage serve to reveal the fact that many of them are none of these things—to reveal weakness that is pathetic, or the transformation of the romantic lover into the domineering husband; to reveal a male egotism, colossal, incredible, and often ludicrous, coupled with a blind selfishness which is a marvel to behold; a childishness at once ridiculous and appealing, and to reveal a false superiority which resents the possession of real intellect or ability on the part of a woman; these are disillusionments which also leave their poison but are not fatal.

"And women! To discover that they are often venomous creatures far more deadly than the male; that jealousy of things both great and small eternally poisons the relationship of woman and woman; that they are actually dull, stupid persons whose interests seldom pass beyond the personal, petty, and material; that even the strongest man is weak in the hands of a clever unscrupulous woman; in short—to discover that human beings are really not admirable creatures at all: all this is sickening beyond description.

"And as to sex—a woman soon discovers that the man quickest to seduce a woman is the one quickest to condemn her for having been seduced; that if a woman has the courage to defy the sex conventions openly, mud will inevitably be slung at her; that if a woman desires that most desirable of masculine traits, strength of personality, she needs must pay for it with constant friction or complete submission; that excellence in mentality does not imply excellence in character; nor does virility in mind betoken virility in body; but the saddest discovery of all is that the majority of women of the world are doomed to live forever unsatisfied sexually and romantically because a good lover is the world's rarest species: these are unjust laws of nature and man which a woman perceives to her sorrow—and endures.

"Then there is herself! When the female of the species discovers that she herself, if aroused, can be more deadly than any male; when she discovers her own limitations, contradictions, and shortcomings and realizes that, however intellectual a passionate woman may be, her body makes insistent and incessant demands which she ignores at her peril: these are painful revelations which can, however, be supported.

"To realize that if she is a thinking woman she is forever cursed with a dual nature: the purely feminine and the intellectual, which are constantly at war within herself, that she has the same desires, fears, and weakness as any other woman, wanting the security, protection, and companionship—and children —which only a man and marriage can offer. Oh, no man knows the misery of that day when she realizes that half her nature will always, with all its primitive might, restrain and retard the grand adventurous mental side; that the very continuance of the human race itself sets an irrevocable limit to her ability in creative pursuits. These are discoveries which leave a bitter poison in the soul. But even these can be borne.

"And after much painful trial and error, to discover finally that the way of happiness lies in being continually drunk on beauty, love, art, passion, or creative work, merely to learn that intoxication can be enjoyed only at the expense of one's nerves and digestion—that is a diabolical law of nature against which rebellion is futile and often fatal.

"To see behind the scenes of the glamorous world; to learn that honesty is not the best policy if one wishes to succeed according to worldly standards; that breeding, sensitiveness, and

intelligence are handicaps in earning a livelihood: these discoveries instill a poison in the young explorer never to be eradi-
cated."

She paused for breath then continued:

"In other words, to have been taught so much sophistry by
the school, the home, the church, and society concerning all the
important matters of life that it requires thirty years of violent
struggle to rid one's self of the burden—that is a bitter thing.

"To see injustice stalk rampant through a helpless world; to
witness man's incredible inhumanity to man; to be taught sentimental sophistries about the beauties and blessings of nature
only to witness her daily indifference and frequent cruelty to
mankind—these too are inevitabilities one can and must sustain.

"To have discovered that this world in which we live is not
the best of all possible worlds as we were taught in childhood,
but a place of strife and misery; that the human race which we
believed to be intelligent and kind is fundamentally neither;
that life is a blind force dealing its blows indiscriminately—all
these poisonous truths I have endured.

"But—" and here the sick girl flared up with redoubled ardor
—"but there is one thing I cannot endure: the failure to fulfill
my own dreams!

"Ah, but it is not the failure of the absurd and beautiful
dreams of my girlhood—those I forego with a smile. For I
know now only too well that I shall never be a great princess
ruling over a great realm with fabulous fame and fortune. I
know Femina will never be wooed by all the greatest men of
the earth, and that her beauty is not such that men die for, nor
will she live in Arabian splendor, nor be loved with immortal
love, as she once dreamed. I know that Tellectina cannot hold
court and have all the philosophers and artists of the world at
her feet. Never shall she be a Corinne proclaimed in the public
forum for her talent and wit. She is not a genius whose writing will set the world on fire, nor will she ever attain the
perfections of which she so confidently dreamed at sixteen—per-

fections of form and face—of knowledge and wisdom—of character and conduct and achievement. Never will she know all things nor be able to do all things as once she so fondly hoped. Those fabulous dreams of girlhood gradually dissolve through the years like a rosy mist.

"Ah, no, it is not for these sweet unattainable and foolish dreams that I weep. It is for the essential, the possible ones. In spite of my disillusioning knowledge of the world, I still thought that I—personally—might soar above mediocrity and could manage to realize at least my two fondest dreams: to write very good, if not great, books, and enjoy a happy, if not perfect, marriage. I am now twenty-nine, and I never doubted for an instant that by now I should have attained both that height where the best view of the world was to be had and a suitable site for my permanent residence in which I could settle down with my own philosophy. I thought I should have acquired my modest but deserved share of both fame and fortune by now, and my more feminine half should have acquired an eminently suitable husband.

"Yet I have done neither. Now for the first time in my life I come face to face with the fact that I may be defeated by life. Others might fail—but that life should defeat me, Tellectina Christian—it's unthinkable—unbearable—impossible!

"Why, why, does life deny fulfillment to me? I do not ask much. I do not ask for a kingdom, fabulous riches, castles and slaves and power and position. No, all I ask of life is within reason.

"I want simply a balanced life: a life of fulfillment, not of renunciation and restraint. I want beauty and balance—health and happiness—joy and zest in all the acts of both body and mind; and comfortable, not luxurious surroundings, where the eye is pleased by all it beholds; and security, security from actual deprivation. I want peace of mind and quiet of body to follow my own thoughts and enjoy my senses—to pursue my studies and creative work. I want congenial companionship, love, a satisfactory lover; a home of my own with pleasant foods and wines; stimulating conversation spiced with wit and wisdom; and a few but deeply satisfying friends. Is that asking too much of life? But are not those things the intrinsic right of every human being? And what do I receive from life? Only pain and bewilderment. It poisons me with disillusionment, and I rebel! Oh, I hate you, life! Do you hear? I hate you!"

Then suddenly the girl's spirit broke—all the rebellion went out of her.

"Failure—failure and defeat! Oh, it is too terrible! It isn't fair, for I have tried, oh, I've tried so hard to conduct my life intelligently! Oh, God in heaven, I cannot face defeat! Why, why, are human beings cursed with desires and ideals and not the opportunity or ability to fulfill them! It's so unjust, so cruel of you, life, fate, nature—whatever your name is! I've struggled so hard to achieve all my fine dreams—in extremity I have prayed to the God in whose existence I no longer believe! Effort, prayer—all, all is futile!"

The girl began to sob hysterically, emitting low, agonized, inhuman sounds.

"Oh, what is to become of me!" she moaned as she lay helpless on her bed all through the sleepless night. "I can neither fulfill my desires nor rid myself of them, and I can't even change them. And yet if they aren't fulfilled I can never be happy! It is an impasse. Death is the only possible solution. Oh, why not? I'm incurably ill in body, mind, and spirit! It's not right to be a burden to myself and others. There is only one intelligent, one right and sensible thing to do—to end my own life voluntarily."

After a night of acute misery, morning found her contemplating the small phial in her hands. At this moment, however, the elder of the two Manhu sisters suddenly entered the room. "A package for you has just arrived. Shall I open it?"

"It doesn't matter," the sick girl replied indifferently, as she concealed the poison under her pillow.

To Miss Manhu's consternation, the package contained straws and prayer books. Lifting out a small brown volume, the older woman carried it to the window to obtain a better light, as the day was one of unprecedented darkness. Tellectina lay staring listlessly out at the black clouds rolling across the sky.

"Well, my dear, aren't you even interested in your gift? It's queer, because it *says* it's a prayer book, but it has some sort of gold horse stamped on the cover. And there is no inscription inside, so you can't tell who sent it to you. What a peculiar way to send a present—and I didn't know anyone knew you were here, anyway." This last she said a little jealously as she turned several pages. "Passages are underlined with a pencil all through the book, yet there is nothing about—yes, wait—here is something about religion. It says: 'For centuries where magic has attempted to coerce Providence, and religion has urged the bribing of Heaven, whether with burnt offerings or good behavior, here the artist has more urbanely adhered to moral suasion, by setting a praiseworthy example for the Demiurge to follow.' Well," the maiden lady exclaimed, "I simply don't know whatever it is talking about!"

Miss Manhu looked up, vaguely puzzled and decidedly shocked, then sampled another page.

" 'But, as an even more remarkable fiction, I consider the new five-dollar bill which I chance this morning to possess. In itself, like the metal disks, it is worth nothing: and its glazed surface chills the thought of devoting it to the one use suggested by its general dimensions.' "

In spite of her pain, the invalid smiled—realizing afterward that it was the first time in two years.

"Humph," was Miss Manhu's only comment. She continued reading.

" 'Even superficial explorations of the charms and the little ways of any unfamiliar and personable young woman, they tell me, is unflaggingly rewarded and incited to fresh exertions by the discovery of some slight novelty or small strangeness. Thighs differ, breasts are always unpredictable, and the piquant mole continually——' "

The elderly maiden lady ceased abruptly. "I won't read such disgraceful things! And all that isn't actually antireligious sounds like nonsense or worse to me. One thing, however, I can see at a glance: it has no real religion in it—for all that it calls itself a prayer book. And I certainly have my opinion of the person who sent it to you. I'm sure you don't want it—I'll just throw it into the fire, where it belongs."

Hope stirred in Tellectina's breast at once. Might not one woman's nonsense be another woman's wisdom? In a casual voice, she replied, "Oh, don't bother. Just lay it on the table here, I'll have a look at it some day. Ah—er—isn't that your sister calling you?"

The instant the spinster left the room the invalid took up the book as quickly as her half-paralyzed condition would permit. She turned first to the back of the book: surely it could be from only one person, the one who invariably inscribed her gifts in the privacy of the back pages. There in a large, almost illegible scrawl was written:

"I've just heard by accident of *your* accident. Sick in bed myself with seventeen ailments, or would come to you at once. This prayer book once saved my life—maybe it will do the same for you. If not, send for me at Smug Harbor.

"Love and curiosity,
"Your unchangeable,
"SOPHISTICA."

"So," the invalid murmured, "she's found me at last. Well, she can be depended on, I think, not to divulge either my whereabouts or condition to my poor dear parents."

Then, quickly opening the brown book, Tellectina began reading the marked passages at random.

"Nobody really needs to notice how the most of us . . . approach toward death through gray and monotonous corridors. Besides, one finds a number of colorful alcoves here and there. . . ."

Like a puzzled, hurt child who has been unjustly punished, Tellectina laid the book down. "But then, why did I think just the reverse? Why was I born with the fond and beautiful belief that life was a gay colorful corridor with only a very occasional gray alcove? Why was I given all these fine hopes and high desires if life never did intend to allow me to realize them? I don't understand—it's so unjust, so ironical. Oh, Lord, is my conception of life all wrong, or is life all wrong—or—or *both?*"

Lifting the small brown volume again, Tellectina continued to read the underscored passages.

"The artist simply does not like the earth he inhabits: for the laws of nature his admiration has always been remarkably temperate; and with the laws of society he has never had any patience whatever."

"Oh, of course, of course! So I am not so great a fool to rebel, after all!" Tellectina exclaimed.

"But those whom life has more deeply disappointed and bored . . . These are the romantics, . . . who, cursed with actual imagination, devoted it in youth to prefiguring what life must be when you became an untrammeled adult. They have faced the reality, they have faced the real and incredible antickry of men as social units. They have faced it with a candor uncharacteristic of common sense."

"Oh, so that's it, maybe," the girl murmured. "That is the secret of all my disillusionment: I am a 'romantic.' 'Untrammeled adult.' Untrammeled, indeed! Oh, adult living is unbearable, reality is unbearable! But what can one do to render life bearable?"

Hopefully she sought the answer in the little brown book.

"It is through consideration of his own unimportance and transiency that man rises to the largest resonance of poetry and wisdom. . . . And Shakespeare rounds off the dirge with the assertion that human living, however full of sound and fury, signifies precisely nothing. . . . Everywhere fine literature . . . tends to voice the futility of man's endeavors."

The young woman gasped and then gulped breathlessly, as though ice water had been flung full in her face. "Unimportant? Is it possible that man—that I—my desires are unimportant?

Does wisdom lie that way? Oh, but—but you mean, sir, that—that there are people who are fully aware of the injustice and futility of life and yet continue to live? But how—do you mean by not taking life too seriously?"

Frantically she consulted the book again. It mattered not at all that she had heard these ideas countless times before. She realized that words, however full of wisdom, fall upon barren ground unless the mind is enriched by experience and understanding.

But when the girl read: "I have embarked in a gaming in which to win is not possible," she felt even more outraged than frightened. "Do you mean that I can *never* win, that defeat is foreplanned? Oh, no, that is too hideously unfair! That would make life unbearable for one second! Surely one couldn't continue to live knowing such a thing to be the truth?"

"And I must be zealous," the little book said, "above all, not ever to regard my beliefs quite seriously. Human ideas are of positive worth in that they make fine playthings for the less obtuse of mankind. That seems to be the ultimate lean value of all human ideas, even my ideas. I must conceal my knowledge of this humiliating fact."

The girl lay absolutely motionless for a long time. Then suddenly she burst into low and prolonged laughter. A strange new joy tingled in all her veins. She laughed till new life and vigor began to course through her deadened limbs.

"So," exclaimed the paralytic of two years, with such a joyful burst of vigor that she unconsciously sat upright in bed, "*that* is my mistake! I take myself, all human beings and their living, too seriously! My pains, my desires, my ambitions are not matters to be taken so—so tragically! I see my fatal error!"

Dusk had fallen without her being aware of it. A servant coming in with her supper was so astonished at the sight before him that he dropped his tray.

The crash of the breaking dishes brought both of the elderly sisters flying to the room. "What happened—what——" But they too stood transfixed at the door, for the sight of the paralytic of two years sitting up in bed was too much to be borne.

"But how—how did it happen—what——" they asked in one voice.

Tellectina sank back weakly against the pillows. "I—I don't know myself. I suddenly felt so much better—almost normal again, and I simply sat up before I realized what I was doing, I suppose." The secret of the little brown prayer book was too precious to share with anyone.

"It's a miracle—nothing less," the first sister whispered piously.

"Yes, it's an act of God," the second one agreed. "Perhaps it's an answer to my nightly prayers."

Tellectina, too excited to sleep that night, lay with her hand on the little brown book beneath her pillow, murmuring over and over again, "Though called a prayer book, this little volume has more magic in it than religion." She laughed softly to herself. "But then religion and magic have always been closely related." Fondly she caressed its rough cover. "You saved my life, but that will remain a secret. Without you despair and illness would have forced me to commit suicide, I verily believe."

Her condition was such that it prevented her reading the book in its entirety, for the perusal of one page strained her weakened eyes, caused a sickening headache and nausea. The very next day, however, she demanded to be conveyed at once to James Branch Cabell, the man who had originally produced that little magic package which Sophistica had sent her. The Manhu sisters divined her secret and immediately became concerned no longer for her body but for her soul endangered by heretical influences. They protested vigorously against her going out-of-doors where the lightning might at any time strike her as it had two years before. And they persuaded a local doctor to pronounce her too weak to undertake such a journey.

Tellectina insisted, however, that she was only partially cured and that perhaps Cabell could cure her entirely, being convinced that he was a magician of no uncertain powers and that nothing short of magic could cure her various maladies now. After reading all the marked passages over again the invalid gained sufficient strength to undertake the trip.

Two black guides who had previously proved themselves invaluable to her in Nithking were employed once more to convey the invalid. They assured her that they could find the way to the mountain top where the magician resided—provided she allowed them plenty of time and rest.

A comfortable litter was prepared by the two protesting Manhu sisters, and to the surprise of all concerned both the sisters and Tellectina found themselves in tears at parting. The patient's gratitude at their prolonged and unselfish nursing was very great; but it seemed to be exceeded by their unspoken gratitude for having been furnished with something for which to live and work.

Early the next day the little party set out on its strange journey. And it was not long before they began to ascend a steep mountain side. As the invalid lay still she would frequently murmur, "After all, though, I was probably on the verge of having such ideas myself as those expressed in the little brown book—otherwise I could not have benefited by them so much; they would have passed over my head just as they did over the heads of the poor dear Manhu sisters. Nevertheless, I shall remain in the debt of the magician and his book for the remainder of my life."

Then she would urge Old Faithful and his brother to hasten. Although they were straining themselves to the utmost, Tellectina was a relentless taskmaster, forcing them to continue even when they were so exhausted that they could scarcely see. Nothing mattered to her now, however, except to reach the mountain where Cabell dwelt.

CHAPTER XIV

THE DISCOVERY OF THE HIGHEST MOUNTAIN IN THE WORLD, AND
THE MANY STRANGE THINGS THAT BEFELL TELLECTINA THERE;
THE END OF HER QUEST FOR MT. CERTITUDE, AND HOW SHE OB-
TAINED THE BEST VIEW OF BOTH WORLDS FROM CABELL'S WIN-
DOWS

THE SICK GIRL was now preparing to traverse slowly the
same ground she had covered in haste two years before.
With pleasant anticipation she looked about her for the eagle's
shadow, which had originally almost passed over her head at
this stage of her journey in Nithking; for she now realized its
significance. It was an augury of better things to come. After
it was finally sighted by her two black guides, one of whom suffered from myopia even more than the other, they followed the
eagle's shadow faithfully until their attention was distracted by
the reappearance of the strange and skillfully wrought figures
of earth which previously had elicited Tellectina's puzzled admiration, and the allegorical meaning of which she was able to
interpret more easily on reëxamination.

Assured now that she had regained Mt. Ghaulot, Tellectina
permitted Old Faithful and his brother a short but much needed
rest; after which they bore the invalid to the same high place
in the middle of which the lightning had struck her two years
ago. As she went over it again, she realized that it offered one
of the most delightful views ever met with in all her travels
through Nithking.

As she drew near the end of the high place, that curious elation which resembled intoxication convinced Tellectina that she
had ascended to a great altitude and was now breathing very

375

rarefied air. Eventually they arrived at Cabell's castle with its white roofs and many brown turrets; and it too proved to be of that rectangular biblioesque style peculiar to the houses of Nithking. It exhibited some nineteen additions which had evidently been made at quite different periods and each of which was sparsely ornamented with gold.

While her guides sought admittance at the surprisingly simple doorway, the sick girl noted with curiosity the figure of "a stallion rampant in all his members" outlined in gold in the lower right-hand corner of the entrance. The brown door swung open, and there before her delighted eyes appeared numerous pages, each of which actually seemed to vie with the other in a unique kind of beauty which, though distinctly masculine, was nevertheless of exquisite delicacy. They introduced the visitor to a most amazing man named Jurgen and then conducted her toward their master, the Prince of Poictesme, carrying her through long medieval passages which she noticed with surprise and delight were brilliantly embellished with exceedingly droll and original artistry.

They bore her into the Great Gallery of Mirrors—a long room elaborately lined with hundreds of exquisite and unusual mirrors scintillating with the reflection of a thousand lighted wax candles. The sick girl failed to notice, at the moment, the departure of Jurgen, but was able to lift her head sufficiently to perceive her host advancing from the far end of the gallery.

Too ill and distraught to be ceremonious even in the presence of a gentleman famous for both his chivalry and his gallantry, the invalid elevated herself slightly on one arm and hastened to inform him of the rumor (coming from the most reliable of sources) concerning the excessive pleasure which he was said to derive from the practice of his magic: a pleasure which, she trusted, justified her belief that her presence was not an unwarranted intrusion. Then the girl rushed on excitedly to explain the causes of her visit, outlining her trip through Nithking and dwelling especially on the magical effects which a small package containing straws and prayer books had produced upon her while ill.

"In short," the girl concluded, "I have been poisoned so many times with such virulence in the last nine years that my system is saturated with it and, as you doubtless know, a supersaturation of Sillidinous in the blood stream creates the worst case of disillusion known to science. I realize the impossibility of curing such extreme cases but there must be some kind of magic palliative, a drug, perhaps, or even a balm with such penetrating qualities that when applied externally would ease internal suffering.

"For I simply haven't the courage or strength to continue living if it means constant misery. Science has failed me. Religion has failed, and philosophy? How can one treat such ailments philosophically? No, no, I'm convinced that nothing short of magic can heal me now!"

The magician waited patiently and politely until the excited girl ceased her supplication; then, accompanying his movements with the words of the incantation, he performed those flourishes and passes from left to right customary in the practise of the Black Art and produced a rectangular brown box six inches by eight, by one and one half inches deep, which evidently he had had concealed about his person all the while. This receptacle he proffered to the sick girl, who discerned the figure of "a stallion rampant in all his members" outlined in gold in the lower right-hand corner of the cover.

Slowly, wonderingly, she opened the top. It was like the Arabian Nights genie and his bottle, for out of this small brown box began to emerge vague shapes which quickly were converted into the life-sized figure of a man and the shadow of an old woman whose head was wrapped in a towel. Tellectina recognized the man in the glittering shirt as not only the same Jurgen whom she had met in the passage leading to the Gallery of Mirrors, but also as that visitor who had so delighted Olev the Third but in whose variety of Reasonese she had then not been proficient enough to understand. He who had conjured them up "did that which was requisite," whereupon the figures became living beings and commenced to speak, Jurgen addressing himself to the shadow thus:

"'Oh, Mother Sereda,' says he, . . . 'many lands we have visited, and many sights we have seen: and at the end . . . I stand where I stood at the beginning of my foiled journeying. . . . You have given me . . . a shadow that renders all things not quite satisfactory, not wholly to be trusted. . . . I concede the jest . . . but what does it mean?'

"'It may be that there is no meaning anywhere. Could you face that interpretation, Jurgen?'"

At these words the invalid moaned audibly, but Jurgen continued.

"'No,' said Jurgen, 'I have faced god and devil, but that I will not face.'"

To which Mother Sereda replied, "'I jest with you. Probably Koshchei jests with all of us. And he, no doubt—even Koshchei who made things as they are—is in turn the butt of some larger jest.'"

Closing her eyes, the young woman on the litter uttered another low moan. "What! someone—something—*above* that which made things as they are! But that only increases the complication! Such words only exacerbate my maladies! But who, what, is responsible for all the unmerited suffering, all the injustice in the world?"

The shadow of Mother Sereda, however, ignored Tellectina's complaints and continued, "'It is as a chessboard whereon the pieces move diversely: . . . There is no discernible order, all to the onlooker is manifestly in confusion: but to the player there is everywhere a plan in the moving, and in each advancement and in each sacrifice of these pieces. . . . So goes this criss-cross multitudinous moving as far as thought can reach: and beyond that the moving goes. . . . The game is endless and ruthless: and there is merriment overhead, but it is very far away.'"

The invalid now lay silent and strangely still. Within herself she said, "So there is no hope: he only confirms my bitterest thoughts—thoughts which I wanted to believe were engendered by illness."

But the voices went on: " 'How do I know there is a word of truth in your high-sounding fancies?' " Jurgen asked.

And the shadow responded, " 'How can any of us know anything? And what is Jurgen, that his knowing or his not knowing should matter to anybody?' "

There was complete silence for a long moment, then Tellectina began to stammer breathlessly, "You mean—you mean, also, that what is Tellectina that her knowing or not knowing should matter to anybody? Or her suffering or her disillusionment or her hopes? You mean, I don't know the meaning or purpose of life and I shall never know and that even my not knowing doesn't matter to anyone? Oh, no, no, this is unbearable! I can't believe it, I don't believe it! It's too—too terrible!" She paused. "And what does it matter that I heard Jurgen utter all these words years ago? Then they were merely so many mellifluous sounds, not cold penetrating truths to absolutely sicken one as they now are. No, no, such ideas will not cure me, they will kill me!" Despairingly the invalid closed her eyes, then opened them again in sudden defiance.

"How dare—how dare anybody make such statements! I *do* matter! I *am* important!" Lifting her head to observe Mother Sereda more clearly, she came face to face with herself in the mirrored wall behind the old woman.

The reflection discovered there startled her. Drawing back, she gazed at it incredulously, objecting stoutly, "No, no, it is not possible!"

While studying herself intently the sick girl was sensible of a momentous change taking place within her. Suddenly she broke into peals of very unladylike laughter. What a ridiculous sight had been presented to her view! In these magical mirrors she appeared as nothing more impressive than a minute chessman. As she gazed at the small ludicrous object before her, she recalled how for twenty-nine years it had been moved about the world like a pawn by an invisible hand. The belief that she had been directing her own life was manifestly ridiculous when one reviewed it honestly. The strange internal transformation, the revivification, rejuvenescence, continued until again laughter welled up from some deep hidden spring. The effect was absolutely tonic. New life and energy commenced to surge through her deadened limbs. She laughed again and then again until such an abundance of renewed vitality charged her whole body that it acted like a magic curative, suddenly enabling the paralytic to sit up briskly. Hoping, incredulous—she waited. Joy gradually redoubled her strength: to her own astonishment it empowered her actually to step down from the litter and order it impatiently from her sight.

Tentatively she took a step forward. It was true then—she could walk! At this knowledge hope buoyed her up. Once more she essayed a step. Then, with eager but hesitant steps, the paralytic of two years walked across the floor.

"Oh, I'm cured!" the girl cried ecstatically. "Magically cured! I can walk again after two long terrible bedridden years! Laughter fills my heart with new hope, my blood with new vigor, my limbs with new strength. It doesn't seem possible! It is incredible! Yet it's true! If in the space of a few minutes you can cure so serious an affliction, it proves beyond question that you are a magician."

Then she lifted admiring and grateful eyes to the magician and the little brown case into the small compass of which the figures he had conjured up had now disappeared again.

"And now——?" She shrugged. "What is Tellectina that her knowing or not knowing should matter to anybody? Even to Tellectina?"

Then once more she looked at the man beside her. "If only there were some service I could render you commensurate with the service you have performed for me!" She thought intently for a moment, then laughed. "But of course there isn't—there couldn't be, owing to the very nature of the circumstances. I hope it's true, however, that you consider the pleasure derived from practicing your magic sufficient remuneration. I am well

aware that you do not indulge in necromancy or even catoptro-
mancy in order to cure perfectly strange young women; but, be
that as it may, I shall remain in your debt forever. Perhaps some
day, somehow I may discover a means of repaying a fraction of
it at least. At this moment, however, I—it is impossible even to
—to——"

Her eyes implored him to understand that which she was
incapable of expressing. And again Cabell seemed to graciously
dismiss such debts as negligible. Tellectina nevertheless continued to stand before him as though some painful necessity
were plaguing her to further speech.

"In the joy of being able to walk again, I momentarily forgot the Sillidinous poison. Due to a treacherously thin skin, as I
explained, this Hynuppa gradually infected my blood. And both
the poison and the rash (see, it covers my hands and throat—
my whole body, in fact)—both, I regret to state, have increased
while I've been in this room. The realization of man's impotence before Koshchei may provide mirth, but does it not almost deprive man of an incentive to live? Does it not cure one
malady only to increase another? For, knowing what he knows,
how is man to support life? What attitude can he adopt toward
the universe, toward mankind, toward himself? What can a person do to render life tolerable when he has become so poisoned
in mind that he actually believes in the indifference and even
cruelty of the life force, the impossibility of maintaining human
happiness, in the inherent stupidity of the human race, in man's
inhumanity to man, in the preclusion of a life of thought or
esthetic pleasure by the mere struggle for existence, and the impossibility of ever realizing one's own fondest dreams?

"I am too proud, too vain a woman to allow my face to become disfigured by Hynuppa, as it inevitably will soon. Surely
you know of some efficacious salve which might assuage the
pain?"

The magician was mysteriously silent for a moment. Then,
bringing out another small brown box, which also had been
concealed about his person all the while, he indulged once more

in those motions by which he produced his black magic and offered the receptacle to Tellectina. Externally it resembled the other, being identical in color and dimensions. In her haste to open it, the sick girl caught only a glimpse of the inscription on the inside of the cover which ended with the words:

"... *The precious life-blood of a master-spirit,*
embalmed and treasured up to a life beyond life."

Immediately there materialized out of the open box a life-sized man whom Cabell introduced as John Charteris. Without for a moment doubting her right to do so, the invalid lifted the box, which now was apparently filled with nothing save an evil-smelling black substance, and commenced to apply it to herself. As she did so Charteris spoke the words of the incantation which was necessary if the balm was to have its desired and magic effect:

"'One moment of clear vision as to man's plight in the universe would be quite sufficient to set the most philosophic gibbering.'"

"Oh, no, no," the girl protested, "such words, such cantraps will only cause my suffering to increase! Please, have you no other incantation that would make the medicine soothing?"

Pausing patiently during Tellectina's interruption, Charteris made no comment, but resumed his original cantrap:

"'Romance is the expression of an attitude which views life with profound distrust, as a business of exceeding dullness and of very little worth; and which therefore seeks for beauty by an abandonment of the facts of living. . . . Beauty, and indeed all the fine things which you desiderate . . . are nowhere attainable save in imagination. To the problem of living, romance propounds the only possible answer, which is, not understanding, but escape.'"

With these words the penetrating properties of the balm began to make themselves felt. Like so many curatives it had stung painfully at first and then become soothing. Eagerly, hopefully, the invalid applied more of the black mixture to the afflicted parts. And as she did so Charteris continued to repeat the words of the incantation:

"'Romance tricks him, but not to his harm. For, be it remembered that man alone of animals plays the ape to his dreams. Romance it is undoubtedly who whispers to every man that life is not a blind and aimless business, not all a hopeless waste and confusion. . . . However extravagant may seem these flattering whispers to-day, they were immeasurably more remote from veracity when men first began to listen to their sugared susurrus; and steadily the discrepancy lessens. . . . And, all the while, man plays the ape to fairer and yet fairer dreams, and practise strengthens him at mimicry.'"

Tellectina interrupted him with unrestrainable excitement: "Oh, look, look, it is already causing the Hynuppa to disappear! This balm is so potent, so penetrating, it is actually counteracting the poison in my blood and magically easing the pain!"

For a long time she stared at the black mixture in the little brown container in her hand. Then slowly she repeated some of the words of the cantrap: "'And steadily the discrepancy lessens'; 'And practise strengthens him at mimicry.' Those are the words that work magic!" The young woman was so overwhelmed that she remained quite motionless for a very long while.

Gradually the slow tears welled up and hung in glistening unheeded drops on the lashes of both her eyes—as was her way when profoundly moved by joy. But Tellectina was not aware of the tears or of Charteris or Cabell, but only of this magic cure which had been effected.

"No longer," she murmured, "is it necessary to attempt to bring myself into harmony with the hideous reality of life, as the stoics contend. I see now that not only is it wise to believe in one's dreams but only by endeavoring to attain them can mankind ever progress. And I readily perceive wherein the race as a whole has advanced; nevertheless, the pain endured by the individual obscures the larger ends of life. Cabell has Charteris employ the word 'dream' in the sense in which most of us use the word 'ideal.' And I have fallen so far short of my own ideals! Will your magic balm soothe that ailment too?"

Once more she resorted to the brown container, and once more Charteris spoke the necessary words:

" '. . . I prefer to take it that we are components of an unfinished world, and that we are but as seething atoms which ferment toward its making, if merely because man as he now exists can hardly be the finished product of any Creator whom one could very heartily revere. We are being made into something quite unpredictable, I imagine: and we are sustained, through the purging and the smelting, by an instinctive knowledge that we are being made into something better.' "

" 'Sustained by an instinctive knowledge'—yes, those too are magic words. For some time I have thought, but been reluctant to believe, that life on earth was no more arranged for the happiness of man than for any other animal. As soon as we realize that man in his present state is not by any means the end and aim of evolution, it explains many puzzling problems which Christianity tries to make all the more puzzling. We cease to expect very much of life, although we certainly continue to want it. And doubtless man will evolve into a being as superior to us as man is superior to the ape. I feel infinitely better now, and I am convinced by the constituent elements and the magic efficacy of this balm that the chief ingredient in its composition is undoubtedly the precious life blood taken from the proper source some time ago. My gratitude is too profound for me to express in words, I fear. I feel, however, that you understand, because you too must have suffered from this same ailment in youth."

She smiled at her benefactor but still made no move to take her departure.

"You may consider that I rather nullify my gratitude when I ask still another favor of you. There is yet a third matter which troubles me. Sillidinous vines are invariably located where one least expects them, it seems; consequently, how am I to avoid falling into them again in the future?"

Her host, who as usual indulged in his little eccentricity of not speaking directly to his guest, smiled and beckoned her to follow him. He walked quickly down the length of the Gallery of Mirrors and so came into the Hall of Armor. Ranged along the wall were fifteen rectangular brown chests, all of a size bearing the figure of "a stallion rampant in all his members" outlined in gold in the lower right-hand corner of the lid. There were also a few irregularly shaped chests. After several pages had opened the brown ones so that Tellectina was able to glance into each, she realized that they all contained the same kind of armor: an unusually light and flexible but indestructible variety composed of gatherulic iron.

His visitor admired the armor exceedingly, declaring that she thought it might be advisable if she acquired a similar kind of protection for herself. Cabell's pages soon brought forth the necessary material, and before she realized it, Tellectina found herself wearing an armor of gatherulic iron, and the Prince of Poictesme instructing her in the art of employing it for her own protection. Although it proved to be somewhat too large and masculine in design for her slender woman's figure, she proudly pretended and protested that it was neither. And Tellectina discovered that whenever she felt herself in danger of losing it a shrug of the shoulders was the quickest and most effective way of restoring it.

And since the Prince was also a magician, he taught her how to render her armor invisible when she so desired, explaining that he had found it inadvisable to display this kind of defense at all times and places; but that even when it was not noticeable to others, she would find it a source of great comfort to herself and an invariable protection through which no thrusts, either human or cosmic, could wound her fatally. In fact, it would even lessen the pain of death in no matter what form it overtook her.

The young woman smiled at her generous host. "Tradition

has it that few women have ever sought the protection of gatherulic iron. It is my belief, however, that I can avail myself of it without appearing masculine, which is indeed my very last desire. After having gradually become skilled in its employment as a defense, I can never again be hurt, no matter into how many treacherous and poisonous vines I fall. Such a protection indeed enables one to laugh at the whole world."

By way of reply the Prince of Poictesme merely smiled in a provocative manner which the inexperienced girl failed to comprehend.

"But my debt to you, sir, mounts steadily. Already, by means of the little package containing straws and prayer books, the mirrors, balm, and armor, you have performed four invaluable services for me. Although these are too much to accept from any one person, I do so because my need is very urgent. One does not like, however, to incur debts without the ability to repay them, or at least to express one's gratitude. And I seem able to do neither."

That he was to render her yet a fifth service would at this time have seemed to his young debtor neither credible nor permissible.

As they left the Hall of Armor and reëntered the Gallery of Mirrors, Tellectina overheard a familiar voice. Jurgen was standing there talking with a beautiful woman whom he addressed as Queen Helen. He was saying:

"'We fall insensibly to common-sense as to a drug; and it dulls and kills whatever in us is rebellious and fine and unreasonable. . . . For within this hour I have become again a creature of use and wont; I am the lackey of prudence and half-measures; and I have put my dreams upon an allowance. . . . I have failed my vision! . . . I have failed, and I know very well that every man must fail——' "

Tellectina stopped abruptly, protesting defiantly but silently: "No, no, surely he must be wrong! I shall not fail, I, who have plunged into every adventure with a whole heart, I, who have scorned half-measures and said they were for puny people!

No, no, it is unthinkable. Surely Tellectina will never become the lackey of prudence—oh, never! Ah, no, fine brave Jurgen, it is too terrible—you can't mean what you say!"

But his words were to haunt her uncomfortably like an evil prophecy. On glancing at her host's face the girl noticed there that same mocking yet strangely wistful smile which to her inexperienced eye concealed more than it revealed. With a shrug Tellectina hastily adjusted her armor and smiled too.

As she accompanied Cabell through the now familiar passages, Tellectina laughed as merrily as a girl of sixteen, albeit with a difference; for under her present gayety could be detected something of metallic hardness. She followed him down the grand staircase to the great hall below where she was to discover the nature of the fifth service to be rendered her by the Prince of Poictesme.

In accordance with a now well-established custom, plays were performed in the great hall in the evenings: primarily, as the Prince insisted, to divert himself rather than to entertain his guests. In contradistinction to the practice among princes, however, he himself wrote the plays, all of which were comedies, and the fame of which had not only spread over Nithking but even down into Err. As a consequence his audiences were as strange a mixture as ever assembled to hear a drama, and some who came to scoff remained to praise.

Tellectina settled herself comfortably into a seat just as the brown curtain—with the figure of "a stallion rampant in all his members" outlined in gold in the lower right-hand corner—was being raised. The play on this particular evening was called *A Comedy of Justice,* in which the leading rôle was taken by the notorious Jurgen who went swaggering drolly across the stage. It being in the nature of an allegory, he was supported by an equally famous cast including Satan and God and Koshchei, Helen and Guinevere, many Philistines—and a wife. Although Tellectina had met all these people in the home of Olev the Third, never had she seen them as actors in a comedy. In fact, she had met Cabell on several occasions previous to this

visit to his castle, but his failure to recognize her neither surprised nor offended the young explorer.

The dialogue was in that form of Reasonese peculiar to the
Principality of Poictesme, with which language Tellectina was
now sufficiently familiar to appreciate the beautiful native accent,
the ironic and erotic innuendoes, inferences, inflections, and
implications; even the Cabellian *double entendre* and word play;
to understand most of the delicate ambiguity, amphibology,
ambiloquy; his equally delightful Atticism, anagoges, allusions,
and even his apologues and adumbrations; but many of his
anagrams, as well as his allegorical and mythological references,
were beyond her.

Judging from the number of people asleep in the seats about
her, Tellectina concluded that the language of Poictesme was
unintelligible to most of the audience. The renewal of her own
health and vigor, however, had so enlivened the young woman's
mind that it was at this time in an exceptionally active state
and peculiarly receptive to this form of entertainment. She
abandoned herself wholeheartedly to enjoyment, delighting so
much in the audacious wit, the subtle wisdom, and the poetic
beauty of the lines of the comedy that she laughed uproariously,
struck the chair in front of her, slapped her thighs, cursed and
wept and gasped for breath. Oddly enough, and fortunately, no
one took the slightest notice of her extremely unladylike antics;
in fact, her misbehavior even went unobserved by her host—
as he invariably remained behind the scenes.

In the first play Tellectina saw that Jurgen sought for justice
but found it nowhere; that he derived "his real, his deepest, his
one unfailing pleasure from the exercise of his . . . intelligence";
and Tellectina saw, also, for the first time in her life, that sex
was a matter for humor not for morals; and saw too how
easily men won women and how quickly they tired of them—
and she made a note of it.

More to her irritation than surprise this audience, like all
others at all plays good or bad, could scarcely restrain themselves while the actors spoke their last lines. With one accord

the majority of them scrambled hastily from their seats and vied with each other in reaching the exit.

"They must be commuting back to Err," Tellectina muttered to herself, "and are terrified for fear they might have to endure Nithking for a whole night!"

After their departure, a group of critics could be overheard discussing both the author and his comedies. The first one was saying, "*Jurgen* is unique in the world's literature. It has taken its place, I think, among the singular and great masterpieces which have been spun out of a richly endowed, wise, critical, and humorous subconscious. Analytically and philosophically it is, I think, the deepest, most prophetic, and most beautiful work of the creative imagination of our period." Tellectina recognized him as Burton Rascoe and his companion as Carl Van Doren. The latter said, "Always Poictesme hangs above the mortal clouds, suspended from the eternal sky, in the region where wit and beauty are joined in an everlasting kiss."

Slowly the excited girl rose and passed from the room, smiling at the tardiness of her realization that the bestowal of a unique and unprecedented pleasure was the fifth gift for which she was to become indebted to the Prince of Poictesme. But she did not for a moment suspect that there might be a sixth.

Every evening she witnessed another play, sitting down to each of the other eleven comedies in shy and fearful eagerness, apprehensive lest the author be unable repeatedly to afford such intense delight. While under their spell, she was torn each night between greediness to get to the end as quickly as possible and the abstemious desire to protract her pleasure as long as possible.

After the *Comedy of Justice,* popularly known as *Jurgen,* came the *Comedy of Appearances,* better known as *Figures of Earth,* in which Tellectina saw the wisdom and the folly of doing the expected thing in the world; and in which she saw, also, how stupid a wife like beautiful Niafer could be, and how far short of man's dream of her woman could fall—and she made a note of it. And there was the *Comedy of Shirking,* called also, *The Cords of Vanity*, in which Tellectina saw how cruelly a man might play at love; and also how easily women were deceived by male flattery—and she made a note of it.

This was followed by *The Rivet in Grandfather's Neck*, a *Comedy of Limitations*, which proved how people's lives were conditioned by their own limitations, whether for good or ill; and which also showed Tellectina how time and intimacy deprive woman of all charm for man—and she made a note of it. And this was succeeded by a *Comedy of Purse-Strings*, better known as *The Eagle's Shadow*, during the performance of which Tellectina observed how money could be a curse; and observed, also, how fine women often love worthless men, and how women's pretty shallowness is to some men transparent—and she made a note of it. Then there came *Domnei, A Comedy of Woman Worship*, in which Tellectina saw woman worshiped by man, who beheld "in womankind High God made manifest in the loveliest and most perfect of His creations," and she saw also the beauty and the bane of the chivalric attitude—and she made a note of it.

The brown curtain was now lifted, and Tellectina witnessed *A Comedy of Evasions*, also entitled *The Cream of the Jest*, which divulged the secret that no man can ever be either permanently or wholly happy with any woman, for all mortal women must inevitably fall short of that dream woman with whom man constantly contrasts her. Tellectina also saw marriage from the man's point of view—and she made a note of it.

A few evenings later Tellectina witnessed the eleventh of the twelve comedies: *A Comedy of Disenchantment*, usually called *The High Place*, in which she saw how man goes forth in search of holiness and beauty and finds them nowhere; and she again saw wherein sex was a matter for humor not for morals, and she saw, too, how quickly after marriage a man becomes disenchanted—and she made an especial note of it.

This was followed in due course by *A Comedy of Fig Leaves*, which most people know as *Something About Eve*, in which Tellectina saw how domesticity and bodily comforts keep men from their high dreams; and she saw also how women lend a hand in both—and she made an especial note of it.

And all the while that the players played and Tellectina laughed (for she knew that even the worst satire on women was true) there lurked under her laughter a poignant note of sadness. And oddly enough she saw at the same time another stage—not visible to those about her—on which other comedies, complementary to those before her eyes, were being enacted simultaneously. And after retiring for the night she lay awake for hours because these companion pieces continued to play themselves out across the stage of her mind—more comedies wherein woman is triumphant; and she laughed in the darkness, and there lurked under her laughter a poignant note of sadness. . . .

Toward dawn Tellectina suddenly sat erect in bed, talking excitedly to herself, "But who on earth is capable of doing it? What woman do I know who could do it wisely and wittily? Not I, surely—nor any woman named Tellectina. To find someone is imperative, for that it must be done 'there is no manner of doubt, no probable, possible shadow of doubt—no possible doubt whatever.' "

Laughing with secret pleasure she rose, and this was a matter which was still affording her delight when she arrived in the great hall that evening hoping a new comedy was to be enjoyed. The producer, a Mr. McBride, soon informed the audience, however, that they had seen all the twelve comedies which Cabell had written; consequently this evening the playwright would come out from behind the scenes and speak to them in person.

After his long seclusion, Tellectina deemed it exceedingly pleasant to see him again. The author said concerning his comedies, that:

" 'The first act is the imagining of the place where contentment exists and may be come to; and the second act reveals the striving toward, and the third act the falling short of, that shining goal, or else (the difference here being negligible) the attaining of it to discover that happiness, after all, abides a thought farther down the bogged, rocky, clogged, befogged heartbreaking road, if anywhere. That is the comedy which, to my finding, the life I write about has enacted over and over again on every stage between Poictesme and Lichfield.' "

He then spoke of the past and future of comedy, saying that at one time " 'the scenery was arboreal, and our comedian wore fur and tail; as before that his costume was reptilian, and yet earlier was piscine. So do the scientists trace backward his career to life's first appearance upon the stage.' "

There followed an elaborately worked out lineage, but Tellectina was scarcely aware of what Cabell was saying now, having been so deeply moved by his previous words. She sat motionless, thinking intently, "Yes, that is true. The first act was set when I was a very young girl in Err 'imagining where contentment exists and may be come to.' I was certain it existed in finding Certitude in Nithking; and so 'the second act reveals the striving toward that shining goal'; and the third act——?"

Turning, she watched the speaker, who had stepped down from the stage and was ascending the great marble stairs of the castle. Almost unconsciously the entranced girl arose and followed him, assuring herself defiantly, however, that the third act of her life would not be "the falling short of that shining goal."

"I'm convinced that happiness exists somewhere. At least, I shall attain a certain quiet kind of happiness when I reach Certitude. Even Ghaulot furnished a form of happiness but are Ghaulot and Certitude the same?"

So concentrated was Tellectina on the thoughts aroused by Cabell that the many hundreds of steps they climbed failed to impress themselves on her consciousness. Her breath, however, came in short little gasps as they ascended the last narrow spiral in the tower. The girl evinced no surprise on discovering that the magician had conducted her to the central tower of his great castle.

Motioning toward a certain opening, he bade her look at

his view. It was, however, not only a very small and very narrow window, but somewhat above her head—a fact of which her host seemed unaware as he proceeded to gaze serenely out another window. Perceiving nothing save a pile of some thirty books in this bare tower room, Tellectina quickly chose the eight strongest volumes and found that with their aid she was able to see Cabell's view with comparative ease. The sight she beheld rendered her breathless. And a very different form of vertigo than that with which high altitudes usually affected her now seized upon the young woman, for this was without doubt the greatest height to which she had ever ascended. The atmosphere was so clear she could see to the very ends of the earth. To the east lay the Forbidden Country of Nithking; to the west, the Land of Err; so that from this vantage point the young explorer was able to review her entire journey through both countries. Ghaulot, however, imparted a new perspective, which radically altered the proportions of many things in both worlds.

The Land of Err, which formerly had seemed to her so large and formidable, appeared now as a small blot on the earth's vast surface; while Smug Harbor gave the impression of a minute flyspeck on the broad green map of the world. The fogs which had once obscured everything in Err were now thin wisps of transparent vapor; and the once illimitable Dead Sea was but a diminutive and stagnant pond. But it was Romanz Isle which afforded her the greatest surprise. That which her childish mind had believed to be a small island was not an island at all: Andersen and Grimm had but conducted her along the coast country. It was in truth an enormous peninsula projecting out from Nithking and extending over the very rim of the earth. There were strange things happening there, too; but Tellectina, making a mental note to inspect it more closely later, turned her eyes eagerly to those areas which she had but recently traversed in person.

On beholding the redoubtable Rocky Mountain of Casuistry miscalled Christianity by some people, she perceived with small surprise that they constituted merely the most recent upheaval in the Great Range of Casuistry which walled in nearly the whole of Err; that these hated mountains actually possessed a kind of beauty when seen from this distance, however, was a fact puzzling in the extreme.

For counter evidence she quickly glanced over to that region of Nithking through which the three white hounds of heaven had given her chase. This entire realm was likewise enhanced by a softening blue haze. Her perplexity increased, but her inquiry as to the meaning of this phenomenon was postponed for the time being.

On distinguishing a small strip of yellow sand dotted with patches of green as the Dotbu Desert, Tellectina laughed outright. How was it possible ever to have become lost in anything so small—or been frightened by it? She smiled ruefully as she descried New Chimera buried in the great jungle, occupying far more ground than she had realized at the time, and exhibiting a certain beauty even in its ruined state. But the formerly turbulent river, Publi Copinion, appeared from this vantage point in Poictesme to be such a small muddy stream that the explorer laughed at herself and the memory of her struggle with it. The tangled net of trails in the Jungle of Otherpeoples-ideas she perceived to be no more formidable than a woman's small hairnet. Although the white light shining about the peak of Manu Mission was discernible even from this distance, its glow was somewhat diminished.

Everywhere in Nithking the verdant and ever green Sillidinous vines could be discerned. No matter what direction an explorer took, it was impossible to escape them: but the view from a great height transformed them into a green carpet on which she saw that one should learn to walk without tripping. Tellectina was amused at the memory of her constant entanglement in them and consequent poisoning. As she shrugged her shoulders to readjust her armor of gatherulic iron, she regretted that the acquisition of such protection had not been made earlier in her expedition.

The house of Olev the Third had fallen into picturesque ruins. The young woman smiled ruefully, but her eyes were moist as she turned them away toward the Seven Siren Islands, which to her amazement proved to be vast continents rather than minute islands. Little had the young explorer realized at the time of her discovery of them how their luscious beauty rendered all the rest of the earth gray and arid by contrast. From this particular angle the Isle of O We Tri was the most alluring of all. But when delectable memories drew her to the Isle of Forta Velo, delight was soon mingled with other emotions. True enough, on the far side of the island men could be seen kneeling in adoration of women in the most chivalric of attitudes. In fact, a curious white light, a sort of mystical radiance, shone about them. The great beauty of chivalry was indeed apparent to Tellectina, who, while admitting that women like Femina enjoyed being worshiped blindly, had reason to believe that the Tellectinas of the world thought differently about it. And she wondered, for the thousandth time since her marriage, if the possession of undue apperception by the feminine sex were not one of nature's great mistakes.

On the near side of Forta Velo, however, in the temple of Ecstaci where she had seen Femina prostrate herself, the light was so harshly bright that it mercilessly exposed all the sordid details of the perspiring devotees in their ecstatic frenzies—especially the females. It was amusing, even ludicrous, and Tellectina laughed—and made an especial note of it.

Even while participating in the Forbidden Mystery, Tellectina had been incapable of ignoring completely its absurd and unesthetic elements; but when so close to Ecstaci and Passino it was difficult to perceive the humor of such proceedings. From Cabell's windows, however, she saw that the Forbidden Ceremony viewed from a detached point of view was neither a subject for religion nor morals but for amusement. But what about the poetry of it? she wondered. Although exceedingly grateful to the Prince of Poictesme for showing her his view, Tellectina, being a woman, observed that from this particular angle the women appeared infinitely more ludicrous than the men—and she made a note of it. With the sudden recollection of her debonair aunt Sophistica's amusing discussion about Entries, there dawned at last both comprehension of that remarkable woman and her delightful point of view.

The next thing which entered Tellectina's field of vision was *The World's World,* which now appeared as a small burlesque show at which the judicious laughed. And she laughed. But on remembering the pain it had inflicted on her, the explorer shook her head dubiously. Perhaps this was merely an intellectual's view and something was wrong with it. In response to her troubled and inquiring expression, the magician bade her look out another window which was both wide and low.

After complying with his suggestion, however, the young woman recoiled instantly. When surveyed from this new angle *The World's World* became an enormous theater which was duplicated innumerable times all over the earth's surface. And the Siren Islands were merely minute green dots in a bleak landscape; the Rocky Mountains of Casuistry appeared almost impassable, Smug Harbor vast and impregnable, and Err one hundred times the size of Nithking. The great sacred river of Publi Copinion was at the flood, inundating miles of territory, obliterating many landmarks of Nithking, sweeping along everything that it touched in its great and merciless stream. And everywhere human beings could be seen toiling and moiling, struggling, suffering—and dying.

The hideousness of this second view sickened the young woman to such an extent that she covered her eyes involuntarily with her hands, protesting, "No, no, it is too frightful! The whole world is gray and forbidding, and life in such a place can be nothing but painful. How has any human being the courage to face reality thus exposed! And yet so it must always look to most of the poor animals cursed with humanness! Very few people ever see the world as it appears through the small high window. How can life be supported by those who are able only to view it realistically? For all of us long instinctively for beauty in some form in our lives!"

The magician assured her that all other human beings found this outlook equally unbearable. "'Living is a drab transaction,'" he said, "'a concatenation of unimportant events: man is impotent and aimless: beauty, and indeed all the fine things which you desiderate . . . in your personal existence . . . are nowhere attainable save in imagination. To the problem of living, romance propounds the only possible answer, which is not understanding, but escape.'"

"And when I heard these words on a previous occasion," the girl said, "escape seemed a very simple matter: indeed, some people are able to escape fairly easily into their own thoughts, or creative work, or the enjoyment of beauty; but the masses of mankind—how can they escape from reality?"

With that habitual gesture of his, the magician made some passes from left to right with his right hand. And so powerful was his necromancy that it altered the view entirely, enlarging Romanz Isle until nothing else was visible. From this vast stretch of land which Tellectina as a child had mistaken for a small island, there now arose a great mountain. It was so high that its peak was lost in the clouds—clouds through which, however, there shone a strange unnatural brilliance. Up the sides of this steep mountain wound many roads on which thousands of people could be seen toiling. Tellectina observed them intently for a long time. Frequently they slipped back, fell by the wayside, were hurt, maimed, weary, ill—and yet they persisted in climbing, lifting their eyes periodically toward the strange light which was evidently their half-seen goal.

And the magician pointed out to her the names of each highway: one bore the word "chivalry," another, "religion," while on still others were the names, "sainthood," "asceticism," "patriotism," "love," or "art." There were numerous roads, but seen from above it was obvious that they all led to the same goal.

"'Indeed,'" Cabell said, "'the most prosaic of materialists

proclaim that we are all descended from an insane fish, who somehow evolved the idea that it was his duty to live on land, and eventually succeeded in doing it. So, now that his earth-treading progeny manifest the same illogical aspiration toward heaven, their bankruptcy in common-sense may, even by material standards, have much the same incredible result.' "

On seeing this third view of the world, Tellectina said nothing but stood very still and tense.

" 'To the problem of living,' " her host repeated, " 'romance propounds the only possible answer, which is, not understanding, but escape. And the method of that escape is the creation of a pleasing dream, which will somehow engender a reality as lovely.' "

At a slight gesture of the magician's right hand, the luminous mountain vanished, leaving only the realistic view of the world. And he said, " 'For it is in this inadequate flesh that each of us must serve his dream; and so, must fail the dream's service, and must parody that which he holds dearest. . . . Thus, one and all, we play false to the dream, and it evades us, and we dwindle into responsible citizens.' "

Tellectina drew back. "No, no, others may play false to their dream, but I—I am not defeated yet! I am aware that our grandest dreams can never be realized, but surely all of them are not beyond our reach. With all my respect for and faith in your words, I must nevertheless endeavor to execute some of my plans."

Almost imperceptibly the magician had once more guided her toward the high small window while he was speaking.

" 'Everywhere, as romance evolved the colorful myths of religion, the main concern of the gods was . . . with the doings of men. . . . Then the demiurge set about a masterpiece, and Christianity was revealed to men. . . . There is really no product of romance more delightful than is the Bible. . . . In this great love-story there are only the two characters of God and Humanity. . . . Can you not see that the story of Christ, the climax toward which the whole Bible-romance moves as its dénouement, is but the story of Cinderella set forth in more impressive terms?—for therein the most neglected and down-trodden of humanity is revealed, not as a tinseled princess, but as the Creator and Master of all things. . . . The story is . . . a triumph of romantic art, in its apotheosis of the Cinderella legend.' "

But the young woman had ceased to listen, not out of im-politeness, but out of overwhelming admiration of the Cabellian views of the two worlds. To herself she began to murmur, "So at long last I see religion as it really is. And even God should be given his due. And now all the scorn and rancor I have nourished for thirty years is dissolved in pity and admiration—principally pity. I was certainly young and intolerant, but Cabell has shown me humanity in a more compassionate light—which brings to view all the beautiful side of all life's worst stupidities, like religion and patriotism and asceticism. From here one can indeed see life whole. What a brave and pathetic and ludicrous spectacle the human race presents when viewed from so great a height! They are like children engaged in a struggle for which they are ill equipped, battling constantly and bravely against terrific odds with every sort of handicap: poverty and illness, earthquakes and floods and fires; injustices from their fellow man, fate, and nature. They play always a losing game, yet they valiantly strive to win."

The woman smiled and shook her head. "Is it any wonder that like frightened children they concoct fairy stories about kind gods and beautiful heavens to keep up their courage? And we might laugh more derisively at the very patent absurdity of mankind if it were not that to understand the human race is to pity it."

Once more Tellectina gazed out each window in turn, and for a long moment incredulity made her speechless. Then, in a voice vibrant with a deep-seated excitement, she said, "Is this not the best, the loftiest view of the world? to see the whole world clearly but with compassion for its strivings and humor for its ridiculousness? From these windows no ugliness is concealed nor any beauty left unseen and unenjoyed. Some people have a detached intellectual view of the world, some a realistic one, while some can boast a compassionate outlook—but who else combines all three by the art of magic? Although each of the three has merit, none of them is sufficiently comprehensive. The extreme complication of human living necessitates its being viewed from more angles than one—if it is to be seen as it really is."

The young woman's face was suffused with admiration as she looked at the man beside her. "Where else does one hear such gallant, such genial and urbane laughter? And where else does one hear man reply to the cosmic comedy with a classic jest? Nowhere—except here! So this is the highest altitude habitable by human beings. It is Ghaulot and Ghaulot is the greatest height attainable by man!"

Passing her hand over her brow in a bewildered gesture, Tellectina gazed steadily at the man beside her with unutterable things in her intent and narrowed eyes. Then suddenly all the strength went out of her. Sighing profoundly, she sank to the floor, murmuring incredulously, "So it's really true! So it's really true! But I'm so tired—oh, so unutterably weary—I'm tired to the very marrow of my bones!"

So acutely conscious was she of the extraordinary views he had shown her that the young explorer actually forgot the presence of the magician himself. Supporting her burning forehead on the cool stone of the window sill, she stared with unseeing eyes at the floor, murmuring to herself:

"So—at long last—I have arrived at my goal, the goal of a lifetime. My protracted journey is now at an end. This is the highest mountain in the world: this is Mt. Certitude, and yet, when one attains Certitude, one discovers that it is Ghaulot. This is the same mountain whose praises Sophistica sang so rapturously some twenty years ago, when she predicted that I might reach it, the same mountain on which most of the people whose views I admire, also, reside at varying levels.

"And at this moment, which I thought would be the supreme

moment of my life, I do not feel ecstasy as I had secretly hoped I might—but only a tremendous relief and an appalling fatigue. Today I am come of age—on this my thirtieth birthday. What a fitting end to one's youth and propitious beginning for one's maturity! And subconsciously I have been seeking Certitude for twenty years—from the time I began to think for myself at the age of ten.

"Yes, a full score of years it required for me to make this journey from Casuistry to Certitude—from Smug Harbor to Mt. Ghaulot. At Manu Mission it was suddenly revealed to me that I was forever freed from the compulsion to believe as other men believed (it was indeed 'the formal liberation of a slave'); I had, however, no slightest conception of what I myself did believe. But now I have attained a positive philosophy: my ideas on all important subjects are clearly defined—surely there are no more problems for me to settle. I know that I know and nothing under heaven can change my convictions on certain subjects, at least. What a deep, thorough satisfaction Certitude gives one!

"It was Mencken who taught me to laugh at the Errorians, at all Puritans; then, while touring Ghaulot, I heard other people laughing at many things—and I smiled, but I could not laugh. I had not suffered enough, for indeed the secret source of humor is not joy but sorrow. It remained for Cabell to teach me to laugh at myself, at all life, even at the laughter of the gods at men. Ah, wonderful Ghaulot! It is to laugh, indeed.

"This mountain and this view I might have attained alone eventually, for it is undeniable that I would have made the same journey through Nithking had I met there no living soul to guide or aid me. And Ghaulot might have been my goal had no James Branch Cabell been born into the world. All the great thinkers I met along the way merely roused into action that which was lying dormant. But for that inestimable service I love them and am forever their debtor. For, paradoxically enough, no great man can give you anything save that which you already possess. Otherwise their words of wisdom pass over your ears like the wind.

"Consciously I sought Certitude, but all the while I was unconsciously seeking another thing as well—perfection, perfection in all things. And nowhere have I found that, and now I know that no human being ever finds it. Yet all my life I have felt that somewhere on this earth there must exist some human beings or at least one who was a beautifully balanced and integrated person; one whose mind and character were equally admirable; a person the every side of whose nature was fully developed in proper proportion: the social and sexual no less than the intellectual and esthetic; and one who possessed a comprehensive and lofty view of the world. Most of the great men of earth have been incredibly deficient in some essential human quality. So many of the great painters, sculptors, and musicians were admirable in nothing except their own art and failed to display keen intellects; the great writers were often socially, or sexually and physically, incompetent, or both; famous scientists are frequently blind esthetically; and greatness of mind and talent has never insured beauty of character. And surely a sense of humor is the mark of a civilized man. And those few human beings who might possess the seven characteristics essential to the perfect man were generally devoid of the eighth quality which made for greatness—talent.

"Emerson chose as representative men: Plato, Shakespeare, Swedenborg, Montaigne, Napoleon, and Goethe—'men who represented the utmost virtues which the human race had so far been given the power to achieve.' Shakespeare and Goethe fulfill all seven—even eight—requirements of the Larice standard, but none of the others do so."

She paused and remained silent for a long time, then suddenly laughed. "And of course, Tellectina Femina Christian, I suppose you were also searching for someone with whose philosophy you could agree! Or rather someone whose philosophy you could swallow whole! Don't console yourself with rationalization. It is a marvelous jest! For I, Tellectina, am not even able to be intellectually independent! I am, after all, a mere woman, and must model my philosophy on that of some man! I say that I might have attained Certitude or Ghaulot alone—then, if I might have, why the hell didn't I? Woman's independence—what a comedy!" She laughed at herself long and heartily, adding, "So furnishing me with a philosophy of life is Cabell's sixth service!" But it would have seemed incredible that he was to render her yet a seventh—and last—service.

Suddenly fatigue overcame her completely, her eyes closed involuntarily as she murmured, "Oh, God, I'm so weary! My spirit seems ten thousand years old, and my very bones ache with fatigue. I shall never be able to rise from here again."

All that day and night the young explorer sat motionless by the window, submerged in a deep coma of fatigue. How much longer she remained thus, she never knew but the sun awakened her by shining directly into her eyes.

She arose to find herself magically refreshed, her strength and courage and confidence reborn. A pleasant sense of elation caused her to laugh happily. "Ah, I feel so well, so strong— the air on this mountain is so stimulating—I feel this morning as if nothing on earth is impossible!"

Rising quickly, she again approached the small high window and stood contemplating the view which had so recently enchanted her. Although she reviewed the remarkable panorama with delight, a thoughtful expression came into her face as her eyes reverted to the Isle of Forta Velo and the house of Olev the Third.

"Yes, I still maintain that this is the finest view I have ever beheld in my life, yet it is a man's view, naturally. And I am, after all, a woman. And I am sure there is a slightly different angle from which it is possible to observe the same scene—and it is there that I shall build my house.

"Although others may seek Ghaulot only when the fogs of Err become too suffocating, I shall endeavor to live at this height always. And others may return to Err to earn their livelihoods and to be with their families (most of whom find this altitude trying, I understand); but I shall construct my house to withstand all weathers; nor do I need companionship nor any more money than I saved while in *The World's World*. I am Tellectina and I shall live alone—sufficient unto myself. All that is necessary is for me to send off for certain books which will serve as companions. Soon there will be erected the most remarkable house ever constructed by a woman—a woman who is free of all things and all people, free to live a life of study and thought and writing. Books and myself—it is enough!"

The young woman raised her arms exultantly then dropped them suddenly. "Oh, damn, I'd forgotten Femina! I presume she must live with me—there is no escaping that curse. But even at her and her need of men I shall now be able to laugh, for this year in Cabell's house has stimulated me so much intellectually that all feminine matters appear inconsequential. I even wish I could reduce my physical life to its simplest possible terms: perhaps live in a cave like a hermit on berries and roots. Before I take my departure from Cabell's house, however, I must attempt to accomplish the impossible and express some fraction of my gratitude to this magician, my most generous host and benefactor for the last year."

She looked about her, but he had disappeared. Someone, however, had deposited beside her an overflowing knapsack supplied with enough concentrated froth-hugot food for a very long journey. "He's quite right. He understands and foresees everything. Cabell realizes that I must continue my journey and that to thank him for the six inestimable services or even to bid him good-bye would be painfully impossible. He has been kind enough to spare me those ordeals."

Tellectina took one long last look at the view from the two windows, gazed fondly about the tower room of Cabell's castle; and, catching up the kit of supplies, rushed eagerly out of the door, down the long winding stairs, out of the brownstone castle, and through the postern gate. . . .

It was not long before she found a satisfactory site near by on free soil and thereon built herself a small temporary shelter. Then she sat down and, extracting paper and pencil from her kit, commenced a very urgent letter.

Mt. Ghaulot

DEAR FEMINA,

At long last I have arrived at my goal, with the glories of which I shall not bore your feminine mind, so-called, but hasten at once to explain wherein you are concerned.

The only solution to what I heretofore considered our accursed dual personality is for you to come and live with me here on Ghaulot. I shall allow you to design and occupy the boudoir of the house I intend to build.

Since Ghaulot proves very trying for most women, you may bring along a man to assist you in forgetting the altitude. It is essential that he possess both intellect and humor, however.

Now as to that ancient matter of our enmity. We have squandered youth and energy by our lifelong feud, so let us arrange a truce and become friendly enemies, at least.

The truth is, something has occurred which has awakened in me an appreciation of your feminine qualities and which, I trust, will likewise open your eyes to my virtues. For the past year I have been visiting in the house of a famous magician and writer of comedies, the Prince of Poictesme. It is a challenge, I should say, which I realize with some consternation you are better qualified to meet than I!

It is not Cabell's personal challenge only, it is rather that he has given concrete and unforgettable form to man's eternal challenge to woman.

I have observed your handling of men for some years and, except in those rare instances where you yourself cared, your success has compelled my reluctant admiration. The rules by which you work should not succeed—but they do. Apparently between the sexes the reverse of all rules holds true. Consequently, I at last concede that there may be instinctive wisdom as well as inherent talents granted to the personification of femininity denied to the intellectual type of woman like my-self. But more of that when we meet.

In all his comedies Cabell has issued a challenge to woman more or less, but unmistakably in *The Comedy of Disenchant-ment* which he calls *The High Place*—a challenge too provoca-tive, too full of delicious potentialities not to be met by some woman at once. I am amazed that no one has attempted to settle this affair of honor before.

Yes, your inference is correct: I have chosen you—you, my dear Femina, the once scorned, to defend the feminine sex—with me as your second, of course.

By the weekly post which leaves here tomorrow I am sending you five of the comedies in book form. I've instructed my mes-senger not to rest until he locates you. I forward only five, as I know you probably wouldn't read more. They are: *The High Place, Jurgen, Something About Eve, Cords of Vanity,* and *Domnei, A Comedy of Woman Worship.*

I repeat that I, Tellectina, find them superb and true; you, however, will be struck by the fact that for all their beautiful woman-worship, the men of Poictesme never regard the actual women they know as anything but toys to be played with and discarded when tired of or domestic drudges to wait on them. But is it not proverbial that every story has two sides?

And are men the only members of the human race who seek for beauty and holiness and fail to find them? and are all wives Meliors and Niafers and Dame Lizas? What of Danaë and Creusa and "all those other minxes who find no husband worthy of them until a god has come down out of heaven, no less"? Ah, yes, thereby hangs many a tale as yet untold!

I presume it unnecessary to call your attention to the ever recurring fact of the mocking ease with which the Cabellian men make their conquests of women and the rapidity with which they tire of them? And that's where *I* come in! You need me as a complement henceforth. For what is the cause of the disenchantment in Cabell's *Comedy of Disenchantment* if not that Florian loved a Femina called Melior and ceased

to love her because she was not also a Tellectina? So there—
you see! And I need you as a lure—no man likes brains in a
woman unless they are concealed by a pretty face! That is
what I mean by our becoming invaluable allies to each other
henceforth.

And in passing, permit me to call your attention to one sad
truth, my dear sister. As long as you are young and pretty you
may never require my assistance to hold any man—you know
your erotica. But now that you are leaving the toothsome
twenties forever, has it occurred to you that old age may not
be, as you have always regarded it, merely a calamity that be-
falls *others?* So don't be so damnably vain and overconfident.
Your coquettish ways of nineteen which men find so charming
even at twenty-nine will at thirty-nine be ridiculous, and at
forty-nine—God spare us! Remember Melior and beware! And
don't be offering me any such specious arguments as "to the
eyes of the lover the beloved is always nineteen." Marriage is
renowned as an eye opener! And you said when I last saw you
that your intentions were strictly dishonorable.

(The letter went on with a lengthy discussion of very private
and very amusing but unmentionable matters, then concluded
with a short paragraph.)

Therefore it may be that what seems to me to be a challenge
to women is not a challenge at all, but merely another proof
that "never while life lasts can the two sexes ever quite understand each other," as Cabell, who is famous for both his
chivalry and his gallantry, assured Ellen Glasgow, whose delightful and deft destruction of the same chivalry on which he
had heaped praise upset him and moved him to make that
sententious remark. Be that as it may, however, just as a simple
little matter of justice, both sides of any story should be told.
But I am already so deeply indebted to him for the seven
services he has rendered me (bringing about my reconciliation
with Femina is the seventh service) that I shall never be able

to repay him if I live to be a thousand. Therefore keep it a secret that I played Judas to so generous a man as J. C. My conscience hurts me.

Always your sister and henceforth your

Faithful ally,

TELLECTINA.

The autumn leaves had fluttered down onto Tellectina's temporary shelter and into the excavations which she was digging for a permanent home when one day a bulky envelope was brought her by the same messenger whom she had dispatched over into Err weeks ago. For the first time in her life Tellectina listened to Femina respectfully.

TELLECTINA—AND MY DEAR SISTER, ALSO:

I find it vastly entertaining that you who have repeatedly assured me that I was too utterly feminine for any use now seek my assistance. I accept your choice, however, and Cabell's challenge. But in strictest secrecy and in advance let me warn you that I shall not win—for a reason I prefer not to divulge.

As to "justice"—there is no such thing between the sexes, and on that score I personally have no complaint to make. If you had appealed to me in the name of "vanity," I would have understood you better.

As to the means by which I shall give the other side of the story, I shall inform you presently. But I should just like to remark in passing that I assure you that I could assure the gay Duc de Puysange that there is magic in the curiously clothed man who is master of himself, the hour, and you: but the prostrate, sweating, and snoring meat in a tangle of bedclothing——! To see a member of the lordly sex who once stood so manfully erect as to arouse any woman's admiration fall so low before her very eyes that he has not the ability to raise his head again—is that not a sight disappointing enough to cause any woman to turn her back on him in disgust?

Ah, that, my dear Tellectina, is the source of one of the

world's greatest comedies—and tragedies. It is seldom that the very men who have themselves aroused a woman's greatest expectations can satisfy her. Yet they strut before you, they boast of their strength and size, they want you to feel their muscle, they look a very pillar of strength, they seem so full-blooded that you think surely their strength is inexhaustible. The instant the occasion arises, they plunge into action so promptly and discharge their duty with such vigor that you congratulate yourself that at last you've come into contact with a man whose strength and endurance are worthy of your most ardent admiration.

But you soon see that sustained effort is impossible—for almost at the first touch of a mere woman their strength ebbs out of them leaving them as helpless as an infant—but certainly not as lovable. And those men whose vitality renews itself with sufficient rapidity to gratify a woman's natural ambitions prove on more intimate acquaintance to be men whose strength is solely of the body rather than the intellect (and every woman admires intellect in a man even if not in a woman). Seldom do two such manly virtues come in one man.

This I consider a subject which never in this man's world has been properly handled by any woman. However deficient they may be in other respects, the comedy with which men furnish women is inexhaustible. The details, though, are suited only to the privacy of our own boudoir—so more anon. But do not reveal to any living male what I really think about the masculine sex—I never do.

But I thoroughly agree with your host when he contends that "there is in every human being that which demands communion with something more fine and potent than itself." And as you sought it in the realm of the intellect, so I have sought it in the realm of love, and have not found—and now know that I shall never find—any man as fine and as potent as I have demanded.

But why, pray, are you so perturbed because the women of Poictesme whom H.R.G. has gathered about him are so beautiful and so brainless? Did he not have the whole world to choose from when he formed his court? He is rumored to have visited every land in every age (that being possible to magicians) and did he see no such persons as Aspasia, or Sappho (I understand she was ambidexterous, so to speak), or Ninon de Lenclos, or Eleonora Duse, or Ellen Glasgow, Edna Millay, Elinor Wylie, or some of the loveliest of the queens, duchesses, and ladies of the salons—mortal women all—who combining brains with beauty and feminine charm were capable of bearing their lovers some issue other than dissatisfaction?

Perhaps you can also elucidate this point: by what rules of what logic do men expect brilliance of the intellect to be concealed in brilliance of the body? Ah, well, maybe by the same logic that leads women to expect strength of mind to be concealed in strength of body in the case of a man! and good breeding to invariably accompany good brains.

I take it, that for all their exceeding great beauty and charm and cunning, in the whole Principality of Poictesme you have yet to find a really intellectual woman. That, however, is a matter in which I am neither interested nor sympathetic; that is a challenge which the Tellectinas of the world will have to answer. But what sort of game is it when the woman plays the winning hand often without trumps? You'll say she cheats. I say that she uses the wits with which nature endowed her; in any case—she wins! And the game of love, the playing of which has no equal for amusement, excitement, and subtlety—until one grows too skillful about the age of thirty—then it becomes a bore. It is a game I know, however, from every possible angle.

And not till now, strange as it may seem, has there been time to stop and discover if my record was in any way remarkable these last ten years. But recently many women have assured me that for any woman of thirty to have enjoyed literally scores of beaus and fifteen authentic proposals of marriage was more than any one woman's share. And having retained the devotion of many of them for ten years, I have at last and reluctantly awakened to the fact that Tellectina—or at least her influence on me —may have played a larger part in my success than I cared to admit. But when you usurped my place I always stood immediately behind you to stop your tongue when necessary! You must admit in turn that it was my "smiles and smirks" as you call them, that captured them in the first place.

As I review my gloriously happy and exciting life from the age of sixteen to thirty I am forced to acknowledge that although brains in a woman are anathema to the majority of men, the only kind of males worth keeping are those who want a dual personality in a woman, a combination of the sexual and the intellectual (named in the order of their importance—to them) a combination of the feminine and the cerebral—in other words, they want a Femina and a Tellectina.

Forgive my modesty if I say I have excellent reason to believe Femina capable of capturing all the men she wants. But it has dawned on me that she may require your assistance in holding them—if they're worth holding, which most of them are not. Most men are so disappointing after a woman has known them a week. It's the sport of the conquest that thrills me.

Thus, you see, you are right, and your blessed Cabell has indeed effected a reconciliation between the feminine and the intellectual, so that henceforth I accept you as my friendly enemy.

Ah, but I wonder if you with your masculine mind, or the mighty males themselves, ever guess how even the woman with laughing lips and eyes is forever seeking the magic circle of a strong man's arms whence no harm can reach her? or that woman is always the mother earth, glad to nourish man, the flourishing tree? And last of all do they know that there has never been in the world and can never be a really happy woman? that no woman can be happy—with one man?—because no man born of woman's dreaming could ever exist. He would have to be—but that is another story.

Genealogy has it that every woman who has ever borne the name of "Femina" has had countless suitors. So I suppose there is something in a name after all. A certain kind of charm goes with it, apparently. And already my mouth waters at the savory bits I shall serve up from my answer to the challenge.

I shall merely toss this comedy of male superiority into the calm pool of masculine complacency and watch for the ripples! If the Prince of Poictesme and his court possess the remarkable sense of humor and fairness with which you so generously credit them, there will be ripples—of some sort!

Henceforth your friendly enemy,

FEMINA.

P.S. But I refuse to live on any cold mountain top the remainder of my life! You come to me! I have several victims for you to examine. I'll sign the treaty of peace, but I won't allow you to dominate me, so you can just save yourself the effort. It is reconciliation without unification.

Tellectina laid the letter on her knee in great annoyance. "I refuse to return to Err! If Femina declines to live up here, I shall live alone. I need neither her nor her everlasting men!" Arising defiantly she continued with the excavations for the foundations of her permanent residence.

Soon all the summer colonists had departed to Err. The days grew colder and colder, until the explorer found it a painful struggle even to keep alive. Suddenly one morning, however, Tellectina discovered means which enabled her to become oblivious of the cold. By combining certain things which had been sent to her in her box of books, she compounded a drug—a hard gray powder applied to the proper medium had the power to drug her for hours on end. And for three months she fell a helpless victim to this stimulant narcotic, Cianite Vitrgrew, which she had taken in mild doses since she was sixteen years of age.

For days she sat in her temporary shelter, scarcely moving: it produced such ecstatic visions that she remained only vaguely conscious of her desire for food and sleep and other periodic requirements of her body—all of which she performed as briefly as possible and always grudgingly. The intensity of her experience during her year in Poictesme had left her nerves in such an agitated state that she was more susceptible to Cianite Vitrgrew than she had ever been before in her whole life. She used up the small yellow cylinders of gray powder one after the other. In fact, this narcotic stimulant so completely swept Tellectina out of herself that months passed before she had any clear idea of what had actually happened to her while under its influence.

Later she pronounced it the most glorious experience of her life, but the days following it were altogether terrible. Her nerves were badly shattered, and without the numbing effects of the drug she lacked the courage to endure her privations. Each day grew more trying, till one morning she lost her footing and descended the precipitous mountain side in an avalanche of snow, broken shrubs, and torn clothing. And later the realization that she had fallen down the western slope and not the eastern, filled her with a mingled sense of shame and relief.

CHAPTER XV

HOW TELLECTINA RETURNED UNEXPECTEDLY TO THE LAND OF
ERR; HER STRANGE ADVENTURES THEREIN AND SUBSCRIPTION TO
THE LAWS THEREOF; AND HOW SHE RESORTED TO AN ESOTERIC
DRUG FOR ALL HER MANY ILLS

WAIT! WAIT! in the name of mercy, wait!" The voice
came from an outlandish figure with its head wrapped
in a makeshift cap of evergreens, and its clothes hanging in tatters about a thin form.

But the sturdy old carriage lumbered on unheeding, the driver
turning a deaf ear to her pleas, and continued along the dim
mountain road which was almost obscured by the heavy snow.
The figure staggered forward, fell, rose, called again, ran on,
slipped and sank to her waist in a deep drift of snow by the
roadside. After struggling resolutely for some time she extricated
herself with the aid of overhanging tree branches weighed low
by ice and stumbled along in the deep carriage tracks, imploring
for help at every step.

Finally the old cabby, whose face was bundled up to the eyes,
glanced over his shoulder but drove on. His indifference so
frightened the girl that it goaded her to one tremendous final
effort, which brought her breathless alongside the carriage.
Convinced that the old driver would not stop, Tellectina
struggled desperately with the handle of the door and then
clambered heavily inside.

Sinking onto the worn leather cushions, the exhausted girl
was overcome almost immediately by profound slumber. She
was never able to estimate the length of time her descent from
the mountain had required, but on awakening noticed that they

414

were on level ground, that there was no trace of snow, and also that she was weak from hunger. At the next inn they purchased sandwiches, at which the ravenous girl snatched the instant they appeared, devouring her share hastily before she even spoke to the old driver, who was seated on the carriage step enjoying his lunch in leisurely fashion.

"I presume you're the famous T. A. Riley whom so many people have assured me I would be compelled to encounter sooner or later."

The old man chuckled, but there was a sinister, inhuman note in his laughter. "That I am, miss—I suspect my fame has spread far and wide."

"But where are you taking me?"

The smile that greeted her was not pleasant. "I convey my passengers to a place where there are shelter and beds and warmth."

"Then take me there, please, please—at once! It doesn't matter where it is, and I'll pay any price you ask. What is your price?"

"Sec Sept Fler."

The girl shuddered, then shrugged. "Oh, well, what does it matter? But that is exorbitant."

The only reply she received was a complete and indifferent silence.

Tellectina laughed mockingly and said, "How have the mighty fallen! What an excellent joke—on me! You see, I thought I was strong enough to live alone on top of the highest mountain on earth, secure in my own little intellectual world, even through the severest weather and trials. When the winter winds descended on me, however, they forced me to resort to a cave. What an experience! I nearly froze to death and starved as well. And then it was that something died in me forever—the spirit of rebellion, I suppose.

"But the worst part of this terrible episode was the loneliness and the realization of my own weakness." The old man wasn't listening but Tellectina found it a relief to unburden herself.

"I discovered that I had adopted the Cabellian philosophy intellectually, but it had not yet seeped deep enough into my being for me to be actually guided by his belief in the necessity of compromise for all human beings. It applied to others but not to me—I thought I was the grand exception, only to find that after all I really wanted to live the way other people do.

"I simply couldn't be unique and self-sufficient and superior. And yet it is some consolation to my vanity to think that if the habits of the human race have proved satisfactory for several thousand years, they must not be so bad after all. But how did you happen to be driving over the mountain at this time of year?" He had turned a deaf ear to all her explanations but she repeated her question, shouting it at him loudly.

"Oh," he replied, "I can often pick up a fare that way. Some young fool is always thinking that he—though not often she, I haven't encountered many females before—can live up there alone and laugh at the rest of the world. But they soon learn!" Here he gave another of his sardonic little chuckles and, rising, brushed the crumbs from his hands and mounted the box again.

As they drove on Tellectina murmured to herself, "I don't care where I go if only once more I can enjoy a few creature comforts and human companionship." On glancing out she noticed that they were passing through a strangely dwarfed forest which appeared vaguely familiar, yet it was so comfortable in the carriage after her recent hardships that she closed her eyes and slept again contentedly.

Each day the weather grew warmer, and when she was not choked with dust she suffocated with an all pervasive fog. After they had passed over the bridge of a clear stream one humid afternoon, Tellectina bade the cabby stop. "I am going down behind those trees at the bend of the river and take a dip—I'm so hot and dirty. You wait here."

"I advise you not to do so unless you have a bathing suit," the old man cautioned her.

The explorer of Nithking turned on him in annoyance. "The very idea! There's nothing wrong about going in naked—I always did in Nithking. I am a free individual—I shall do as I please—damned if I won't!"

"You'll be damned all right, but you won't be pleased."

"You're the rudest old man I ever saw in my life!" she exclaimed. "But you wait right here just the same."

Glancing at him scornfully she hastened down the river bank and had just removed her clothes and was gazing at the cool water with longing eyes when masculine voices on the roadway came to her ears.

"Well," one voice was saying, "if any smart-aleck foreigner thinks she can come into this country and break our laws she can have the pleasure of changing her mind—in jail! Go down and arrest that female right now," the sergeant said to his two assistants.

Donning her garments quickly, Tellectina returned by another route, hoping to escape the officers. As she climbed the embankment some poisonous vines tripped her up, but extricating herself with a laugh, she readjusted her invisible armor and hastened on to the carriage. The sergeant who was awaiting her there barred the door of the carriage with his arm.

"Well, miss, you think you've very smart, don't you?"

Tellectina drew herself up with offended dignity. "I think that you're forgetting yourself, and I also think that your laws are——"

The officer interrupted her by thrusting a large sheaf of papers almost in her face. "I can tell by your accent and conduct that you're one of those foreigners. Now, if you want to stay in God's Country you've got to sign these papers and swear to obey the laws."

In consternation, the young woman glanced at the heading printed across the top of the papers in large letters:

THE LAWS OF THE LAND OF ERR

At the word "Err," Tellectina turned sick and leaned weakly against the side of the carriage. "Yes," she murmured, "I've been suspecting this for a long time. I just could not bear to admit it to myself!"

"Better read them," the officer urged.

Tellectina's smile was a little awry. "It isn't necessary. I know them by heart."

"But you talk like a foreigner."

"No, I'm a native of Err. It's only that I've been traveling in another country for a long time. I wonder if——" She glanced hastily over the papers. "No, no important alterations—not even in ten years."

The two men stood chatting in loud voices while she flicked meditatively through the papers, musing upon what had occurred. "So, I'm the person who was never going to set foot in Err again! I was going to live in Nithking always, alone and free on a mountain top, was I? I was going to be different, superior to my fellow man, and now——" She laughed.

Old T. A. Riley turned to her. "It's very simple. I can't see why you dreamy-eyed visionaries make such a blooming fuss about what sensible people accept without protest. If you want creature comforts and human companionship (and all people do) you can obtain them most easily in Err; and if you would live in Err in peace you must subscribe to its laws. It's an obvious truism. And reality eventually brings every human being to this point. If you don't want the same kind of unpleasant incidents to recur daily—you'd better sign."

For the first time Tellectina listened respectfully to the old cab driver. Again she looked at the list of laws in her hand and silently commented, "Stupid, childish, insulting, contradictory, inconsistent, and endless! How degrading to subscribe to such idiocy! There is only one thing more degrading—and that is the willingness to subscribe." She stood lost in thought for a long moment; then sighed heavily. Aloud she said very politely to the officer, "Where do I sign, please?"

And taking the pen which the old cabby held out to her, Tellectina signed her full name on the dotted line, "Tellectina

Femina Christian." And as she wrote it carefully and legibly, she felt the curious eyes of the officer watching her tongue move slowly inside her cheek. When she handed the signed document back to him, he tipped his cap obsequiously, saying, "Excellent, madame, excellent. Now you have the honor to be a citizen of this wonderful Land of Err once more—of God's own country."

The young woman smiled. "No one is more keenly aware of that fact than I."

"You know, it's quite a coincidence. I remember, about four years ago, a young woman—a foreigner, or rather an expatriate, like you—signed these citizenship papers, and she had a name almost like yours—and even looked something like you except that she was pret— I mean, was she a relative by any chance?"

"Yes, and a very sensible one. Her name was Femina Christian." The other two officers of the law now came up breathlessly. At a signal from the sergeant all three touched their caps and swaggered off.

Wearily, Tellectina climbed into the carriage again. "Drive on, cabby, until I see a house I might like to live in. But wait a moment." Suddenly she saw the old man with new eyes. "So your name is not T. A. Riley!"

"No, miss. People call me that because it sounds better! No one likes to call me by my right name, it seems, any more than they like to look on my face bare. They all insist on my keeping it muffled up all the time." Pulling down his soiled old scarf, he revealed his whole face.

Tellectina gasped. "No, no, don't turn away. I should have made your acquaintance years ago. Now I know your real name —though I suspected the truth all along. And now that I've come face to face with you at last I take a sort of masochistic pleasure in gazing on your hideousness. But why—why must you be so ugly?"

The old man was totally unmoved by her insults; he laughed as if frightening people gave him a sort of pleasure. "Ask my maker."

"There's nothing I should like better! And nothing so impossible! But what is the name of this highway on which I have been traveling for some time?"

He pointed his whip at a large signpost. "Can't you read?"

His passenger had grown accustomed to his rudeness by now, consequently she leaned out and read the large newly repainted signpost: Expiedway Ten.

Tellectina made a sound, but as laughter it was not convincing. "Oh, to think that I, Tellectina, should ever deliberately have chosen to follow such a road!"

"Don't take it so hard, miss. Everybody must travel on it sooner or later or starve to death, as you were in a fair way of doing when you had sense enough to climb into my carriage! Believe me, I've taken every degree of person over this route at some time or another—from the highest to the lowest persons. All roads lead to Err. This is merely the most traveled because it's the easiest way to travel. So be sensible, don't rebel against the thing you are powerless to prevent."

"Rebel and powerless? Those two words describe me a little too well! I am now a powerless rebel."

"Then if one is powerless, is it not folly to rebel?"

"It is futile, at least," the girl replied wearily. "And I presume that means it is folly." And suddenly there echoed in her mind the words of Jurgen, pronouncing her doom:

" 'We must live by politic evasion; . . . we fall insensibly to common sense as to a drug; and it dulls and kills whatever in us is rebellious and fine and unreasonable. . . . Within this hour I have become . . . a creature of use and wont; and am the lackey of prudence and half measures.' "

The young woman laughed. "I—I, Tellectina, whose motto was 'Half measures are for puny people—it's whole heart or none for me!' It is a fine jest—that much I do admit!" But oddly enough she failed to accord it the kind of laughter which a fine jest merits. Instead she merely bade the man on the box drive on.

Gradually the fog grew more oppressive, so that when they stopped on a slight promontory to have lunch, Tellectina was barely able to discern a city lying under the thick blanket of white mist. "What's that ahead of us?" she inquired.

As usual an unpleasant chuckle preceded T. A. Riley's answer. "That's the largest, oldest, and most prosperous seaport in the world. This highway leads right into the city."

"Make haste, then. I long to sleep in a real house on a real bed with real sheets once again."

"Yes'm, that's what they all say."

He flicked the horse with his whip, and soon they entered the city. It was not long before Tellectina eagerly leaned out from the window. "Stop, driver, here's a very comfortable-looking house. Maybe I could arrange to live there or even purchase it by degrees." The old coachman's face appeared at the window, and she continued, "You see, I had always intended to build a unique and beautiful house of my own, but it might save a great deal of time and energy if I chose one already built. Besides, I couldn't build one half so substantial by my own efforts only. And, after all, it surely can't be a disgrace to occupy a house merely because it was constructed by someone else. And all these mansions look the very epitome of comfort and very securely built, too."

"That they are, miss, and hundreds of years old, if they're a day. Stood the test of time and all weather too, to say nothing of the attempts of every generation to pull 'em down."

"Of course, I could redecorate the interior in the modern manner to suit my own personal taste."

"Aye, miss, you could try, but I thought you said you were looking for peace and comfort. Whatever you do, don't alter the exterior—take a tip from an old man who's seen a lot in his day. Speaking of tips——"

His passenger shook her head vigorously. "No, indeed, no more for you." She stepped out of the carriage. "You have no right to extort Sec Sept Fler from your passengers. And I've already paid you in advance, you old swindler!"

Such insults merely amused the hardened old man. "That you have, miss, but I never had a lady passenger so reluctant to pay the price agreed upon. Remember my stand is right here in this street, so——"

"I thought as much, and I presume there is no law to prevent it. Drive on a bit, though, will you!"

But the cabby merely hastened to open for her the tall iron gates which led into a large and lazy old boxwood garden. The peaceful charm of it caused her to forget her annoyance with T. A. Riley for a while. "Ah," she murmured, "I can imagine no scene in the world more delightful to look out on for the rest of one's life than this!"

Strolling on admiringly through the winding walk, she was suddenly stopped short by the faint sound of voices coming from the veranda. There was something vaguely familiar about these surroundings—was it possible——? Instantly she reassured herself: "No, no, *that* is not possibly possible!"

She could now see the house even better, though not in its entirety. "I ask nothing better in life than to be able to remain here always—except with summers spent on Mt. Ghaulot, of course. Yes, there is something familiar about this fine old boxwood and the locust trees."

Peering through the trees more closely, she saw on the wide south veranda an elderly couple rocking leisurely. Tellectina's heart stood still, a wave of sickness swept over her. She fell forward, her foot caught in a tangle of vines, but she managed to steady herself against the broad trunk of an oak.

"Oh, dear God in heaven!" She buried her face against the tree in the bend of her arm. "It's not fair—it's not possible—but it's true!"

Lifting her head, she stared about her, then shrugged her shoulders. "So I am back where I started from, back in Smug Harbor, back to the house of my Fathers' Fathers, the ancestral home of the indomitable Christians, back to live among the Rationalizers! I have only described a circle in my journeyings. This, then, was my ultimate goal!" Her laughter was not a pleasant thing to hear. "Was it for this that I went exploring in Nithking, risked my life, broke my leg, scaled mountains, was poisoned, shipwrecked—died and was born again? Is this the reward for all my aspiring, my fine dreaming, my courage and effort—to arrive at the place from which my fathers have never departed?"

She looked up at the serene and indifferent expanse of gray sky. "Yes, your irony is superb!" Then a flicker of her old rebellion flared up once more. "But why, why, did you curse me with such hopes, such dreams when you knew that defeat was foreplanned? You lie and cheat and trick the young Tellectinas of the world—and they don't discover it till it's too late.

"For the third time the fact is forced upon me that I am just an ordinary human being like any other with the same desires and weaknesses and needs. And I must not only return from Nithking, but accept the ways of my fathers as well, because I was unable to live a higher and better life! The independence I dreamed of was but a farce!

"Seventeen years ago I stood under this very tree on my thirteenth birthday and said I was just beginning to live. There's something in that—" she smiled—"perhaps there's everything in that."

As she turned away from the tree, Tellectina perceived that she had been standing in a deep bed of Sillidinous vines—but to her delight the Hynuppa increased very little. As she extricated herself with a laugh, she patted her armor fondly, "You stood me in good stead this time, certainly." Then she smiled wearily.

"Surely this is the final disillusion—beyond this there can be nothing. For certainly I have been caught in every disillusionment in the world—there just can't be any more—and that is some consolation. But how has it all happened? I must analyze this terrible dénouement when I am rested; but the chief thing now is—why, the chief thing now is that I'm very hot and very tired and the one thing in the world I want most at this moment is—is a large glass of iced tea with mint in it—the way the old cook at home used to make it in Smug Harbor."

As she started up, however, she stumbled on the gravel walk.

The noise brought her astounded and overjoyed parents rushing off the porch to help her. Amid inarticulate cries of joy they assisted her indoors.

As she lay sipping her tall glass of iced tea with a fresh sprig of mint in it, the Christians were so pathetically overjoyed at the prodigal's return that Tellectina was almost destroyed by contrition and pity. "People have no right to bare their hearts in their eyes that way—it's too painful to behold!" she protested to her tea as she stirred it violently and blinked back the tears. "I'm just a sentimental fool—who hasn't sense enough not to drop tears into her tea—that's the whole trouble with me—and I can't help it if I love my own parents, can I? I suppose that isn't any disgrace!"

Having heard the commotion, Sophistica came quickly into the room, as gay as ever. The young woman sat up eagerly to greet the older one, then suddenly dropped her eyes in guilt.

Placing her hand under her niece's chin, Sophistica lifted it and smiled tenderly into her eyes. "Dearest child."

"Child! I'm a battered old explorer of thirty!"

"Oh, Daughter," John Christian interrupted in a voice which he made valiant and vain efforts to control, "I feared you—you would nev—never return!"

Sophistica blinked back her own tears impatiently. "And I assured these poor worrying dears a thousand times that you would return to Smug Harbor in due course of time."

"But——"

"You see, I've known T. A. Riley intimately, oh, very intimately, for a good many years now, and he can generally be relied on to bring headstrong young explorers back to Err."

But Mary Christian could contain herself no longer. "Well, I, for one, think it's very unladylike for a girl to go gallivanting all alone all over those foreign countries. Why didn't you write to your poor parents all those terrible years, Tina? You nearly broke your mother's heart! But I forgive you now that you've come home at last. But why didn't you at least notify us that you were returning?"

"Oh, I'm so sorry, Mother dear, I realize now that my prolonged silence was cruel. But I knew least of all that I was on my way home. I'm still a bit dazed by the discovery."

"Do you mean you didn't intend—— But never mind, you're here now. But didn't you at least recognize the street leading to your own home, child?"

"No, Mother, I either saw it with different eyes as a child, or I'd never been on it before."

"Well, what roadway did you come on, for heaven's sake?"

"It's called the Expiedway Ten."

"Well, I don't know why you've never been on it before: it's the widest and most traveled of any street in Smug Harbor. But you just lie there, honey, and rest—here, have another glass of iced tea. Yes, take it—it will do Mother's poor baby good. Father, you tell Amanda to bring some more ice to Miss Tina, quick. I'll go down and speak to the cook and tell her to make some of that nice orange ice Tina used to like so well. Come on out, Sophie, and let her have a good nap before supper. I know my poor baby is worn out, what with all that terrible traveling."

She bustled out, but neither John Christian nor his sister Sophistica moved. They sat silently watching the girl who lay with closed eyes—but who had never felt more wide awake in her life.

An elaborate dinner was prepared to celebrate the return of the prodigal daughter, and relatives and friends were hastily invited in.

Later, when they were passing into the dining room, Sophistica whispered in Reasonese to Tellectina, "It's going to be a damned difficult dinner for you! But don't discuss your travels if you wish to avoid inflicting pain. Talk about the weather— it's the only safe topic in Smug Harbor—and the favorite one."

Tellectina smiled. "I am now prepared to be an appreciative audience for the first time in my life."

The older woman looked at her with surprised pleasure in her eyes. "It's a wise child that knows its own family."

The rich and abundant dinner was considered by some a

great success. The effort of John and Mary Christian to impress the returned traveler with the wonders and virtues of Smug Harbor and prove its superiority to all other spots on earth was a remarkable feat deserving of a better cause. The only contribution made to the conversation by Tellectina, the world traveler, was a repeated, "Is that so?" and "Well, isn't that nice!" But with Sophistica she exchanged many a surreptitious and significant glance.

As they rose from the table Mr. Christian placed his arm fondly about Tellectina's shoulders. "Daughter, my dear, you don't know how happy it makes your mother and father to have you safely back in Smug Harbor, or how deeply we've grieved over your absence. And I'm certainly glad to see that you—like Sophie here—have come to your senses at last and returned to Err and given up trying to speak that foolish foreign language that no one could understand, anyway. Reasonese, didn't you call it? Halfish ought to be good enough for any Errorian."

Tellectina bit her lips and smiled as best she could as the procession formed to march out to the shady veranda and the inevitable rocking chairs whose gentle rhythm lulled thought to sleep.

After John and Mary Christian had retired that night, Tellectina slipped into Sophistica's room exactly as she had done ten years before—on that memorable night before she started on her journey into Nithking. Just as formerly, the older woman laid aside her book and settled herself against her pillows to listen while Tellectina sat, not eagerly on the edge of her chair, but resting quietly in it.

"You know, Auntie——"

"I think you are old enough to call me Sophie now."

"I do feel that we are the same age, somehow—er—Sophistica. Twenty years' difference. It surely isn't possible!"

"Age, my dear, as you must know by now, is not so much a matter of time as of mentality."

"Merciful heavens, I wish I didn't know it! That realization has been forced on me since my return to Smug Harbor. Honestly, Sophie, I never had such a strong maternal feeling toward anyone in my life as I now have toward my own mother and father! And I genuinely admire and respect them for their honor and integrity and kindness. And I love them, but—well, you see, it took me an unflattering number of years to learn that fine characters could exist independently of fine minds."

"And you consider the former without the latter trying to live with—is that it?"

"Exactly."

"And it would be equally trying to live with a fine mind which existed independent of a fine character."

"Don't remind me! The Land of Nithking is too full of such monsters. I love them—my parents, I mean, and I'm as loath to hurt them as I would be children; but I'm constitutionally incapable of speaking Halfish, yet I can't keep my mouth closed for the rest of my life!"

"No, you don't deserve such extreme punishment. But has not your tolerance grown broad enough to encompass even their intolerance of you?"

"Yes, but——"

"Ah," Sophistica raised two fingers as though in a pontifical blessing. "Greater love hath no man."

"But, damn my heathen soul, Sophie, love is not enough in this world! You can love people and yet be bored by them to the point of murder. One must have congenial companionship, too—friends who speak one's own language."

"There are a great many people even in Err who speak your language—secretly, more or less, as one always must in an enemy country. I've come to feel, however, that it doesn't matter where I live as long as there are two or three gathered together in the name of Reasonese—and I am there in the midst of them. Come, my dear, you can live in my wing of your father's house. I feel badly that I did not keep track of you all these last ten years, but I was too deeply involved in marriages and other misadventures."

"Oh, I'm terribly sorry—but there's no escaping marriage, apparently, for a woman—she's damned if she does and damned if she doesn't. But you're an angel to want to take me."

"Angel? God forbid!"

"But this damnable fog. Does one ever get used to it?"

"No, but better still, one finds it the source of constant amusement: watching others wander blindly in the fog through which one can see so clearly one's self."

"And when it grows unbearable, one can always seek Ghaulot, I suppose," Tellectina said, then suddenly covered her face.

"I know, Tina, the idea of seeking the mountain top brings back unpleasant memories to you—eh?"

"Oh, yes, I feel I'm such a fool!"

"Aren't we all? Come, Tina, tell me about your adventures in Nithking. Can't you see I'm more curious than the proverbial cat?—for I infer that you made some fascinating discoveries in that strange land."

Tellectina leaned forward in her chair. "Well, certainly the greatest discovery I made was that Nithking offers the most exciting adventure that can be experienced by a human being."

"But you can't expect the ordinary person to regard it as an adventure."

"Of ordinary people, my dear aunt, I expect nothing but ordinariness. But, hell's bells, it's an expedition that every thinking young person must make—especially those brought up as Puritans in a Smug Harbor."

"Never mind the other thinking young people, I have a sort of weakness for this one. Tell me more of her experiences."

Tellectina drew in a deep breath and began. "I believe firmly, however, that mine was a universal experience. At first my only desire was to escape from Err. I rebelled against the whole established order, against all the prevailing conceptions of everything (except four things); against organized religion, government, morality, sex and woman's status, art, the institution of marriage, the family, and the state. Though unfortunately I still believed for a while in their optimistic sophistry concerning love, mankind, God, and the world. Then later I came to rebel not only against the laws of Err, but against all law, and was consumed with desire to find Certitude—which I believed to be the highest peak in the world."

"Wait! Wait! You go too fast for an oldster like me. Finish with Err first. After you left here what did you first find in Nithking?"

Tellectina smiled at her fondly and said, "Before I go into details, let me sum it all up by saying that I discovered that the truth about the facts of life as one is taught them in Err is just the reverse. And yet there is a germ of truth in the Errorian teachings too."

"That sounds paradoxical enough to be true. But specify and elucidate."

"I mean specifically that the world, mankind, God, love, and marriage prove to be the five great disillusionments."

"You only found five? You lucky girl!"

"Five major ones but innumerable minor ones. And the four great joyful surprises for the young Puritan explorer are beauty and art, the pursuit of knowledge, and sex. No one gives her an inkling of the intense joy those four things can give her. But life's greatest surprise for a Puritan woman is—passion!"

"Ah, I see you've been fortunate in lovers. So you really ought to be grateful, for the skilled ones are as rare as—as corsets in the South Sea Islands."

"You forget that I am Tellectina, and for me sex is not enough. The trouble is that the pain of the five disillusionments far exceeds the pleasure afforded by the four great joys. Woman's desire for love and a happy marriage in the everyday world is stronger than her desire for beauty, creative achievement, truth, or even pleasure."

"Oh, hell, Tina, I was in hopes that that was one discovery you wouldn't make in Nithking. But you expected too much of life and that miserable insect known as humanity. I was never the mad idealist that you were. I was born in the shape of a question mark—I have always doubted everything—and I've generally been right." But she smiled tenderly at her niece with that same look in her eyes which had so puzzled Tellectina when she saw it first in her father's, fourteen years ago—that same look which so delighted Femina every time she saw it in men's eyes.

"Oh, I know I was a young fool, for, incredible as it sounds now even to my own ears, I not only wanted everything good, I unconsciously expected everything good as my natural due. I expected constant happiness, perpetual pleasure, romance, and beauty. I dreamed of perfection—of perfect love, a perfect man, a perfect marriage, perfect friends—of infallible wisdom and unfailing goodness and justice."

The older woman lifted her hands. "Dear God in heaven!"

"Oh, I know, I was an idealistic young fool!"

"Did you say idealistic or egotistic?"

"But I believe in egotism—it's necessary for human progress," the younger woman stated.

"Don't you admire the ingenuity of the human mind in inventing justifications for its desires? But I digress. What I intended to say was that all these perfections you did experience —for fleeting golden moments, perhaps. You made the mistake of expecting them to last a lifetime."

"Please——"

"But if you wanted everything, as you said, everything includes sorrow and pain—they too enrich one's nature. You never can see the beauty of your ideals till they lie in glittering fragments about your feet, you never know what love is till your heart is broken, and only brutal reality has the strength to crush the finest fragrance from your dreams. Did you not make any such discoveries as these in Nithking?"

By way of answer Tellectina drew from out her breast the battered waterproof diary which she had been keeping all through her expedition in the Forbidden Country and tossed it onto Sophistica's bed. "Cast your sophisticated eye over that, will you?—while I go and indulge in another cold bath—in a real human tub."

When she returned her aunt gazed at her with fond approving eyes. And all through the long spring night they sat and talked about their respective journeys through Nithking, completely oblivious of the thick white fog rolling in from the Dead Sea at the foot of the Christian garden.

"Then, as I said before, Sophie, when I got farther and farther into Nithking, I came to rebel against all law: the laws of the universe, of nature, of my own human nature, and of mankind —only to return now and accept everything! What a farce it is!"

"Accept—but with a difference."

"But even that precious difference doesn't prevent me from appearing a fool and a weakling in my own eyes. For of the universe I expected, if not benevolence, at least justice; only to find it implacable, inscrutable, and indifferent and unjust to the point of absolute cruelty—though perhaps with its eyes on so large, so magnificent a design that the individual threads of human lives are negligible. I even rebelled against the injustice of natural forces. What madness! for what is man's thin wailing against the anger of the storm and the cruelty of the lightning? I refused furthermore to be a slave to any custom, any act or thought ever accepted by the human race."

"What a gesture!" Sophistica murmured.

"I thought I would live as though I were the first human being inhabiting this earth, only to discover that the human race is not as stupid as I in my abysmal ignorance considered it; only to discover that it is exceedingly pleasant to be sheltered by houses, to eat cooked food, to sleep in soft beds, to protect the naked body with warm coverings cut to accommodate the body in action and to have some mode of transportation other than one's own two feet."

"And you discovered that you must condescend to accept the help of others if you wish to enjoy these comforts?"

"Yes, and forfeit my independence for life. I also rejected all governments, all religions, only to learn that they are absolute necessities to most people, and that one small person is power-

less against them, anyway. I questioned all conventions, all customs, only to find that they very pleasantly lubricate the wheels
of social intercourse. I expected equality and independence for
women only to discover that they could attain neither."

"*Et tu, Brute!*"

"I discarded the prevailing notions of morality and——"

"And still do I hope—secretly!"

The younger woman smiled and nodded. "I discarded the institutions of marriage and family and state."

"Another brave and futile gesture."

"Only to find them both convenient and pleasant."

"There I disagree with you—having been married twice since
I saw you ten years ago—but continue."

"And, finally, I rebelled against my own nature, only to learn
that I was a slave to my body. I could neither think nor write
nor read without being forever interrupted by the periodic demands of the flesh: to feed it, or bathe it, or exercise it; to dress
it, or rest it, or let it sleep; to eliminate something or copulate
with somebody."

The older woman laughed. "Ah, yes, the eight demands of
the human body, that tyrant which keeps constant and jealous
guard over the human mind that it may never progress too far.
I am overfamiliar with that tyrant."

"But, Sophie, I resent these bodily demands so vehemently.
And I resent the emotional demands, too. I am a slave to my
own desires for human companionship and love, for accomplishment and the respect of myself and my fellow man."

"So what are you going to do about it?"

"Nothing."

"That's what we all do."

"Nothing can be done about it. Submission—we must submit!
I've tried to deny every one of those demands. And denial costs
more in the long run than submission. One is not a free agent:
free will is just a pretty conceit. I thought the human will
omnipotent, only to find it the slave of a dozen masters. All our
lives are conditioned by circumstance, by our own limitations—

mental and physical. Oh, it's all so mortifying after all the fine dreams I cherished for myself!"

"But, my dear Tellectina, you shouldn't be ashamed of yourself—but merely of being a human being. That's nothing to be proud of, goodness knows, but if shame loves company, you have plenty of it. Expiedway Ten is not only the most traveled highway in Smug Harbor but in the whole world. We all follow it sooner or later, for the very excellent reason that it leads us to many of the things we desire."

"Ah, my desires! Don't mention them. I desired so ardently to live on a higher plane than the ordinary person—live more beautifully, more naturally, more independently, more esthetically, and intellectually, and more honestly."

"I understand you a little too well, in spite of my seeming skepticism. The superwoman is an ideal which many of us have striven for—and relinquished—more gracefully, shall I say? than ——" A shrug and a smile completed her sentence. "And who, pray, is this little Tellectina who defies both nature and human nature as well?"

"You should have said 'defied'—used the past tense, for she is merely a deflated little ego now. For since I am unable to live in a world of ideas different from the majority of people there is only one sensible thing to do."

"Grin and bear it?"

"Yes, because the time and energy consumed in defying even the most stupid laws of Err would leave one no time for anything else, and as it happens there is another thing which I wish to accomplish much more than that."

"I know, we'll return to that later."

"So I have decided to accept what I want of the man-made world and——"

"And a damned lot you don't want."

"But of course," Tellectina agreed. "And since one must eat and sleep and live under roofs and wear clothes and bathe and pay taxes and pretend to live and love and think and marry and copulate just like other people, then——"

"I notice you put love before marriage and copulation after it. Have you turned conventional as well as cynical?"

"We'll hold a special session on those three subjects—you and I. But since, as I was saying, expediency brings us to this conformity, we can at least perform all these human necessities as attractively as possible."

"Hedonism is the second tenet of my creed, also. Peace is my first. And what other antique truths did you excavate in Nithking?"

"But they are new to the young explorer," Tellectina protested.

"Don't listen to me, child, continue."

"I discovered that woman's independence is a farce."

"Comedy is a prettier word."

"Comedy, then," Tellectina agreed.

"But one laughs at comedies."

"I am laughing."

"Oh, my error. Apparently my hearing isn't what it once was."

"It is a comedy because she can't be independent of the established order; she can't be independent of men either emotionally or intellectually. The intellectual woman thinks to attain an original and personal philosophy of life. And what happens? Ninety-nine out of every hundred women merely adopt some man's philosophy all ready made!"

"Ninety-nine women out of every hundred aren't capable of having any philosophy. One woman out of every hundred (the percentage is generous) may with effort be able to adopt some admired male's point of view."

"Why, Sophie, you are even more cruel than I."

"The truth is often cruel."

"Nor can a woman free herself from her own inherent limitations and weaknesses. Independence? Bah! There is only one kind of independence women have ever achieved so far—and that is financial."

"Thank God for that! For without financial independence

woman can never attain any other kind. Make no mistake on that score."

"But that doesn't satisfy."

"Nothing does. But don't blame woman's failure to be independent solely on the fact of her being a woman. She fails because she is human. What man is free of his desire for love and sex and companionship? What man is free of his need for creature comforts? (Have you forgotten *Something about Eve* so soon?) Nor is he free of the pressure of the social group. You ask the impossible."

"But a real man is practically free of other men intellectually."

"Yes and no. Have you never read of Shakespeare's indebtedness to Marlowe, as well as Milton's; Goethe's to Spinoza, Tolstoy's to Turgenev, Shaw's to Butler—etcetera ad infinitum?"

"But men are more free of women emotionally than women are of men."

"Or men simply make less noise about it. I've seen women both make and break fine men. Nothing on earth can wreck a man so thoroughly as a heartless hussy!"

"Ah, but, Sophie, women have endured so much injustice at the hands of men. Men have abused their power."

"Don't give them the power. In other words, don't marry. There's no panacea for the conflict between the sexes, but that's the best preventative. What men want when they marry is not a companion, as they so convincingly tell you, but merely a combination of mother, nurse, servant, and harlot. Pretty combination, isn't it? It simply leaves a woman with a mind and personality of her own out of the picture."

"I know, and outside of marriage women could learn to be happier if they wouldn't take sex so seriously."

"And if they'd take birth control more seriously—man's greatest gift to womankind."

"Oh, Lord, yes, and by learning to have affairs without regrets and without love."

"Or tears. Women cry too damned much. If they'd only learn to laugh and swear—both sexes would be better off. Modern surgery should remove the tear ducts entirely—tears only spoil a woman's looks and digestions."

"And they should learn to take an interest in their work—whatever it is—as men do."

"Let work be their main existence and men a thing apart, to modernize Lord Byron."

"And learn to derive their happiness through things, as men do—not entirely through people, as they have in the past. The trouble with women is that all through the ages they have done nothing but wallow in love."

"*And* childbirth," Sophistica added.

"Oh, hell, Sophie, do you suppose women can ever be the equal of men?"

"Never!"

"Never?"

"Never."

"But, Sophie——"

"Never as long as they have female organs that bear babies."

"I know, biology is dead set against her. If we can't compete with them physically, how can we expect to do so mentally? We've lost the race before we even start."

"Then admit it and laugh. A great deal of amusement can be got out of being a woman, nevertheless. Your gatherulic iron armor is too frequently invisible, I fear, little Tina. Nothing in the world is worth taking very seriously—not even one's self."

"I know it, and yet the hellish part is that the desire, the ambition to equal men has been awakened in some women so strongly."

"How prettily you flatter our sex, Tina."

"You don't believe women want to be men's equals?"

"Not many of them—not much—not yet."

"You are cynical, Sophistica!"

"I'm fifty."

"You're right. I suppose the majority of women past twenty-five want marriage and children more than anything else on earth. And yet there seems to be a sort of neuter sex coming into existence who want neither men nor babies nor marriage, and they appear quite healthy and happy."

"Simply a newer and healthier and happier type of spinster, that's all. But women as a race will never be able to accomplish any great and enduring work in the world until babies are conceived and born in test tubes in the chemical laboratories. Hundreds of years from now the human race will look back and laugh at the old-fashioned custom of women giving birth to babies. Copulation will become a means of pleasure only, as it is with so many women today. Already the mammary glands of the higher type of human animal are ceasing to function. Women's breasts will in time doubtless become of no more use than the clitoris—only let us hope they will retain their exquisite sensitiveness—even if not their beauty and softness. And when old Dame Nature finally obeys man's dictates and adjusts woman's organs to perform no more of the reproductive function than man's now do—women will be really free for the first time in their history, free to commence to live the life of a civilized animal instead of that of a mere breeding animal."

"But I see that nowadays many actresses take time out for a year, have a baby, get some trained nurse to take efficient care of it, and return to their jobs as good as ever."

"Not as good as ever. Their endurance and appearance and Ports of Entry have been impaired. Whereas, when a man begets a baby, the only effect it has on him is to improve his appearance and appetite and disposition."

"Oh, it's all so damnably unfair!"

Sophistica laughed. "I suspect the horses and chickens and other domestic animals think life is unfair, too. Woman was born lower down in the animal scale than man—but evolution may do strange things to her yet."

Tellectina sat puffing her third cigarette meditatively. "Do you know, Sophie, that the stage (dramatic and musical) has been the only career in the history of the world (unless we count the rare cases of queenship) for which women have willingly foregone husbands and homes and children?"

"Yes, when women pursue any of the other arts, they don't give them up, they neglect them."

"Physically only, though, they make better wives and mothers, mentally speaking."

"No male wants a mental wife or mother."

"But some women feel the absolute necessity of a mental life of their own. And yet—and yet, I, who considered myself the most independent female who ever graced the earth, see now that I was strongly influenced by whatever male was in the ascendancy of power over me at the moment. First, there was my father and his conservatism; then Olev the First and his romanticism—though his influence was brief; then Olev the Second and his mysticism; and lastly Olev the Third and his cynicism. Then finally there was the intellectual influence of Cabell, of course. When, oh, when will women learn to think for themselves! Where is our self-confidence?"

"So you won't even give the child time to grow up?"

"You mean——"

"I mean that women have always been treated as children—it made them so much easier for the males to handle. You expect women in one generation to arrive at the same stage of maturity, so called, that it has required men several thousand years to achieve? Come, be reasonable—and laugh. Are not the pathetic and amusing attempts of children to behave like adults always a matter for indulgent laughter?"

"I am still too serious, I know. I thought that on Mt. Ghaulot I had really learned to laugh at all things; and so I have, but only periodically."

"Of course, some people have never considered women to be human beings at all, you know." Sophistica drew a large black-and-gold volume from the shelf near her bed and said, "No less an authority than Cabell himself says that the romantic male 'even when of the embittered variety, perhaps cannot ever, quite, regard women as human beings. Now to do this is, of course, the signal attempt of the twentieth century. . . . For so great a while they were but conveniences, equally for housework and copulation. Then, as the more talented courtesans were evolved, women here and there began to be ranked among the luxuries and adornments of life. . . . But the apex was reached in the medieval notion of domnei, . . . whereby women became goddesses . . . Yet . . . domnei was always a cult limited . . . to the upper classes. . . . Side by side with domnei, . . . persisted always the monkish notion of woman as a snare of the devil, and the bourgeois notion of woman as a false and lustful animal. . . .

"'The lady . . . grows nowadays as rare as the horse; these two, who were formerly the dearliest prized chattels of every well-bred male, now race neck and neck into extinction.' He also points out other matters concerning the regard in which women were held, 'In common with all the non-human creatures such as gods and fiends and ghosts' . . . There, you have briefly the history of woman."

"That may be their past, but their future will be quite different."

"I wonder if it will. There's a certain factor you've omitted that seems very important—at fifty."

"Age?"

"No, looking one's age, if one's a woman."

"But you don't look a day over thirty-eight, Sophistica, you're remarkable!"

"I'm perhaps the exception. I prove nothing—except that every new lover a woman takes makes her five years younger."

"You've had a lot?"

"Yes, thank God! All intelligent women do, unless they're happily married—which no intelligent woman can be. But we'll return to that, it is a subject which deserves volumes. The other factor against women is not so much the fact that they age earlier than men; but that the basis of their attraction for men is physical appearance."

"Yet men remain attractive to women till they have one foot in the grave almost, and their appearance and youth are not the basis of attraction anyway. Oh, it's so unfair."

"Certainly it's unfair. But don't fret over it—that will only make you more unattractive. Laugh."

"But even laughter gives women wrinkles around the eyes!" Both women laughed long and heartily and secretly counted the fine wrinkles around each other's eyes.

"Oh, nature is so unfair to women, that's what angers me so!" Tellectina exclaimed.

"My dear child, the whole trouble really is that when a thing designed solely for a breeding animal suddenly decides it wants —to write books, let us say—what can you expect but incongruity and disappointment?"

"But then who the seven dying devils infused the poor breeding animal with this incongruous desire?"

Sophistica shrugged. "Ah, who made the world? The answer, you see, is very simple."

"Well, I have it on good authority that even 'the most prosaic of materialists proclaim that we are all descended from an insane fish, who somehow evolved the idea that it was his duty to live on land, and eventually succeeded in doing it.' So that now his baby-bearing progeny manifest the same illogical aspiration toward intelligence, their bankruptcy in common sense may, even by men's standards, have much the same incredible result."

Sophistica shook her head in mock severity. "He may not like that."

"I don't think any men are going to like it! All of them count intellectual women among the blights of the earth, but I know of only one who has had the honesty to admit it. No master relishes the idea of giving up his slaves. Why should he? He wouldn't be human."

"True enough, for although men prefer to do most of the adoring before marriage, they generally expect the woman to do most of it after marriage."

"Marriage! What on earth is going to happen to it if women

do succeed in becoming really intelligent? There can't be two masters in one house."

"I suspect the fatter purse and the stronger personality will rule the nest regardless of sex (to mix my metaphors as badly as a senator)."

"But if the woman's the master, she has no respect for the man, and if he's the master, she has no respect for herself."

"A pretty impasse. I have been married twice since I saw you —once to a weak man who adored me, and once to a strong one —whom I adored. Neither worked. Having lovers and writing books is much more satisfactory."

"Femina could have the lovers, and I could write the books. But she wrote me that she had grown to hate that way of living and wanted to marry again. So it really isn't a satisfactory way for a woman to live, is it?"

"Who said it was?"

"But I thought you said——"

"I said it was more satisfactory than marriage. That doesn't mean it is satisfactory—nothing is."

Tellectina gazed quizzically at the older woman, who laughed and said, "I understand. You're merely too polite to ask it. When a woman gets too old to have lovers, what then? Is she not lonely? Yes, most women would be—unbearably. But there is always one way——" and here she whispered in the younger woman's ear. "And even if one did that the lovers without the books would be hard to bear. Writing books takes the place of both husbands and children if one cares enough about the books —but they don't take the place of the lovers. By the way, speaking of books, the time is now ripe for me to present you with my masterpiece, *The Chastity Myth Exploded.*" She took down another volume from the shelf beside her bed.

"Oh, thanks so much, Sophie. I know I shall love this now. Heretofore I had always felt that your books were too—too satirical. Now satire seems the most civilized way of dealing with the human scene, doesn't it? Books have been everything in the world to me during the last ten years."

"I know—books can be houses to rest in, boats to ride in, food, drink, and shelter."

"The only kind of books of which there seems to be a tragic shortage is books on the art of love."

"Yes, and most men need a whole course in that subject. My chief complaint of men is that they are seldom skilled enough to give a woman pleasure on the connubial couch or any other kind."

"That's what Femina says, too. But since Steckel proves convincingly that there is no such thing as a frigid woman, men should be forced to learn—there ought to be a law!"

"No, there ought to be a school. What the world needs today is an art school for men where the lost art of love could be taught. And I could be the head mistress."

"There's more truth than humor in that, I suspect, my dear Sophistica."

"But the latter is of equal importance, remember." She laughed, then said, "And now that all's been said and done—by both of us—you think life's not worth living?"

"One's mind says it's not, but one's senses say it most emphatically is! As long as there are two things left in the world, life can never be too terrible to me. I mean beauty and ecstasy, I mean the two great sources of beauty and the nine great sources of ecstasy."

"Godsky, if you've known them all, young lady, you should be grateful to whatever gods there should be."

"Grateful? Hell's bells, I'm exultant! For I have known them all save two. Shall I tell you what I've discovered to be the secret of life?"

"With that ecstatic look on your face, I presume you mean only one thing—love!"

"Love!" Tellectina was scornful. "It is not to my sister Femina you speak (though she's coming tomorrow to plague me with all her troubles and all her men!). Remember I am Tellectina, and to me love is but one of many passions—an inexplicable fever that makes the heart tremble with joy one minute and cruelly lacerates it the next. No, it is not of love I speak. Passion —that is the secret of life!"

The older woman raised amused and quizzical eyebrows.

But Tellectina held up a deprecating hand. "No, no, not that kind, sexual passion is merely one of many."

"The purest, though, you'll admit?"

"Well, the most intense and the most fleeting, certainly. But I mean passion in all things is the secret of living well."

"Whereas the Greeks thought it was moderation, and the Chinese, restraint."

But the younger woman was swept on by the power of her own emotions. "Yes, to do everything in life with whole-hearted intensity—whether it's loving or hating; whether it's the pursuit of a rainbow or the peeling of a potato—that is the way to live richly. Thus we bring upon ourselves great disappointments, griefs, and joys, but never do we bring upon our heads the real tragedies of life. For the real tragedies are not heartbreak, sorrow, and disillusionment, but emptiness, denial, frustration, repression and suppression, dullness and monotony. If we're going to have sorrow, let us have a big one that we can get our teeth into, so to speak—one that is a worthy opponent of a self-respecting person—one that will test our strength and courage to the utmost so that, if we win it will be a great and glorious victory, and if we lose at least we can have the satisfaction of having been conquered by a giant."

"Yes, but——" Sophistica protested.

"I have, as you yourself once advised me, been wise and rushed in where fools feared to tread; I have denied myself nothing. I have lived—lived, I tell you! to the fullest, to the uttermost limits of human joy and anguish, to the last limit and beyond that! I am ripe and rich and full. I've scorned half measures and plunged into life with a whole heart, and I'm glad—glad!"

Tellectina rose and walked back and forth across the floor, exultant. The dark circles under her eyes, the fine lines at their corners, the gray hair at her temples—all were forgotten. Her face became luminous, her very flesh glowed with the inner fire of her ecstatic spirit, her slender body seemed transparent—incandescent.

"My body and my senses—my mind and heart and spirit, no less, have been like a hundred æolian harps. All the winds of life have played sweet music on them. All my being has been attuned to the most exquisite and heart-rending melodies; the strings so tightly strung that they vibrated to every vagrant breeze of emotion and thought. Is there a note, a chord, any possible combination of harmonies or discords which have not been sounded again and again upon my spirit?"

"And is this the little Puritan who once believed beauty and joy to be sins?" Sophistica asked.

"Ah, yes, the Puritan became the dancing Bacchante drunk with life! My whole life has been a series of drunken orgies."

"And with all the miserable aftermaths too, I'll warrant. There's no escaping them."

"Yes, but——"

"But to the world you showed a sober enough face, I suspect. You, like me, were one of those secret and solitary drinkers, I think? The very worst kind!" And her companion shook her head in mock disapproval.

"And the best—for to feel with consuming intensity, to tingle with emotion to your very fingertips, to the very ends of your hair—that is the important thing. To feel every atom of your being dancing with life—even if it's with misery; to have your blood race and sing, your very flesh tingle with joy—that is to live! That's it—the zest for life—that is the greatest gift of any god to any mortal!"

"Yes, if——"

"Zest, ecstasy, passion! To feel intensely—to feel everything— to experience all the emotions possible to a human being. And I have run the gamut. I have known the heights and depths of which a human being is capable: love, despair, pity, passion, anger, fear, hatred, and joy! My life is like a great storehouse of treasure—I have only to put my hand into my past to know how rich I am."

"Only if——"

"I have experienced great love and received great love. I have known such violent hatred that my fingers trembled with the exquisite agony to kill; passion has carried me up into a mystical union with the very universe itself; the ecstasy of artistic creation has flowed through my slender body like celestial wine; I have suffered such illness that I have welcomed the face of death; sudden intellectual insight has swept me up to the cold, luminous mountain top; and the sight of great beauty has so dissolved my being that I have merged in fearful joy and sorrow with the very elements themselves!"

"All that can be true if——"

But Tellectina rushed on: "Ah, yes, the Tellectinas of the world are not afraid; they do not, like Pater's Botticellian people, shrink from their own greatness. Their experiences, ecstasies, and griefs are not normal, thank God; but an 'extension of the normal'—like Sullivan's Beethoven's! My spirit too has soared like the lark into the heart of the sun, for I have also tasted 'that ruinous mad moment of communion there in heaven.'"

"Well, really——"

"Ah, yes, ah, yes, at thirty I feel ripe and rich, for I have experienced seven of life's nine great ecstasies: love and passion, the intoxication that comes from beauty, from wine and drugs, from moments of high heroism and religious exaltation, from thought and artistic creation."

"And the greatest of these is creation!" Sophistica asserted.

Tellectina suddenly looked down in shy guilt. "I—I am beginning to realize that too." Then she rushed on again: "No, no, life can never be too terrible as long as there is beauty in the world, and the capacity to enjoy it!"

"If, Tina—now wait, damn you, I'm determined to say it this time—if our indigestion will permit. The seat of philosophy is not the brain, remember, but the stomach, and a sour outlook on life is engendered by a s——"

"Spare me," the other protested. "But be that as it may, I still say, let fate do its worst; life can never be too bad as long as we have the sweet intoxication of spring, the ripe voluptuousness of summer, the strange exciting sorrow of autumn, and the comfort of winter firesides; as long as we can enjoy the mystery of moonlight on old gardens, the sight and sound of the eternal sea, the sigh and caress of the light loving winds, the golden warmth of the sun, the lavish grandeur of its setting, the dignity and dearness of trees, and the unutterable loveliness of flowers; as long as we have the dear awkwardness and sweet grace, the ineffable appeal of young things at play, of children and kittens and puppies; the beauty of sequestered pools, of mauve twilights, and mountains languishing under the blue haze of dusk, and the poignant sweetness of singing birds."

"Yes," Sophistica drawled, "the beauties of nature are surpassed only by her cruelties. But, thank goodness, you had the honesty and good taste to omit snow—for of all the hideous, loathsome, messy——"

But Tellectina was drunk on her own words. "All people, no matter how dense and dull, respond sometimes to the beauties of nature, but the beauties created by man remain stimulants to the few.

"A fragment of beauty captured in color or held captive forever in one perfect line; a high moment of perfection caught forever in unchanging marble; mountains of stone, handwrought, great masses looming against the sky, surpassing the dignity and beauty of nature's mountains.

"Sounds that ebb and flow and carry our happiness with them like flotsam on the sea; small magic marks on white paper revealing to man a new heaven and a new earth.

"Designed vistas of trees and fountains uttering the final esthetic word; singing sounds that enkindle, enrapture, soothe, or sadden human emotions; and spoken sounds that enkindle, enrapture, soothe, or sadden human emotions and human thinking; the nice gesture, the subtle expression, engendering complete satisfaction; woods carved and curved, fabrics cut and colored—to continually delight the eye."

"Yes," her companion said, "the beauties mankind exhibits are more in its handiwork than in itself."

"But even human beings—what is so subtle and complicated, so varied as human nature? What so fascinating as to weave or trace the intricate patterns of human thought; to follow or form the subtleties of speech; to witness the dramatic contradictions of human actions and reactions; what so incredibly sweet as the ineffable look of love in the lover's eyes, the unutterable tenderness between lovers, the perfect physical beauty of young girls —breath-taking and ultimate; the quick sure strength of men; rich human laughter, and the lilting voices of happy children?"

"Which sounds lilting for the first five minutes—after that— God spare us—because their mothers won't."

Disregarding her, the young hedonist rushed on. "And all the pleasure one derives from one's self: the sweet rhythmic motion of one's own moving muscles in dancing, walking, swimming, copulating. The joys of eating, drinking, bathing, talking, dreaming, wondering. The caress of the comb in the hair, the warmth of the bed, the silk dress on the ankles and thighs— innumerable small sweet pleasures! The unaccountable and ever fascinating drama of one's own emotions and the sweet sure ways of one's own thinking."

"Narcist!"

"No, hedonist! This living is a continual drama without beginning, without plot and without end, but full of comedy, tragedy, beauty, and pathos—with the greatest virtue of all dramas—it is never dull."

"So I was wrong. Tellectina thinks life is a grand and glorious affair."

"At moments!" The younger woman laughed gayly as she pirouetted about the room.

"Ah, these songs of Tellectina, this ode to beauty and hymn to passion—they make me retract," Sophistica said. "You remind me of something. Not all the Greeks nor even the Latins believed in moderation. There were two poets, Sappho and Catullus, in whom we find more ardent natures, keener sensibilities, and a sensuality so intense as to be noble. They also possess profounder and more subtle minds."

Lifting her eyes, she gazed with intent significance into those of the younger woman, which lowered in pleased embarrassment. "Yes," Sophistica said softly, "and we also meet with another woman whose capacity for intensity of enjoyment amounts to genius."

Suddenly her namesake looked at the clock and sprang up. "God help me, if I haven't kept you up till three in the morning! Forgive me—forgive me!"

"I shouldn't have forgiven you if you hadn't!"

Tellectina smiled and, kissing her aunt on the top of her head, danced merrily out of the room crying, "I'm so happy, so happy! Good-night! Good-night!"

The older woman looked after her with a tender but dubious smile, murmuring, "Wait till tomorrow, when the reaction sets in! There'll be the devil to pay."

Sophistica was far more moved by her niece's rhapsodic outbursts than she cared to show. Making no attempt to sleep, she sat by the window and looked out over the old garden full of gray ghosts in the fog, and thought of many things. Toward morning there could be heard a low sound of moaning. Tiptoeing down the hall, Sophistica located the door from behind which it was issuing. It was Tellectina's.

Turning the handle softly, she entered and in the dawn light could discern the girl tossing on the bed.

"Oh, Auntie, I haven't slept a wink! I'm glad you've come— I thought you were asleep. I'm so sick, so miserable, I wish I could die!"

"I expected this. I thought you were too intelligent to be happy very long. But what can I do?"

"Nothing, nothing. There is no cure for my maladies, I fear."

Sophistica leaned closer and peered at the girl in the dim

light. "Oh, you look quite ill! Why, Tina, you're hot and fever-ish. That horrid old Hynuppa has broken out afresh and come clear up into your face now!"

Tellectina hid her face in the pillow. "Oh, I feared it was chronic! And I'm too vain to have my face spoiled with it—too proud to let the whole world see that I suffer from an incurable affliction."

"Then your happiness last night wasn't real?"

"Oh, yes, it was. It was real but only momentary, temporary—that's the trouble. When I'm talking to you like that I forget all my other pains for the time being. I told you the truth but not the whole truth."

"Come on, I can stand anything—going to have a baby?"

"God forbid, Sophie! Women who've been in Nithking be-come impregnated with worse things than spermatozoa! That's nothing compared to this—this thing that plagues and torments me hourly, incessantly—except when I'm drunk."

"Then get drunk."

"I have, I was tonight—on the sound of my own words while talking with you about beauty and ecstasy and joy. Ah, but you see they are merely the foam on the wave—iridescent, lovely, transient, fleeting—gone in the instant of their forming. Don't speak of them!"

"I didn't. But what about this whole truth and this Hynuppa? Something should be done about the latter, because you really look terrible. But why didn't the armor of gatherulic iron Ca-bell gave you, and of which you boasted so proudly, protect you a little better?"

"Oh, I acquired it too late, the harm had already been done, the Sillidinous poison was already in my blood. I shall wear it to protect me from future harm, however; but nothing except drunkenness or drugs relieves this Hynuppa pain. Yet I can't be drunk all the time on wine, or love, or passion, or even beauty—it ruins my nerves. And the long intervals of soberness are too painful to be borne. I don't know what to do."

"Well, let me put my wits to work. But first, what about Femina—will she interfere with you?"

"Oh, she's coming tomorrow to live with me permanently. We have decided that we may be invaluable to each other— complementary halves, so to speak. She, however, wants men and love all over the place."

"Then she would object to your using this remedy which I was going to suggest for your Hynuppa and blood-poisoning?" Sophistica asked.

"Oh, to hell with Femina! I can keep her quiet if I supply her with plenty of suitors. Oh, help me, Sophie, surely there must be in the world somewhere some kind of remedy for this painful and disfiguring malady. I thought Ghaulot had cured me, but it's chronic; it recedes but invariably returns with increasing pain."

"A physician can prescribe only after she has diagnosed her case."

"I don't understand."

"I shall be obliged to examine you in order to determine the cause of your Hynuppa and the particular form which is afflicting you."

Sophistica proceeded with her own particular method of examination, talking while she did so. "It's not that you can't endure suffering, I'm sure. It is only that you deem it unfair for human beings to be doomed to a life composed more of suffering than of anything else; that the proportion of pain and pleasure is wrong. If only it were half and half, but human living is composed of one fourth pleasure, one fourth active pain, and the rest is just damned dull, but even dullness and boredom are painful, aren't they?"

"Yes, yes," Tellectina moaned as she lay with her eyes closed, submitting to her aunt's extraordinary method of examining her patient.

"No matter how intense or how frequent our joys, they are always outweighed by sorrows. Joy comes in golden moments interspersed among black hours of misery and gray days of drabness. And even if life offered one endless pleasure, the human body, you say, is limited in its capacity for enjoyment?"

"Yes, dammit! Oh, Sophie, at times like this, when I am sleepless, or tired, or ill, I feel that life is too horrible for anybody to face!"

"There, there, my dear, be calm, you only make your Hynuppa worse. I think I've diagnosed your form of this malady correctly and can prescribe—not something which will cure you, that is impossible—but something which will at least alleviate your suffering. I must prepare you for it, however, before I give it to you. You don't seem to realize how fortunate you are, for this medicine cannot be taken by all patients."

"Fortunate?" Tellectina opened her eyes in amazement.

"Yes, for I haven't examined you for nothing, nor have I watched you and heard you talk all night—to say nothing of the information which I gleaned from your travel diary—without perceiving your susceptibility to this drug."

"But the medicine—the drug!" the sick girl begged fretfully.

"My dear, patience is not one of your virtues, is it? You will have to listen to me before I can give it to you, however irrelevant my remarks may seem to you at this moment. You must admit in your saner moments that you revel in your own griefs —you enjoy your own suffering?"

Tellectina dropped her eyelids in guilty haste.

"You revel in the tragic and comic drama of your own life. Through all the dark tapestry of your disillusionments has run a bright golden thread of joy. It is the joy of the artist, detached, impersonal—watching—waiting—making notes. So the artist is the most fortunate person on earth; he is the only human being who is able to enjoy his own sorrows."

Tellectina smiled and turned her face away. "But what is the medicine you propose to give me? And what has my—has one's being an artist to do with this drug?"

"Everything. Now, just you lie still in bed for a minute and I'll go and get it. It's just when the patient is in this excited, feverish condition that the best results are produced."

She left the room hurriedly but soon returned with two objects in her hand and, locking the door, said, "Here it is, my dear. It is a stimulant narcotic which will at least give you temporary relief. It is a drug which renders you unconscious of yourself so completely that all ills and troubles dwindle, fade away, and are not; which fills you with a strange ecstasy the like of which is produced by no other narcotic in the whole world."

"But where is this wonderful drug? I'm in such misery—please hurry. Where is it?"

"Here in this little black cylindrical case is your anodyne." She held up the small black object tipped with gold at one end.

"A drug in that?"

"S—sh!" She placed her fingers on her lips. " 'Drug' is a barred word. The mediocre people of the world look askance at anyone who uses any kind of drug, remember! Only by the use of this, however, can man rise above nature; because the greater part of it is a mixture of human blood, tears, and sweat which—" the patient shuddered—"which by a subtle alchemy are transformed into a palliative. Thus are the gods cheated at their own game, cheated for a few brief hours, at least. For this drug not only produces visions like other morphias, but even makes one feel a veritable god one's self, who creates new worlds and peoples them to suit her own fancy."

"But," Tellectina objected, "it looks like an ordinary little——"

"Ah, it *looks!* That is to deceive stupid people." She lifted a little gold lever, whereupon a black fluid flowed out the point.

"But I swear it's a clever deception! Most people would use it as an ordinary——"

"Of course they would. But the way a person applies it is the whole secret of its efficacy as a narcotic." She showed the sick girl how to apply it, adding, "But you can't deceive me: your diary reveals that you have used this drug in some form before."

"Well—er—look in my desk drawer there. That little yellow container with the gray powder in it. I have taken this drug, though I hesitated to confess it to anyone. People hate abnormality in others."

"I suspected that Tellectina had enjoyed the pleasures of Cianite Vitrgrew before—that's why I recommended it to you. Form the pernicious habit now more strongly than ever, for although in the end it will probably ruin your health—for even the strongest constitutions degenerate under its constant use—this—with the wearing of the gatherulic iron armor—is the only way to render life tolerable. It will give you, with continued use, a pleasure that none of the other stimulant narcotics—wine, passion, and morphias—can give."

The invalid was turning it slowly in her hands, a strange slow smile on her lips, while her companion stood staring out the window at the approaching dawn. Softly Sophistica said:

"It is better than hashish or opium, which transport you to a land of pleasing visions. For when you take this Cianite Vitrgrew it lifts you to the land of the Trista, where, I repeat, you feel a veritable god. You find the earth without proper form and void. So you create a new heaven and a new earth, you create man in your own image, male and female create you them. You form men and women of the dust of the ground and breathe into their nostrils the breath of life, and they become living souls. And then you look forth upon your handiwork, and behold, it is very good, and you rest from all that which you have made.

"And in this land of the Trista, since you are omnipotent, there is none to oppose you. You may create men in the likeness of your worst enemies and there is none to say you nay. You may create gods in your own likeness. You can bring into being lands as fair as a dream; you can assert your opinion on all subjects and there is none to contradict you. What greater satisfaction can man, or woman either, want? And for those who cling obstinately to their own opinions but are too lazy to defend them, the land of the Trista is ideal. It is the place where you can enjoy complete self-expression—the thing we all desire.

"Finding the world you inhabit imperfect, you can create a

new world nearer your heart's desire, you can people it with fair creatures—lovers who never cease to love, friends who never betray or grow dull, you can fashion a veritable paradise. You can make people here speak not as they do but as they should —poetically, wisely, and wittily—as well as rhetorically. Life has nothing better to offer than this. For as long as you remain under the influence of Cianite Vitrgrew you continue to inhabit this paradise of your own creation. The ugliness that surrounds you fades away, the pain in your body, the ache in your heart, disappear. You have no need for riches, nor food, nor sleep, nor love—you possess the world and all that's in it. You know neither fatigue nor illness, for you are a god. The fretful shortcomings of those about you fade into oblivion; you are filled with adventure and romance and beauty indescribable. . . . And thus endeth Sophistica's hymn to creation."

She paused, then shrugged and added, "Yes, you can be a god —until your nerves rebel, until the drug wears off and you come down to earth with a crash. True, 'the state of your nerves is deplorable' but it was worth it."

Suddenly Tellectina sat up in bed with glowing eyes. "Now I can make my confession. I have been bursting with it for a long time. You are the only one I would dare to tell—other people might think I was insane or merely ridiculous. I know that you are right and that the weakness for Cianite Vitrgrew runs in our family. I have been mildly addicted to it ever since I accidentally discovered its joys at sixteen, at which time I frequently used to remain under its influence till two in the morning. Of course, when my mother discovered this unhealthy habit in her child, she took drastic means to break her of it. But I continued to indulge secretly. Some of my young schoolmates, but particularly my English teacher, who seemed to have a good eye for such irregularities in young people, commented on the results it produced.

"I have succumbed to it periodically ever since. But I led such an active and exciting life that I seldom allowed myself the leisure and peace which its use requires, although I was constantly haunted by the idea that I would eventually fall a helpless victim to it. But little did I dream of the astounding, incredible power or pleasure it held until I accidentally got an overdose on Mt. Ghaulot.

"It was not until I attained Certitude that I felt a desire to sit down and remain inactive for a while. The high altitude and the exciting experiences in Cabell's house had left my nerves in such an agitated state that I felt it was absolutely imperative to resort to Cianite Vitrgrew. An irresistible desire seized me. I grasped the little yellow container which I always kept at hand, and the thing which happened to me after that is indescribable and glorious beyond words. As I sat there I was filled with sudden unaccountable joy. I began to see the most ravishing visions. A whole new world opened up to me. . . .

"For hours on end I forgot to sleep or eat or rest. Wherever I went the vision stayed in front of my eyes. When I walked I seemed to float, I seemed to have no weight, no body. I forgot the time of day, I forgot the cold, I knew no fatigue. The last thing I saw when I finally fell into an exhausted sleep each night and the first thing I saw when I opened my eyes every morning before the sun was even up was this vision.

"I took another injection. I was too happy to sleep much, too excited—and this lasted for weeks, waxing and waning, but the glow did not die away for months.

"It left me ill and exhausted, but it was perfect; more glorious than any sensation a human being can experience. I used to sit there motionless sometimes and feel such great waves of this shining ecstasy surge over me that I was frightened. I thought I was losing my mind or would the next minute be translated, like Elijah, and borne straight up into heaven. Once I felt like the Virgin Mary when the angel of the annunciation came to inform her that she was to give birth to a god! Everything was illuminated as with a great invisible light, a shining radiance of its own like the masterpieces of the holy family and the saints. Ecstasy descended on me out of the shining luminous nowhere, seized upon me, shook me, left me limp and indescribably happy, leaving in its wake a sort of orgasmic satisfaction deeper, more profound than any physical sensation could ever be.

"Ah, the very memory of that phenomenal experience re-awakens my desire for Cianite Vitrgrew!" Oblivious of the other's presence, Tellectina began to apply the drug in the proper manner.

Gradually her fever subsided, the Hynuppa disappeared from her face. And as Sophistica stole noiselessly out of the room, an ineffably happy smile slowly spread over the sick girl's face—that smile peculiar to the victims of Cianite Vitrgrew. . . .

Hours passed. . . .

Then a knock came on the door, and Sophistica's mocking eyes showed in the opening. "Sorry, but there's a young man downstairs who wants to see Femina. He seems quite convinced that he is her fiancé."

Tellectina turned unseeing eyes on the intruder. Slowly that far-away look faded, and not till then did she speak, "Oh, damn Femina and all her men!"

But she laid aside the black cylindrical container with far more alacrity than was to be expected in so ardent an addict to Cianite Vitrgrew and hastily began to don her most feminine and seductive underwear.

AFTERWORD

GLOSSARY

WORKS CITED

For
Claire Myers Spotswood Owens
1896–1983
and for the friends and colleagues
whose love and care
perpetuate her memory

AFTERWORD

CLAIRE MYERS SPOTSWOOD OWENS
A "GRAND AMOUREUSE"

Miriam Kalman Harris

> You may think that when you die, you
> disappear, you no longer exist. But even
> though you vanish, something which is
> existent cannot be non-existent.
> —Shunryu Suzuki

February 2, 1991
Rochester, New York

W E DECIDED not to light the white candles. After all, the
sun was still shining outside, and the candles looked so
attractive positioned on the mantle next to the portrait. Claire
must have been in her fifties when this was painted. Elegant,
still beautiful, no . . . handsome—I stepped back to get a
better look—I would describe her as a commanding presence:
white evening gown, white roses in her greying hair, set against
a deep scarlet background.

My first introduction to Claire Myers Spotswood Owens had
been through a different portrait, the mate to this one, of an
earlier Claire: a woman in her middle years, early forties, holding a book and seated beside several more, wearing a grey suit
and a hat made of pink roses. What attracted me? Some dynamic life force that flowed from the painting and captivated
my imagination? My kind of colors perhaps, mauve, purple,
green. Or the books? Books were her life. Books, learning,

knowledge, laughter, and love. Oh, yes—love. Claire was ever
and ever in love.

The guests begin to arrive. Margaret, Marion, Geoffrey, Barbara—Claire's friends at the end of her life and members of the
Zen community here in Rochester. Most of them appear as characters, all under pseudonyms, of course, in *Zen and the Lady,* her
last published book. The occasion for this gathering at the home
of Audrey Fernandez has come to be known as the Annual CMO
tea held to commemorate her birthday. This year it is held one
week early, to accommodate my travel schedule. On February
11, she would have been ninety-five. May 7 of this year will
mark the eighth anniversary of her death.

"When she moved here she must have been seventy-four,"
Audrey recalls. "But she never seemed old. She had such an
expansive spirit. She never seemed confined by her body the way
many older people are, hunched at the shoulders. She had a
good physique, held herself well, and just did not seem old. She
said she always thought of herself as in her forties." We are
waiting now for Dwain Wilder, referred to as Dexter in *Zen and
the Lady.* In his absence, he becomes the center of our conversation because he had been the center of Claire's final years and
the catalyst to her move here, a move that defined her as no less
an adventurer in her old age than she had been in her youth.

The themes of her writing are the themes of her life: youth
and age, love and work, women's rights and self-definition. A
woman in her seventies meets a man in his twenties. Sparks fly!
Who can believe it? How am I, her biographer, to understand
this? Having met Claire Owens three years ago, first through
that portrait, next in the boxes of books and manuscripts, letters, photographs, and tapes at the Blagg-Huey Library and
then deciding to make her writing the subject of my own, I
made this trip to Rochester to try to solve this one last mystery
and to meet her friends, one friend in particular.

"Society accepts sexuality between older men and younger
women," Audrey is saying, "but never older women with

younger men. But now we have a glut of people in the world and maybe we can begin to regard women in other capacities than their reproductive one." Audrey and I have explored this issue in depth into the late hours of the previous night. She is filling the rest of the group in on our discussion. It occurs to me, however, that this circle of friends had accepted Dwain's and Claire's attraction to one another at the time, though certainly they each had their own speculations.

"In a society where women are valued for the span of their whole lives and not just for their childbearing years," Audrey continued, "there may exist the possibility of new types of relationships. We'll begin to see older women and younger men and not be shocked. We'll be able to talk about it in polite company."

Geoff:	My sense, though, with Claire, when she told me about it, was that what happened between her and Dwain was just so karmic—for both of them it was karmic—that it was just irresistible. And yet painful because of the age difference, and they were just so taken with each other.
Margaret:	It seems to me that she had a great enjoyment in flirting, the power to attract.
Marion:	Isn't that characteristic of a southern belle?
Audrey:	Yes, and with Claire, there was an extra quality when the men were involved. With women she was straightforward, as if to say, "I don't have to use my wiles with you." But with men there was the sense of a challenge—yes, that's how she was brought up—and there was always an extra sparkle.
Margaret:	She loved to talk about men and women. In my memory that was one of her favorite topics— the polarity, the tension, the search for a resolu-

tion. She loved to talk, loved to visit with friends. But never small talk. Always deep philosophical issues.

The energy that was Claire lights their faces as each tells a favorite anecdote, recalls a special moment spent in complex intellectual discussion seasoned with laughter.

Barbara: There was always laughter around Claire. She had such a wonderful laugh.

The room grows quiet and still, each person lost in private reminiscences. A warm glow from the setting sun slants through the living room shutters. Audrey brings forth a fresh pot of tea and sets it down next to the remaining lemon tarts. Margaret breaks the silence: "She would just love today. It seems so funny not to have her here with us." And I answer, "But she is here."

To understand Claire and to appreciate her as a character, a protagonist of her life story, who transforms rather ordinary circumstances into an extraordinary life, we must understand the significance of the underlying dichotomies shaping the nature of her struggle. The struggle is built on a paradox, and the roots of the paradox grow out of Texas soil and her southern heritage. As she tells it: "I was born in the Deep South in the heart of Texas; most people think of Texas as being a western state with cowboys and large ranches. But that's the *western* part of the state. I never saw a live cowboy in my life." Her voice bounces with youthful vibrancy as she speaks in a taped interview from 1979 with Kenneth Ring, professor of psychology at the University of Connecticut, at her home in Rochester after the publication of *Zen and the Lady,* which she began writing the day she turned eighty. "My roots are in central Texas, the black belt, and that means rich black land good for growing cotton. Half of our town was black," she says, acknowledging the double meaning of the word. "But our whole town was submerged in old southern traditions" (Owens 1979b, cassette no. 1A).

Born in 1896 in Rockdale, Texas, Clairene Lenora Allen Myers's childhood home was in nearby Temple, a small town situated in what was known not only as the black belt but also as "the heart of the bible belt." Her youth was influenced by the lingering traces of old Virginia plantation life perpetuated through the moralistic teachings of her mother, Susan Allen Myers, and her maternal grandmother, Laura Smith Allen, who were primarily concerned that their young charge "grow up to be a proper southern belle, a lady." Claire describes her grandmother as a woman who considered herself an "exile of Virginia" and who tried to inculcate in her "not just the ways of southern aristocracy but [also] the southern values in the days before emancipation, the days of antebellum south" (Owens 1979b, cassette no. 1A).

She characterizes her mother as intuitive in contrast to the rather fierce intellectuality of her father, Coren Lee Myers, and remembers her as very civic-minded: once a group of townsmen came to the house to ask her mother to run for governor. But her father, a schoolteacher and principal, wouldn't have it at all. It was not the proper role for a lady, and her mother demurred in good southern fashion.* She was a woman of exceedingly conventional values, "friendly toward people who shared her belief systems, yet very intolerant of those with differing beliefs" (Owens 1979, cassette no. 1A). Claire had to resist her

---

*Susan Allen Myers must have been approached to run for governor after 1920, the year women were given the right to vote in Texas. In the tapes, Claire recalls the moment as if it occurred in her childhood, though typically, she is unspecific about dates. It is possible that the incident occurred during one of Claire's visits after she moved away. For example, she came home for a three-year period during the 1920s following an unhappy love affair with a sculptor, who was separated from his wife. Texas was the ninth state to approve the Nineteenth Amendment, on August 20, 1920. "The first five years of the 1920s were . . . the woman's day in Texas," according to Anne Firor Scott in A. Elizabeth Taylor, *Citizens at Last: The Woman Suffrage Movement in Texas* (Austin: Ellen C. Temple, 1987), xiii. The first woman governor of Texas was Miriam (Ma) Ferguson, who served two terms, 1925–27 and 1933–35. No other woman served as governor until Ann Richards took office in 1991.

family's attitudes in order to develop her own values, a set of beliefs that taught her to rebel, frequently in ways that nurtured others.

She writes often and painfully that even in early childhood, her mother never loved her. Favoring Claire's more traditional brother, Coren Douglas, Susan Myers was emotionally distant from her daughter. Undemonstrative and critical, she filled young Claire with strict Puritan admonitions against pleasure, beauty, and love. Sex was duty for women, pleasure for men; dancing was strictly forbidden; divorce was an unthinkable disgrace. The highest virtue for a woman was to be "ladylike": "Daughter, can't you run more . . . quietly," she scolded when she discovered Claire running in the wind, her "favorite sport" (Owens 1935, 24; Owens 1958, 41, 47).

Still, for Claire, her great love and respect of family resided in her memories of her father. "He was a born teacher and a very religious man. But he rejected the precepts of the church. He said he just couldn't understand them and when no preacher could explain them to his satisfaction, he took to the woods." Her father's response dismayed her mother and grandmother because they were both "ardent Baptists—even fundamentalists." "The woods were my father's cathedral and he walked and explored and communicated with nature" in a way Claire came to appreciate, years later, as that same deeply spiritual relationship with which she communed with the universe (Owens 1979b).

She describes her father as strictly domineering but with a gentle soul, "the iron hand in the velvet glove." He spoke to Claire in a way that showed he valued her mind and shared her deep reverence for books. Still, when she longed to go to the University of Texas in Austin and study literature and philosophy, her father resisted and delivered her to the steps of the College of Industrial Arts in Denton, now Texas Woman's University, where her archive now resides.

Again, her father's actions present something of a paradox. His teachings, his love of literature, his staunch belief in Jeffersonian democracy, and his acknowledgment of Claire's intellectual promise ignited in her a deep love for education, ethics, and universal justice; yet his belief in old southern traditions and his dominance over the women in his life narrowed the options for both his wife and his daughter.

It didn't matter. Claire loved college and hungrily devoured every course from physics, geology, and anthropology to literature and philosophy. Her unfinished and unpublished "Autobiography," which spans most of her eighty-seven years, captures the cultural and historical atmosphere of life at a woman's college in her day:

> Our society teaches us that women's lives must be lived through some man. We accepted this without question in 1912. The importance of intellectual pursuits held up to us as an ideal by the faculty had small chance against society's pre-determined role for women.
>
> In our leisure we strolled about the campus . . . talking endlessly about men, marriage, love, and romance—always romance. Never sex in broad daylight. That was considered very bad taste—if not immoral. We were all waiting breathlessly for a tall dark handsome man to appear and sweep us off our feet and to be married. We wasted many a precious hour . . . dreaming about romance.
>
> In books, men—even great men—have recounted their constant preoccupation with sex. But it is romance with which women—even middle-aged, married women—are preoccupied. Even in this day of the women's liberation movement, the only books that sell in the millions are novels of romance. Maybe this is women's curse: not menstruation like my mother said, but romance. (Owens ca. 1970–80)

The library soon proved to be a refuge from the unceasing giggling and chatter of girls, to which, she writes, "I added more than my share." Here, in the presence of "so many books and quiet," Claire's intellectual hunger was a catalyst for transcending the confining mores of her era. She had to conceal from friends, both girls and boys, her interest and excitement in "intellectual matters." But looking back she realized that college aroused in her an awareness of the possibility of "living an intellectual life." During her senior year, when most of her classmates were fluttering about deciding which beau to marry, Claire broke her engagement. After graduating with a bachelor's degree in domestic science, she returned home; her liberated ideas concerning her future collided with the values of two matriarchs and one patriarch planning her social debut.

At age twenty in 1916, Claire left home with a dream in her heart to "save the world overnight and . . . to abolish poverty and suffering immediately" (Owens 1979b, cassette no. 1A). When she informed her parents of plans to leave Temple and go to work, her father disinherited her. "A lady never works." She loved her father, but she loved freedom more and felt a compulsive need to discover "her true self," though she had no idea what that meant at the time.

In a recent conversation, John White, Claire's literary agent during her life and literary executor after her death, characterized her as a "pioneer: sweet, cultured, high-minded. When she left Texas in 1916, she left with a sense of daring and risk for something nameless and intuitive, something only felt, a search for an expansive life" White calls a "heroic enterprise" instead of a "goal-oriented move" (White 1990). "I had never read anything about a girl, a lady, going out to work," Claire said. "See, we were way behind the times. I'd never read about social service. When I left, I left with just a wind of desire and no clear plan" (Owens 1979b, cassette no. 1A).

No plan, but a sense of adventure. I have come to realize after these several years of studying Claire's work that an adventure is a journey without a map; it is inherently unpredictable. Leaving Texas when she did, tossing away the map of predictability awaiting her in Temple, she transformed the journey of her life into an adventure, an unpredictable adventure.

During those early years dramatized in *The Unpredictable Adventure*, "Claire did settlement house and social work in Chicago, New York City, and in an Alabama mining camp. Her wide range of experiences included living in a commune in the Blue Ridge Mountains of Virginia" (White 1983). She eventually moved to New York, worked at Dauber & Pine and several other well-known New York bookshops, wrote reviews for *Publishers Weekly,* and organized a rigorous, disciplined work schedule that permitted her to write her book and socialize with her many "beaux" among New York's literati.

In the early thirties, working in bookstores, she was struck by two trends that she found deeply disturbing. "All the popular non-fiction books were concerned with physical adventure like safaris in Africa, climbing Mt. Everest, or swimming the Hellespoint *{sic}*. Physical adventure was considered life's supreme adventure. I felt outraged. Surely the supreme goal in life was the intellectual search for certitude, for ultimate truth embodied in a work of art, preferably literature—novels, drama, poetry, or essays" (Owens ca. 1970–80). Furthermore, Claire noticed that adventure books always had male heroes. Where were the female adventurers? Claire knew only too well where they could be found. She decided to take matters into her own hands. Goaded by these popular trends in what she considered the wrong direction, she felt a "strong urge to write a different kind of book" (Owens ca. 1970–80).

Creative writing, she soon discovered, was the most exciting experience she had ever known, "more exciting than love or passion or popularity."

> To write creatively, I learned, is to run the gamut of experiences. To pursue elusive thoughts is more exhilarating than a fox hunt. To disentangle a tangle of ideas is as exciting a challenge as stopping a street fight. . . .
>
> Creating a novel is an architectural process. The writer pushes and pulls, inserts and removes, rejects and rearranges. Words, phrases, sentences, paragraphs become like blocks of marble. Unlike marble, however, they acquire a will of their own. One polishes the exterior and hopes it will become a thing of beauty. . . .
>
> Gradually one erects an enormous edifice, its inner framework concealed from the eyes of others. One's book assumes a person-

ality of its own, a life as real as that of a beautiful woman—it seemed feminine even to me the most feminine of women (Owens ca. 1970–80).

She began to write every Sunday and holiday, finding that "the creative writer ceases to care if she ever sees her friends, or men, or theater, has love or passion, ever rests or sleeps or eats. She forgets time and place, what day it is, what hour, whether she has eaten or not" (Owens ca. 1970–80). Enamored with the physical joy of writing, she eventually began accepting week-night dinner dates on the condition that her escort would have her home by eight o'clock. "They protested but submitted, ungracefully" (Owens ca. 1970–80).

From this regimen arose her adventure novel, an allegory modeled on the Jurgen books by James Branch Cabell, but with a female protagonist searching for the highest mountain in the world, Mount Certitude. "Her name was Tellectina, the intellectual woman. Her twin sister however was Femina who cared only for love, romance, men, and marriage. She was a great deterrent. But a third woman mysteriously emerged from nowhere, unplanned, uninvited, unwelcome. Aunt Sophistica. She pranced through the pages full of laughter and cynicism" (Owens ca. 1970–80).

In many ways Sophistica represents the voice and experience of the author speaking back through time to her younger self, as characterized by Tellectina and her shadow, Femina. Interestingly, Sophie doesn't speak directly to Femina—they would not speak the same language—but speaks to Tellectina in a voice that foreshadows both women's concerns, a voice that represents wholeness. Perhaps Claire found the delightful Sophie unwelcome and intrusive because in life she was not really there. After all, this is an autobiographical novel fictionalizing the events of the author's life through age thirty. In interviews and in writing, Claire often complained of the lack of models in life and in literature. Fairy tales offered misleading and unrealistic promises. Novels ended in marital bliss. Claire had to learn the ways

of the world on her own. She had no mentors, no sense of precedence for the choices she made, only foresight, intuition, and
guts.

On the other hand, even in her thirties Claire had not reached
the level of sophistication she portrays in Sophistica. That is,
not yet. Sophie is the "not-yet" of utopian fiction: mentor,
model, and goal—the ideal woman Claire hopes to become as
she writes her into existence—a "grand amoureuse." Thus the
journey from southern belle to grand amoureuse is, predictably,
an unpredictable adventure.

Subtitled, "A Comedy of Woman's Independence," the novel
explores society's double standards that divide woman against
herself. Tellectina, the protagonist and heroine, leaves Smug
Harbor, her hometown in the Land of Err, where the only language spoken is Halfish, to travel in the Forbidden Country of
Nithking, an anagram for thinking, where Reasonese is spoken.
Anagrams establish an allegorical pattern; people and places become symbols of obstacles, insights, goals, and psychological
conditions. The heroine strives to reach the top of Mount Certitude, where she hopes to look out upon "Truth" and attain her
ultimate goal of self-realization. A *künstlerroman* ahead of its
time, *The Unpredictable Adventure* hums with feminist yearnings
for freedom, autonomy, career, and marital relationships with
nongender-defined roles and daringly explores female sexuality
to the point that it was banned by the New York Public Library
shortly after its release.*

---

*This novel lends itself to an archetypal study, informed by Jungian anal-
ysis. For useful feminist theories, see Kim Chernin, *Reinventing Eve: Modern
Woman in Search of Herself* (New York: Harper and Row, 1987). See also Jean
Shinoda Bolen, *Goddesses in Everywoman: A New Psychology of Women* (New
York: Harper and Row, 1985); Penelope Washburn, *Becoming Woman: The
Quest for Wholeness in Female Experience* (San Francisco: Harper and Row, 1977);
and Carol S. Pearson, *The Hero Within: Six Archetypes We Live By*, expanded ed.
(New York: Harper and Row, 1989).

The protagonist, like her author, is a rebel with myriad causes, ranging from female independence to outcries against political corruption, social injustice, war, and religious hypocrisy. Yet here lies another touch of irony: Claire published the book under the name Claire Myers Spotswood to exploit her prestigious connections to the eighteenth-century Virginia governor Alexander Spotswood, whose lineage traced to Martha Washington, even though the values she satirizes include those she had definitely left behind.

Aunt Sophistica takes pride in her protégée's courage. Reversing the truisms common to Tellectina's fundamentalist and Puritan background, Sophie advises her *not* to be careful but to "be wise and rush in where fools fear to tread," *not* to let conscience be her guide, but desire. "Throw yourself into this expedition with a whole heart—half measures are for puny people. Abandon yourself recklessly to the passion of living, for it is the grand passion. . . . Be the grand amoureuse of life—for you receive from life, your lover, only what you give him. And the best lovers reside in Nithking, of course" (Owens 1935, 73–74).

The name Tellectina Femina Christian embodies aspects of the protagonist's psychological identity. Tellectina, the intellectually curious, aggressive, male-*modeled* self, is pitted against Femina, the passive, ladylike, nurturing, seductive, and male-*identified* self, antagonistic to all worldly pursuit. These two "natural sisters" meet unexpectedly during Tina's first day at college and, throughout the rest of the novel, emerge and converse with one another as separate selves, each arguing, foiling, and tricking the other in an effort to win control. Once Femina appears, she exists as if she were a separate character. Because the novel is set in the realm of the fantastic, the paradox seems plausible. Neither persona, however, can develop into natural wholeness because each has been split off from the other through the moralistic upbringing represented by their surname. "Christian" functions as a superego or patriarchal conscience by structuring the two personae, which appear, disappear, divide, and reunite throughout the novel.

"One is not born, but rather becomes, a woman. No biological, psychological, or economic fate determines the figure that the human female presents in society; it is civilization as a whole that produces this creature" (de Beauvoir 1952, 301). And what kind of creatures are we? Creatures divided and fragmented into bundles of tensions in opposition to each other, a morass of binary splits spinning in turmoil. Male against female, thinking against feeling, religion against spirituality, intellect against intuition. In each dichotomy, society privileges the male-associated trait over the female-associated trait.* What is a thinking woman to do? "To be a Tellectina is at once a blessing and curse" (Owens 1935, 15). Given the autobiographical context of the novel, it becomes clear that a woman, with a free spirit who is living life as an adventure, is not only a heretical creature but also a physical impossibility.

"What have you done to me?" Tellectina asks Femina. "Must I be divided into two people just because I think one thing and feel another? Which am I?" (Owens 1935, 47). Tellectina loves "to read and study better than anything"; Femina loves "to flirt and make boys fall in love." Sensing her power, Femina announces her intention that she will not "be kept imprisoned any longer!" She will not be repressed. Yet Tina knows that Femina's presence renders her powerless; society will oppress both of them.

The answer is to change society, to restructure the world into a community "where women can live in perfect freedom, perfect equality, and perfect love" (Owens 1935, 99). But first come the questions. Noequists rebel against traditional society represented by the land of Err. The woman Noequist is a symbol of the feminist question as it prevailed in debates in *fin de siècle* society. Women questioning the "gender arrangements in soci-

---

*For discussions of binary or oppositional thinking by feminist theorists, see Genevieve Lloyd, *The Man of Reason: "Male" and "Female" in Western Philosophy* (Minneapolis: Univ. of Minnesota Press, 1984) and Rosemarie Tong, *Feminist Thought: A Comprehensive Introduction* (Boulder, Colo.: Westview, 1989).

ety and culture," Carolyn Heilbrun explains in her definition of feminism, "[work] to change them; the desired transformation gives more power to women while simultaneously challenging both the forms and the legitimacy power as it is now established" (Heilbrun 1990, 3).

The cooperative community of New Chimera empowers women; indeed, the colony is established around the worship of Freewoman and Freelove, two icons of female sexuality. For Tellectina, freedom is an absence of the constrictions associated with institutionalized matrimony, religion, family tradition, and morality. Trained experts care for children, leaving women free to work and become "men's equals." The segment functions as a tragi-comic search for the New Woman's place and role in society.*

Claire anticipates the fundamental tenet of contemporary feminism: that the personal be viewed as the political. Tellectina's visit to the City of Famous Women becomes a search through literary history for models. Although Tina "admired, respected, and envied" the women she encountered, such as Madame de Staël, George Sand, and George Eliot, she considered their courage in taking lovers defective, "being a desire for pleasure rather than an assertion of freedom." Tina is looking for politi-

---

*Carol Farley Kessler considers this depiction of the "Colony of New Chimera, where free women worship the Goddess Frewo," to be a "critique of the 1920s Flapper" because the *free love* they revere as the Priestess Frelo turns out to be a deception" (1984, 15). This chapter, and the novel as a whole, dramatizes the struggle of the New Woman to break from the constraints of the Victorian world view and establish new codes of behavior. For discussions of the Woman Question and the New Woman in *fin de siècle* society and literature, see Elaine Showalter, *Sexual Anarchy: Gender and Culture at the Fin de Siècle* (New York: Viking, 1990); Gail Cunningham, *The New Woman and the Victorian Novel* (New York: Harper and Row, 1978); Patricia Stubbs, *Women and Fiction: Feminism and the Novel, 1880-1920* (New York: Harper and Row, 1979); Martha Vicinus, *Independent Women: Work and Community for Single Women, 1850-1920* (Chicago: Univ. of Chicago Press, 1985); and Lillian Faderman, *Surpassing the Love of Men: Romantic Friendship and Love Between Women from the Renaissance to the Present* (New York: William Morrow, 1981).

cal commitment reflected in the personal lives of her would-be heroines. She does not find it. Their life-styles, not their literary contributions, fail; thus "there were none who were true worshipers of either Freewoman or Freelove and all were consequently outside the fold of the saved." Unfortunately, in her disappointment, Tina neglects to take heed of the exemplary life of Mary Wollstonecraft, "the one woman prepared to direct them" and leads the expedition away from the city (Owens 1935, 106).

Even in the pages of women's literary history, a philosophical framework is needed to recognize the lessons and to read our past into our future. Adrienne Rich writes, "What does a woman need to know to become a self-conscious, self-defining human being? Doesn't she need a knowledge of her own history, of her much-politicized female body, of the creative genius of the past . . . doesn't she need an analysis of her condition, a knowledge of the women thinkers of the past who have reflected on it . . . of women's world-wide individual rebellions and organized movements?" (1986, 1–2). Women look to their past for guidance, and it just isn't there. Tellectina misses the signals and discredits the writers as role models in the City of Women because she lacks an educated feminist consciousness. Deriving from a Puritanical background and the restrictions of a woman's college, she is a product of that gap in education that deprives women of their own heritage. Recognizing a similar lack in her own experience, Claire had to start from the beginning by creating a new consciousness out of the void.

In the chapter on New Chimera, Claire uses humor to satirize the possibility of constructing a utopian society; for as the name indicates, New Chimera represents a monster built out of ignorance and zest. In order to achieve a utopian state, one must first construct a utopian self built on a combination of self-knowledge and experience.*

---

*The assumptions found in chapters 5, 9, and 10 that "dark-skinned" natives are closer to nature and more sexually free, and had something to teach

"Feminist Utopian visions help us frame a new consciousness permitting the exploration of a more complete range of human possibilities," writes Carol Farley Kessler (1984, 6). Thus the failure of New Chimera indicates that utopia is an outgrowth of the process of self-discovery, not a society structured to create a utopian self. For Clair the not-yet is not a place but a way of being in the world. The not-yet dissolves away through the lived experiences of the adventure to make room for a new way of being, one the young intellectual dreams of discovering.

Doing, even through failure, is part of becoming. "Follow your bliss," Joseph Campbell advises; "deserve your dreams," offers Octavio Paz, for, according to Carol Farley Kessler, "as we dare to dream of the not yet known, we change our mindset concerning the possible. As we try to imagine the unimaginable—namely, where we're going before we're there, we move ourselves toward new and as yet unrealized ends" (1984, 7). What is possible must be fashioned by making the not-yet exist. As Tellectina resolves near the end of her journey, it is "wise to believe in one's dreams but only by endeavoring to attain them can mankind {sic} ever progress" (Owens 1935, 383).

Leaving New Chimera and her unhappy union with Olev the Second, a consequence once again of a woman being deprived of vital information, Tellectina is off in search of her dreams of discovering Certitude, her hope for the absolute truth regarding a way to function in the world as a self-realized woman. Through all her adventures, she holds fast to her philosophy of free love

---

the "white woman" reveal an underlying racism that was part of cultural perceptions in general and the author's upbringing in particular. The underlying homophobia, expressed in Tellectina's relationship with Ray Niviso and in other brief passages, reflects the influence of the writings of Richard Krafft-Ebing and Havelock Ellis on the author. In her lifelong quest for enlightenment and self-realization, Claire struggled to transcend the narrow-minded stereotypes inherent in society and in her background. She would embrace and reject many theories, but her drive for a broad understanding of the human condition remained part of her character for her entire life.

and communal living. Femina ensnares men with her feminine charms and Tina struggles to hold their interest through reason and idealism, without sacrificing her autonomy.*

Although Tellectina falls for Elam Domitann, he loves Femina. Throughout this tempestuous affair and brief marriage, they argue in diatribes that explore issues of female dependency; he calls her "inconsiderate" for wanting to work. She insists that he doesn't want a "real person" but a "bowl of jelly" he can press into his "particular mold": "As long as a woman permits a man to support her," Tina rages, "it's in the very nature of the bargain that she must pay in return . . . by subservience" (Owens 1935, 201–2). Indeed, her marriage to Elam represents a compromise of her convictions as a free spirit; she agrees to marriage only when rumors of their adulterous relationship, perpetrated by the narrow-minded college community, threaten their teaching careers. While Elam's death frees her, it does not resolve her split personality. Tina sets out into the world again while grief-stricken Femina disappears, and the two halves remain divided.

No matter what the circumstance, no matter what the place, Tellectina eventually returns to her central concern: how can I relate to a man with my feminine, intuitive, and sensual self, without losing, camouflaging, or compromising my masculine, assertive, intellectual capacities and my goal of functioning as a sexually free, financially autonomous woman? She repeatedly faces dilemmas that force her to choose one self over the other, Femina or Tellectina. Society, religion, and cultural mores keep her forever divided.

Kim Chernin writes that her search for self evolved into a search for the ancient mother goddess, a quest for a pre-Judeo-

*The concept of relational autonomy as a feminist ideal replacing the concept of male autonomy obtained through separation is discussed in theories developed in Catherine Keller, *From a Broken Web: Separation, Sexism, and Self* (Boston: Beacon, 1986); Evelyn Fox Keller, *Reflections on Gender and Science* (New Haven: Yale Univ. Press, 1985); and Carol Gilligan, *In a Different Voice: Psychological Theory and Women's Development* (Cambridge, Mass.: Harvard Univ. Press, 1982).

Christian Eve that becomes a search for the "Woman Who Is Not Yet." According to Chernin, "when a woman, divided within herself, seeks for wholeness and authentic power . . . the mother goddess speaks. From dreams, from nature, from memory, she leads our development forward by guiding us into the past, to a reexperience of the time we knew the mother in her majesty, before we split off this knowledge, losing with it the fundamental roots of female being" (1987, 77).

In Tina's case, the call of the mother goddess comes from the Seven Siren Islands, a world of mythical proportions designed in an elaborate metaphorical and anagrammatical scheme. Here Tellectina is initiated into the "native orgies," and here Femina's personality rises to its greatest strength. In a temple that monumentalizes female anatomy, Tina discovers, to her dismay, that Femina has already engaged in rituals with the high priest Passino in their worship of the God Ecstaci.

The erotic symbology reverses our expectations and describes rites of passage designed by a woman to satisfy her own secret fantasies. This section is written in a language that moves between the satiric and poetic and is filled with humor, innuendoes, and double entendres. The author invents a sexual mythology celebrating woman's natural creative power, as she explores female passion and desire and her need to express herself freely, guiltlessly.

Tellectina's apprehension in the face of the "indecent beauty" of the island and the unbridled passion of the rituals reflects her failure to overcome the repressive remnants of her moralistic upbringing. Although she has been involved in two intimate relationships with men, all the while arguing rigorously for women's sexual freedom, Femina interceded each time to experience the romantic and passionate moments, leaving each persona dissatisfied and the dichotomy between morality and sensuality unresolved.

When Femina chants "The Vaginae," the "Woman's Song of Ecstasy," she teaches her sister to celebrate female creative power. "I am a flower, full blown . . . a bed of lotus blossoms opening wide voluptuous petals . . . his eyes and lips and hands a swarm of hungry bees that sip and rifle me of all my honey. I am . . . the parched and hungry earth . . . wherein all the rivers of all the world fill and rise and rush headlong to the primal sea, when ecstasy moves within me" (Owens 1935, 285). She is woman giving; she is woman taking. In the transcendent "moment of moments," the ecstasy of sexual union, she becomes mother and mistress to man; he becomes child and lover. Each gives and receives pleasure and in so doing perpetuates the harmony and balance of the cycle of life.

Finally Tina, reluctant but primed, follows Femina and the priest into the temple for the final initiation ceremony. Tina struggles to keep "her eyes open and her mind calm, but her lids were heavy and her thoughts rose and fell upon delicious waves of sensation." She is swept away as Femina's voice whispers in her ear: "In this moment of white heat we become one . . . united, irrevocably and forever. The twain shall be one flesh—godlike—hermaphroditic . . . a divine—dual oneness without beginning and without end—perfect and whole" (Owens 1935, 286–87). At last in the temple of Yeta-bu, in the presence of Ecstaci, Femina and Tellectina merge into one being for the first time.

Tellectina cannot let go for long; such emotional intensity threatens her conviction that she still has much to learn. She escapes on a freighter, the *Esse McMoonn*, and sets out to scale the heights of Mt. Certitude. But the sisters, touched by the powers of the mother goddess, are forever transformed. As Tina departs the Siren Islands, she leaves Femina, by now a religious fanatic dedicated to Ecstaci, on an island chanting joyfully of "fulfillment and radiant bloom."

But the central quest is for *both* authentic fulfillment and reunification. The book is about healing the fractured self, the divided consciousness, the wounded world. The dichotomies between male and female, thinking and feeling, religion and spirituality must coalesce. Tellectina must learn to value her female principle, to use it not to ensnare men, but to experience life as beautiful, sensual, creative. Femina must learn to value her intellectual sister, not just to hold men and keep them interested but also to establish an autonomous existence. "Sexual pleasure, wisely used . . . may prove the stimulus and liberator of our finest and most exalted activities" (Owens 1935, 325). Living creatively involves knowledge and experience, method and madness, commitment and passion.

The novel ends as the author began, with theories of writing and passion and passionate writing. "Having lovers and writing books is much more satisfactory than marriage," Tellectina tells Aunt Sophistica:

> Love is but one of many passions—an inexplicable fever that makes the heart tremble with joy one minute and cruelly lacerates it the next. [Not love but] Passion—that is the secret of life! . . . Ah, yes, ah, yes, at thirty I feel ripe and rich, for I have experienced . . . love and passion, the intoxication that comes from beauty . . . from moments of high heroism and religious exaltation, from thought and artistic creation . . . life can never be too terrible as long as there is beauty in the world, and the capacity to enjoy it! (Owens 1935, 442–45).

It is not surprising that the book received rave reviews throughout the country when it was first released. Nor is it surprising that it was banned. As Murat Williams claimed in the *Richmond* (Va.) *News-Leader* on October 21, 1935, *The Unpredictable Adventure*, which sought "to tell the literary world about woman's search for happiness" showed prospects for financial success until it was banned by the New York Public Library because "it was too risque for its shelves. The author . . . said too much about the strange affairs of Tellectina in the Land of Nithking." The *Los Angeles Times*, October 27, 1935, hailed the novel in one sentence as reminiscent "of *Pilgrim's Progress*" with "double meanings, anagrams," and in the next followed with a more ambiguous description: "Lightly amusing, intelligent, mildly wicked, enough to shock the rigid-pious, this allegory of a woman's adventures in life is more instructive than most manuals about what a young girl ought to know." Not only do we learn what women need to know about themselves throughout this book but we also observe the repression of knowledge necessary for women to become "self-conscious, self-defining human being(s)" with "a knowledge of [our] own history" (Rich 1986, 2).

With a contract from Doubleday to write seven more books in the series, Claire envisioned that such scandal would bring her the fame and notoriety enjoyed by James Branch Cabell. She wrote in her "Autobiography," "I had hoped it would be banned like *Jurgen* and I would become famous overnight" (Owens ca. 1970–80). But despite the book's notoriety, fame eluded the author. The underlying message was clear. When a man rebels, he is an adventurer and a hero. When a woman rebels, she is a disgrace and branded as immoral. Years later, when Claire gave copies of *The Unpredictable Adventure* to friends and associates, she would inscribe the book with a disclaimer: "This novel is a bit naughty and rebellious. . . . I was young—a woman—and Southern—which means I was twenty years younger than anyone else of the same age," she wrote in Kenneth Ring's copy. In Elizabeth Snapp's copy she wrote: "This is my first book. It was written in the early 1930s when literary America was under the influence of the satirists: H. L. Mencken, Sinclair Lewis, and James Branch Cabell. I am not by nature a satirist, Nowadays I am deeply religious in the broadest sense, I hope. I feel compassion for people's shortcomings and awareness of the good innate in all people." Similar explanations are found written on extra copies in the archive.

These apologias reflect two things: first, Claire, like many other writers, offers a disclaimer that recognizes the gaps in her early thinking and seeks to justify her naïveté; second, and here I speculate, Claire seems to have internalized the criticism she experienced when the book was banned. Could it be possible that even in the 1970s and 1980s, a vestigial sense of "shame" still clouded her earliest accomplishment? Nevertheless, because

almost everyone she felt close to received a copy of the book
with a similar inscription, a part of Claire had to be proud of
this younger self revealed by the novel. Furthermore, when published, the book received more praise than negative criticism.

The Fifth Avenue Bookshop where she worked for five years
displayed entire windows of her books; laying in front of them
were the letters she received from literary dignitaries. James
Branch Cabell called *The Unpredictable Adventure* "indubitably a
masterpiece"; Carl Van Doren, of the The Book of the Month
Club, wrote, "a beautiful book, one of my favorites"; Aldous
Huxley called it "a remarkable book," and invited her to "come
to see me if you are in England." Burton Rascoe, Claire's advi-
sory editor at Doubleday, and the book's dedicatee, called the
novel "original, profound, and audacious" (Owens ca. 1970–
80). An article featuring Claire at work on a new book quotes a
letter from Rascoe: "I think your first novel will make a great
stir. I consider it a fine and unusual piece of work. . . . It is the
sort of a book no women have had the courage to write, although there is no doubt many have been dying to, and many
would have written it if they had had the talent" (*Hartford Daily
Times*, May 18, 1935, 9).

"Then it died a quiet death." Claire took a small apartment
on Ninth Street beside Mark Twain's old house on Fifth Avenue
and began to "write like mad. I felt justified as I could not get a
job" (Owens ca. 1970–80).

Stories, stories, stories. Book reviews, a monthly column for
Today's Woman magazine, three unpublished novels centering on
domestic issues written in the 1940s, one unpublished and three
published autobiographical accounts of her journey toward self-
realization, numerous articles and essays on transpersonal psychology and Zen, a full-length manuscript, "Varieties of Self-
Realization," and the unpublished "Autobiography" that wraps
itself around all the writings stored away in boxes in the Blagg-
Huey Library archive.

But the utopian series of seven fantasy-adventure novels contracted with Doubleday never came. Perhaps the best explanation lies in the course Claire's life took. Like the journey of
every heroine, the pattern of the quest is cyclical. Claire would
consistently lose and rediscover her values, face and overcome
the same kinds of obstacles until she learned to hold onto her
insights in all kinds of circumstances that tested her.

In 1937, Claire married H. Thurston Owens III, a wealthy,
aristocratic businessman and descendant of the Van Horn family
of New York; soon after they moved to New Haven. Life was no
longer an adventure. It was predictable and safe. Her marriage
to Owens brought privilege and grace, yet the arrival of this
privilege was not without its consequences. Once again, Claire
found herself enmeshed in the trappings of aristocratic living
she had fled in her youth. Claire never bought into this new life
completely. Characteristically, she held herself apart from it and
questioned society's tyrannical hold over women [and herself]
using the allure of material values. "Why did I need three
closets full of clothes? I was sick to death of straining every
nerve to wear the latest fashion . . . the competition and rivalry
among women was idiotic. Why in the name of common sense
did we allow this invisible monster—society—to tyrannize our
lives? Material things determined our social status, not our
characters, brains, talents. How ridiculous; how false" (Owens
ca. 1970–80).

Claire understood that "for women, all privilege is relative"
(Rich 1986, 4). She chastised herself for allowing her husband
to heap expensive clothes, jewels, and furs on her, to praise her
female attributes extravagantly, and to tell her she was beautiful
and good in bed. "He praises you as a sex object. Yet he never
reads your books or articles, never reads your fan letters, resents
your going up to your study to write, prevents you from talking
to other men. Like most husbands, he prevents you from devel-
oping into a whole human being—keeping you in a luxurious
cage where you cannot try your wings. He even sings you the
old song about the bird in the gilded cage" (Owens ca. 1970–
80).

Is it his fault or her own, she wonders? Or is it the fault of this patriarchal society that breeds woman to be an object? Angry at herself, she is angry at all women who, whether as a result of "biology or custom," place too high a value on love. "Byron the poet was right: 'To men, love is a thing apart; it is woman's whole existence.'" Did she, in marrying Owens, choose the "Expiedway Ten" and relinquish her hard-earned spot on "Mount Certitude"? Claire's choice provokes amazement; it is so antithetical to a woman who, only a few years earlier, had written: "domesticity and bodily comforts keep men (and women) from their high dreams" (Owens 1935, 390–91).

But romance and high adventure in fiction are one thing; in life all those obstacles, all those defeats for a few victories, cease being fun. Claire needed a respite. Two failed marriages and one failed long-term romance, events partially treated in the novel, preceded this marriage.* Twice divorced, she had suffered condemnation from her parents, especially her mother. Claire felt she had failed in her goal to be successful as a wife and a writer, in love, and in work. She was forty-one years old. She wanted to try again.

And although her thirty-two-year marriage had its flaws, like many long marriages, it had its high points, its moments of bliss. For the most part, Claire was happy and in love with her "Thursty." She sacrificed her staunch conviction that women needed their financial independence and thus compromised and lived according to common sense, the drug that "dulls and lulls" whatever is fine and rebellious; yet Thurston's wealth pro-

*Claire engaged in a companionate marriage with Leo Saidlo, fictionalized as Ray Niviso, around 1918. Even though the marriage was never legalized or consummated, she discovered, after they parted, that it was considered common law. She obtained a legal divorce, most likely in 1925. In July 1931, she married George Wanders, a reporter for the *New York Herald Tribune*. Legally married for five years, they lived together only briefly. In May 1936, Claire went to Reno, Nevada to obtain a divorce. Because no legal documents have surfaced, these dates are approximate and based primarily on letters in the archive.

vided her a room of her own on the third floor of her New Haven home, servants to take over the domestic chores she despised, and time to do the "kind of writing" she wanted to do without the worry of monetary compensation. Besides, her nature didn't change: she lived her whole life with zest and intensity, "abandoning herself to the passion" of writing. What she wrote and the way that she wrote it demonstrate she was a rebel at heart.

In 1949, Claire underwent a spontaneous Great Awakening, a peak experience of spiritual enlightenment that "changed [her] entire life" and the focus of her writing. She was, so to speak, lifted off Expiedway Ten and set once again on the steep mountain road in search of Certitude. *Awakening to the Good: Psychological or Religious?* describes the day when her "Reason united with [her] Intuition and Feeling and [she] was made whole" (1958, 20). On Christmas morning, she awakened in a state of depression that had been plaguing her for some time. She attributed this bout of despair, which she calls "the dark night of the soul," to the "political chaos of the world" and its ethical decline. To further complicate her emotional turmoil, she had been betrayed recently by her best friend. Overcome by the hypocrisy of the headlines in the morning paper, "Peace on Earth, Good Will Toward Men," she dragged herself up to her study and collapsed. "Great waves of desolation washed" over her; she felt she was dying (Owens ca. 1970–80). "Suddenly the entire room was filled with a great golden light . . . nothing but light. . . . The ordinary 'I' ceased to exist. . . . It felt as if some vast transcendent force was invading me . . . as if all the immanent good lying latent within me began to pour forth in a stream. . . . It was a mystical moment of union with the mysterious infinite . . . a confrontation with Ultimate Reality, an overwhelming indescribable experience, the ecstasy so intense it was unbearable, the rapture . . . ineffable" (Owens 1958, inserts following 170). This moment of bliss could have lasted a minute or an hour; she would never know. When she regained consciousness, she realized that she had experienced death and rebirth of incredible magnitude, a culmination of the small moments of ecstatic transcendence that had been part of her life.

Partially motivating Claire to write this book and its sequel, *Discovery of the Self*, was her desire to recover that state of bliss she lived under for twelve years, not just for herself, but because "'awakening to the good' that is inherent in all people, she saw the key to overcoming perennial problems besetting humanity" (White 1983). The other motive, equally important, was Claire's innate intellectual need to explain an event that happened intuitively, emotionally. Her research opened for her a new world of learning and brought her into the humanistic and transpersonal psychology movements at the time of their inceptions with founders Abraham Maslow and Anthony Sutich, along with Aldous Huxley, who, over the years, came to respect her work and value her friendship.*

In 1949, Claire had to start from scratch. Just as she had no mentor, no models, when she left home at age twenty, Claire now had no language, no tools with which she could recount the phenomenon she had experienced. There was no movement, no philosophy, nothing she had ever read to explain what had happened. For eight years, she spoke of it with no one, fearing she would be thought mad. Meanwhile, quietly and secretly, she began her private search through the labyrinthine passages of avant-garde writers like Aldous Huxley, Abraham Maslow, Anthony Sutich, F. S. C. Northrop, William Sheldon, and Sigmund Freud.

"Finally I discovered Carl Gustav Jung and his books saved my life" (Owens ca. 1970–80). Difficult to read, even more difficult to understand, he was the one person writing at the time who provided scientific explanations to spiritual phenom-

*Letters from Abraham Maslow, Aldous Huxley, James Branch Cabell, Havelock Ellis, Robert Briffault, Richard Aldington, H. L. Mencken, Burton Rascoe, and numerous other writers and thinkers (usually men) commenting on all four of Claire's published books and other matters, personal and professional, are part of the archival holdings at Texas Woman's University.

ena in a way that allowed Claire to assimilate all her disparate research. She discovered the personal unconscious and the deeper level of the universal; in short, she discovered a language, a system of communication through which she could express something ineffable in concrete terms. Form follows function. Now in order to tell her stories, she would have to invent her own form and pour the words of her experience into it.

Awakening to the Good is divided into brief sections describing events, moods, and circumstances deeply affecting the writer's psychological state. "Winter" describes a lonely night during her unhappy marriage in the early 1930s to George Wanders; "Sea and Sand" captures her blissful union with Owens. "Wind" resonates with the sexual energy of a ten-year-old discovering the erotic but recalled by a woman in her fifties. Interspersed among these personal reminiscences are philosophical speculations seeking to explain the events. The last section of the book summarizes research the author did in an effort to understand the small ecstasies and the great awakening experience. The author's rhapsodic voice dances across years and events, with the theoretical passages interrupted by explosive and passionate personal observations. The result is a collage that juxtaposes event with research, mind with emotion, science with art.

From the first, I loved it, but I did not know what it was nor what to make of it. I called it too emotional, didactic. It all seemed to be too much, larger than life. Yet I could not let go of it; I could not dismiss either book as insignificant. Passages stuck in my brain, like phrases of poetry but not exactly poetry, patches of narrative like a novel but not exactly a novel, exposition, perhaps, but no. Something else. "Myth is not invented; it is experienced. It formulates itself from an urge to understand what has happened in the dark mystery of the past and what may happen in the unknown and unknowable future" (Wickes 1963, xv). In her effort to light the darkness, Claire created a mythology out of her own life story. The person became part of the persona, a heroine larger than life.

By writing herself out of the darkness, she wrote her *self* onto the page. And I, reading these two books for the first time, simply did not know what to think. Here, at last, was a woman's voice uncensored, spilling out her most intimate insights, feelings, and secrets. I had read Virginia Woolf on women's writing; I had read Anaïs Nin on "writing from the womb"; Hélène Cixous's admonition that "woman must write her self: must write about women . . . [the] body must be heard" (Cixous 1981, 245, 250). Claire was doing women's writing! Confronted with it here in these books in its raw state, I did not recognize what I was seeing. I, a true believer, a devotee, had almost missed the signal.

Awakening to the Good and *Discovery of the Self* each adopts the utopian quest to invent the unknown. These writings are not exactly autobiography, though they are accounts of true life experiences; not exactly memoir, though they look back on a specific time, place, event; not exactly scholarly research, though Claire researches extensively to validate scientifically her spiritual awakenings. "Not exactly" is to the search for a new form of expression what "not yet" is to the search for a new structure of society. Inventing a new form, the author invents a new self, a new way of being in the world. In the process she becomes the woman who is not yet, the Sophistica of her first novel, a grand amoureuse.

She didn't know it, would have denied it, did in fact scorn it. In her "Autobiography" she recalls her personal interview with Carl Jung at his home in Geneva and sheds light on her ambivalence regarding the concept of an *amoureuse*. The article she wrote describing the interview was published in the *New York Herald Tribune* Paris edition, won a prize, and was eventually anthologized. But the article does not capture the trauma the writer suffered in meeting her hero.

Still in the process of writing *Awakening to the Good*, still searching for answers to explain what had happened to her, Claire believed this visit was the perfect opportunity to conduct her research in person. Unfortunately, she was so in awe of this great man and his giant intellect that all the questions she had planned to ask him flew out of her mind, and she was silent. He began to explain the principles of his system. But she knew all that he was telling her from having read and studied his books. Too modest to tell him about her own book on spontaneous self-realization, she writes with regret: "I might have made a friend for life but to him I appeared to be a tongue tied young woman in a red hat. I did have the presence of mind to show him the paper dust jacket of my one published book. He smiled at the nude woman riding a centaur and read the blurb and talked a great deal about my being an amoureuse. This was not what I wanted at all!" (Owen ca. 1970–80).

I have been using the word *amoureuse*, as Claire did in her novel, to describe the ideal woman, the woman who is not yet. And I have realized all along that *amoureuse* is a word loaded with potential controversy in feminist circles. "Love has been assigned to woman as her supreme vocation" writes Simone de Beauvoir in *The Second Sex*. Associating the role of the *amoureuse* with the destructive source of a woman's dependency, de Beauvoir (with Jung and perhaps Claire) believes love "represents . . . the curse that lies heavily upon woman confined in the feminine universe, woman mutilated, insufficient unto herself. . . . Through twenty years of waiting, dreaming, hoping, the young girl [and surely, we can add, the young southern belle] has cherished the myth of the liberating savior-hero, and hence the independence she has won through work is not enough to abolish her desire for a glorious abdication" (de Beauvoir 1952, 743, 773).

The image of *amoureuse* Claire conveys in her novel is quite different and demonstrates a significant aspect of Claire's approach to binary thinking. Caught in the tension between the powerlessness of the southern belle and the dominating power of male independence, Claire's struggle became the search for a resolution. She loved being a woman, she loved playing belle to her beaux. At the same time, she could not bear to be considered helpless or empty headed. She dealt with this struggle throughout her life; it informed all of her writing.

Grand amoureuse represents an ideal of female wholeness that invents a model for a new kind of woman, a woman with an intellect (Tellectina) who can enter the world of thinking (Nithking) and, by abandoning herself recklessly, passionately, to the project of living, can expect to receive back what she gives: love and fulfillment, relationship and work. Wholeness.

The ideal of grand amoureuse metaphorically establishes the possibility for a way of being in the world that transcends the limitations of traditional roles open to women. For de Beauvoir "if we want to be all that we can possibly be as individuals," we must passionately dedicate ourselves to the *projects of our lives;* but "we must first clear the social space" for the projects (Tong 1989, 211). And this is exactly what Claire/Tellectina did in leaving home. It is what she did, though in a different way, when she married H. Thurston Owens III and moved from her beloved New York City to New Haven. And it is what she did finally when, after their thirty-two-year marriage ended with Owens's death, she gave up her lovely home and servants and moved with a group of young rebels, Yale students, to Rochester to join the Zen community. In keeping with her predictably unpredictable ways, she awakened on the morning of her eightieth birthday and began to write that story.

Zen and the Lady, which traces her journey to Zen as a means to recapture spiritual enlightenment through meditation, is a passionate account of the universal questions about old age. For, in an intellectual and emotional sense, Claire never grew old; she kept rebirthing herself. Beginning with Owens's death in June 1969, she recounts a reawakening of her sexual energy when, in her seventies, she finds herself wildly and erotically attracted to young male Zen students in their twenties. Though never physically consummated, these relationships formulate a path toward a new understanding of female sexuality where the quest for an intellectual conception of human spirituality provides the momentum for a new kind of physical and emotional joy.

The focus of the book, however, is not Claire's young men.

Zen and the Lady is a marvelous, energetic, autobiographical account, smoother and more refined than her previous two works. Claire seems more comfortable with this form, which she has invented, without necessarily realizing it. Indeed, by the time she wrote *Zen and the Lady,* she had completed a major book using a highly polished version of this new technique. "Varieties of Self-Realization," an unpublished manuscript of over four hundred pages, explores a wide variety of scientific and philosophical theories on enlightenment and self-realization using the same kind of personal experiential approach found earlier, in the more experimental *Awakening to the Good* and *Discovery of the Self.* "Meditation and the Lady," yet another unfinished manuscript in the archive, is a sequel to *Zen and the Lady.* With these works, Claire brings her life's journey full circle as she defines a Western approach to mysticism and describes the new worlds she discovered through meditation. East meets West, spirituality meets religion, life meets fulfillment, Claire meets wholeness, and youth meets age.

Still, I had trouble reconciling myself to such passages as this one: "The first moment our eyes met across the room a spark was ignited between us that flamed and later flared until we were both almost consumed. Soon he began to arrive at my house before the others and remain after they had all departed" (Owens 1979b, 20).

Social conditioning had me convinced it simply could not be true.

It is growing dark outside. Audrey closes the shutters, turns on an extra lamp, and, moving them away from the portrait on the mantle, lights the two white candles. Voices grow quiet, Geoff takes a polite leave. All of us begin to doubt that Dwain will arrive before our gathering disperses.

Dwain? Readers should now be squirming in their chairs—a feminist discussion of a woman's novel that turns on the arrival of a man? The former young love interest of an older woman?

What kind of feminism is this? This is feminism still asking
questions about gender-power relations; feminism still questioning the roles assigned women; still concerned with what women
"ought" to know, need to know; still fighting against constrictions in what society allows us to know. This is feminism still
concerned with issues regarding the dichotomy between public
and private spheres, and the degree or quality of our sexual freedom. And this is feminism now questioning the ways women
over fifty (or forty?) have been socialized into believing they are
no longer sexual beings, no longer valued as useful, vital, and
productive.

In *Zen and the Lady*, Claire writes autobiographically about
her mixed feelings at Dexter's wedding. Accompanied by Lance,
the second of the three young men depicted in the book, Claire
reveals maternal instincts mixed with jealousy, pride, hope, and
understanding. Her feelings suggest the depth of familial commitment that developed between them, a friendship from mutual giving and receiving, of love, joy, desire, and passion representing complex feelings difficult for me to describe, much
less to accept.

At last Dwain arrives and begins, unself-consciously and ener-
getically to guide me in an exploration of their relationship so
that I will be able to write about it. We refill our teacups and
plates and, with Claire looking on from her vantage point on
the mantle, resume our discussion.

Dwain: We just hit it off—like that.
Margaret: Do you remember the first time you actually
            saw her, that first moment?
Dwain: Oh yes, walking into her house.
Miriam: She opened the door?
Dwain: Yes, and there was an immediate electricity. I
            was there for a sitting—she opened her home to
            our Zen group—and I guess I was a few min-
            utes early, maybe twenty minutes or so. We
            immediately fell into this conversation, and

when she found out I was from Texas, well, within twenty minutes we were just spilling out our hearts to each other. No one else was there and then people would come in, and she was ignoring them and opening the door and pointing them upstairs for the sitting.

Marion: What did you think about age, or did you?

Dwain: The only thing I thought about age was that if she was twenty years younger or I was twenty years older we would have had a raging affair; that's the only thing I thought about age. Somehow I sensed that we were twenty years out of range of each other. So I must have thought that she was fifty or sixty. I was about thirty.

Miriam: In *Zen* she writes that you asked her age, calling her—none of the others would have dared—by her first name. Her answer was smooth:

"How old do you think?"

"Oh, about fifty."

"Fifty is a nice age. I always feel a permanent forty."

You were twenty-nine and she was seventy-three.

Everyone laughed. But the relationship was no laughing matter. Suddenly, seeing Dwain sitting across the room talking about his love for this woman known and loved by each of us, something clicked. After all these years of pondering the questions, thanks to this visit, thanks to my late-night discussion with Audrey when we together began to pound out a theory, I finally understood.

Claire's relationship with Dwain set a precedent for the young men who followed and established for us a means by which we can expand the meaning of *amoureuse* into a concept to be approached with honor and appreciated as a new way of understanding the role older women can play in younger men's lives. Those young men were looking for refinement; they were attracted to her worldliness, her dignity. Her sophistication suggested the demeanor of a goddess, but her sexuality, that ever-present erotic energy, supplied the impetus for the relationship.

Claire's integrity established a sense of trust. Her humor and childlike approach to living made their hours together seem light and unthreatening; it took the edge off learning and made intimacy seem like a social encounter. Yet her fervent intellect and probing curiosity about mutual philosophical interests drove through to deep self-understanding for both Claire and her young men. Claire was a woman of culture who could help these men refine themselves, a sexual being who was not a genital object. The erotic energy functioned as a catalyst that kept them coming back for more. Refraining from acting on the erotic teaches self-control. For a boy to become a man, he must harness his sexual impulse and learn to see a woman's other side, not simply the sexual object or mother, wife or child, but the person or human being whose life may span a century and encompass a multitude of roles. Claire is a model for a new kind of relationship between men and women. Man must now learn these things from Woman; he must go back to the mythical and the primitive associated with the priestess, the wise woman, the goddess.

Barbara:	People put her on a pedestal, made her into a kind of goddess. But Claire wasn't a goddess. She had doubts.
Miriam:	What kinds of doubts?
Barbara:	Doubts about her writing, doubts about her life choices.

For the last year of her life, Claire suffered from an extremely painful form of diverticulitis. Audrey speculates that, near the end, Claire must have suspected she had cancer. She could find no relief. During one of their many discussions, Barbara recalls,

Claire wondered if her physical suffering was a form of retribution for her having lived such a privileged life. Dwain elaborates: "I had no idea what I was asking of her when I talked her into coming here. I was too young to realize what she was giving up, her home, friends, status in the community, servants. I never once considered the risk or the courage it took for her to leave, start over. Looking back now . . ."

Looking back, we all see her as a heroine, embarking on yet another adventure. But it occurs to me that they really knew her in the flesh, as friend and philosophical companion. I know her only as icon or myth. Suddenly, it seems unfair. Barbara, it turns out, was one of the few people who could decipher Claire's handwriting. She had been typing "Meditation and the Lady" when Claire died and was the one who could perhaps transcribe the numerous diaries I cannot read. I asked about the unfinished, ongoing "Autobiography"; I asked about "Varieties of Self-Realization," trying to establish the years they were written. Barbara was not familiar with either text. "All I can tell you is that she wrote every day of her life. It was an exercise for her. She was a writer, a real writer."

Claire's writings speak louder when augmented by the feminist theories propounded today. Her works address issues of ageism, classism, and sexism, even though her need to rise above such biases is part of her journey of self-discovery. The focus of all of her intellectual probing, finally, rests on validation of self and of a method with which she could intellectually explain what happened in the spiritual and intuitive process of self-realization, when science is merged with art, psychology with philosophy. Her approach to life, love, self, and writing turns on a philosophy of closing the gaps, healing the wounds of the world, and reconciling the tension built into socially structured oppositionals. "The value of oneness," she wrote in *Zen and the Lady*, "is the obliteration of duality—the cause of all man's {sic} troubles" (1979b, 142).

Like myth, Claire's end was beyond time and place, glorious and painful, extraordinary and mundane. Her physical condition had deteriorated to become a source of constant pain. To spare her friends as much grief and discomfort as possible and with her mind still lucid and sharp, she meticulously planned her death. On Mother's Day, May 7, 1983, Claire ended her life as she had lived it: in choice, dignity, and self-control.

In accordance with Buddhist belief, Claire requested that her body be kept for three days to permit the mind energy to separate from the body. Audrey carried out her last wishes. On the third day, she came to the crematorium carrying a large yellow tulip, a small bell, and a brass gong. "The funeral director must have thought I was insane. I sat and chanted the 'Prajna-paramita' and the 'Kanzeon Chant' in English, Japanese, and Chinese." The Buddhist ritual is meant to propel the energy released by death to the next stage and signifies that form is emptiness and emptiness is form. There is no death. There is transformation. The cremation took about an hour and a half. "I felt renewed after this private ceremony," Audrey told me. "I felt there was nothing but life, nothing but transcendence."

The funeral director brought the red damask box containing Claire's ashes to the Zen Center where it was placed on the altar for the memorial service held several days later in the Buddha Hall, in front of the great golden Buddha. Over a hundred people assembled, primarily members of the Zen community. Claire left detailed instructions for the memorial ceremony and reception and requested that her remains be buried in a beautiful garden. Audrey describes the "fine spring day, cool, gray, and rather overcast," with all the trees and bushes "blooming and lovely." Everyone remarked about the profusion of blossoms, pink crabapples and pink magnolias, as if nature, in honor of this auspicious occasion, remembered Claire's favorite color. After a couple of weeks, Geoff and his wife, Kathy, Dwain, and Audrey met at the Zen Center. They took the red damask box that held Claire's ashes from the altar and went out to the garden. With a small hand shovel they dug a hole, bowed, and put the ashes under the dogwood tree.

A deep stillness seasoned the crisp, winter air the morning

Audrey took me on a tour of the Zen Center. We stood in the garden on a path facing two trees, one large and one small. Their bare branches cast shadows on the blankets of snow that hugged their trunks. Naturally, I walked toward the tall one, unconsciously connecting it with Claire's stature and dignity.

"No, not that one," Audrey called out. "This one, the dog-wood." I turned.

"Why did you choose the smaller tree?" I asked.

"Oh, we never even discussed it. It just seemed natural, I suppose, because it has more time left to grow."

In Zen, past and present are one. The end is the beginning. And the beginning is an unpredictable adventure.

GLOSSARY*

Astte: Taste.

Austen, Jane: (1775–1817). English novelist whose ironic narratives celebrate intellectual feelings and moral sense in her heroines. She wrote in the common sitting room in the midst of an active family life and, according to Virginia Woolf, "wrote as women write, not as men write . . . [and] ignored the perpetual admonitions of the eternal pedagogue." She rejected the traditional male sentence and devised a sentence proper for a woman's use.

Awr: War.

Bashkirtseff, Marie: (1860–1884). Russian painter and diarist who exhibited in the salons of Paris. She was famous for her *Journal* (1887) describing childhood feelings, fantasies, and ambitions; her analyses of adolescent sensitivity give a vivid psychological self-portrait.

Bee Leaf: Belief.

---

*Anagram "translations" are my own in collaboration with Stanley R. Harris and Claire Myers Owens's notations. Information about literary figures or other allusions has been taken from the following sources: William Rose Benét, *The Reader's Encyclopedia,* 2d. ed. (New York: Thomas Y. Crowell, 1965); Virginia Blaine, Isobel Grundy, and Patricia Clemens, *The Feminist Companion to Literature in English* (New Haven: Yale University Press, 1990); Sandra M. Gilbert and Susan Gubar, *The Norton Anthology of Literature by Women: The Tradition in English* (New York: Norton, 1985); C. Hugh Holman, *A Handbook to Literature* (Indianapolis: Bobbs-Merrill, 1980); Jennifer S. Uglow, ed., *The Continuum Dictionary of Women's Biography* (New York: Continuum, 1989); Barbara G. Walker, *The Woman's Encyclopedia of Myths and Secrets* (San Francisco: Harper and Row, 1983).

Biblioesque: Booklike.

Bli Du: Build.

Bodtu: Doubt.

Briffault, Robert: (1876–1948). English anthropologist. He was author of *The Mothers: A Study of the Origins of Sentiments and Institutions* (1927), a monumental, three-volume work that investigates the origins of social instinct. Briffault believed that the social characteristics of the mind were related to the functions of the female and that society owed its existence to maternal instinct. *The Mothers: The Matriarchal Theory of Social Origins* (1931), a history of matriarchy and marriage in primitive society, further develops the theses of his earlier work.

Cabell, James Branch: (1879–1958). American novelist and essayist from an old Virginia family. His first book, *The Eagle's Shadow*, appeared in 1904. Thereafter, he created his own mythical country, the medieval French province of Poictesme. With the publication of *Jurgen* in 1919, Cabell received popular success, largely from attempts to suppress his book on the grounds of immorality.

Cape Coverture: Protective shelter, the legal status of women during marriage.

Carpenter, Edward: (1844–1929). English poet and writer. Originally a clergyman, he left the church because of his strongly held socialist views. He had a nostalgic vision of a primitive and free moral society. A strong supporter of the feminist movement, he saw the personal and the political as inseparable and hoped that freedom of sexual experience would lead to the emancipation of homosexuals. A disciple of Walt Whitman.

Casuistry: Specious reasoning; subtle use of false logic or ethics to gain an argumentative end.

Catulus: Claire's spelling of Catullus (87?–54 B.C.). Gaius Valerius Catullus, a Roman lyric poet born in Verna, went to Rome as a young man. Through his charm and precocious brilliance, he gained easy admittance to the refined and prodigal society of the day. Because of his ardent susceptibility, he fell disastrously in love with a young Roman matron who became the Lesbia of his poems.

Cerebral Lethargica: Idle thinking, dreaming, questioning, a condition leading to dangerous activities cured by the drug Cianite Vitrgrew.

Cessneray: Necessary.

Ceve-Peri: Perceive.

Chimera: Illusion or fabrication of the mind; an unrealizable dream. Also a monster compounded of incongruous parts. *See* New Chimera.

Chotu: Touch.

Cianite Vitrgrew: Creative writing.

Ciro-nange Clouds: Clouds of ignorance.

Colette: Pen name of Sidonie Gabrielle Colette (1873–1954). An influential French novelist, she initiated important ideas about gender relations, sexual politics, and the links between sexuality, history, and the family.

Cooco: Cooperative community.

Corinne: Title character in the romantic novel, *Corinne* or *l'Italie* (1807), by Madame de Staël. (See Madame de Staël and Madame de Récamier.)

Cumsi: Music.

Cynosure: Center of attraction or admiration. A name given by the Greek sect, Cynics (or "Doglike Ones") to the pole star or North Star, which they believed would move from its place as the still point of the turning heavens when doomsday was near. A prime navigational star, it became the "cynosure of all eyes."

Dotbu Desert: Desert of doubt.

Eco: Economic independence.

Ecstaci: Ectasy, the god who serves the goddess Yeta-Bu.

Elam Domitann: Dominant male. Olev the Third.

Eliot, George: Pen name of Mary Ann(e) (later Marian) Evans (1819–1880). English novelist who introduced a new realism and psychological seriousness to English fiction. Among others, her novels *The Mill on the Floss* (1860), *Silas Marner* (1863), and *Middlemarch* (1871) enjoyed financial and critical success. Her feminist significance arises from her portrayal of the limitations imposed by the social, cultural, and familial structures of her day. Her adoption of a male pseudonym links her to George Sand and is also a tribute to her literary mentor and lover George Henry Lewes, a married man unable to obtain a divorce. Their decision to cohabit caused a scandal.

Ellis, Havelock: (1859–1939). English psychologist, essayist, and art critic, best known for his pioneering, and at the time scandalous, studies in sexual psychology, including *The Erotic Rights of Women* (1918). He championed women's rights and mutual desire. His ambivalent views, expressed in *Sexual Inversion* (1898; banned in England), influenced some of the current negative stereotypes of homosexuals. Excerpts from *Little Essays of Love and Virtue* (1922, 1931) are quoted in *The Unpredictable Adventure*.

Equi: Equal rights.

Ese: See.

Esse McMoonn: Common sense.

Expeidway Ten: Expedient way.

Fanecedi Tree: In defiance.

Femina: Feminine woman. The archetype or stereotype of female virtue and sexuality. Negative implications align woman with nature in an absence of intelligence. This concept sets up a dichotomy between thinking and feeling, intellect and emotion.

Forta Feli, Isle of: Art of Life.

Forta Velo, Isle of: Art of Love.

Frelo: Freelove.

Frewo: Freewoman.

Gatherulic Iron: Ironic laughter.

Ghaulot, Mt. Ghaulot: To laugh.

Glasgow, Ellen: (1873–1945). American novelist whose work dealt primarily with the South. Born to an old Virginia family, Glasgow was expected to make a debut and to live the life of a southern lady. Instead, she revolted against the "sanctified fallacies" and wrote novels that explore the vagaries of southern society, like *Barren Ground* (1925) and *The Romantic Comedians* (1926). Her friend, James Branch Cabell (also a Virginian), praised her writing. Her novel, *In This Our Life* (1941), received a Pulitzer Prize in 1942.

Godidea: The idea of God, perpetuated by Judeo-Christian tradition.

Godsson: God's son.

Gribble, Francis Henry: (1862–1946). Biographer of George Sand, Percy Bysshe Shelley, and Jean Jacques Rousseau.

Halfish: Half-truths; language spoken in the land of Err.

Hancce: Chance.

Hearn, Lafcadio: (1850–1904). American journalist and author known for the poetic prose style of his exotic and fantastic tales. He dedicated himself to "the worship of the Old, the Queer, the Strange, the Exotic, the Monstrous." *Chita* (1887) is a novel about a young girl who survives a tidal wave on a small island.

Huxley, Aldous: (1894–1963). British novelist whose early works satirized the intellectual posturing of the 1920s. His later works reflected an interest in mysticism, the occult, and alternative medicine. After he moved to California, he became associated with Buddhist and Hindu groups. Claire called him "the man of tomorrow" in her unpublished, romantic poem "Basic Encounter," which dramatizes a lunch meeting with Huxley in the late 1950s or early 1960s after the publication of her work on spiritual awakenings.

Hynuppa: Unhappy.

Jurgen: A novel by James Branch Cabell (1919) that became a cause célèbre and brought the author popular fame. It is part of a series of novels set in the imaginary realm of Poictesme.

Kamdinn: Mankind.

Karreza: Claire's spelling of Karezza. Restraint. Specifically, coitus reservatus, sexual intercourse without male orgasm. Its purpose is to increase a man's spiritual powers by keeping seminal secretions in his body, while he absorbs the power engendered by his partner's multiple orgasms.

Koobish Roan: Bookish roan.

Krafft-Ebing, Richard: (1840–1902). German neurologist whose writings in *Psychopathia Sexualis* (1882) influenced the work of Havelock Ellis. Claire's spelling of his name is "Kraft-Ebing."

Künstlerroman: A form of the apprenticeship novel in which the protagonist is a writer or an artist. Like James Joyce's *Portrait of the Artist as a Young Man*, the protagonist is on a journey from childhood to maturity, struggling to overcome antagonistic forces both in the world and within the self.

Lenclos, Ninon de: (1620–1705). Also known as Ann Lenclos. French courtesan, subject of a biography by Emile Magne [1926]. Famous for her wit and beauty, she had many lovers, including La Rochefoucauld. Her life was the inspiration for Madeleine de Scudéry's Clarisse in her novel, *Clélie* (1654). Claire considered Lenclos an *amoureuse*.

Li-Ngam: Lingam or penis. A stylized phallic symbol of the masculine cosmic principle. Hindu symbol of any god, usually Shiva. The lingam-yoni is the supreme symbol of the vital principle, representing male and female genitalia in conjunction. Its verbal equivalent is the Jewel in the Lotus. Sometimes, the lingam appeared as a phallic pillar in the Holy of Holies, the core of the temple, which stands for the goddess and is called womb.

Magnitation: Imagination (an imperfect anagram, one letter off). Imagination gives birth to nervous disorders and works with Karreza to give birth to Sublimation. Used ironically.

Manhu Sisters: Human sisters.

Manlig: Lingam. See Li-Ngam.

Manu Mission: Formal emancipation from slavery.

Mar-it-al: Marital, the institution of marriage. It becomes ironic as an anagram for *martial*.

Marotily: Morality.

Mean Ingless: Meaningless, a deadly cobra.

Mencken, H. L.: (1880–1956). American journalist, editor,

GLOSSARY 503

and writer for the *Baltimore Herald* and later the *Baltimore Sun*. He excelled at hurling insults at the "booboisie" and attacked Puritanism, conservatism, and religion. Although admirers exalted Mencken for his satire, some critics considered him crude and intolerant. His *In Defense of Women* (1922) depicted "Women-Righters" as "man-eating suffragettes," though at times he championed women's rights.

Mill, John Stuart: (1806–1873). English philosopher, economist, and advocate of women's suffrage. He was author of *The Subjection of Women* (1869), a work influenced significantly by the intellectual contributions of his colleague, feminist Harriet Taylor (later Mill).

Millay, Edna St. Vincent: (1892–1950). American poet noted for her verse celebrating life, love, and moral freedom. After graduating from Vassar in 1917, she lived a bohemian life in Greenwich Village and became a celebrity of sorts among artists and intellectuals. Her prize winning poem "Renascence" (1912), which captures a mystical awakening, influenced Claire's understanding of her own awakening in 1949. Millay's volume of poetry, *The Harp-Weaver*, won the Pulitzer Prize in 1923.

Mllse: Smell.

Mount Ghaulot: *See* Ghaulot.

Nartso-tiva: Starvation.

Nesse: Sense.

New Chimera: The colony founded by Tellectina and Olev the Second based on communitarian living and the worship of the goddesses Frelo and Frewo.

Nithking: Thinking, The Forbidden Country.

Noequists: Questions; radical party of political outcasts from Err, Wandering in Dotbu Desert, who speak Reasonese.

Noailles, Comtesse Anna de: (1876–1933). French poet, who published nine volumes of lyric and romantic poetry and an autobiography.

Norancegi Bamboo: Ignorance bamboo; used with Zest leaves to build huts—a dangerous combination.

Olev: Love.

Onegod: One god.

Ophe Bamboo: Hope bamboo.

Opia Nut Tree: Utopian tree.

Otherpeoplesideas: Other people's ideas.

O We Tri: O write.

Parides Tree: Despair tree.

Parker, Dorothy: (1893–1967). American writer known for her caustic wit and satire; served as drama critic for *Vanity Fair* and later *The New Yorker*. She was a central figure of the Algonquin Hotel Round Table, and her reviews and short stories regularly appeared in *The New Yorker* between 1926 and 1955. Parker's stories expose the isolation of women.

Passino: Passion, priest to Ecstaci.

Pater, Walter: (1839–1894). English essayist and critic. Pater was a leader in the nineteenth-century revival of interest in Renaissance art and humanism. He formulated a doctrine that art and aesthetics are, in themselves, the chief pursuit of life. His philosophy involving "living for the moment," decadence, and the New Woman became linked in *fin de siècle* popular culture.

Poictesme: An imaginary country of medieval France, setting for many of the romances of James Branch Cabell.

Publi Copinion: Public opinion.

Pur Poses: Purposes.

Quma: Question mark; leader of the woman Noequists. *See* Woqu.

Rascoe, Burton: (1892–1957). American author and Claire's editor at Doubleday. Several of his books greatly influenced Claire: *Titans of Literature: From Homer to the Present* (1932), a history of world literature, encompassing, among others, Homer, Sophocles, Rabelais, Voltaire, Mark Twain, and Anatole France; and *Prometheans Ancient and Modern* (1933), a literary history including such diverse authors as Saint Mark, Apuleius, Friedrich Nietzsche, D. H. Lawrence, Theodore Dreiser, and James Branch Cabell. Although a few women are discussed, all chapters focus on male authors.

Ray Niviso: Visionary. Olev the Second.

Récamier, Madame de: Jeanne Françoise Julie Adélaïde (1777–1849). French salon hostess. Known for her wit and beauty, she influenced the most important people in politics and the arts, including Chateaubriand. She was a close friend of Madame de Staël, who portrayed her in *Corinne* or *l'Italie* (1807), and she became the subject of Edouard Herriot's two-volume biography *Madame Récamier* (1926).

Reha: Hear.

Renan, Ernest: (1823–1892). French critic, writer, and scholar. While preparing for the priesthood, he lost his faith in orthodox religion after being influenced by German philosophy and Semitic philology. As a tolerant skeptic, he realized that no one system of religious, scientific, or historical knowledge could claim absolute truth. His *La Vie de Jésus,* published in 1863, was the first of a series called *Histoire des Origines du Christianisme, 1866–1881.* This influential work offered a new perspective on religious history and approached the subject matter as biography and psychology, not merely as factual history.

Rolland and Christophe Expedition: Referring to any of the *Jean Christophe* novels by Romain Rolland (1866–1944), especially *Jean Christophe In Paris* (1911).

Rote Hill: O Thrill. The name of the college, portrayed as a carnival, Tellectina attends. Ironic if interpreted as rote learning.

Sakti: Hindu god or goddess, sometimes male, sometimes female. Also Saki, Saci, and Shakti. In Hindu texts, Saci is the goddess power whose wine meant life and energy for all the gods. In Tantric Indian texts, Shakti goddess power is that which causes all action to occur. *See* Yo-Ni.

Sand, George: Pen name of Amandine-Aurore Lucille Dupin, Barrone Dudevant (1804–1876). A prolific writer, she argued for the right of free love for both women and men in her early novels. She was famous for her independence, outspoken manner, and crossdressing, as well as for her love affairs with Alfred de Musset and Frédéric Chopin. Her assumption of a male pseudonym influenced George Eliot.

Sappho: (ca. 610–580 B.C.). Poet-priestess of Lesbos, the "isle of women," dedicated to the goddess Aphrodite. Sappho is one of the most famous lyric poets of all time. Once married and mother of a daughter, Cleis, she devoted her later life to the love of women and was the leader of a group of young girls who were devotees of music and poetry. She was called the Tenth Muse and revered even above Homer. Only fragments of her work remain because her books were later burned.

Scei Dui berries: Suicide berries.

Schimpflexikon: Refers to *Menckeniana: A Schimpflexicon* (1927), compiled from unfavorable press notices about H. L. Mencken. *See* Mencken, H. L.

Sec Sept Fluer: Self-respect.

Seedd: Deeds.

Semsianic Vineyards: Messianic vineyards. Wine makes Tellectina a spiritual leader.

Seva Doxnel: Sex and love. A goddess with two faces, like Janus or Anna. However, she possessed two bodies as well.

Sexu and Sexu: Twins—sexual union and sexual purity.

Shicspy: Physics.

Shiw-mats: Wish-mats.

Shyfell: Fleshly.

Sillidinous Vines: Disillusion vines, which remove the protective film from the eyes of Smug Harboreans.

Simery: Misery; a rash from the poison of sillidinous vines.

Sin: Single standard.

Sinecure: Literally, "without cure of souls." An official position that gives the holder profit or honor without work attached.

Sithory: History.

Staël, Madame de: Anne-Louise-Germaine Necker (1766–1817). French novelist, literary critic, political writer, and philosopher of history. Unhappy with her arranged marriage to Baron Eric Magnus de Staël-Holstein, she had many love affairs, including a turbulent one with Benjamin Constant. de Staël published two novels, *Delphine* (1803) and *Corinne or l'Italie* (1807), in which Madame de Récamier is a character. She opened a salon in Paris and was influential in European politics.

Stopes, Marie: (1880–1950). Scientist and birth control pioneer. She was the author of *Married Love* "to increase the joys of marriage," *Wise Parenthood* (ca. 1918), and *Radiant Motherhood* (1920). In 1921, she opened Britain's first birth control clinic, Holloway, in London.

Sub: Sublimation.

Swernas: Answers.

Swinburne, Algernon C.: (1837–1909). English poet. Swinburne was known for his rebellion against Victorian social conventions and religion, his sympathies with the movements of political revolution of his time, and for the pagan spirit and musical effects of his poetry.

T.A. Riley: Reality.

Tellectina: Female Intelligence, Intelligent Female, Thinking Woman.

Thruts: Truths. The forest of half-grown thruts gives the name Halfish to the language of Err.

Tni-Pa: Paint.

Trisalic: Satirical.

Trista: Artist.

Tru-Sce-Plu: Sculpture.

Vomo: Voluntary motherhood.

Wharton, Edith: (1862–1937). American novelist and short story writer. Wharton was known for her examination of the tragedies and ironies of life and for depicting strong, rebellious heroines of middle-class and aristocratic New York society in the nineteenth and early twentieth centuries. *The House of Mirth* (1905) exposes hypocrisies of old New York society; *The Age of Innocence* (1921) won a Pulitzer Prize.

Wollstonecraft, Mary: (1759–1797). English author. A foremother of contemporary feminism, she is best known for her *Vindication of the Rights of Woman* (1792), an argument for equality for women. She died in childbirth with daughter Mary, later Mary W. Shelley, author of *Frankenstein*.

Woqu: Woman Question. Woqu is Claire's shorthand for the expression from the 1830s through the 1880s used in discussing the role of women in society and challenging the traditional values of marriage, work, and family life. These examinations of the nature of women in society included debates on suffrage and sexual emancipation, which certainly were of dominant interest to women by the end of the nineteenth century. Also, during this time, Eleanor Marx (daughter of Karl Marx) and Edward Aveling published *The Woman Question* (1886).

Yeta-Bu: Beauty, goddess of the Seven Siren Islands.

Yo-Ni: Yoni or Vulva, the primary Tantric object of worship, symbolized variously by a triangle, fish, double-pointed oval, horseshoe, egg, or fruit. The goddess Kali personifies the Yoni and bore the title of Cunti or Kunda, root of the now pejorative word "cunt." The Yoni Yantra or triangle was known as the Primordial Image representing the Great Mother as source of all life. Also, the formal symbol under which Shakti is worshiped; the dynamic or cosmic energy personified as the female consort, and implying power, ability, prowess, and genius.

WORKS CITED

Beauvoir, Simone de. 1952. *The Second Sex.* Translated and edited by H. M. Parshley. New York: Vintage.

Bolen, Jean Shinoda. 1985. *Goddesses in Everywoman: A New Psychology of Women.* New York: Harper and Row.

Chernin, Kim. 1987. *Reinventing Eve: Modern Woman in Search of Herself.* New York: Harper and Row.

Cixous, Hélène. 1981. "The Laugh of the Medusa." In *New French Feminisms: An Anthology,* edited by Elaine Marks and Isabelle de Courtivron. New York: Schocken Books, 245–64.

Cunningham, Gail. 1978. *The New Woman and the Victorian Novel.* New York: Harper and Row.

Faderman, Lillian. 1981. *Surpassing the Love of Men: Romantic Friendship and Love Between Women from the Renaissance to the Present.* New York: William Morrow.

Gilligan, Carol. 1982. *In a Different Voice: Psychological Theory and Women's Development.* Cambridge, Mass.: Harvard Univ. Press.

Gilman, Charlotte Perkins. 1973. *The Yellow Wallpaper.* Old Westbury, N.Y.: Feminist Press.

Harris, Miriam Kalman. 1990. "Rediscovery: Claire Myers Spotswood (Owens)," *Belles Lettres* 5 (Winter 1990): 15.

———. 1991. *Mirrors: A One Woman Performance.* Produced and performed by Linda Comess, Dallas, Tex.

———. 1992a. "Claire Myers Spotswood Owens: From Southern Belle to Grand Amoureuse." *Southern Quarterly* 31 (Fall 1992): 50–69.

————. 1992b. "The Pressure of the Choices." In *All Sides of the Subject: Women and Biography,* edited by Teresa Iles. New York: Teacher's College Press: 68–79.

Heilbrun, Carolyn G. 1990. *Hamlet's Mother and Other Women.* New York: Ballantine.

Keller, Catherine. 1986. *From a Broken Web: Separation, Sexism, and Self.* Boston: Beacon.

Keller, Evelyn Fox. 1985. *Reflections on Gender and Science.* New Haven: Yale Univ. Press.

Kessler, Carol Farley. 1984. *Daring to Dream: Utopian Stories by United States Women: 1836–1919.* Boston: Pandora.

Lloyd, Genevieve. 1984. *The Man of Reason: "Male" and "Female" in Western Philosophy.* Minneapolis: Univ. of Minnesota Press.

Nin, Anaïs. 1967. *The Diary of Anaïs Nin.* Vol. 2, *1934–1939.* New York and London: Swallow Press and Harcourt Brace Jovanovich.

Owens, Claire Myers [Claire Myers Spotswood]. 1935. *The Unpredictable Adventure: A Comedy of Woman's Independence.* New York: Doubleday, Doran.

————. 1958. *Awakening to the Good: Psychological or Religious?* Boston: Christopher.

————. 1963. *Discovery of the Self.* Boston: Christopher.

————. 1970s. "Varieties of Self-Realization." Claire Myers Owens Collection. Blagg-Huey Library, Texas Woman's Univ., Denton.

————. ca. 1970–80. "Autobiography." Claire Myers Owens Collection Blagg-Huey Library Texas Woman's Univ., Denton.

————. 1977. "Horns Blowing, Bells Ringing." In *C.G. Jung Speaking,* edited by William McGuire and R. F. C. Hull, 237–39. Princeton: Princeton Univ. Press.

————. 1979a. *Zen and the Lady.* New York: Baraka.

————. 1979b. Interview by Kenneth Ring. Sound cassettes 1–6. Vol. 17. Claire Myers Owens Collection. Blagg-Huey Library, Texas Woman's Univ., Denton.

————. ca. 1980–83. "Meditation and the Lady." Claire
    Myers Owens Collection. Blagg-Huey Library, Texas
    Woman's Univ., Denton.

Pearson, Carol S. 1989. *The Hero Within: Six Archetypes We Live
    By*. Expanded ed. New York: Harper and Row.

Rich, Adrienne. 1986. "What Does a Woman Need to Know?
    (1979)" In *Blood, Bread, and Poetry: Selected Prose 1979–
    1985*. New York: Norton, 1–10.

Showalter, Elaine. 1990. *Sexual Anarchy: Gender and Culture at
    the Fin de Siècle*. New York: Viking.

Stubbs, Patricia. 1979. *Women and Fiction: Feminism and the
    Novel, 1880–1920*. New York: Harper and Row.

Suzuki, Shuryu. 1990. *Zen Mind, Beginner's Mind*. New York:
    Weatherhill.

Taylor, A. Elizabeth. 1987. *Citizens at Last: The Woman Suffrage
    Movement in Texas*. Austin, Tex.: Ellen C. Temple.

Tong, Rosemarie. 1989. *Feminist Thought: A Comprehensive Intro-
    duction*. Boulder, Colo.: Westview.

Vicinus, Martha. 1985. *Independent Women: Work and Community
    for Single Women, 1850–1920*. Chicago: Univ. of Chicago
    Press.

Washbourn, Penelope. 1977. *Becoming Woman: The Quest for
    Wholeness in Female Experience*. San Francisco: Harper and
    Row.

White, John. 1983. "Foreword." In *Small Ecstasies*, edited by
    John White. San Diego: ACS Publications.

————. 1990. Telephone conversation with Miriam Kalman
    Harris, Sept. 8, 1990.

Wickes, Frances G. 1963. *The Inner World of Choice*. New York:
    Harper and Row.

Woolf, Virginia. 1957. *A Room of One's Own*. New York: Har-
    court Brace and World.

Utopianism and Communitarianism
Lyman Tower Sargent and Gregory Claeys, Series Editors

This new series offers historical and contemporary analyses of utopian literature, communal studies, utopian social theory, broad themes such as the treatment of women in these traditions, and new editions of fictional works of lasting value for both a general and scholarly audience.

Other titles in the series include:

The Concept of Utopia. Ruth Levitas
Low Living and High Thinking at Modern Times, New York. Roger Wunderlich
The Southern Land, Known. Gabriel de Foigny; David John Fausett, *trans. and ed.*
Unveiling a Parallel. Alice Ilgenfritz Jones and Ella Merchant; Carol Kolmerten, *ed.*
Women, Family, and Utopia: Communal Experiments of the Shakers, the Oneida Community, and the Mormons. Lawrence Foster
Women in Spiritual and Communitarian Societies in the United States. Wendy E. Chmielewski, Louis J. Kern, and Marlyn Klee-Hartzell, *eds.*
Writing the New World: Imaginary Voyages and Utopias of the Great Southern Land. David John Fausett